F

"Fourth Echelon has more than enough non-lethal options in their loadouts, Dad. The hard way... your way... is not the only way."

He gave a nod. "Fair point. I just want to be sure of your reasons. I don't want you following in my footsteps for my sake."

Sarah gave a derisive snort. "With all due respect, Dad, get over yourself. All the horrible things our family has been through, it showed me the hard truth about what's out there. Along the way, it took something from me."

A slight tremor resonated through the deck beneath their feet and both of them felt the change in the Paladin's attitude. The jet started a slow descent, curving in to follow the coastline.

"Here we go." Sarah checked her watch. "Right on the clock. A simple father-daughter day out, right? Just like Colorado."

"Same hunt," said Fisher, "different prey."

ALSO AVAILABLE

TOM CLANCY'S
SPLINTER·CELL
FIREWALL

JAMES SWALLOW

ACONYTE

First published by Aconyte Books in 2022

ISBN 978 1 83908 114 9

Ebook ISBN 978 1 83908 115 6

Cover art by Larry Rostant and Shutterstock

Distributed in North America by Simon & Schuster Inc, New York, USA

Printed in the United States of America

9 8 7 6 5 4 3 2 1

ACONYTE BOOKS

An imprint of Asmodee Entertainment Ltd

Mercury House, Shipstones Business Centre

North Gate, Nottingham NG7 7FN, UK

aconytebooks.com // twitter.com/aconytebooks

For Rich Dansky; gentleman,
scholar & were-sasquatch

Author's Note

Firewall takes place in 2015, two years after the events depicted in *Splinter Cell: Blacklist,* and four years prior to the *Operation Watchman* mission in Bolivia (seen in *Ghost Recon: Wildlands*).

ONE

Gunterfabrik – Kreuzberg – Berlin

It took four days for them to narrow the search.

Four cold days on the streets of a stone-gray city where the spring seemed unable to take hold, the season still warring with the last overcast remains of a winter unwilling to give ground.

They got close to the target on the second night, tracking a hand-off in the U-Bahn at Alexanderplatz, but a wild scramble that saw them changing trains and sprinting down rain-slick platforms netted nothing but irritation. Their quarry – designated with the codename *Treble* – avoided the team with an ease that bordered on insulting.

Later, Lynx had earned hard looks when she suggested that the target had deliberately drawn them in to get the measure of the operatives sent to capture him.

Her companions reacted predictably. Gator, the stocky corn-fed ex-Ranger, took it as a personal failure on his part and spent hours staring into his coffee and squaring away his kit to hide his frustration. Buzzard, the wiry New Yorker forever pent up with nervous energy, played with his knife and pored over a map of the city. Neither man seemed to sleep that much, both always awake when Lynx rose each morning, in their dingy safe house off Karl-Marx-Strasse.

She wasn't like them. Of average build, with dark brown shoulder-length hair, she could have blended into any crowd of tourists without making a ripple. But if you gave her a second look, meeting those sharp green eyes, you might have sensed something of the hard focus she kept hidden.

The others had been career military before their recruitment, although Buzzard was circumspect about what branch. Lynx guessed Navy, but he wouldn't confirm or deny, and when he posed the question to her, she was equally tight-lipped. Gator decided she was former police, and she allowed him to believe that. The truth was more complex.

The secrecy – even from each other – was part of the program. Sometimes active missions meant working with people you knew next to nothing about, finding a way to mesh together into an operable unit at short notice. Hence the codenames and the lack of personal small talk. The people in charge wanted this op to be about the takedown, not a team-building exercise for agents in the field.

Lynx was fine with that. Having seen Gator and Buzzard out in the world over the past few days, she had her doubts that either man had the right mindset for collaboration.

Still, they managed to track Treble to his staging area, a victory of sorts. Lynx studied the derelict building across the street, through the windshield of their rented VW Golf, the brutalist five-story block of concrete and graffiti-covered glass rising behind a corrugated metal fence.

Against the whirl of fine rain falling from a low night sky, the place had an unlovely look to it, the typical silhouette of utilitarian East German architecture. The sign over the entrance was still visible despite decades of decay. The place had been a textile factory turning out sports kits for kids playing soccer inside the Deutsche Demokratische Republik, but that had been before the fall of the Berlin Wall and *Die Wende*, what the Germans called *the turning point*.

Lynx looked around, checking her sector for traffic, finding nothing. This whole area on the bank of the river Spree had been just inside the wall in the bad old days of the Cold War, and you could see the legacy of it in the buildings. Like a lot of Berlin's riverside real estate, the fate of the factory would be to get gobbled up by some property developer, then razed to the ground so some new modernist construction could rise in its place. Or maybe they would keep the exterior intact, playing on its Communist-era retro chic. She wondered what the DDR stalwarts of the past would make of that. For her, those people and that time were ancient history, something that only existed in movies and documentaries.

"No visual," drawled Gator, down low in the passenger seat with a pair of low-light goggles held to his face. He peered at the factory's lightless windows. "Treble could be masking his signature."

"He's smart," offered Buzzard, leaning forward in the VW's backseat. He carefully screwed a long sound suppressor into the barrel of a Glock 17 pistol, before loading it with a magazine of blue-tipped bullets.

"More than you know," noted Lynx. "He practically wrote the book on this."

"You a fan?" Gator gave a derisive snort and a pointed look, then went on. "There's only one of him. All you gotta do is make sure you don't repeat the screw-up at the subway."

"Don't put that on me," she said. "You're the one that spooked him."

"And you're the one supposed to mark him." Gator checked his own weapon, before stuffing it into his overcoat.

"He got past us all," Lynx snapped. "Like I said, he's top tier."

Buzzard drummed his fingers on the doorframe. "So, we do this different," he said. "The mistake was leaving him a way out at the station. This time, we split up, cut off his escape routes."

Lynx shook her head. "Wrong. We need to come at Treble in force. It's the only shot we have at taking him down. Remember the briefing." The thin document that operational command had given them talked in no uncertain terms about their target's superlative skillset, easily the equal of the best the Spetsnaz, SAS, or SEALs had to offer.

"I got my force multiplier right here." Gator smirked and patted his gun.

Lynx pulled a face, but clearly the other two had already made up their minds, and she knew it would be a waste of her time trying to bring them around. Buzzard elected to go up the drainpipe on the west side of the factory and work his way down from the roof, while Gator would go in from the riverside. That left Lynx with the front entrance. Her scowl deepened.

Buzzard pulled up the sleeve of his jacket to reveal a device that resembled a smartphone clipped to the inside of his forearm. The screen blinked on, and he tapped it experimentally. "All right. Synchronize OPSATs."

"Copy." Lynx and Gator had identical tech of their own, part of a clandestine network that gave near-instantaneous communication to the chair-warmers back at command. The Operational Satellite Uplink, to give it its full name, could be slaved to a strategic mission interface for real-time tactical data exchange, but for the duration of this action, most of those functions were inactive.

The three operatives keyed in their identity codes, and their OPSATs vibrated against their skin. Next, Buzzard handed out the last items of their gear: flexible ballistic cloth facemasks and low-light monocles that fitted over one eye. Suitably equipped, with hoods pulled up over their heads, the trio became faceless.

Lynx checked her pistol one last time as Gator slipped into the rain, then she followed him out, taking care to close the door quietly. Buzzard was a step behind, a gray shape in the steady downpour.

"*Comms check.*" Gator's gruff tones sounded in Lynx's ear, relayed through a tiny radio bead inside her earlobe.

"Lynx," she replied, her voice picked up by a dermal microphone taped to her throat.

"*Buzzard.*" The other man followed protocol, and from the corner of her eye, Lynx saw him dash across the empty street and vanish around a wall.

"*Good copy.*" At the other end of the block, Gator hesitated and threw a look in Lynx's direction. Illuminated by the dull glow of a streetlight, he gave her the sketch of a salute and melted into the shadows.

Lynx got to the front entrance in quick steps, taking care to avoid the deep puddles where the rain collected. Drawing her weapon, she squeezed through a narrow gap in two sheets of metal fencing. A truck rumbled past, headlights briefly throwing a wash of white over the building's tumbledown façade, and she froze, letting it pass before moving on.

She checked the edges of the door and found no sign of sensors or booby-traps. That meant Treble had either neglected to place any – unlikely, given what she knew about him – or that he'd placed them so well she couldn't see them on the first pass.

Lynx flicked down her low-light monocle and examined the entryway more closely. As she did, she heard a grunt from Buzzard.

"*Ascending.*"

"*Copy,*" replied Gator. "*At the rear door. Tripwire. Made safe.*"

As he spoke, Lynx caught sight of the same thing. A nearly invisible length of line at ankle height had been placed inside the entrance vestibule, and she followed it to a primed nine-banger stun grenade, cleverly hidden under some debris.

"Same here," she whispered. Lynx chose to leave the trap in place and stepped over it with a gymnast's ease.

She moved slowly, steadily, spreading her weight with each footfall. A narrow and tall atrium, the entrance had a central staircase choked with rubble and broken furniture. High above, a cracked skylight allowed runnels of rain to fall the distance and spatter against the tiled floor.

Lynx stayed low, moving from cover to cover, pausing every few moments to survey her surroundings. The view through the monocle cast everything in fuzzy shades of sea-green and corpse-white, as if she was at the bottom of a lake.

She held her breath. In the distance, somewhere in the

direction of Engelbecken Park, police sirens wailed, then grew faint.

In short order, Lynx moved from room to room, looking for anything that indicated Treble's presence, coming up empty. "Ground floor, no contact," she announced.

"*Basement, no contact,*" said Gator. "*Proceeding to first floor.*"

"*Roof, no contact.*" Buzzard seemed out of breath, then he corrected himself. "*I mean, I found a spotter perch up here but no spotter.*" He sighed. "*Descending to fifth.*"

"Copy." Lynx considered that for a moment. Had Treble been up there, watching them before they made entry? She sucked in a breath of musty air, and then set off, making for the stairwell at the end of the corridor. "Proceeding to second floor."

Buzzard climbed into the building through a gap that had once held a skylight. The swollen and cracked wood took his weight, and he dropped into a cat-footed landing on damp, mold-blackened carpet. The office space he descended into was empty, everything not nailed down long gone, leaving only bare walls covered in dirt and graffiti tags layers deep. The concrete floor beneath the rancid carpet meant no creaking floorboards to betray his movements. The only sound was the rain.

Or was it?

Buzzard turned his head in the direction of a ghost of a noise. He caught an electronic mutter, like the sound of static from a poorly tuned radio. It was frustratingly indistinct, but he didn't dare ignore it. The noise was a sign of life, and that meant they were right about Treble hiding out here.

Keeping to the shadows, Buzzard crept forward, out of the office and on to a long landing. More ruined flooring squelched under his boots, the edges of the mildewed carpet tiles curling up like decayed flower petals. He fixed his sights on the source of the sound, bringing up his pistol, resting his finger on the trigger.

Through his low-light monocle, he spotted a knife edge of illumination emerging from beneath a half-closed door a few meters away. The sound came again, clearer this time. The burble of a voice on the other end of a phone.

So Treble was in there, talking to someone. That meant he would be distracted. Vulnerable.

Buzzard hesitated, tapping his throat mike three times, the code for *target sighted*.

"*Can you confirm?*" Lynx whispered in his earpiece.

He frowned. The only way he could do that was to kick open the door and put a round in Treble's chest. Buzzard didn't reply. He had to be quick and quiet, or the element of surprise would be lost.

He was within arm's reach of the half-open door when his movement triggered the proximity sensor of a device hidden under a fold of rotted carpet. In a fizzing burst, the concealed shocker released the full stun charge stored in its dense battery core, hitting the operative with punishing force.

Buzzard's muscles locked in agony, and he toppled forward like a felled tree. His body sang with pain, as if he had been dipped in fire. His shuddering hands clutched at the air and his mouth locked open.

He heard Gator in his ear, calling for an update, but all Buzzard could do was lie in a trembling heap and scream silently as electricity shot through him.

•••

"Buzzard, respond?" Gator hesitated at the edge of the first-floor atrium, waiting for a reply that didn't come. "Buzzard, key your mike if you can."

"You think Treble got him?" Lynx ventured the question on both of their minds.

"Maybe." Gator released a breath. "I'll draw him out."

"Bad idea."

"Didn't ask your opinion." He brought the Glock close to his chest and picked a direction, moving down the corridor to his right.

The floor opened up into a grid of office cubicles with tumbledown wooden partitions. The space had high ceilings deep with shadows and Gator scanned for movement among the hanging pipework and broken ducting. Opportunistic thieves had been through here in the past, ripping up the walls and the flooring for the building's copper wiring. The drifts of debris everywhere made it hard to move without making noise, and Gator strained to listen over the constant ticking of the rain on the grime-coated windows.

He would have been hard pressed to put it into words, but Gator had *an inkling*. Some sixth sense trained into him by his drill instructors at Ranger School, warning him he wasn't alone. Treble was in here with him, he could *feel* it, like an itch between his shoulders.

And that meant a trap, waiting for him to put the wrong foot forward. His lip curled. That had to be what Buzzard had run into, some fake-out set by their target to thin the ranks of his hunters.

A voice in the back of Gator's head asked him if maybe Lynx had been right all along. If Treble wanted to pick them off one by one, they had given the man exactly what he wanted.

Re-evaluating his situation, Gator started a slow retreat, moving back the way he had come, as another truck raced past down on the street. The vehicle's headlights threw a fan of light through the windows, and for a moment the jumping shadows took on the shape of a man.

Gator fired without thinking, putting two rounds up into the dark figure. The Glock's stifled cough echoed through the open space, and spent brass pinged off the wooden partitions, but he hit nothing.

The shadow was just that, a hazy black form that melted away as the truck carried on its journey. Gator cursed inwardly, angry at himself for letting his eagerness get in the way.

His patience waned, and he decided to even the odds. The Ranger felt for the cylindrical shape of a flashbang grenade clipped to the inside of his jacket. If Treble *was* in the room, it was the best way to force him into the open.

He fumbled for the grenade as a low whistle sounded from above him. Gator twisted, spinning around to bring up the gun, and he had the impression of a figure suspended in the gloom, dangling from one of the pipes.

Before he could get off a shot, the man was on him, gravity bringing them together with enough force to put the thickset Ranger down on the floor.

Gator fought to keep control of his pistol, but his assailant snaked a wiry, muscular arm around his neck and pulled him in close. Unable to call out a warning to Lynx, his air choked off, Gator's vision began to fog as the sleeper hold took effect.

He jerked the Glock's trigger and the shot went wild, pinging off the floor. He had the dim impression of a black-clad stalker, of rasping breath sounding near his ear. In a last-ditch attempt to break free, Gator kicked and punched, feeling his blows hit body armor.

Blood roaring in his ears, Gator desperately tried to fight back as the color bled out of his world and the shadows closed in. He pulled the flashbang's pin in a last act of defiance – but as the cylinder rolled away from him across the floor, he had already lost consciousness.

Lynx heard the stun grenade go off on the floor below her, and saw the brief flash of oxide-white light through cracks in the concrete.

In the wake of the sound-shock, she caught the crunch of booted feet moving away, and burst into motion, tracking them.

He took down Gator.

She didn't question the thought, overlooking the sharp realization that she was now the last hunter standing. Her target was heading to the northeast corner of the building, in the direction of the river. There was a bridge that way, she remembered, and if he could get outside and across to the other bank, Treble would vanish. The city turned into a warren over there, and alone, she had no chance of tagging him.

If she didn't stop him here inside the factory, he'd be as good as gone.

A few meters away, a rough-edged hole in the floor where part of the structure had collapsed formed a pool of blackness leading down to the level below. Lynx made her choice without hesitating, dropping into a sliding motion that took her over the edge and into the dark.

It was a risky ploy, dropping into the unknown, but she took the chance that she wouldn't fall feet-first on to a pile of rusted rebar or another booby-trap. The drop was longer than she expected, and Lynx landed off-kilter, stumbling as she tried to recover her balance.

In the pitch dark she fumbled to adjust her low-light monocle. Everything through her right eye's vision showed green and white. Every support pillar or fallen wall stood out, complicating her sight picture.

Treble could not have missed her entrance, and from somewhere across the open space, Lynx heard a faint click and then a high-pitched whine, like a camera flash charging.

She fired in the direction of the noise, not so much to score a hit, but more to force a reaction. Bullets sparked off the wall, and a piece of the shadows broke off and dove behind cover.

There!

Finding her momentum again, Lynx pulled herself over one of the low partitions, half-rolling, half-diving, gun close in and ready. She landed sure-footed this time, firing another two rounds into the space where Treble had gone. But he'd faded away.

She pivoted on her heel, instinct screaming at her to watch her back.

Treble had set up the three operatives to draw them close at Alexanderplatz and he had done it again. The target intuited how the team's dynamic operated and turned that against them. *Isolate and neutralize.* Good tactics.

Lynx evaded the short, hard punch that came straight at her, flinching away, but not fast enough to get off cleanly. Treble's gloved knuckles kissed her cheekbone with a glancing hit that took her monocle with it, ripping the device from her masked face.

She ducked low, bringing up her gun, but Treble slammed the heel of his hand into her solar plexus, blowing the air out of her lungs in a pained rush. Lynx staggered back a step, and Treble's shadowy form kept coming, out of the dark and into the half-light. He reached out and snagged her wrist, bending it the wrong way. She hissed in pain and lost her grip on the Glock.

The gun fell at her feet, but Lynx had no time to think about it. Treble moved on her, firing rapid blows out of the gloom that she deflected more by the sound than by seeing them.

She tried to extend the distance, but he wouldn't let her, keeping up the pressure, forcing her to dance to his tune.

Anger flared, and Lynx used it to fuel her, feinting right, avoiding a chopping blow aimed at her throat. She pushed in closer, moving inside Treble's guard, and landed return blows on his belly, chest, and throat.

Her attacker growled and lost a step as he soaked up the hits, passing through a shaft of moonlight from a broken window. Lynx glimpsed a craggy, unshaven face hidden behind insect-like night-vision goggles, and a loose coat over matte black tactical gear.

She kept up the momentum, using her edge in speed and agility. Treble was easily twice her mass, and one well-placed blow from him could put her down hard. But each hit she sent his way was guesswork and instinct. Fighting in the dimness was like boxing smoke, and she couldn't be sure if she could hold her own.

"Lynx...?" Buzzard's voice echoed behind her, and she looked without thinking, snared by the distraction. "You there?"

The wiry young man stood in the passage, groggy and slow, supporting himself with one hand up on the doorjamb. In the weak light, he looked pale and unsteady. Whatever Treble had used to put him down, he felt the effects of it.

The target made a *tsk* noise under his breath and moved like lightning. He snatched the seam of Lynx's hoodie and yanked her off balance, pulling her to him. Pressing her back to his chest, he put one arm at her throat and started the slow business of choking her out.

Part of Lynx realized that Treble had been taking his time with her in the exchange of blows, playing it out. At the same time, he had drawn a gun with his other hand, bringing it to bear on Buzzard.

Lynx tried to shout a warning, but a strangled gasp emerged from her lips.

Treble's silenced pistol chugged, and a blue spark burst on Buzzard's chest. He gave a cry and fell out of sight.

The instinctive action for Lynx would have been to wrestle the man's hand away from her neck, to take a desperate gulp of air before she blacked out – but she fought down the animal panic rising inside her and felt for her only remaining weapon.

Her fingers found the black polymer combat knife tucked into a sheath-pocket at her thigh and pulled it free, twisting it around in her grip. Her blood thundering in her ears, Lynx put her energy into forcing the blade up and back, until the point pushed into the soft flesh of Treble's throat.

She applied steady pressure against his Adam's apple, and

felt her opponent stiffen. The slightest motion of her hand would open his throat to the air.

Treble's grip slackened and Lynx fought the urge to stumble away and suck in air. She kept the knife in place, making it clear where the balance of this fight now lay.

Treble slowly put away his gun and spoke in a low voice full of rough edges.

"OK," he allowed, then pressed a microphone tab at his neck and repeated the same word three times. "*Endex. Endex. Endex.*"

TWO

Gunterfabrik – Kreuzberg – Berlin

"All right, you heard the man. This training exercise is concluded."

Anna Grímsdóttir removed the wireless headset she had been using to monitor the radio channel, stepping back from the bank of surveillance monitors inside the rear of the unmarked Renault truck. Her gaze raked over the gang of field technicians waiting for her word, each one carrying gear with which to sanitize the site. None of them would move without her order.

Grim – as most of her colleagues knew her – instilled that sort of obedience in her subordinates. Firm, no-nonsense and pragmatic, the tall, henna-haired woman's official title was "technical operations officer", a deliberately vague euphemism that could cover a multitude of clandestine works. In the real world, that translated into mission command for one of the best kept secrets on the planet – Fourth Echelon, a covert anti-terror and counter-intelligence unit that lived in the deep black.

"I want this location cleaned up inside of fifteen minutes," Grim told the techs. "Move."

The team – each one dressed in deliberately nondescript street clothing – scrambled to obey. Emerging from the rear of the truck, they made their way to the derelict Gunterfabrik building, while Grim followed on behind at a more leisurely pace, checking up and down the street with a clinical, experienced eye.

No police, no watchers. All clear… For now.

She didn't need to tell the techs that they were operating in-country without the blessing of the German government or their intelligence services. If the Bundesnachrichtendienst – the BND – knew that a Fourth Echelon Splinter Cell deployment was happening right in their backyard, their reaction would be, to put it mildly, *unpleasant.* Thus, it was vital to pick up after themselves and leave no traces that they were ever here. The Splinter Cells were shadows, the knife in the dark that no one saw coming.

That's practically the 4E motto, Grim thought, with a rare smile.

This hunt-and-trap mission was part evaluation, part live-fire exercise. The added wrinkle of working in a non-permissive environment was one more test for Grim's latest batch of recruits from the Farm, the training facility for the Central Intelligence Agency and other elements of America's covert apparatus.

Gator, Lynx, and Buzzard were the only three potentials who had made the cut for Fourth Echelon's punishing training regimen, and all three were potentially looking at a failing grade.

•••

Grim entered the factory through the front door, passing one of the techs at work making a tripwire safe, and found the night's senior instructor waiting for her in the atrium. He rubbed at a sore spot on his throat, his expression thoughtful.

"Sam." She gave him a nod.

"Grim." Sam Fisher returned the gesture, removing the distinctive tri-focal vision goggles from atop his forehead and stowing them in his coat. "Enjoy the show?"

"You know me," she replied. "I'm always watching."

Grim nodded to where another tech recovered one of dozens of wireless camera pods that had been secreted inside the Gunterfabrik building for the purpose of monitoring the night's events.

"No doubt," allowed Fisher, the briefest flicker of a wry smile crossing his face, then vanishing.

Tall, but not overly so, beneath the big coat Fisher had a spare, lean build that men half his age would have killed for. With a closely cut beard and short hair turning from black to gunmetal, he could have been anything from fifty to sixty years old. Hard eyes and the lines around them told the tale of a life lived in the fight, and a will to keep up the contest until the bitter end.

A former Navy SEAL before he became a CIA paramilitary officer, Fisher had been one of the first recruits in the early Aughts to what would eventually become Fourth Echelon. In that time, he had forged a reputation that few knew of, but all who did respected. In many ways, Grim reflected, he set the benchmark for every Splinter Cell operative who had followed in his wake. It was a testament to Fisher's tenacity and resilience that the work hadn't yet put him in the ground.

"So?" She made a circling gesture with one hand. "Do you have any good news for me?"

"I'm always a ray of sunshine, Grim."

"Right." She drew out the word. As one of the most experienced operators in the field, Fisher's evaluation of the trainees could make or break them. A single word from him would see a recruit out, and he had failed more potential new agents than any other instructor.

But high standards were what made Fourth Echelon an exemplary unit. Existing beyond oversight of all but the President of the United States, the group drew intelligence and resources from the top tier of the National Security Agency, operating in the espionage world's most rarified air. It might have been a cliché, but the Splinter Cells really were the best of the best at what they did.

"The skinny kid," began Fisher, nodding toward Buzzard, who was being helped to his feet by a medic. "Showed some grit, shaking off a shocker like that. But he still needs some seasoning."

Grim sighed and called out to the younger man. "Rybicki, you're a fail for this evaluation." Buzzard couldn't manage any more response than a shaky nod of the head, almost grateful for the excuse. The shock-tipped training round Fisher had put in his chest had robbed him of his voice.

Gator – whose real name was Michaels – passed them by as two more techs carried out his unconscious form between them. Grim didn't have to ask about that one. When the moment came, his hesitation had cost him dearly. The Ranger would join Rybicki on the next transport back to the States. Fisher gave a shrug and said nothing.

The two young men would never know exactly who or what they had been auditioning for. The terms "Fourth Echelon" and "Splinter Cell" had not been uttered in the presence of those trainees. They'd rotate back to their units with a story they could never tell, about a shady recruiter who had pulled them off the line one day for a training mission in Germany that nobody could explain.

The only member of the trio still able to stand under their own power was Lynx, but even so she limped visibly as she came into the atrium, one hand pressed to her masked face, and dark hair spilling out over her neck. The blade she'd managed to put to Fisher's throat was nowhere to be seen.

"What about her?" Grim eyed him. "She almost cut you a new smile, Sam."

"Quick," admitted Fisher. "Good instincts. Definitely the best of the three." He sighed. "Green light."

Grim raised an eyebrow. "You're passing her?"

"You think I'm wrong?"

"No. In fact, I'm in full agreement with you, it's just rare to see it." Grim folded her arms. "Two fails, one pass. Not getting soft in your old age, are you?"

"You know better than that."

Grim frowned. "I do. But it's important I make sure your evaluation is on point. Especially in this case." She raised her hand and beckoned Lynx over to them.

Fisher's eyes narrowed. "What's that supposed to mean?" He knew Grim well enough to sense when she was hiding something.

"Don't get mad," she said. "And believe me when I tell you, I'm doing this for the best of the agency." As Lynx warily approached, Grim gestured at the younger woman's face. "Take off your mask, please."

Lynx reluctantly peeled away the covering, revealing herself in full for the first time. She managed an awkward smile in Fisher's direction.

"Hey, Dad," she said.

"*Sarah.*" Fisher froze, and his gaze turned flinty. There was a new contusion on his daughter's face that he had given her only moments ago, unaware of the fact that the woman who came closest to killing him in the mock engagement was his only child. "What the hell is this?"

"This is Trainee Lynx, aka Sarah Burns, aka Sarah Fisher." Grim stood her ground, waiting for the storm she knew would come. "Now you know why I insisted on anonymizing the recruit data for this exercise."

"Clear the room." Fisher addressed the order to the techs who were still at work in the atrium, and when they hesitated, looking to Grim for confirmation, he let out a growl. "Did I stutter?"

The techs departed in short order without stopping to pick up their gear, leaving Grim, Sam, and Sarah in the echoing, rain-damp space. Fisher's daughter sighed and drew a breath. "Dad, will you let me explain?"

"Wait your turn." Fisher turned on Grim. "You put her in a live-fire exercise. You kept this from me? What were you thinking?" He didn't raise his voice. His cold and stony annoyance was enough.

"I can't allow good potential to go to waste, Sam," replied Grim.

"Thought those fight moves looked familiar," Fisher

muttered, shooting Sarah another look. "I taught you that, after…" He trailed off.

After she was kidnapped, Grim thought, twice in as many years. Despite her father's attempts to isolate Sarah from the harsh realities of his clandestine career, her life had been marred by incidents when his dark world impinged on her civilian existence.

Fisher reframed his thoughts. "When I agreed Sarah could take a role with Fourth Echelon, I wanted her to be an *analyst*." He put hard emphasis on the word.

"You might have agreed to that," Sarah said quietly. "I didn't. I make my own choices." Before her father could respond, she continued. "Kicks and punches aren't the only thing you taught me, Dad. I learned responsibility. I learned about duty. You taught me to see things as they are, and not to be afraid of them."

Fisher scowled. "I wanted to keep you safe!"

"Like I said, my choice." Sarah met her father's gaze.

Fisher turned back to Grim. "If I had known she–"

"If you had known Lynx was Sarah, you wouldn't have treated her impartially," Grim spoke over him, her voice like a whip-crack. "I concealed her identity from you so you would test her like Michaels and Rybicki, and push her as hard as she needed to go." She opened her hands. "And you did just give her a passing grade."

"He did?" Despite her fatigue, Sarah's eyes lit up.

"Rescinded," said Fisher. "Red light."

"Too late for that," Grim said firmly. "Sarah's in the top percentile of our evaluation. She's excelled in all areas."

"In simulations," he insisted.

Grim allowed that. "True. But she was the only one of the trainees who came close enough to put a mark on you. Tell me, Sam, how many times has that happened?"

Fisher said nothing, his lips compressing into a thin line.

Grim relented. "I'm sorry I didn't give you the whole picture. But Sarah has the skills we need. And I defy you to tell me otherwise."

Fisher's silence lengthened. He had no response to Grim's statement because he knew it was true. Sarah wasn't a callow, bookish student anymore, she was a capable young woman, and she clearly had the innate instincts perfect for a covert operative. Finally, he spoke again. "You sure about this, kid?"

"I want to do more," Sarah saw an opening and pounced on it. "Like you and Uncle Vic did. I can make a difference."

"We're not like Vic's organization," Fisher told her. Sam's old friend and Sarah's ersatz "Uncle" Victor Coste ran Paladin Nine Security, a private military contractor that handled everything from high-end bodyguard duties to kidnap and recovery operations. "What we do makes that PNC stuff look like the bush league."

Sarah hesitated, and for a second Grim thought she saw her wavering. Then Fisher's daughter straightened. "Your instinct is to protect me, and I love you for that. You're not sure I can do this, I get it. But there's only one way to find out."

Fisher gave a shake of the head and cast a glance in Grim's direction. "You like being right, don't you?"

"No doubt," she admitted.

"Then don't make me regret this." It was as close to an admission of acceptance as Sam Fisher would ever give, and Grim decided not to push it any further.

He would come around. And if he didn't … He'd have to live with it. Grim's directive was to keep Fourth Echelon running at maximum efficiency, not to keep Sam Fisher happy.

Drew, one of the techs, came back into the atrium brandishing an encrypted satellite-comm handset. "Call from the bird," he explained. "It's urgent."

Grim took the handset and pressed it to her ear. "Go for Grímsdóttir."

"Ma'am, this is Kade. What's your status there?" Lea Kade served as one of the operational crew aboard the C-147B Paladin, Fourth Echelon's mobile airborne mission hub. Currently, the black jet was parked in a secluded hangar, several kilometers away at Ramstein Air Force Base. The Paladin's crew were looped in on the exercise, along with Grim and her cadre of technicians.

"We're wrapping up. Is there a problem?"

"We need you and Treble back here ASAP," Kade replied. *"We have a priority, eyes-only communique for the attention of you both."*

Grim frowned, and Fisher caught the look in her eye. He knew it of old: something was up.

"Origin?" Grim asked the question, but she already knew the answer.

"The Black Box," said Kade, and left it at that. The nickname had only one meaning in this context – the priority message had come directly from the NSA's headquarters at Fort Meade in Maryland.

THREE

GreenSea Incorporated – Canary Wharf – London

The pen spun around in Charlie Cole's fingers, gaining speed until it became a silver blur.

"You know the problem with me, Jan," he said to the air, as he typed one-handed on the illuminated keyboard in front of him. "There's too much gray hat in me. I can't stay in my lane."

The pen reached escape velocity and flew out of his grip, clattering across his desk and into the shadows, but Charlie paid it no heed. In the darkened office, the only light came from the skyline of glassy skyscrapers surrounding the building and the soft glow of a computer screen. On the display, endless lines of blue-on-black text scrolled past as Charlie ventured deeper and deeper into layers of secured data.

He leaned in, both hands on the keyboard, and kept talking. "Would I have even spotted this if you hadn't brought it to me? Yeah, probably. I mean, I'm always sticking my nose where it doesn't belong." He drummed out another command string without taking a breath. "I'm the kid who keeps pestering the magician to explain the tricks, right? Peek behind the curtain, look in the box. That's always my instinct."

Charlie turned in his chair, toward a smartphone sitting on pile of books nearby, its screen blinking to show an open line. Jan had still not picked up, and that wasn't like her, not at all. Three rings and she answered, every single call. This was the first time that Charlie had ever spoken to her voicemail, and he found it hard to stop.

"Listen," he said, his tone turning serious. "I think this is something bad, even worse than you said. There's more here than some routing errors and weird email trails. I have to take this up the line to Borden." He threw up his hands as if Jan stood in the room with him, anticipating her reaction. "I know, I know, like you always say, the guy's a *knob-head.*" He chuckled. Jan's favorite description of the company's senior security executive sounded strange when uttered in Charlie's East Coast American accent; something about Jan's cut-glass English delivery of the insult always made it land perfectly. "But I gotta. I gotta," he said. "Can't sit on this. I mean, that's what they hired us for, right?" He paused, his brow furrowed with worry. Still no pickup. He didn't want to admit how much it bothered him. "OK, so you call me back the moment you get this. Right? *Right.*"

Charlie leaned over and tapped the END CALL tab, and the phone went dark. In the moment of quiet that followed, he drew in a long breath, then raised his head to look out of the window.

Most of the other office buildings in this quadrant of London's Docklands development were empty this late into the evening, with a few floors working as the international trade and banking concerns continued to do business with Moscow, Mumbai, Tokyo, and Beijing. GreenSea's offices were always carefully lit at low levels, as part of the company's ecologically-aware mission dedicated to conservation, energy efficiency, and renewable power sources. In the dark mirror of the windows, Charlie saw himself reflected, along with the other staff in their glass-walled workspaces.

His youthful face – still boyish into his thirties – was marred by his concern for his friend. An itching, crawling sensation gathered at the small of his back, a sure sign of his fear index ramping up.

The last time I felt like this…

Charlie killed the thought before it could fully form. He did not want to dwell on those days, getting bombed and shot at. They were part of a life he had left behind.

Jan Freling had been headhunted by GreenSea's recruiters around the same time as Charlie, she from a major banking conglomerate in Dubai and he at the end of his contract with a certain three-letter-acronym division of the US government. As he understood it, Jan was the errant daughter of some ultra-rich British bluebloods, who had discovered an aptitude for computer mischief at boarding school and parlayed that into a career in information security. Charlie's upbringing mirrored the whole "computer mischief" bit, but his origin story came from the broken cogs of the American social services system, and a childhood of adoption with families who never quite got him. Few people did, but Jan was one of them.

She described their working relationship as *the crass Yank and the slick Brit*, and together they made an excellent team working to keep GreenSea's networks digitally secure. One of the world's top three eco-technology corporations, GreenSea specialized in building hyper-efficient windmills and wave-farms. Their patents were worth billions of dollars. Company CEO Edward Morant wanted that intellectual property protected, and paid Cole and Freling very well to bring their expertise to his security department. For Jan, the job had been a way to prove herself; for Charlie, it was a way out of the clandestine world and back to something grounded. Something *safer*.

He blew out a breath and sent the data he had gathered to a secure tablet, rising to stand as the progress bar filled. Charlie looked up, in the direction of the corridor that led straight to Gary Borden's massive corner office. Once he did this, there would be no turning back. People would be angry. People would lose their jobs. People would go to jail.

Charlie knew this because of what Jan had discovered on a sweep through the company network infrastructure. Someone inside the GreenSea Corporation had been secretly transferring money and assets to another company and doing it for quite a while. They were hiding it from the sight of the board members and the external financial regulators alike. Millions of virtual dollars, vanishing unseen into the digital ether. The transactions were buried so deep that only someone with the singular focus of an obsessive – say, like a pair of high-functioning tech geeks – would be able to track them.

The tablet pinged, signaling completion of the data transfer. Charlie stood straight and plucked the device from its charging cradle, tucking it under his arm as he marched down the corridor toward Borden's office.

Along the way, Charlie became aware that the floor seemed busier than usual. Faces from the other departments were around, hushed conversations were happening. Something important was going on, and it dawned on him that he was out of the loop. He wondered what he had missed.

He rapped on Borden's door, peering through the frosted glass to catch sight of his boss perched on the edge of his desk. Borden had a Bluetooth headset looped over one of the misshapen ears that sat low on the man's head, and his lips curled when he saw Charlie's face. He held up a single finger, in a *just one minute* gesture, and Charlie had to work not to shake his head.

Borden always made the people he considered his inferiors wait. Charlie guessed he thought it was some kind of power move, but all it really did was show off what an irritating person he was.

Eventually, Borden finished his call and granted Charlie entry. "Cole," he began, setting the terms of the conversation before the other man could even speak. "I don't have a lot of time, it's all hands on deck here. What do you want?" His voice had a nasal register that made everything he said sound dismissive.

Charlie held up the tablet computer. "I have something you should look at."

"Can it wait?" Borden waved in the direction of a monitor on his desk, which showed a live feed from the conference room in the main atrium. In the middle of the screen, the lectern on the dais in front of the GreenSea logo stood vacant. From the camera angle, Charlie could see the room filling with people wearing visitor lanyards, patiently waiting for something to happen.

"Is there a press event?" For a moment, Charlie lost focus on his reason for being there.

Borden rolled his eyes. "Do you ever actually read the memos you're sent, Cole? Or do you sit back there having a wank and playing videogames all day?" He nodded in the direction of Charlie's workspace. "For crying out loud, you need to pay attention to the outside world!"

"Rude," managed Charlie.

"Where's your pal Freling, eh?" Borden looked up, surveying the corridor. "Usually when you come in here bothering me, she's along for backup."

"I don't know," Charlie admitted. "She didn't come in today. I don't know where she is."

"Better not be throwing a sickie," said the other man. He sighed. "Look, write up a memo and send it to my inbox, I'll read it tomorrow."

Charlie shook his head. "This really can't wait."

Borden scowled at him. He had made no secret of the fact that he hadn't wanted Morant to bring on Cole and Freling to bolster GreenSea's IT security. He viewed them as dilettantes, little better than the hackers they fought to keep off the network. Even though they had been in place for over a year and done great things, the man refused to change his mind.

"Spit it out, then." Borden folded his arms across his chest, taking on a haughty air. "I'll give you one minute." He looked at his wristwatch. "Tick-tock."

Charlie sucked in a breath and launched in. "Jan conducted a security review of our redundant servers and she found something off."

"I didn't authorize any reviews," Borden snapped. "That sort of thing has to go through me first."

"Kind of the point," Charlie retorted. "You authorize it, it gets logged in the system, and if any outsider has software implants in our system, they know about it too. This was totally on the D-L."

Borden said nothing, reluctantly accepting the logic of that, and made a *keep going* motion.

"So, the sweep detected an anomaly in the redundant memory of the company financial database." Charlie gestured with the tablet computer in his hand. "Jan brought it to me, and we dug into it. We found a bunch of transaction trails that had been erased after the fact, but there was partial data in the headers. Enough for us to reconstruct them."

"What, you're telling me someone's stealing our money?" Borden snorted with derision.

"Not just money. Hardware and a bunch of other stuff, even some land deeds, all being diverted off-grid."

"No chance. This network is airtight."

"Nothing's airtight," Charlie said firmly, with the certainty of hard-won experience behind the words. "Believe me."

Borden snatched the tablet out of his hand and swiped across the pages it displayed, barely reading what was written there. "If someone hijacked GreenSea assets, we'd have spotted it by now…"

"Not if they made it look like nothing was missing," insisted Charlie. "Faked the entries."

Borden made a disinterested noise and looked past Charlie, watching some of their colleagues through his office window. The tempo around whatever was going on tonight had peaked, and he saw movement on the monitor screen. Down in the conference space, Edward Morant had taken the lectern, speaking animatedly to members of the press.

"You know what your problem is?" Borden continued.

Charlie straightened. "I'm sure you're gonna tell me."

"You like finding complications where there aren't any. It's conspiracy theory thinking, adding two and two and getting … a unicorn!" Borden waggled his finger. "This isn't spook country, Cole. You don't work for the CIA anymore, there's no Reds under the bed."

"*NSA*," he muttered, "I never worked for the CIA." But Borden wasn't listening.

"If you're so certain there's an issue here, then riddle me this." The other man discarded Charlie's tablet on his desk and fixed him with a look. "Who's behind it? If there's malfeasance afoot, it means sod all without any attribution."

Charlie fell silent. This was the question he'd been dreading, not just because the answer he had was sketchy, but because of the wider implications if it turned out to be correct.

According to the data Charlie and Jan had scraped together, the illicit transfers had flowed through a web of shell companies and blind servers, ultimately leading toward a single locus; another corporate entity on the far side of the world, known as much for its bleeding-edge technology as for its unwillingness to follow convention.

"*Teague.*" Charlie said the name. The Teague Technical Group – more commonly known as T-Tec – were the biggest of the new beasts in the world of next-gen technology and computing, currently engaged in consuming most of their competition on the way toward global dominance of the social media datasphere. If the threads of half-deleted files Jan had discovered were authentic, it meant that T-Tec were not just engaged in their usual raft of dirty business tricks, they were actively engaging in criminality.

"And there he is," said Borden, with a smirk. He pointed at the monitor as a fresh-faced, well-tanned young man in a designer jacket stepped into view.

Brody Teague. The founder-CEO-wunderkind master of T-Tec, the man running the company stealing from GreenSea, and he was *right there*, on the screen. In the building, in fact, five floors down from where they currently stood.

Charlie gaped, and for a second it was like his world inverted itself. How was it possible for him to say Teague's name, and then have him appear, like a summoned monster?

Borden threw Charlie a sneering look. "What's the matter with you, Cole? You look like you're having a stroke!"

"What … ?" Charlie forced himself to concentrate. "What's going on?"

"Like I said, you need to read the bloody memos!" Borden tapped a button on the side of his monitor and the volume came up.

"*–such an amazing development for GreenSea!*" Edward Morant was in mid-flow, gesturing with both hands, smiling tightly. "*As of today, our company's new partnership with the Teague Technical Group represents the next step in its evolution, the start of a synergy that will take our vision for Earth-friendly technology to a whole new level.*" He seemed to be reading the words off an autocue, and the stiff smile didn't reach his eyes.

"Partnership?" Charlie echoed the word suspiciously. Suddenly, the reason behind the frenzied activity in the office became abundantly clear. He really *had* been way behind the curve on this, so lost in the investigation with Jan that news of it had never reached him.

"More like *takeover*," Borden said, with a snort. "Teague Technical swallows up competitors like a shark going after chum, *chum*." He followed that up with a shrug. "Morant's trying to save face, make it look like it's amicable, but it's a forced buy-out, pure and simple. I don't care, though. My shares are going to triple in value."

On the screen, Brody Teague had decided to take the spotlight, and he came up to the lectern, into a storm of camera flashes, gently sidelining Morant before the other man was aware of it. In his ten thousand dollar suit, Teague was the epitome of the alpha geek, the kind of slick smartass guy that Charlie contemptuously thought of as a *"bro-grammer"*. Athletic and trim, aggressively intelligent, and totally unhindered by any moral compass, he was what you would get if you spliced a Silicon Valley tech dude with a Hollywood-handsome frat boy.

"What a great day," Teague said, with a glib smile, beginning with the words that had become his signature catchphrase. *"A great day for GreenSea, a great day for our shareholders."*

The insincerity oozing from Teague's voice was like nails drawn down a blackboard for Charlie, and he hit the mute button, ignoring Borden's scowl as his mind raced to assimilate this alarming new development. "Listen to me, we have a problem."

"Another? Still waiting for you to explain the first one." Borden's attention went to the corridor as the elevator arrived in the nearby reception area, and a group of new arrivals emerged.

Charlie looked in the same direction and saw two dark-suited bodyguards wearing augmented reality-enhanced glasses and radio earpieces. The pair flanked a harried-looking Indian executive, while another man in dark clothes, impossible to see clearly from this angle, hung back by the elevator.

Borden made for the door, but Charlie blocked his exit. "Gary, for crying out loud, have you not been listening?" He made a point of using Borden's first name to emphasize his seriousness.

"To be honest, I don't pay much attention to what comes out of your mouth," retorted the other man.

"The security breach," insisted Charlie. "It has T-Tec's stink all over it! Something is not right—"

Borden shook his head, cutting him off. "The company that just bought out GreenSea is also stealing from it? Do you hear yourself? Does that make any sense? As of now, Brody Teague owns all this, from staplers to servers!" He gestured at the building around them. "You really want to make waves with the new boss *ten seconds* after he takes over?" He didn't wait for a reply, and pushed past Charlie, out into the corridor.

Lost for words, Charlie snatched up his tablet and followed him, moving woodenly. "What just happened?" He asked himself the question, his hands finding one another as he tried to keep hold of the unfolding events.

"Hello, hello!" He heard Borden's voice take on an uncharacteristically cheery tone as the other man greeted the new arrivals. "Gary Borden, GreenSea systems security senior executive. A pleasure to meet you!"

"Samir Patel," said the Indian man, without accepting Borden's offer of a handshake. His tone was brisk and distracted. "You can consider me Brody's second-in-command. I want a tour of your setup, Gary. It's imperative we ensure that everything is adequate while Brody is on site."

"Of course!" Borden led Patel away in the opposite direction. "Shall we start with our operations center?"

"I suppose so." Patel's voice echoed down the corridor as they moved away, sounding equally terse and indifferent. Charlie saw him turn toward the man lurking by the elevator. "Mr Stone, if you could join us?"

The man called Stone moved out into the atrium, and Charlie felt an odd chill run through him as he caught sight of his face. Narrow and gaunt, with a hawkish nose and cold eyes, the final member of Patel's entourage was tall and intimidating. He wore a dark coat better suited to a chilly climate, and with every step he took, he seemed to be evaluating everything around him.

When the man looked in Charlie's direction, he couldn't help but turn away, suddenly fearful of making eye contact. The reaction was strange, almost primal. He'd felt the same thing when he was a kid, trying to avoid the gaze of a neighborhood bully, and again much later, when men with guns had held his life in their hands.

There was something else familiar about Stone, not just a face that rang a distant bell of memory in Charlie's thoughts, but in the way the man carried himself. He moved like a predator stalking prey.

Only one other person Charlie Cole knew had that same aura about them, that razor edge hiding in plain sight; but it had been a long time since he had seen Sam Fisher.

FOUR

GreenSea Incorporated – Canary Wharf – London

Brody Teague leaned forward over the lectern and scanned the faces of the gathered journalists, picking out the ones he knew to be shills and easily swayed.

"Now, I'm not saying I know everything…" He smiled a perfect, movie star smile and received a scattering of chuckles in return. "Who am I kidding? Yes, I am! I know exactly what I am talking about."

He felt the heat of the room's attention on him and soaked it in. It wasn't as good a serotonin hit as he felt from working the big auditoriums, like the theater-size space at T-Tec's campus in Palo Alto or the hall in the Lisbon tower, but he still wanted it. It never got old, feeling every person out there hanging on his words, no matter if they loved him or hated him.

"People look at me and they say, *who the hell does this douchebag think he is?*" Teague pressed on, past the nervous laughs, dialing up the intensity. He could sense GreenSea's CEO nearby, shifting apprehensively as he continued, but

Teague couldn't care less about the man's concerns. He was on a roll. "People see some good-looking punk and they think I'm an immature man-child who lucked into a billion-dollar IPO. Those people are wrong. Because what I have is *vision*." He prodded the lectern as he said the last word, reeling in his audience's curiosity with it like a fishing lure. "I'm talking about building better todays to have greater tomorrows. A world where we cross off the worst experiences of humankind and be our best."

He paraphrased the opening chapter of his book, *Great Days: The Brody Teague Way*. He hadn't actually written the book. The text had come from a learning program he created that had sampled his speeches and synthesized something that vaguely resembled a manifesto. Not that it really mattered. Teague's legion of fans and consumers around the world made it a bestseller, as he'd predicted they would. From the start, he'd had a good eye for the thing that would sell. It was one of his strengths.

"Let me tell you what my vision is." He held for a dramatic pause. "I want to see poverty *gone*. And I'm not talking about food in bellies, folks. I'm talking about poverty of energy, poverty of education, poverty of justice, poverty of opportunity. All that grows out of a level playing field, you know? A world where we take down the walls, heal the wounds and just..." He paused again, letting his eyes get a little misty. "Just give back, right?"

The conference room was silent, and for a moment Teague wondered if he had leaned too hard into fake sentimentality. He forgot he was playing to an audience largely made up of Brits and Europeans, and these guys were so stiff, they didn't succumb to the same emotional manipulation and *rah-rah* that got the blood pumping back in the States.

He changed tack. "I see a future of technology unchained. Reset! Freed to make the world better. A world where nobody has to worry about keeping the lights on or staying warm. A world where information is truly open, and so are we." Teague pivoted, clapping Morant on the shoulder. "This merger with GreenSea will bring us a step closer to that world. Believe it! We have great days ahead!"

And then, as he felt the first twitches of his interest waning, Teague stepped off the dais and away, ignoring the torrent of questions yelled at his back by the reporters. His last sight of the conference room was one of his subordinates taking his place at the lectern to spout some pre-scripted post-statements to keep the investors happy.

Another of his assistants, a pale, willowy redhead in a black pantsuit, stepped seamlessly into pace with him as he strode along the corridor. He'd mentally labelled her "Number Eighteen" . It didn't really seem worthwhile for Teague to learn their names, as the people who carried out his whims were largely interchangeable and not really of interest to him. Teague only remembered people who were useful, annoying, or amusing. The rest of his world was made up of nobodies.

"The Prime Minister would like to meet you for dinner," said Eighteen, consulting a digital notepad.

"The what?" He frowned, taking a bottle of chilled ice water offered by her, swigging noisily from it.

"The Prime Minister of Great Britain," she added.

Teague shrugged. "Do I care?" He looked around at the other members of his entourage trailing after him, including

Morant. "Do we care?" No one responded, so he shook his head. "I don't think so."

"Well," Morant spoke up, "it might be–"

"You want to do it? Go ahead. Where's Stone? I want him here." Teague stopped and gave Morant a level look. "You. Where's your office?"

The other man blinked, having difficulty keeping up with Teague's grasshopper mind as he leapt from thought to thought. "On the top floor. The express lift…" He gestured at a bank of elevators as they approached the atrium.

"Oh, good." Teague looked at Eighteen. "So, we're meeting there, make it happen."

"Understood." She immediately began tapping out a message on her computer.

Teague entered the waiting elevator, with his personal security in tow. Morant and his aide moved to follow, but Eighteen gave them a withering look and shook her head.

"Brody will let you know if your presence is required," she told them, as the elevator doors closed in their faces. "Have a great day."

Stone was not his real name.

It was only the current identity he operated under, nothing more than a cover which he would discard in due time, like the others he had adopted over the years.

The man calling himself Stone preferred to live his life in a manner where his identity did not come under any scrutiny. Content to remain a shadow moving along the dark edges of the world, he only ventured into the light when a kill had to be made. And even then, if he could strike unseen, he did so.

He refused the offer of a drink from the lithe young woman attending them, and she retreated. He did not enjoy being summoned to meet the client, like some errant courtier called to appear before a capricious king. He was a professional, and he expected those he worked with to be the same. The etiquette for these matters kept a barrier of deniability between his work and those who paid him.

But this man Teague did not care about any of that. He perched atop the desk in the opulent office, contemptuously considering the photos and mementos belonging to GreenSea's CEO, before finally turning his attention to his guest.

"What are we doing, huh?" Teague leaned forward, staring intently at the older man. He shrugged, his hands moving in the air. "I thought we had bought quality here. Your reputation said you were the best at this."

"Every sanction has its complications," offered Stone, softening the rough vowels of his Iron Curtain English. "All contracts so far have been executed to completion."

"*Complications.*" Teague said the word like he didn't understand what it meant. "Complications bore me. Brody Teague doesn't do complicated. He does *complex*. There's a difference."

Stone frowned and spread his hands. "Why are we talking?"

"Because it's what I want." Teague glanced up, shooting his colleague a look.

The Indian, Patel, said nothing, keeping his back to one of the large windows looking out over the river Thames. Stone understood that Teague's long-suffering companion had been his friend from their days as students at the Massachusetts

Institute of Technology, the only one of their company's founder members who remained after Teague had ousted the rest.

Stone gave a slow shake of the head. "You do not want me to be here. You pay me to stay in the shadows. We should not be in the same city, let alone risk being seen together." He had completed his work in London, and he should have been on a plane out of the country by now.

"I pay you to do what I say. I say *be here*." Teague found his momentum, and he continued onward. "I say *get rid of my problems*. But you don't, Stone, or whatever the fuck your real name is. You cause problems for me."

"Ah." At last, he understood the reason for this meeting. "You are referring to the sanction in Montreal."

A week earlier, he had been in Quebec to end the life of one of Brody Teague's "problems" . While the operation had gone as planned, a swift murder on a snowy highway late at night, there had been an unexpected complication. A local police officer happened on the scene, and Stone had been forced to eliminate her as well. In the end, he folded the additional kill into the scenario he left behind for the investigators and exfiltrated the same night. But there was the possibility that his likeness might have been caught on the officer's body camera and uploaded to the police precinct's cloud server.

"Brody, we, uh, we dealt with that," insisted Patel, speaking up for the first time.

"Did we, Samir?" Teague turned his ire on the other man. "Are you a hundred percent sure?" He didn't wait for Patel to reply and snapped back to Stone. "This is a critical juncture, you understand? Critical. Even the smallest mistake can derail my project at this stage, and I will. Not. Have. It." Teague punctuated his words by rapping his fist on the CEO's desk. Then he shook his head and rose. "Are you getting sloppy because you're old? I mean, what are you compared to me? Fucking ancient. Old enough to be my dad, or something."

"Perish the thought," said Stone.

"We don't do sloppy at T-Tec!" Teague snapped, his color rising. "I don't tolerate it. We do clean and fast!"

"You keep your hands clean," Stone corrected, taking on a lecturing tone. "The rest you outsource." He met the younger man's gaze, his glacial patience diminishing. "Mr Teague, you fancy yourself as some sort of self-styled 'disruptor' of established order and accepted methods. But all you do is attempt what other, wiser men have already tried and learned from." Stone let the words hang for a moment, briefly glancing in Patel's direction. "Find some wisdom now. Leave me alone and let me do my work. In the long run, it will be better for both of us."

"No." Teague shook his head. "I'm not happy with my service. Zero star rating. I'm unconvinced." He jabbed a finger at his two bodyguards, who stood impassively at either side of the executive elevator. "Retire him," he demanded.

The two men exchanged looks. "You mean... here?" One of them ventured the question, as his colleague drew a Beretta M9 semi-automatic from beneath his jacket.

"Right here on this shitty rug," shouted Teague, his voice cracking. "So I can see!"

The bodyguard with the gun took two steps toward the leather sofa where Stone sat, raising the pistol to aim it at the back of his head.

As he had been taught, Stone had automatically assessed the room upon entering it regarding various factors – ease of escape, potential threats, opportunities for cover and so on. That training had kept him alive on more than one occasion, and he did it as effortlessly as breathing.

Stone moved, much faster than one would have expected from a man of his age. He shifted in place, one hand coming up to snag the barrel of the Beretta, giving it a savage twist. The bodyguard grunted in pain as his wrist bent the wrong way, bones grinding against one another.

He had a weapon of his own, of course. He never traveled without it. But he saw no need to draw it here, for a matter so trivial. His momentum pushed him up out of the chair and he continued the move, drawing a wet snap from the man's wrist. With his other hand, he fired a punch into a nerve plexus at the base of the bodyguard's throat, robbing him of the chance to cry out. Wheezing and gripping his broken wrist, the bodyguard stumbled backwards.

The M9 grasped in his hand, he flicked it around in an adroit show of dexterity and had it pointing at the second bodyguard even as the other man's gun cleared its shoulder-holster. Teague's assistant covered her ears and yelped as a single shot cracked loudly. Stone put the 9mm round through the second bodyguard's kneecap, crippling him. The CEO's office was soundproofed, so he could have discharged the entire magazine, but one bullet was enough to make his point.

He disarmed the second man and turned back toward Teague, who laughed and clapped as if he were a child at the circus.

"All right, all right! That's what I'm talking about!"

"Many people have tried to… *retire* me," he explained. "I have buried them all."

"I believe it!" Teague gave a whistle. "This pair of pricks, they'd smoke any ordinary old guy, but not you, huh? Cool. I take back what I said, your skills are sharp!" He sighed, then smiled. "Honestly, I was thinking you'd kill them both. But you have control as well as edge, don't you? Impressive. *Five stars!*"

"I said he was worth the money," offered Patel, moving gingerly out of the corner he had backed into.

"Yeah, yeah, yeah," Teague waved Patel into silence. "I wanted to, like, see some of it up close." He rocked forward, off the desk, advancing on Stone. He seemed unconcerned by the fact that the other man still had a pistol in his hand, with enough rounds in it to kill everyone in the room. "OK, the Montreal thing? Already forgotten. But I need to know you can give me what I need, right?"

Teague snapped his fingers in the woman's direction and nervously she handed over a digital tablet. The younger man thrust it at Stone.

The device showed a few pages of information and a photograph of a man in his thirties with short, dark hair and a full face. A target package, identical to hundreds of others the assassin had seen in his time. Another problem to be solved.

"Your work in London isn't finished, yet." Teague tapped the tablet with a finger. "This guy, he's nosing around where he shouldn't be, just like his friend was. Get rid of him. Make it look like an accident, or a mugging…" He laughed and threw up his hands. "Whatever is good! I don't want to mess with your process."

"Charles Cole." Stone read the target's name aloud.

"This one's a gimmie," Teague said, with a nod. "Easy mark. He's in this building, right now, as a matter of fact! Practically giftwrapped for you."

"Uh, Brody…" Patel looked up from swiping across the square tile of his smartwatch screen, his tone doubtful.

"*Uh Brody.*" Teague mimicked Patel's manner. "Shit, Samir, every damn time you say that, I know it's going to piss me off. What?"

"According to the building's security system, Cole's ID card was logged out eleven minutes ago. He's gone."

Before Teague could say any more, Stone held up his hand. "That is not an issue. I will complete the contract." His tolerance for his current employer's behavior was waning, and he wanted to be gone. Handing the Beretta back to the man whose wrist he had ruined, he nodded at the second bodyguard, who lay gasping on the bloodstained rug trying to staunch his wound. "You should have that looked at."

As he stepped into the elevator, he heard Teague chuckle. "Try not to get your picture taken this time, yeah?"

FIVE

Ramstein Air Force Base – Kaiserslautern – Germany

A haze of pre-dawn pink gathered at the horizon, signaling that sunrise was not far behind, and the air held the chill of rain damp even though the clouds were gone and the sky was clear.

Hoisting his gear bag over his shoulder, Fisher crossed the dark asphalt of the runway, moving toward the tall sliver of light spilling out of the hangar before him. He cast around, scanning down the flight line. Painted ghost-gray, lines of US Air Force C-17 Globemaster and C-130 Hercules transport planes sat waiting in their staging areas, ready to set off back across the Atlantic, or in the opposite direction toward operational zones in the Middle East.

Casual observers would have seen little difference between those aircraft and the large machine hidden inside the hangar. Fourth Echelon's airborne operations center sat somewhere between the C-17 jet and its bigger brother, the monster-sized C-5A Galaxy, but unlike those Air Force birds it was night-black and bore no identifying markings beyond a registration number.

The Paladin was all cutting-edge stealth technology and covert power projection. With a radar cross-section as small as a Piper Cub, it still managed to pack in enough hardware to run 4E's most sensitive missions from anywhere on the planet. It could masquerade as a civilian cargo carrier or make combat landings on improvised airstrips, and only the discreet blisters and antennae along the lines of the fuselage hinted at other secret capabilities. Fisher didn't know the details, but that matte black skin was some kind of advanced composite, recently improved to make the aircraft virtually invulnerable to electronic warfare and cyberattacks. To his eyes, it gave the Paladin the look of a bull shark; big, sleek and dangerous.

The command staff at Ramstein knew the drill. They had assigned the Paladin to the remotest hangar on the base, far away from any curious onlookers, making sure that what few maintenance techs they did supply knew to keep their mouths shut and their eyes down while they fueled the plane. Black jets meant only one thing – *if I tell you, I have to kill you.*

Fisher gave the ground crew a wide berth and made his way to the rear cargo ramp, climbing aboard. He passed Lea Kade, finding her at work securing a gear case on the deck. Kade gave him a respectful nod which he returned – the stocky young Polynesian woman had been a Marine, but Fisher didn't hold that against her. One of a handful of 4E field agents recently assigned to the Paladin, the ex-jarhead specialized in communications and cryptography.

"She on board?" Fisher nodded toward the front of the plane.

Kade knew who he meant. "Sir, yes sir."

Fisher took that in with a frown. "Told you before not to 'sir' me, Kade."

"You are technically an officer, sir," she replied.

"Don't remind me," said Fisher. "What's so damn important you had to reel us back here?"

Kade looked away. "I'm not cleared to know message content, sir. I just see that TOP SECRET banner and raise the flag."

He accepted that with a reluctant shrug. "Carry on, Marine."

Fisher moved up the aircraft. Inside, there was a series of cramped modular compartments – among them crew quarters, an armory, a workshop, and a small infirmary – but the main event was the command-and-control area, a cut-down version of the bigger C&C center back at NSA headquarters. Every square centimeter around the perimeter of the compartment had been outfitted with computers, monitors, and hardened server stacks, the middle of the space dominated by the strategic mission interface, or SMI. The crew nicknamed it "the pool table", a virtual plotting surface that could present text, maps, video, or any other kind of mission-critical data.

Grim stood at her usual place at the head of the table, arms folded across her chest, watching him expectantly. Anna Grímsdóttir was, he could not deny, the most coolly efficient person he'd ever met. She had more ice-water in her veins than most tier one operators of his acquaintance.

He glanced around. His daughter had been with Grim when they split up, following standard operating procedure to return via different routes, but now there was no sign of her.

"Sarah's getting a hot meal and a cot at the visiting officer's quarters, courtesy of the Air Force." Grim sensed the question before he voiced it. "She deserves it."

"And after?"

"Then it'll be orientation, and I'll look at making her operational as soon as possible."

Fisher made a negative noise. "You're really going through with this?"

"I really am," Grim replied, "unless you can give me a good reason why I shouldn't?" She didn't wait for him to think of one. "With all due respect, Sam, you're not getting any younger, and we need new blood." She gestured at a screen showing a world map projection, highlighting a dozen hotspots that were of interest to Fourth Echelon. "Briggs is in Shanghai chasing arms dealers, Loskov is in Moscow surveilling that Russian bio-scientist, and the others are in transit or already embedded... We have all our Splinter Cells deployed right now, and that operational tempo is not viable in the long term. Rainbow and SHD aren't letting me poach any of their people, so I looked for someone else to fill the gap. Call it a temporary reassignment if you like, but until further notice, Sarah stays."

"You want me to be OK with putting my only child in the field?"

"That train has already left the station," Grim said firmly. "At least here, you get to keep an eye on her." The woman's expression softened slightly. "She has your determination, Sam. You can either get in the way of that or you can help her achieve her potential."

Fisher's lip curled. As always, Grim had a clear-eyed view of the matter. But it would take a lot more than a few choice words for him to make peace with the situation. "Good speech. You practice it?"

"Never had the need." Grim leaned forward and tapped the digital chart table, waking it from standby. For now, the "Sarah" part of their conversation was clearly over.

"Langley briefed me on the road," she began, making a flicking motion across the screen. A fan of virtual pages lined up in front of Fisher, each one presenting a new piece of intelligence. All bore the seal of the Central Intelligence Agency. "Our friends in Virginia have been tracking a series of targeted killings. Each victim was involved in high-level information security."

Fisher put his elbows on the edge of the table and craned over to study the pages. The CIA files were drawn from several different police reports and coroner's records. Faces of the dead looked up at him, some scans of passport pictures or family photos, others stark black-and-whites taken post-mortem.

Grim pointed to the pages one by one. "A top flight penetration tester. A lecturer in artificial intelligence at Berkeley. A software engineer from Finland. A former Fancy Bear hacker."

Fisher raised an eyebrow at that last one. "Say again?"

"I don't come up with the codenames," Grim admitted. "Fancy Bear is Unit 26165, the hacker team operated by the GRU. State-run black hats working at the behest of the Russian government. The dead guy was one of their top guns before he turned freelance." She pulled up the locations of the killings on a world map. "These are just the confirmed ones."

"Sad as this is for the families of these people," said Fisher, "why does Fourth Echelon care about their deaths?"

"The woman from Berkeley caught the CIA's attention. She had high-level security clearance, she previously worked on some DARPA advanced drone projects for the Department of Defense. At first, they thought it might be connected to that, but the prevailing theory is that these kills are part of a planned program of assassination, specifically targeting individuals with a common, high-level skill set. With the DoD link in the mix, that's enough to suggest a potential national security threat."

Fisher considered that. While Fourth Echelon was created to be an independent, deep-black counter-terror unit, its roots were in its predecessor; Third Echelon had been an initiative run as a covert action branch of the NSA, the signals intelligence bureau of the US government. The unlawful termination of information security experts would have been right in the old 3E wheelhouse, but these days it wasn't really their remit. Grim knew that as well as Fisher did.

When he spoke again, there was accusation in his tone. "That's thin motivation for the Company to rope us in. There's more to this you're not telling me."

"There are details above my pay grade." That was as much an admission as Grim would ever make. "But you're right, there's a specific reason why you are being read in on this."

Here we go, thought Fisher. Grim dealt out another set of pages, as a croupier would pass out cards over a blackjack table. The new images were a mix of grisly close-ups of stab wounds and virtual reconstructions of the weapon that had made them.

Recognition flashed in the depths of Fisher's memory. The blade in question was the common denominator in each killing. He reached forward and pinched the edges of a digital frame, pulling it apart to enlarge the image.

"The CIA may be struggling with the motive for murdering these people, but they do have a correlation on the assassin's modus operandi," said Grim, offering the bleak truth of it to the empty compartment. "All close-in attacks using the same small, double-edged knife. A single strike to the throat or the heart, the blade twisted so the wound won't close. Massive blood loss resulting in death."

Fisher gave a nod. "I know this weapon. I've seen it before. Russian made, issued to KGB field agents back in the day. They call it a *karatel*."

"*Punisher*," said Grim, translating the word. "Two days ago, the Montreal municipal police put out an advisory that got picked up by Interpol and the agency." She dealt out another set of pages. "A civilian and a cop killed at what looked like a routine traffic stop. Single fatal stab wound in each case, from a small double-edged knife."

Fisher's expression turned stony as he saw the murder scene photos, with patches of bright crimson on the dirty gray snowbanks along a highway. "Let me guess. This fits the profile of the other kills."

"The civilian was an engineer working in processor design for advanced, cutting-edge computers."

"The cop was collateral damage. Must have come on the scene unexpectedly."

Fisher walked through the assassination in his mind, gaming out the scenario. In the past, he had been called upon to do similar work by his government, silent terminations of individuals who represented a threat to the United States and to global security. He considered how he might have fulfilled the same mission brief, if things had been reversed. But however it would have happened, he drew the line at taking the life of an innocent.

Whoever was behind these murders did their work up close and personal. There were easier ways to take out a target, cleaner methods with far less risk of blowback. A shot from a sniper rifle or a suppressed pistol would have given the same result, and at greater range.

But that's the point, isn't it? This assassin wanted to see the light go out in their target's eyes. They wanted to hear the last breath, feel the hot blood spill over their hands when the blade went in.

"He likes the kill," said Fisher. "Maybe a little too much."

"And it got him into trouble," agreed Grim. With an index finger, she pushed out one last image across the table-screen. "This is from the cop's body camera."

He saw a grainy frame-grab from digital footage, recognizing a watermark in one corner with codes and text identifying the date and location where it had been shot. A partial sliver of a man's face was visible in the corner of the image, an arc of pale skin in the black depths of a heavy coat.

A flicker of dim, nagging recognition pushed at the back of Fisher's thoughts. "I know him."

"If he is who the CIA think he is, then *yes*, you do."

Fisher gave her a hard look. The hastily terminated training operation in Berlin, the urgent recall back to the jet, the eyes-only secrecy of the message, it was starting to come into focus now. "Don't play games with me, Grim. Spit it out."

She sighed. "Partial facial recognition from this still,

combined with the assassin's M/O and the signature murder weapon, brings up one name as the most likely suspect. *Dima Aslanov.*"

"Aslanov's dead." The reply came instantly, and Fisher shook his head. "I was there."

"Did you see a body?"

"That would have been difficult." He closed his eyes for a moment and thought back to that day. The sense-memory of it came to him with full force – the dull stink of cordite and concrete dust in the air, the low rumble of the detonations as the airstrike flattened the enemy outpost. "It was Desert Storm. I was still a SEAL back then. Word comes down out of nowhere one morning, a high-value target is in our area of operations. When I heard it was Aslanov, I damn near hijacked the Black Hawk so I could go along. I wanted to be the one to bring him in."

Fisher recalled the mission in flash-frames, snatches of sand, fire, and smoke. "But it went to shit. We lost the helo. Aslanov had been working with the Iraqi Republican Guard, they fell back to a strongpoint, and we couldn't get close. Command called the game, and the next thing we knew, they had a flight of RAF Tornadoes come in and carpet-bomb the site. There wasn't enough left to put in a thimble, let alone a corpse we could identify."

"But you saw him, right? Aslanov. On that day."

He nodded, glancing down at the still image. "He was there. I put lead down range as we went after him, but never came close." Fisher stared at the ghost-face, questioning a reality that he had accepted and lived with for over two decades. "We closed the book on Aslanov. Crossed him off. Moved on."

"You may have been premature. Because if that was not Dima Aslanov in Montreal, then it's someone mimicking his profile down to the last detail."

Annoyance coiled through Fisher, turning into motion as he pushed himself away from the table. He did not want to accept that an enemy he thought long dead and buried was not only alive, but that the man had been continuing his grisly trade in the same shadows where Fisher worked.

Could it be true? Had he crossed paths with Aslanov after Kuwait and never known it? The man was a dark mirror of Fisher, and something about the Russian had always unsettled him whenever they had faced one another. Fisher feared that Aslanov was what he might have become without a code, without a conscience.

"The CIA read us in because you're the nearest we have to an authority on this man," said Grim. "Four documented contact incidents over a ten year period starting in the 1980s—"

"Five," Fisher corrected. "Closest I ever got to him was Budapest in '89. He dodged me there, killed two men on the way out. That was after he'd quit taking a paycheck from Moscow and gone pay-to-play."

Grim made a note on the screen. "Sam, everyone else who crossed swords with this guy is dead. The CIA need your insight, so as of now Fourth Echelon is officially collaborating in this ghost hunt." She paused, framing her next words carefully. "Do you want to tell me what's so personal about this?"

He looked up, meeting her gaze. "I don't let things get personal."

She smiled thinly. "Who do you think you are talking to

here? After all we've been through, I'd assume you wouldn't bullshit me. It insults my intelligence."

Fisher bit down on a growl. The woman was more perceptive than he would have liked. They shared a unique bond, and at the core of it was the inability to lie to one another. Some days it could be a good thing, but other times – like now – not so much.

She waited for him to respond, and at length Fisher shrugged off his jacket before helping himself to a steaming mug of coffee. "I don't want this on the record," he told her. "Understood?"

Grim nodded. "Keeping secrets is what I do, Sam. So why don't you start from the beginning?"

SIX

1984

French Embassy – Tbilisi – Soviet Socialist Republic of Georgia

"This damn suit," said Fisher, pulling irritably at the too-tight collar cinched around his neck. "Feel like a prize turkey in this thing."

At his side, Regan Burns gave him a wry smile, pausing to brush a speck of lint off his immaculate dinner jacket. She appraised him with a long, challenging glance. "You look good in black, Sam. You ought to dress up more often."

He couldn't resist returning the smile. "Nobody's going to be looking at me tonight, not with you around."

Regan cut a stunning figure in the cold evening air, decked out in a form-fitting off-the-shoulder gown colored midnight blue and shot through with sparkling threads of silver. She had her dark hair up for a change, and she could have stepped right off a fashion show catwalk. His hand found hers and they continued walking, up the wide stairs and into the ornate atrium at the front of the building.

The French Embassy was an elegant, well-kept pile behind ten-foot high walls in the nicer quarter of the Georgian capital. Inside the keep, you would have been forgiven for thinking you were in some upscale Parisian arrondissement – but drive a few miles and the reality of the surrounding country set in.

Jammed against the Turkish border and the Black Sea in one direction and the greater mass of the USSR in the other, the nation-state had long been a buffer zone between conflicting ideologies. Tensions had risen in recent years, as leaders with anti-corruption and nationalist agendas caused friction with the Communist Party apparatchiks in Moscow. The Soviet old guard were intent on maintaining the status quo in Georgia, but their adversaries in the West saw an opening to be exploited. In such conditions opportunities bloomed for anyone who worked in the shadows, criminals and spies alike.

As the couple entered, they passed through a discreet security arch concealed by velvet curtains. Out of sight, a French soldier watched a monitor for any warnings from the hidden metal detector.

Fisher disliked being out in the field without a weapon to hand, but to carry anything larger than a fountain pen would be to risk a pat-down, and that would draw more attention than he wanted.

He handed over their monogrammed invites to an aloof woman waiting at reception beneath the paired flags of France and Georgia. The woman ticked their names off a checklist, but he caught the brief look she gave him as they walked away, like she knew something he didn't.

It was likely that anyone who needed to know who they were, did know. Fisher had yet to deal with the French in any operational capacity, but he'd heard they took a thorough, if hands-off, approach.

"Let's get a drink." Regan led him into the building proper, finding the way to the ballroom.

Paneled in dark wood and lined with oil paintings of pastoral scenes, the wide, open hall had a curved glass ceiling high above, dotted with raindrops. Well-dressed men and women moved with their cliques, chatting and laughing to the accompaniment of a string quartet playing some classical number that Fisher didn't recognize.

They received a nod from the American ambassador as they passed his group. Other clusters of attendees stayed in the orbit of their fellows, with only the French moving between them, greasing the wheels of the gathering. Fisher spotted the contingent from Moscow, the stiff and unsmiling men in military dress uniforms with their willowy, ex-ballerina wives. But, for the moment, he saw no sign of the one face he was searching for.

Regan plucked two flutes of champagne from the tray of a passing server and pressed one into Fisher's hand.

He sipped the drink and frowned at it. "Can I get a beer instead?"

"Live a little," she replied. "I intend to. This is my first real time off in weeks! I'm going to enjoy it."

She clinked her glass against his and took another sip, eyeing him over the rim. Regan had that look that Fisher couldn't pull away from, like everything she said was *daring* him.

She was unlike any woman he had ever met. Sure, there had been others, but no one so sharp, as vital as Regan Burns. Smart, funny, and uncompromising, she might have been too much for a man of lesser character. But Sam Fisher had never shied away from a challenge in his life.

The two of them had first crossed paths at an office mixer just after Fisher had been posted to Tbilisi – she worked in the American embassy's pool of translators, and he was in the country as a diplomatic aide. Neither of their official roles told the full truth about them, though.

While Regan *did* translate documents for the ambassador and his staff, she was also working as a low-level cryptanalyst for the NSA, splitting her time between embassy business and decoding low-priority signals gathered by the listening gear hidden in the US residents' compound.

Fisher knew this because his post as a diplomatic aide was an equally thin veil over another reality. He had been posted to Georgia at the behest of the CIA, operating in an "official cover" capacity. The moment he had shown any interest in Regan Burns, Fisher's supervisors back at Langley had quietly run the woman's life under a microscope, to be certain of her loyalties. With approval granted, Sam and Regan started dating.

They didn't talk about their other jobs. They didn't need to. But Fisher suspected Regan had an inkling of why he was really in the republic.

At times, he felt like it was obvious to everyone. Sam Fisher, on secondment from the Navy, standing tall and straight, hair slicked back, his youthful face clean-shaven. Anyone who looked twice could see there was a wolf in his sheep's clothing. For his part, Fisher still wasn't sure if this secret agent stuff was the best fit for a gung-ho squid looking to make a name for himself. But it had its benefits.

The couple lived in the moment, and so far, that was working. It wasn't all plain sailing, of course. Only a few months old, their relationship had already weathered a few storms. Fisher had to admit that Regan kept him off balance, but rather than back away from that, it made him want to know her even more. She was a puzzle to him, at times frustrating, at other times dazzling, but he couldn't deny that she could compel him with a flash of those dark eyes and a sly laugh.

"What?" Regan cocked her head, studying him.

Fisher realized he'd been staring at her. "Nothing. Just... thinking how lucky I am to be with the most beautiful woman in the room."

"In the whole wide room, huh? Wow," she teased. "Thanks, handsome. It's a little corny, but I'll take it."

"That's not, uh, I didn't mean..." He stumbled over his words, belatedly realizing he could have picked a better compliment. Fisher dried up, uncertain what to say next, and then he grinned. Regan could always do this to him, disarm him with just a few words. She laughed and so did he.

Damn, am I falling for this woman? He pushed the question away before the weight of it could settle.

And then Captain First Rank Maxim Belov of the Soviet Black Sea Fleet crossed Fisher's line of sight. The Russian naval officer fiddled with a packet of cigarettes as he made his way toward the atrium.

A switch flipped in Fisher's head, as if he had become a weapon locked onto a target. Belov was his reason for being here, the mission behind the masquerade.

Fisher checked the bulky "canteen" style Navy watch on his wrist. Belov was running late.

When he looked back at Regan, the smile on her face had gone. She followed Fisher's line of attention, catching sight of the Russian as he disappeared through the doorway.

"You know that guy?"

"Never seen him before." The lie came automatically, and the moment he said it, Fisher knew she saw right through him.

Regan put down her glass and stepped closer, speaking in a low voice so only he would hear it. "Are you… working tonight? Is that why we're here?" Her buoyant mood faded.

In that moment, anything he could say would be the wrong answer, and he knew it. But his silence was no better a reply.

"Well, shit." Regan shook her head. "Here I thought you were going to show a girl a good time, but I'm not your date tonight, am I?" There was genuine hurt in her eyes. "I'm your cover."

"It's not like that."

"Really, Sam? Don't patronize me."

Frowning, he looked at his watch again. He had to give Belov time to make his way up to the smoker's terrace on the floor above, and light up a cigarette. It was vital to be discreet. One wrong move would alert the KGB minders mingling with the reception's other attendees.

"You know we can't talk about it. Not here." It was the closest Fisher had ever come to admitting the truth to her.

"I know," she said. "I just…" Regan trailed off and gave a tight, fake smile. "I don't know what I thought. Never mind. My mistake."

He wanted to explain it to her. He wanted to tell Regan how he felt, but the words retreated, and frustration uncoiled in him. "I have to go," he said finally. "This won't take long. Don't leave without me."

"Sure," she said coldly. "That would look bad, wouldn't it?"

He left her behind in the ballroom and set off in Belov's wake. With a deep breath, Fisher closed off the echoes of the conversation in his mind and put his focus into the mission.

It was an effort to keep his pace unhurried, the anticipation of action tingling through him as Fisher made his way up the marble staircase. Reaching the last flight leading to the terrace, he slowed.

Tall glass-paneled doors led out on to the dimly lit terrace, but a heavyset pug of a man blocked them. He wore the same outfit as the servers carrying trays of drinks, and gave Fisher a sideways look, almost a smirk, before waving his hand like a traffic cop at an intersection.

"No entry," he said, in heavy Moscow-accented English, adding a *shoo*-ing gesture for good measure. "Come later."

Fisher looked past the man, trying to see out into the evening, but the panes in the doors were mottled and he could only make out shadows.

His thoughts raced. If Belov was out there and being kept isolated, then the operation was already blown.

Had the Russians noticed the naval officer acting suspiciously? Had Belov done something to tip his hand in the past few days? It had taken weeks to set up this rendezvous, painstakingly earning Belov's trust after a CIA operative had made a clandestine approach at another diplomatic function.

The word was Maxim Belov had displeased his superiors and, knowing his time was running out, he had opted to take the only path still open to him. He wanted to defect to the United States.

To sweeten the pot, Belov offered up critical data on the Black Sea Fleet's surface ship capabilities. If secured, the material would be an intelligence coup for Langley. With his naval background and – as far as the Russians were concerned – his relatively clean profile, Fisher had been chosen as point man on the mission.

Tonight was supposed to be the first handoff from Belov, the French Embassy picked as neutral ground where both sides could mingle freely without raising suspicions.

But now the plan was unravelling. Fisher should have walked away. That was what his instructors back at the Farm would have told him, had they been here. *Your source has been burned. Cut your losses and disengage. Write it off and move on.*

But failure did not come easily to him. The notion of leaving a man behind, even a turncoat like Belov, stuck in his craw. It wasn't how he was wired.

"You not listen?" The man in the server uniform took a step closer. "Go way." The smile slipped off the Russian's face. "Tell your people, this not your business."

"I think it is," said Fisher, making the decision. He shot a bullet-fast punch into the other man's neck with enough force to send him reeling back.

Keeping up the momentum, Fisher body-checked the Russian, shoving him through an adjoining door and into a walk-in janitorial closet. He landed more blows on the other man, but it was like punching a sack of meat.

The Russian gave an angry-dog snarl, grabbed at the first available thing he could use as a weapon – a carpet broom – and swung the long handle at Fisher's face and neck.

Fisher took a hit and blocked another, hearing wood splinter as his attacker's makeshift baton broke under the impact. Trapped in the tiny space of the service room, neither man had room to maneuver. They moved in circles, locked in a violent, brutal dance.

When the broom handle came at him again, Fisher snagged the damaged end and wrenched it the other way. A piece of the shaft came away in his hand and he tried to swing it at the Russian's face, but the other man reacted faster than he expected.

Using the broken end of the broom like the tip of a spear, the Russian jabbed Fisher hard in the chest, the impact cracking a rib. Wheezing, Fisher stumbled backward over a tin mop bucket and lost his balance, falling into a rack of cleaning supplies and then down to the tiled floor.

The Russian heaved a grunt and wound up for a knockout swing aimed at Fisher's head, but the other man still had his splintered piece of the shaft in one hand.

Fisher lurched forward and jammed the jagged wooden rod into the Russian's knee-joint, drawing a gasping, pain-filled moan from his attacker.

He rocketed forward and up, taking full advantage of the strike to grapple his opponent. Before the Russian could react, Fisher had his arm snaked around the thickset man's bull neck, and he pulled tight. Choking off the Russian's air, he put his weight into the hold and held it until the smaller man went limp.

Collecting himself, Fisher peeked out through the half-open door and back into the stairwell. The sounds of conversation, clinking glasses and classical music filtered up from the lower floor. No one had heard the melee.

Leaving the unconscious man in the service room, Fisher

straightened his jacket and walked out on to the terrace. He ignored the pain in his chest, working to even out his breathing.

A light rain fell around him, ticking off the awnings that extended over the wide stone platform. Fisher looked past the ornamental planters and sculpted balustrade, searching for any sign of Belov.

For one worrying moment, he was afraid that the would-be defector might have gone over the stone rail that edged the terrace, risking the steep drop to the glass roof of the ballroom below. But there was nobody down there.

To the left, the space was poorly lit, and Fisher instinctively gravitated in that direction. As he stepped out of the glow of the windows, he caught sight of movement in the shadows at the far end of the terrace.

Two figures, one close to the other, almost like lovers embracing.

The closest of them, with the narrow-shouldered profile of an athlete, turned in place to look in Fisher's direction. He saw an older man with a gaunt, narrow face and dead eyes.

The man had Maxim Belov up against a wall, one black-gloved hand pressed against the naval officer's chest. Belov caught sight of Fisher and started forward, desperation writ large on his features.

The gaunt man shoved Belov back, and silver light flashed off the wicked edge of a knife in his other hand. Before Fisher could take a step, the gaunt man thrust the small blade into Belov's throat and twisted it, fatally severing his carotid. The killer calmly turned the dying man's head away so the arterial spray would miss him.

Fisher froze. Even from this distance, he knew he could do

nothing to save Belov's life, and with no weapon to hand, he could not avenge his murder.

The gaunt man withdrew his hand and allowed Belov to slide down the wall and collapse in an untidy heap. Keeping one eye on Fisher, he carefully placed the bloody knife in the dead man's hand, closing his fingers around it. Fisher recognized the distinctive shape of the blade, the double-edged knife the Russians called a *karatel*. He drew up his hands into a defensive stance, ready in case the gaunt man came at him, but the assassin was in no hurry.

"A traitor's death," he said. His accent had a measured, Slavic edge to it. "Maxim failed in his service to his country. He will do better as a lesson to others, yes?" Then he bent down and recovered something from the dead man's jacket, a small gray metal rectangle that he turned over in his fingers.

The object was a Minox LX camera, the Cold War standard for covert photography on both sides of the Iron Curtain. On the film cartridge inside would be the bounty of intelligence that Belov had promised as the down-payment for his freedom.

Fisher felt sick inside. Belov had trusted him, and now the man lay in a puddle of his own blood, his life brutally cut short.

The killer glanced up, intuiting Fisher's thoughts. "You Americans do not lose well. It is not something they prepare you for, I think." He pocketed the camera and stood up.

"We're not done yet." Fisher stepped into the other man's path. "Give me the camera or I'll take it from you."

"Oh?" The killer considered the threat. "An understandable demand. With that, you might at least salvage something from this debacle. But no." He shook his head. "Tonight, you go home with empty hands, Mr Fisher."

He stiffened at the mention of his own name but did not respond.

"Are you surprised that I know exactly who you are, Samuel? Perhaps you thought we did not know the identities of all the official cover operatives in Tbilisi." The other man frowned, as if disappointed. "I hoped the situation would not progress this far. My comrade at the door, did you...?"

"I showed some restraint," Fisher broke in. "More than you gave Belov."

"Of course. Easier to imagine yourself as the hero that way. But you will find that after a while, the expedient choice becomes the custom." He buttoned his jacket and walked slowly toward Fisher, arms at his side, maintaining an unthreatening posture. "Step aside, please."

"You think you can walk away?" Fisher stood his ground. "You just murdered a man on French sovereign territory."

"He took his own life," corrected the killer. "Those of weak character frequently do." He sighed and glanced at his wristwatch. "This is how the game is played, my friend. Belov made himself inconsequential the moment he spoke to the CIA. He will fade away, and the French will make no noise about this business. They have too much to lose." The man paused, then moved to stand at the balcony. "And so do you." He looked over the edge and nodded. "She's quite attractive. I can see why you like her."

Fisher's blood turned to ice. He stepped to the edge of the terrace, glancing down, through the glass roof below and into the ballroom. He found Regan immediately, still holding the flute of champagne. She was talking to another woman, a striking blonde in a jet-black ensemble. The woman toyed with a thick bracelet around one of her wrists.

"I thought you would be intelligent enough to walk away," said the killer. "But I pride myself on preparing for every eventuality." He nodded at the blonde. "My comrade in the dress specializes in sanctions using toxins. She has a needle in that bracelet loaded with a chemical... I do not know the name, but I have seen the effects. The victim is barely aware of it. They become sleepy. They lose consciousness. Once they close their eyes, they never open them again."

Fisher stiffened as he watched Regan and the other assassin share a joke. The blonde woman briefly placed her hand on Regan's shoulder, then glanced at her watch.

"Believe me when I say I take no pleasure in causing unnecessary collateral damage. It is unprofessional. But if I do not leave in the next two minutes, Captain Belov will not be the only tragedy tonight," said the killer. "Do not blame yourself. Your mission was always going to fail." His manner was reasonable. "The only thing you can control is how many people will die."

Fisher's hands tightened into fists. His fury seethed beneath the surface, and for a giddy moment he wanted to let it out, to take this man and beat the life from him.

The killer must have seen a flash of that murderous impulse in his eyes, and he backed off a step, momentarily surprised, steeling himself for an attack.

But Fisher forced that rage back into the darkness. He had put Regan at risk for the sake of the mission, and now he was paying the price.

He turned his back on the other man. "Next time I see you,"

he growled, "I promise, you won't have an innocent woman to hide behind."

The killer said nothing, and Fisher heard his footsteps fade away.

When Regan returned from the ladies' room, her new friend was nowhere in sight. She frowned, taking up a fresh glass of champagne, and looked around the ballroom.

"Huh." She made a face. "Ditched twice in one night. Something I said?"

"Regan." Sam pushed through the attendees toward her, and there was an expression on his face she had never seen before. It was *fear*, or something like it, and she instantly felt a chill wash over her. "Do you feel OK?"

"What do you mean?"

He came in close and took her arm, discreetly checking her wrist, then her shoulder. "You feel tired? Any pain?"

"No. I'm fine." Regan pulled her arm out of his grip. "Sam, you're scaring me. What's wrong?" She looked around for the Russian guy he had been scoping out earlier and didn't see him either. "Did something happen … ?"

"We're leaving," he told her, putting a hand between her shoulder blades and applying gentle pressure. "Right now."

Regan let him guide her out of the embassy and on to the street. Sam flagged down a taxi, and soon they were rushing away, back in the direction of the apartment block where many of the US embassy staff in Tbilisi lived.

Sam spoke quietly. "I'm sorry," he said. "I wasn't honest with you. Tonight, I made you a part of something you shouldn't have been involved in."

Regan had never heard him sound as vulnerable as he did in that moment. She rested her head on his shoulder, and her pulse quickened as she saw tiny crimson dots of blood on his shirt. From the very start of their relationship, she had known there were darker parts of Sam Fisher he kept hidden from her, but now a sliver of that reality was revealed, and she didn't know how to react to it. "If I ask you, will you tell me what happened back there?"

"Don't ask me," he told her. "Please don't. Just know I would never let anyone hurt you."

The taxi rumbled on for a few more miles before they spoke again. Regan looked him in the eyes, and she felt she was on shifting sands, the surety of their relationship suddenly in jeopardy. "What are we doing, Sam? You and me. I need to know if we're going to make a go of this."

He sighed. "Before I joined the Navy, I was a dumb kid. A fuckup waiting for his cards to fall the wrong way. But I found something in the military. A path out of that. Regan, I'm no white knight. But I'm trying to be a better man. Tonight, I put that and you at risk. I can't let that happen again. I need to keep you safe."

"Then just... *be with me*," said Regan, and she pulled him closer.

SEVEN

Ramstein Air Force Base – Kaiserslautern – Germany

Fisher fell silent, closing out his story, coming back to the moment with a solemn nod.

Grim had rarely heard him speak so openly about, *well*, anything. For the most part, Sam Fisher was the textbook definition of terse, and she admired that about him. But tonight, Grim had been granted a brief glimpse beneath his armor, to see the human within.

It was a testament to the bond between them that he'd been willing to open up to her about this. What they shared wasn't exactly *trust* – that word was too simplistic to encompass the facts of it – more like a mutual respect.

Grim heard footsteps and looked up to see Lea Kade entering the Paladin's commandand-control center from the rear hatch. She caught the Marine's eye before the other woman could take a step over the threshold and gave her a curt shake of the head. *Not now.*

Kade got the message and retreated back the way she had

come, closing the hatch behind her and leaving them to their privacy.

"What about afterward?" Grim offered the question into the silence that followed.

Fisher leaned back from the glow of the mission interface table, fading into the dimness of the compartment. "The Belov defection was a failure and got black-booked. I was pulled from Georgia a week later and my official cover was rescinded."

"Tell me about Aslanov."

"Found out his name when the agency debriefed me," said Fisher. "They had a jacket on him. Dima Pavlovich Aslanov, one of the KGB's top assassins. He had a few years on me, all of it serious work. Specialized in close-quarter kills." He made a throat-cutting gesture. "Blades, mostly. Trained as a covert infiltrator, zero footprint. When the Russians wanted to send a message, they called him in. For a while, he stayed in when the KGB switched over to being the FSB, then he went freelance."

"What about Maxim Belov?" Grim glanced down at the screen, studying the ghostly image of the man's killer. "Was there any blowback from his death?"

"None," Fisher said, with disdain. "What Aslanov said to me was right on the money. Nobody wanted to risk an international incident over one unimportant officer. The KGB just... took Belov out of the story. His wife and son turned up a month later, lying in a ditch with their throats cut. They were a warning to anyone else thinking of jumping the wall."

Grim knew Fisher well enough to guess that he blamed himself for the deaths of those innocents. She pushed on with her questions. "And Regan?"

Fisher's expression softened slightly as he thought of his

wife. "She left Georgia too. We tried to put it behind us. It was good, for a while. Married her. Then we had Sarah…" He trailed off. "You know all that."

"I do," said Grim, tacitly giving Fisher consent to leave the next part, the sorrowful part, unspoken.

Sam and Regan had exchanged their vows less than a year past that night in Tbilisi, and their daughter had come along soon after. The heartbreak of it was that Regan did not live to see Sarah grow into an impressive young woman, her future stolen by the aggressive cancer that took her life while her daughter was still a teenager.

Fisher stared into nothing, caught on the pain of his memories. "There's only a few times in my life I've felt powerless. First time was out on that terrace at the embassy. Second time was when Regan…" He faltered, unwilling to finish the sentence. "Figured I could do something about one of those things."

"It's always a mistake to take on a crusade, Sam." Grim shook her head.

"Sometimes it's not a choice," he shot back. A familiar razor-edge returned to his tone. "I made it a duty to find Aslanov and put him down. To get a measure of justice for Belov and his family, if nothing else."

Grim had looked over the heavily redacted files that the CIA had supplied on the Russian assassin, and formed a picture of a rare thing – an adversary who was a match for Sam Fisher.

A few years after Georgia, Fisher had volunteered for a risky sortie during his deployment to Senegal, after learning that Aslanov was in-country. Neither man had been able to neutralize the other on that occasion. There were equally unsuccessful encounters after that, then finally the operation during Desert Storm that saw Fisher's nemesis officially declared dead. But despite the years of resentment, ultimately there had been no cathartic moment of confrontation. No justice.

Dima Aslanov's file was closed. The world moved on. If it hadn't been for one tiny lapse of tradecraft on his part, the assassin's survival would have gone unnoticed.

"You were effectively the last person to see Aslanov alive," said Grim.

"Yeah," said Fisher, "through the scope of my CAR-15."

"The folks at Langley want your interpretation of the intel they've gathered, if it is Aslanov. They want the benefit of your experience."

"You mean they want to pump me for any insights and then send out some Ground Branch yahoos to hunt him down," Fisher corrected. "No deal. Aslanov's a ghost. They'd never get close to him. The agency doesn't know who they're dealing with."

Grim could see what was coming. "But you do?"

"You're damn right." Fisher came back into the light. "If he's out still there, I'm the one who's gonna end him. I'll drag whatever he's doing out of the shadows so the whole world can see."

"Sending a lone Splinter Cell operative after a highly motivated killer and whatever organization has the funds to back him, without knowing their motive and endgame…" Grim shook her head again. "No offense, Sam, but even without your personal issues with the man in the mix, that's a hard sell."

Fisher nodded at the global threat board, where indicators showed the active deployments of Fourth Echelon's other agents. "I'm the best option we have to neutralize him, and you know it."

"Not true," she countered. "You want to do this? I'll back you. But we run it on my terms. Two operatives. That way, I make sure you stay on-mission."

"This won't wait for Briggs to finish up in China," said Fisher. "I need to go active right now. Aslanov will know he left a mark in Quebec; he'll be twice as cagey from here on. We can't let him set the tempo."

"I don't disagree," said Grim. "That's why I'm going to provisionally activate Sarah. She can act as your overwatch."

"No. *Fucking*. Way." Fisher rarely cursed in front of her, but now he ground out the words like bits of broken glass. "I'm not putting my girl in that man's crosshairs."

"She's not a girl, Sam," Grim said harshly. "She can handle herself. If you took off the daddy-blinders for a moment, you might be able to see it." He opened his mouth to protest, but she pushed on. "You want this guy buried? This is how we make it happen. It's that or we watch from the sidelines. *Your call*."

A nerve jumped in Fisher's jaw as he held his silence. When he spoke again, he did nothing to hide the bitterness in his tone. "Sometimes I forget how cold-blooded you can be."

"Comes with the job," she told him. "Are you in?"

He nodded.

"Good." Grim cleared away the digital pages on the SMI table with a sweep of her hand over the touch-sensitive surface. "To sell this to the President, we'll need a solid angle of attack.

How do we track down a man who's been a shadow for the last two decades?" She leaned over the world map, willing it to offer up some indication of where to start looking.

Fisher considered that for a moment, then reached over and used the table's controls to zoom in on northwestern Africa, until the Kingdom of Morocco grew to fill the screen. "There's someone we can ask," he noted, tapping the display, "but I guarantee he won't be pleased to see me."

Grim allowed a small smile to form on her lips. She would need to get the green light from Washington, but as Fisher had noted, time was of the essence – and sometimes it was better to seek forgiveness after the fact, than to ask permission first.

"I'll get us flight clearance," she said. "Get your gear together. Wheels up within the hour."

Jubilee Line (Westbound) – London – England

His face hidden in the shadows of a black SeV hoodie, Charlie hunched forward in his seat, retreating into himself.

He was hemmed in on one side by an elderly, dozing Asian woman in a voluminous sari, and on the other by a gangly youth in a tracksuit talking animatedly to his similarly dressed friend. The tracksuit guys spoke machine-gun fast, but Charlie only heard the top of their conversation, the yelps of laughter and the odd curse. The rest of their words were eaten by the hissy rumble of the subway train as it rocketed through the tunnels of the London Underground.

Jan had insisted that he call it *the Tube* like the locals did, and not *the Metro*. It made him sound like a tourist, she said. *A noob.* And he didn't want that.

Charlie's feet tapped out an aimless rhythm on the floor of the train carriage, unconsciously venting his nervous energy. His gut wound tight, and he tasted metal in his mouth. A flavor of fear that he had hoped was forever behind him curdled like bile, threatening to bubble up.

He took a shuddering breath and tried to put his thoughts in order, staring blankly at the screen of his Enduro notepad computer. He held the thing on his lap, bent over it like a holy book from which he took benediction.

Things were getting away from him, he could feel it happening. From the moment he had spoken with Gary Borden at the GreenSea office in Docklands, the comfortable pieces of his world began to break open. Borden wasn't interested in the data Charlie and Jan had uncovered; he didn't care about the very real possibility that GreenSea's new "corporate partners" at T-Tec had been secretly plundering the company for months. The specter of illegal dark money dealings didn't register. It rapidly became clear that Gary was only interested in sucking up to the new boss and covering his ass.

But this was a big deal, the kind of thing that would rope in the British National Crime Agency, the FBI, and Interpol. They had evidence of financial crimes across national borders, and much more.

We've only scratched the surface. Jan had said that to Charlie the last time he saw her in person, over a week ago now. She wasn't someone given to exaggeration.

The darkness flashing past the carriage windows gave way to a haze of light as the train pulled into Canada Water, and Charlie's head jerked up. He saw blurred posters for theatre shows and movies resolve as they slowed and the roar of the train ebbed. A polite, synthetic voice speaking cut-glass received-pronunciation English announced the station's name and warned those disembarking to mind the gap between the train and the platform.

The carriage doors hissed open, in synchrony with a second set of doors on the platform. Charlie vaguely remembered from one of Jan's spontaneous pro-London rants that the silver-liveried Jubilee line was the only Tube route with the double doors. She liked to expound at the drop of a hat about her hometown, from the big details to the small ones, and Charlie was always happy to listen.

Thinking about Jan only amped up his worries. After three days of no calls returned, no updates on her Facebook status, and no new Twitter posts, it was like the ground had opened up and swallowed her whole.

"Come on. Come on." While passengers filed on and off the train, Charlie's fingers beat out a tattoo on the back of the tablet computer as it tossed out a line to catch the station's Wi-Fi network. The deeper you went into the London Underground, the harder it was to get any bars, and with the train three-quarters full of people trying to do the same thing and log on to their social media feeds at once, maintaining a wireless connection to anything became a crapshoot.

Out in the Cloud, there was a virtual email server that only Charlie Cole and Jan Freling knew about, a tiny private island in the World Wide Web's sea of data that they had fenced off for extracurricular use. Mostly that meant working as an offline store for whatever hot new TV shows Charlie torrented off pirate sites, but it was also a place where they could communicate in secret, if need be.

After Jan's extended silence, there were only two places he could think of to look for her; the server was one, and the other was her apartment, off a side-street near Waterloo. He glanced up at the banner showing the stations along the Jubilee line. There were a few more stops before he reached the nearest station, and from there Jan's place was a five-minute walk.

If she's even still in the city, he thought morosely. Perhaps she saw something that scared her so much she fled.

Charlie tried to re-connect to the server, but the link was slower than dial-up. Still, this time he felt a surge of elation as the email client pinged successfully and dutifully informed him that an encrypted video file had appeared in his inbox. The file was ominously tagged as *999.mp4* – triple nine being the telephone number for the British emergency services.

Charlie licked his dry lips and tapped the download tab, but as soon as the progress bar started to fill, the polite announcer voice told everyone to stand clear of the closing doors, please. The train juddered and started moving.

"No, no, not again…" Charlie shook the tablet, as if that would somehow keep the connection stable.

It didn't help. He watched his bars wink out one by one, and then a pop-up on the screen helpfully informed him that he was now offline, and his download had been cancelled.

"Shit!" said Charlie, with feeling.

His cursing attracted the attention of the track-suited youth, who raised an eyebrow in his direction. "You all right, bruv?"

"Wi-Fi sucks," he explained.

"Yeah, it's peak," agreed the youth, then he grinned and nodded toward the other end of the carriage. "The Fed's using it up, innit?"

Charlie automatically turned to get a look at the Fed – *the cop* – that the youth blamed for stealing the bandwidth, and he flinched.

Halfway down the train carriage sat a man with a hawkish face and a dark coat too thick for the temperate London climate.

Stone.

The cold-eyed muscle that T-Tec's CEO had brought with him to GreenSea. The same man whose presence had set alarm bells clanging in Charlie's mind as he struggled to remember where he had first seen his face.

Stone held up a smartphone, as if watching a video on the screen, but he could just as easily have been recording Charlie's every move.

How long has he been sitting there? Charlie tried to shrink into the depths of his hoodie and vanish from sight. *What the hell does he want?*

He had no answers for the questions cannoning around in his thoughts, and he could feel himself starting to spiral toward panic. Charlie couldn't escape the sense that this man was here for him, he was out to do him harm.

It was an instinctive reaction, something bone-deep and primal. A prey animal recognizing the predator stalking it. Fear surged up through Charlie's chest in a hot flood and he was suddenly on his feet, propelled by dread. His body moved of its own accord as he tried to put more distance between himself and Stone. Ignoring their complaints, he pushed past the two youths, back to the doors connecting this train car with the next one in line.

Warning signs on the metal door forbade passengers from

using them, but Charlie didn't care. He grabbed the handle and wrenched it down, pushing through into the trailing carriage. His actions earned him a few judgmental looks from the other passengers, but no one stopped him.

Charlie kept moving back down the train, gripping the tablet in one hand. He chanced a look over his shoulder and saw that Stone was following. The man in the dark coat made it look casual, he didn't even glance in Charlie's direction. But he didn't need to. This carriage was the last one, ending in a blank door that only the driver could open.

Charlie sank down into a vacant seat, aware of Stone standing in a vestibule at the corner of his vision. A word wandered through his mind, looking for something to connect with. *Russian.*

Stone was a Russian asset, Charlie was convinced of it. That had to mean he had come across his stalker's face while he was in the employ of the US government. Maybe a file somewhere, or a mention in a half-remembered briefing? It infuriated him that he couldn't remember the details, but his fear fogged every thought in his head.

"The next station is. Bermondsey," said the automated announcer, before mentioning which side to exit the train.

Charlie kept his head down, staring at the floor, but he could see the nearest double-doors as they parted, and out past them, a series of steel-lined passages leading into the station proper. On the far side of the space, more passages opened on to another platform for trains traveling in the opposite direction, and he heard the rumble and whine of a train pulling in across the way.

He gave his notebook screen a last look – still struggling to connect, he saw – before stuffing it deep in his hoodie's pocket. Charlie slid his feet back until they were braced against his seat.

Am I going to do this? The question echoed in his mind as the seconds ticked on. *I am going to do this.* He didn't dare look in Stone's direction.

"This station is. Bermondsey," repeated the announcer, alerting Charlie that departure was imminent. "This train terminates at. Stanmore." Then a high-pitched beeping tone issued out, and both sets of doors began to close.

Charlie exploded from his seat with enough speed that a passenger near him cried out in surprise. Charlie was skinny but nimble with it, and he snaked through the narrowing gap of the closing doors in a wild rush, the soles of his sneakers hitting the platform with a loud slap.

His forward momentum was momentarily arrested, and he pulled hard, yanking out the hem of his hoodie from where it had caught in the doors.

He stumbled, losing his footing; and that was when he saw Stone, his face tight with effort, as the Russian fought to hold another door open at his end of the carriage. The man strained to force his way through, stuck half-in and half-out as the door's mechanism tried to slide home.

They locked eyes and Stone's pitiless gaze bored into Charlie. He knew then that the Russian intended to end him.

From the opposite side of the station, the eastbound train's automated voice made its pre-departure announcement, spurring Charlie back into motion. He sprinted through the connecting passage and past the handful of commuters making their way to the exits, on to the other platform, even as the beeping tones sounded again.

He made it to the train in time for the doors to slam closed in his face. Unable to stop, Charlie collided with the barrier and bounced off it, falling to his haunches. The eastbound train raced away into the tunnel and vanished.

Ice flooded into Charlie's gut and his heart hammered in his chest. He spun back in the direction he had come, fighting down a surge of fright. The westbound train had left too, the doors to the platform closed, but he couldn't see if Stone had made it off before it departed.

The sound of the trains echoed and faded, and the station fell silent in the brief lull between arrivals. Charlie retreated into one of the passageways and held his breath, his back pressed to the cold metal of the curved steel wall. He felt sick with fear.

The platforms were long and there were a few places to hide, but aside from boarding another train, the only other way out led up to street level.

Charlie strained to listen, hearing nothing but the whir of air-conditioning, uncertain of what to do next. If Stone was on the westbound train, he would likely ride up one stop to Southwark station and then double back, soon arriving on the platform where Charlie now stood. But if Stone had disembarked here, if he was waiting for Charlie to show himself…

Then he heard a man speaking, one half of a conversation over a cellphone.

"I have lost sight of Cole." The voice grew fainter as it continued, moving toward the exit. "No. It does not matter. I will re-acquire." The conversation became indistinct as another pair of trains approached, blotting it out.

Charlie risked a look out from the passage. There was no

sign of Stone anywhere on the lower level, so he raced back to the westbound platform and scrambled aboard the next train, sinking into the first vacant seat he found.

Trembling with adrenaline, he checked himself over to make sure the tablet computer was still safe in his pocket as the train began to move. As he touched it, the device vibrated.

Gingerly, Charlie drew it out and studied the screen. A pop-up announced DOWNLOAD COMPLETE: DECRYPT FILE Y/N?

His eyes widened in surprise. Clearly, the obedient device had continued to try to reconnect with the server while Charlie had been hiding on the platform. He plugged in a set of headphones and opened the 999 file, clutching it close to him as his trepidation built.

A video window opened and Jan Freling's face appeared against the background of a dark room, ghostly pale from the glow of the smartphone she'd used to record the message. She looked strung out and terrified.

"*Charlie, it's worse than we thought,*" she said. "*Remember this name: GORDIAN SWORD. I think it's the key to everything.*"

EIGHT

Waterloo – London – England

Charlie exited the station, casting furtive glances right and left as he dodged traffic and jogged down the side street near St John's Church. Jan's apartment was a couple of blocks back from there, one of a dozen flats built into the shell of what had once been a Victorian-era warehouse.

The recording of Jan's voice whispered in his ears as he walked, her tones low and intense as she explained in fine detail what she had done in the shadowy depths of the dark web. Charlie held his notepad tablet in one hand, gripping it tightly.

"*The illicit money transfers we uncovered, well, I thought that would probably be the sum of it, but guess what?*" It was like Jan was walking along with him down the narrow avenue. "*Brody Teague, world-renowned, Olympic-grade arsehole and amoral tech-dude is either turning a blind eye to this nasty stuff, or he's in it up to his perfectly tanned neck. I know which.*"

"Yeah." Charlie nodded in agreement, throwing a wary look back over his shoulder. No one had followed him out of

Waterloo station, and he saw no sign of Stone or anybody else as he passed over an intersection. He turned left and kept going.

"*First, we had dark money moving around, plus technical assets being signed over from one place to another for no reason.*" On the recording, Jan continued to speak. "*I even found the deeds of ownership for some of GreenSea's reclaim sites being shuffled over to T-Tec. No idea what that's about.*"

Charlie frowned at that. One of the side-projects championed by GreenSea's CEO Edward Morant was the reclamation of old industrial facilities – a shuttered paint factory in Canada, a dry-hole oil rig in the North Sea, an aging chemical plant in India, and several others – all bought up and painstakingly cleansed of run-off and contamination so they could be repurposed for new development. He couldn't imagine what T-Tec would need those for.

"*So I kept digging,*" said Jan. "*All right, maybe I shouldn't have. But I did. And then this codename, this Gordian Sword thing, pops up. Everything seems to connect back to that, it's some secret pet project of Teague's.*" She sighed. "*You know me, I'm nosey. I found some files on a remote server. I took a look…*"

Jan fell silent and Charlie pulled the tablet from his pocket, afraid the file had ended abruptly. But Jan remained quiet for a long moment, her pale features hanging in the gloom. She blinked, sniffed, and pressed a tear from the corner of her eye.

"*I wish I hadn't. Charlie, they've killed people. I don't know how else to put it. I found encoded documents about these two researchers. A pen tester from the States called Sally Drake and this Finnish bloke named Virtanen. They were being paid by GreenSea, on the orders of T-Tec!*"

Charlie thought about what that could mean. Teague used

Morant's company like a cut-out, as a shell through which he could work without drawing attention. But why change that now, why take over GreenSea? The only logical reason he could think of was that Teague had finished with whatever he was doing, and he was cleaning up the loose ends.

"*These people… they're both dead.*" Jan looked away. Her voice thickened with revulsion. "*There are images of their corpses! Like whoever killed them took photos to prove it was done. I feel sick thinking about it.*" She shook her head.

Charlie put the tablet back in his pocket and moved off. Jan's place was close by, and he rounded the nearest corner, where the patrons of the local pub were milling around outside and chatting. None of them paid any attention as he passed.

"*Why would they pay these people off and then have them murdered?*" Jan's fear briefly gave way to indignant anger. "*There's no way to know who's in on it. We have to find someone we can trust with this, it's a big deal. I'll copy everything I found to another directory so you can read it. Or chuck it in the river if you want, I wouldn't blame you.*"

He threw another look over his shoulder. He was still alone.

When Jan spoke again, the fear had returned. "*I think I might have messed up going too deep into those files. I'm worried they'll be able to track it back to me. So, I'm going to go dark. I'll reach out to you again when I'm somewhere safe. You should do the same thing.*" Charlie heard a soft chime picked up by the smartphone's mike. "*OK, I have to wrap this up. My ride-share is here.*"

As he reached the end of the terrace of houses, Charlie turned on to the street where Jan's apartment block stood, and the flash of strobing blue lights dazzled him.

A few hundred meters away outside the building, two Metropolitan Police units were parked next to one another, with a black van nearby; the words *Private Ambulance* were visible on the side, which meant it belonged to a coroner. Uniformed constables stood around the communal entrance to the apartment, keeping the locals on the far side of a line of warning tape.

"*You get out of there, get away,*" said Jan's voice in his ear, as the recording concluded. "*And whatever happens,* do not *come to my flat.*"

Charlie staggered to a halt, and before anyone could catch sight of him, he retreated into the nearest doorway. He felt light-headed, an ugly and familiar fear filling him.

Taking a deep breath that failed to calm his racing pulse, he chanced a peek out, in the direction of the apartment. Figures rendered unidentifiable by white all-over bodysuits emerged through the entrance, carrying a body bag between them.

"Jan?" More than anything, he wanted to believe that it wasn't his friend in there. But the dreadful reality was overpowering. He was too late. Jan's loss hollowed him out, smothering all hope. She was dead, and nothing he could do would change that.

Struck motionless, Charlie could only watch the figures in white take their burden to the coroner's van and load it inside. He mutely watched the vehicle pull away and depart.

As the van passed by a group of bystanders on the far side of the road, one of the faces caught his eye, and Charlie jerked back in shock.

Stone, his expression a blank mask of studied disinterest, stood among the curious neighbors and onlookers.

In a giddy rush, a snatch of Stone's overheard phone conversation from earlier that night came back to Charlie. *I have lost sight of Cole. It does not matter. I will re-acquire.*

At once, he understood why the Russian had left the station, instead of tearing it apart looking for him. Stone knew that Charlie would come here. He was waiting for him to show up at Jan's apartment, and when that happened, her fate would be his.

Charlie reached deep into himself, searching for the resolve to stay calm. If he gave in to panic now, it would all be over. He considered walking up to the police and asking for protection, even calling out Stone to them – but there were too many variables. One wrong move and he wouldn't live to see another day.

His skin crawled. More than once, in his past life at the NSA, Charlie had found himself in situations as bleak as this one, but foolishly he'd believed that was all behind him. There was a cold irony to the fact that the "safe" job he'd taken with GreenSea had now put him right back into danger.

It took all his effort to fight the urge to run full tilt, and instead walk calmly away back in the direction he had come. With every step, he was convinced he could sense the Russian's hard gaze boring into his back.

On the main street, Charlie jumped on to the first bus that passed and found a quiet corner in the upper deck where he could figure out his next move.

If Stone knew where Jan lived, then he also knew about Charlie's apartment in Camden Town. He couldn't go back there. He needed to go dark, like she had said.

But more than that, he needed to find someone he could

trust – and there was only one person he could reach out to who fit that bill.

Charlie switched his tablet to cellular mode and started recording a voice message to be sent to an unlisted telephone number with an American dialing code. He only hoped that after all this time, it was still active.

"It's Charlie Cole," he began. "If you're hearing this… Grim, I really need your help."

C-147B Paladin – Mediterranean Sea – Altitude 29,000 Feet

Having spent most of his lifetime on deployment, Fisher had learned to snatch any opportunity for shuteye that presented itself, and so he spent the first few hours of the flight to Rabat in one of the Paladin's crash-bunks, his sleep deep and dreamless.

A little over an hour out from landing, he awoke to the keening whine of the engines and the creaking of the fuselage around him. Glancing out through an oval window, he saw an endless expanse of white clouds lit by a low sun, and through occasional breaks in the cover beneath, the glitter of blue sea.

Fisher stretched out the stiffness in his limbs with a short walk that took him to the jet's workshop and armory compartment, intending to check over his gear for the mission ahead.

His daughter was already there, doing the same thing. She had a sniper rifle in her hands, closely examining the weapon's action, and she didn't meet his gaze as he approached.

Fisher studied the rifle with a professional's eye. It was a Paladin 9 SNR, a custom-made model employed by Victor Coste's private military contractor. With a complex scope and a blocky suppressor on the barrel, it was configured for low-observable, long-range operations.

Sarah hesitated, looking around for something. "The rounds you want are in the green case," he told her, guessing her needs.

"Oh, right." Sarah walked to the container he had indicated and examined the tight rows of .338 ammunition inside. "So, you're still talking to me?" She asked the question without looking up, pre-loading magazines for the SNR.

He ignored the question, exchanging it with one of his own, still studying the rifle. "This is what you're using? Fourth Echelon has better hardware."

"I don't doubt it. But I'll stick with what I know."

"Fair enough." Fisher picked up the SNR, gauging the weapon's weight and balance. "Grim says your marksmanship numbers are good."

"Better than good," she insisted. "I got top score in training."

Fisher weighed his next words carefully, changing tack. "Skills on the range are one thing. Skills in the field are something different." He looked down the rifle's scope. "If it comes to taking a life, are you ready for that? Could you do it?"

Sarah took the gun from him. "Are you asking me that because I'm new to this or because I'm your daughter?"

"Both." He looked at Sarah and saw her as two images laid over one another; the first the uncompromising, defiant woman in front of him, the second the young girl he had left behind at home while he fought in dozens of covert conflicts. "That's not the question. I know you can shoot and hunt. I taught you how."

"I remember."

"There was that trip in the spring, to Colorado. The deer we tracked. And when the moment came, you wouldn't pull the trigger."

Sarah's face clouded. "I won't kill what's not my enemy. If the day comes when I have to cross that line… I'll do what's right. That's the other thing you taught me."

He took a step nearer. Fisher was a closed book to most who knew him, and even with his own flesh and blood he found it difficult to be open. But he pushed on, knowing he could not stay silent. "Sarah… I love your empathy. It's the best part of your mother in you. But it could get you killed."

"Part of the job is knowing when to pull the trigger and when not." She looked away, across the racks of weapons and equipment. "Fourth Echelon has more than enough non-lethal options in their loadouts, Dad. The hard way… *your way*… is not the only way."

He gave a nod. "Fair point. I just want to be sure of your reasons. I don't want you following in my footsteps for my sake."

Sarah gave a derisive snort. "With all due respect, Dad, get over yourself." She sighed. "Sure, I want to make you proud…"

"You do," he insisted. "Always have."

"But there's more to it than that. I want to make a difference in the world. All the horrible things our family has been through, it showed me the hard truth about what's out there. Along the way, it *took* something from me."

Fisher felt a knife of guilt pressing into his heart. He couldn't deny what Sarah was saying.

"The thought of some other person going through that makes me cold inside." She shook her head. "So, what I want…" Sarah trailed off, unable to find the right words.

"You want to make sure it doesn't happen to anyone else," he said.

"Yes." She put down the rifle and folded her arms. "Being a victim can make you feel powerless. I want to take back the power taken from me, and use it against the monsters out there in the darkness."

Fisher let her words sink in. It was hard to hear, but he understood. *She's more like me than I ever realized.* Still, one last question preyed on his mind. "However you want to cut it, Fourth Echelon, and Third Echelon before it, were responsible for a lot of that darkness you talked about. Why would you want to be a part of that?"

Sarah's focus shifted, a new distance in her eyes. In her youth, Fisher's daughter had suffered through abductions and attacks, through the faking of her death and years of living under a false identity, all because of her father's connection to that clandestine world. Now she was stepping into those same murky shadows of her own accord.

"I don't have a good answer for you, Dad," she said. "I guess, after everything that happened, I need to see it from the inside. All those times when you called me from the middle of an operation, when you couldn't tell me where you were or what you were doing... I have to walk that path myself. So I can understand." She made a face, shaking off the emotion of the moment. "Does that make sense?"

"More than you know." He was strangely heartened by her answer.

A slight tremor resonated through the deck beneath their feet and both of them felt the change in the Paladin's attitude.

The jet started a slow descent, curving in to follow the line of Morocco's Atlantic coastline. They planned to masquerade as a cargo carrier and put in at an airport near Rabat. It was a thin cover that wouldn't stand up to a second look, but Fisher didn't plan for them to be on the ground long past nightfall. Whether he wanted to or not, the man they had come looking for would soon be taking an unscheduled trip.

"Here we go." Sarah checked her watch. "Right on the clock. A simple father-daughter day out, right? Just like Colorado."

"Same hunt," said Fisher, "different prey."

NINE

Rabat-Salé-Zemmour-Zaër – Rabat – Morocco

"Look at this place," sneered Nabil, peering through the window of his pearl-white Escalade. "He lives in a villa like a Sultan's palace."

Nabil's vehicle rode in the middle of three identical SUVs that passed through the automated gates to the walled compound, the convoy kicking up dust into the evening air as the sun dipped beneath the horizon behind them.

He scowled at the guard by the entrance – some dead-eyed Eastern European muscle gripping a Bizon sub-machine gun – and surveyed the elegant, sharp-angled forms of the big house at the end of the drive.

"It is an insult," agreed Lasri. "A foreigner should not have a home like this."

Nabil's muscular associate was a heavy, rotund figure that the unwary might have thought fat and slow, but that illusion hid muscle and a mean spirit. Lasri had wrestled in his youth, and Nabil had taken him on as his second-in-command after seeing the man crack a policeman's skull with his bare hands.

If he hadn't been in his car, Nabil would have spat in agreement. "The man is a wretched dog. But animals have their uses, eh?"

Lasri chuckled, anticipating the coming events.

In contrast to the bigger man, Nabil was tall and thin, so much so that his enemies and allies alike called him "*the Crane*". The nickname amused him, and he played into it by wearing white kaftans with black and gray accents.

Their partnership had led the two men to a profitable life in Morocco's illegal drug economy, and between them they currently controlled most of the cannabis trade in the north of the Kingdom. All had been well for a time, until a certain Saharawi gang had come into their territory. Loud and disrespectful, they had traded in their camels for sports cars and made pacts with the South American cartels, who smuggled their cocaine into Europe via the Moroccan gateway.

For a time, their leader, Delim, had kept out of Nabil's way, but two lions could not prowl the same lands without coming into conflict. Now their gangs were six months into a street war that had encompassed drive-by shootings, car bombs, and arson.

The situation was untenable. Profits were down. Nabil's clients in Europe and America were putting pressure on him to stabilize it, and he had to reluctantly admit that they could not afford to keep bleeding out men and money.

Delim accepted the offer of a ceasefire, of course. He was in the same boat, with the cartels breathing down his neck, and his workers and soldiers dying at the hands of Nabil's thugs.

Both gangs needed the war to end, but to do it in a way where both sides could save face.

Here, the dog came in useful. True, he was an outsider, possessed of a transactional nature and loyal only to his wallet. But he had happily sold guns to both sides in this confrontation, and that made him a rare commodity – someone who could facilitate a gathering like this, where the two gang-lords might meet on neutral ground and hash out a solution.

Nabil's convoy pulled up outside the long, low shape of the villa, a modernist rendition that deliberately echoed the ancient El Badi Palace of Marrakesh. Delim's men were already there, indolently standing around a cluster of armor-plated Jeep Gladiators, their vehicle of choice.

"You know where to park," Nabil told his driver. The man nodded and reversed the Escalade back until the rear of the vehicle faced the shallow stairs leading up to the villa's portico.

Lasri lumbered out of the SUV and came around to open Nabil's door. As the tall man stepped into the cooling evening air, he looked around, out over the manicured grounds. His host had showed good judgment for once and dismissed most of his guards for the evening.

Nabil's cold-eyed gaze crossed over Delim's men, and they stared back at him blankly. He kept his expression neutral, but inwardly he loathed their presence. None of them dared show disrespect by openly carrying weapons, but he suspected that guns were close at hand, in the Jeeps.

"Nabil! My man! *As-salamu alaykum*!" a voice called out, and he turned to see a man come jogging down the stairs.

Like his guard on the gate, their host was from Eastern Europe, but his accent had an American twang to it that the gang-lord had never warmed to. His short, oiled hair grayed at the temples and he had a face like a fox, all teeth and smirks. Gold chains glittered at his throat beneath a gaudy silk shirt, and he smiled with the confidence of someone who could smell money. He was being paid well to accommodate this gathering.

"Listen to the dog bark," muttered Lasri, so only Nabil could hear him. "It thinks it is people."

Nabil detested Delim and his crew, but he had a special dislike for this individual. He concealed it behind a false grin and offered his hand. "Andriy Kobin, my good friend," he lied. "Thank you for your invitation."

"My pleasure!" Kobin slapped Nabil on the back, his forced bonhomie already starting to grate. "Welcome to my humble abode. Come inside, Delim is already here. This is going to be great! Believe me!"

"I do," said Nabil, falling in step with Kobin as Lasri followed on behind them. "I believe this will be a memorable evening."

"All call-signs, this is Panther. Confirming asset on site."

Fisher's words were picked up by the microphone pad at his throat and broadcast across the encrypted mission net.

From the shallow ridge beyond the villa's grounds, he had a good view of the whole west side of the building, his tactical suit's camouflage blending him into the dull tan and green of the landscape.

"*Paladin Actual copies,*" said Grim.

"*Lynx copies,*" echoed Sarah. "*I have him in my sights.*" He heard the curl of her lip in her voice. "*Well. Andriy Kobin. That prick is still alive.*"

"*Hard to believe,*" added Grim, equally dismissively.

"He's a survivor, I'll give him that," said Fisher.

Kobin had first come to his attention in the thick of a conspiracy that had seen Fisher disavowed and his daughter declared dead. Former Ukrainian *bratva*, a career criminal with the morals of a jackal, Kobin had graduated from drug dealer to international arms trafficker before forcibly becoming a Fourth Echelon asset during the Blacklist attacks a few years ago. He'd proven his value over those days, enough that the CIA were willing to put the man back on the street, albeit with a long leash. But he wasn't to be trusted.

Fisher put those thoughts aside and swept his binoculars over the other men in the compound. They had formed into two groups who glared at one another. All of them had the distinct twitchy look of street killers with poor impulse control.

"Reckon Kobin's odds might be running a little thin tonight," Fisher noted.

"*That's the second group of guests to arrive,*" said Sarah, his daughter's voice a quiet whisper in his ear. "*Who are these guys?*"

Fisher looked off to the south, toward where she hid under a camo web, sighting toward the villa through her rifle scope. He saw nothing but dusty scrubland, evidence of how well his daughter had concealed herself.

"*Panther, Paladin Actual. Give me a slow pass over their faces.*"

"Copy." Fisher raised the binoculars again and did as Grim asked, dwelling briefly on each of the gun-thugs, catching them as they talked, smoked cigarettes, or snarled into a smartphone.

Remote imaging circuits in the binos captured each face and transmitted it back to the Paladin, where Lea Kade would process the silhouette through a vast facial recognition database of terrorists, criminals, and known troublemakers.

"*Good capture,*" said Grim. "*Should have something soon. Do not enter the building without my go. Meantime, we're getting into the local cell tower network, back-tracing the phones of everyone on site.*"

"I'm moving up." Fisher slipped out of his hiding place in a crevice of the rocks, and moved into a low sneak pattern, crouching to stay out of sight.

Quickly and carefully, he made his way to the base of the outer wall and ran a gloved hand over the bricks. His fingertips found places where the mortar between the blocks had crumbled, and he visualized his next moves before he made them: up to the top of the wall, a low roll over, a cat-fall into the grass on the other side.

Faint threads of conversation in Arabic reached him on the breeze. He couldn't make it all out, but whoever was speaking was severely pissed off about being here tonight. His earlier estimation of the men on the other side of the wall was correct. They were spoiling for a fight.

"*This complicates matters,*" said Grim, returning to the radio net. "*Facial recog got a bunch of hits with Interpol and the DEA. Those nice gentlemen at Kobin's place are members of two rival drug gangs, currently involved in a local turf war.*"

Sarah asked the pressing question. "*So why aren't they killing each other?*"

"*According to phone intercepts we pulled, Kobin's acting as middleman for an old-fashioned sit-down between these scumbags.*"

"Playing both sides against the middle," said Fisher. "Should've guessed."

"*It seems he's expecting a big payday for being a peacemaker,*" Grim went on. "*We're drilling down for more details as I speak. This is go or no-go. It's your call, Panther.*"

Fisher cursed silently. "Nothing's ever simple with this guy."

"*He's supposed to be alone in there,*" said Sarah. "*Now we have to snatch him out from under the noses of a bunch of feuding gang-bangers?*"

"Yeah." Fisher began his ascent. "Cover me, I'm heading in."

Fisher climbed over the wall and vanished into a section of long pampas grass. Snaking across the distance toward the villa, he picked out his route as he moved. A security camera high up on a lintel slowly panned left to right, leaving a fractional four-second blind spot that Fisher could use to cross the distance to the side of the building.

The problem was the man with a Bizon SMG loitering right in that spot. One round to the forehead from Fisher's SC-IS pistol would solve that in a heartbeat, but a corpse lying in plain sight was as bad as leading a marching band down the driveway.

Fisher found a thumb-sized pebble amid the roots of the tall grass and flicked it so it landed close to an ornamental bench. The guard with the Bizon heard the noise and took the bait, wandering over.

The setting sun was at Fisher's back, which meant the guard was looking right into it as he came closer. Shading his eyes and blinking, he approached the bench and bent to look under it, unaware that an intruder lay less than a meter from where he stood.

Fisher timed the moment for when the camera turned away,

then struck cobra-fast. He shot out and grabbed the guard's legs, yanking him off balance. The guard fell on his back, too shocked to even cry out, and Fisher dragged him back into the grass, jamming his forearm across the other man's throat.

He leaned on the guard's carotid artery, sliding his other hand behind the man's head. "Quiet," Fisher admonished, as the man struggled against him. He kept up the pressure, and the guard's movements became sluggish and uncoordinated. Finally, he went slack and passed out.

Fisher looked up as the camera came back on the return sweep and hesitated. The guard's SMG lay where he had dropped it, in plain sight. Acting quickly, he hooked the strap with his foot and pulled it under the bench.

The camera went to the apex of its move and then started back the other way. Leaving his unconscious victim in the long grass, Fisher counted down the seconds before he would make the short sprint to the house.

A low, insectile buzz reached his ears, coming closer. He chanced a look up and saw a blur of motion in the darkening sky.

Fisher keyed his throat mike. "Lynx, you have eyes up?"

"*Negative, Panther.*" Sarah carried a tri-rotor drone in her kit, a compact micro-UAV that could be hand-deployed in the field to give operatives their own aerial recon capability; but what was flying around the villa did not belong to Fourth Echelon. "*Wait, I see it. Quadcopter, your six o'clock. Looks like it's being manually operated, likely by Kobin's security.*"

Fisher weighed his options. The 4E tactical suit's stealth capabilities might be enough to hide him, but if Kobin's drone had thermographic, heat-reading vision, the operator would be able to pick out the unconscious guard lying hidden in the grass. But taking the little UAV out of play would alert the guards that something was amiss. There was no good option.

"*It's coming your way*," said Sarah, making the choice for him. "*I have a bead.*"

"Send it," Fisher told her.

The suppressed report of Sarah's rifle didn't reach the walls of the compound, but the round she put through the security drone's center mass was perfect. The drone's buzzing became a death rattle and it tumbled out of the air, bouncing off a gurgling fountain and into a koi pond.

Fisher didn't wait around to see if anyone had heard the machine fall. The camera faced away, and he burst out of his cover, crossing the open distance to the villa in heartbeats.

Pressing himself to the wall, avoiding the pools of light cast by the windows, he moved to a boxy drainpipe that went all the way up to the roof. The men standing around the cars in the drive were too interested in glaring at one another to notice him making the short climb.

"*Guard on the roof, west corner*," reported Sarah. "*I don't have an angle.*"

"I got it."

Fisher rolled on to the top of the villa, his boot scraping the tarpaper as he moved. The motion caught the eye of the guard and the man turned in his direction. His instincts were better than his counterpart in the pampas grass, automatically bringing up his Bizon to aim the barrel-shaped SMG toward Fisher.

That made him a bigger threat, and it cost him his life. Fisher led with his sidearm and planted a double-tap in the guard's throat, the gun's integral silencer turning the sound of the shots into an indistinct clatter. The SC-IS pistol was the perfect tool for the Splinter Cell operative, an evolution of the FN Herstal Five-Seven semi-automatic that he could wield like a scalpel.

Blood gushed down the guard's shoulders and the man fell to his knees, then flat on his face. Fisher closed in, pulling the body into the shadow of an air-conditioning unit. Aside from a splash of crimson, there was no sign the man had ever been there.

"*No alerts,*" said Sarah, offering the information before he asked for it. "*Panther is clear to proceed.*"

"It's just a minor inconvenience," said Kobin, stretching out his best, most accommodating smile. "Just biz. You understand, right?"

Nabil stared at the guard with the metal detector wand like he thought the guy might shove it up his ass, but he relented. "Sure, sure," said the Moroccan, reluctantly raising his hands so the guard could wave the scanner over him.

The wand made electronic squeaking noises, but nothing that signaled the presence of any dense metal objects – no blades, no guns – and Kobin clapped his hands together in thanks.

"There! Painless!" He nodded toward Nabil's guy Lasri and the guard scanned the big man with the wand for good measure. He too was unarmed, and it encouraged Kobin to think tonight's participants were taking him seriously.

Nabil's violent rival, Delim, sat on a leather sofa close by, in sight of the villa's entrance, and he too had been unwilling to be patted down. But the Saharawi gangster had agreed when

Kobin explained that it was a pre-requisite for the meeting to go ahead.

Nobody inside the villa was armed except Kobin's own guys, and there were only a handful of them. That way, the two gang-lords and their thugs had to at least *consider* settling their beef by using their words. If things did degenerate, they could only whale on one another with their fists or the heavier items of Kobin's interior décor.

That was the plan, anyhow. Kobin only got paid if both sides left here tonight with a peace treaty, but he was convinced he could make it happen.

I'm a broker, Kobin told himself. I trade guns, drugs, whatever I want! I can broker peace just as easily, right? A stray voice in his thoughts wondered if his bottomless confidence was more a product of the pinch of methamphetamine he had done in the bathroom, but he ignored it.

Kobin was clear-eyed enough to know that while he wasn't liked by either Delim or Nabil, he had made himself valuable to both men by getting them the weapons they wanted. It was a step down from how it used to be, he had to admit that. Once upon a time, Kobin had been auctioning off jet fighters and tanks to third world dictators. Now he'd been reduced to bulk-buying surplus AKMs for a pair of squabbling drug kingpins.

But tonight's deal would change things. It would put Andriy Kobin back on the grid. It would show people that he was smarter than he looked.

"Food, drink, dope, on the house," he told his guests, acting every inch the genial host. "Help yourselves, guys. Then we'll get down to business, eh?"

"Andriy." With a feral grin on his face, Nabil hove back in his direction and placed a thin hand on his shoulder. The man's fingers were like the talons of a hawk. "Come. I want to show you something."

"Uh, sure…" Nabil applied pressure, and Kobin felt himself being steered over to the windows looking out across the driveway.

One of Kobin's guards intercepted them and leaned in to whisper urgently in his ear. "Boss, maybe something?" The guard spoke in Ukrainian, a language that none of the Moroccans understood. "The drone has gone down. Might be the battery, might be something else…"

"So?" Kobin glared at him, affronted to be disturbed in the middle of his work. "What do I pay you for? Deal with it!" A notion occurred and he added an afterthought. "And do a radio check, just in case!"

The guard nodded and backed away, leaving Kobin and Nabil alone. "Staff trouble?" said the other man.

"Nothing to worry about," Kobin said smoothly, glossing over the interruption.

Nabil's hand gripped his shoulder again, pressing him forward. "Look. Look! Do you like my new cars?" He gestured at the shiny white Escalades outside the villa. With black-tinted windows, neon under-lighting, gold wire rims on the wheels and other shiny accents, Nabil's vehicles were as unsubtle as he was.

"Nice," said Kobin, with a nod, uncertain where the conversation was heading.

"I paid a lot of money for them," Nabil explained, his tone turning flinty. "Let me ask you, Andriy. How much are *you* getting paid?"

"Uh, well…" Kobin made a *what-can-you-do* gesture. "You know the answer to that! A small consideration from you and Delim for setting this up–"

Nabil's fingers dug hard into Kobin's shoulder, and his dark gaze bored into the other man's eyes, promising violence. "Forgive me. I meant to say, how much are you getting paid to fuck me over, you cur?"

Fisher crouched at the corner of a rectangular panel cut into the villa's flat roof, one of several designed to let in the light of the day. Through the glass, he could see Kobin in that ugly shirt of his, standing out like a sore thumb.

The gunrunner's eyes were wide with fright, an expression Fisher had seen on the man more than once. *Something is very wrong down there.*

"*Paladin Actual, all call-signs.*" Grim's voice broke through Fisher's musings, and the tone of her words carried a warning. "*We've got the take from the phones these creeps are using, and their text message chains make for interesting reading. They're planning a doublecross to wipe out the opposition.*"

"Which gang?" said Fisher.

"*Both of them,*" noted Grim. "*And Kobin's right in the middle of it.*"

TEN

Rabat-Salé-Zemmour-Zaër – Rabat – Morocco

Kobin's eyes widened as he tried and failed to get free of Nabil's vise-like grip. He tried a different tack, faking good cheer as best he could.

"Nabil, buddy! You think I want to screw you over? No way!"

"You lie as easily as you breathe," growled the criminal.

"I don't!" Kobin's voice went up an octave. He really *wasn't* lying about the whole break-bread, kiss-and-make-up plan he had for Nabil and his archenemy Delim.

At first, having a turf war *was* good for his business, pulling in the cash for Kobin as he sold guns and ammo to both sides of the conflict. But soon the battle spilled over into the streets and started eating into his bottom line.

Peace between the Moroccan drug gangs was preferable to chaos – and while Kobin could easily have put his weight behind one side over the other, that was a short-sighted strategy. Helping Delim kill Nabil or Nabil kill Delim would leave only one kingpin in charge, which meant fewer customers for Kobin. Two factions would always have a healthy paranoia about one another, which he could milk for a long time by keeping both sides well armed.

Nabil clearly didn't think the same way. He released Kobin and banged his fist on the window that looked out on to the villa's drive, in a pre-arranged signal.

The taillights on the white SUV closest to the front door flashed brightly and the vehicle roared into high-speed reverse. Kobin's guard on the portico leapt out of the way as the Escalade mounted the steps and rammed backward through the doors, smashing them to matchwood.

Panic erupted in the hall as the vehicle slammed aside a table and skidded to a halt on the tiled floor. The SUV's rear hatch lifted open, and as Kobin watched in shock, Nabil and his sidekick Lasri grabbed for the large weapons concealed in the trunk. To his increasing alarm, Kobin noted that the weapons were the pair of belt-fed PKM machine guns he had sold to the gang-lord a couple of weeks earlier, each loaded with a heavyweight box magazine.

Delim and his entourage were scattering, frantically searching for cover and cursing Kobin for doublecrossing them.

"This isn't my idea!" he shouted, as Nabil and Lasri opened up with the machine guns, spraying rounds wildly.

Bullets shredded the expensive Italian leather of Kobin's sofa and reduced a dozen of his *objets d'art* to splinters, and when Lasri turned a PKM in the gunrunner's direction, his panic broke and he fled.

•••

"Report," demanded Grim. *"What's the situation?"*

"Bad," snapped Fisher, aiming his pistol down through the skylight. "Someone brought the wrong kind of favors to Kobin's party."

Along with the hail of bullets inside the villa, gunfire started up out on the drive, as the loitering men from the two criminal gangs drew iron and tried to kill each other.

"The asset is no good to us dead," said Grim. *"Can you still extract him, or do we abort?"*

Fisher spotted a flash of movement below him, as Kobin zigzagged between pieces of furniture as he tried to make his escape. Other gang members were coming in through the obliterated doorway, complicating the battlespace.

"Negative abort," he said. "I'll get him."

Down in the hall, Kobin scrambled over a low table and sprinted deeper into the villa, heading toward the rear of the building. He didn't see the stocky guy with the PKM coming after him, taking his time, drawing a bead on the fleeing criminal.

But Fisher did. He raised his SC-IS pistol and fired three shots, the first to gauge deflection and shatter the glass, the second and third instinctively correcting to strike the gunman in the chest and head. In the chaos, no one caught on to where the shots had come from, and the stocky man went down.

"You're welcome," muttered Fisher, as he broke into a jog, paralleling Kobin's movements beneath him.

More skylights marked out the path of the long hallway below, and Fisher glanced down as he passed them, tracking Kobin's path. Other armed thugs who had broken in from outside were following him, intent on finishing the job their comrade had started.

Marking each threat in his mind's eye, Fisher took up a firing position and executed a series of pinpoint kills through the skylights, shooting down into the hallway, crossing off Kobin's pursuers in short order.

At best it was a holding action. The building swarmed with furious gang members intent on wiping each other out. The flashy, overblown villa had become a warzone.

A shout of alarm from below warned Fisher that he had been spotted. Automatic fire raked the ceiling and shattered the remaining skylight, forcing him to duck back. He responded by lobbing a pair of grenades – one white smoke, one lethal fragmentation – through the broken glass, before moving forward again. The detonations would discourage anyone from chasing Kobin, at least for a moment.

Fisher needed a better solution. "Panther, Lynx. How copy?" He pressed his throat mike as he ran.

"*Lynx copies.*" Sarah's voice came back immediately. "*What do you need?*"

"There's an external generator on your side of the building," he replied, between sharp breaths. "Get to it."

"*Lynx is moving.*"

"*Panther, what's your plan?*" Grim's voice held an edge of concern.

"Making it up as I go," Fisher replied, as he reloaded on the run. "Just be ready for that extract."

"Ah, shit!" Kobin tripped over the edge of a rug as the shock from an explosion pushed a wall of cordite-choked air down the villa's long hallway. "Who's throwing grenades?"

He recovered, barely stopping himself from going over,

careening off a tower of shelves and back into a stumbling run. Up ahead, another doorway led to the garage and the rear of the building. If he could get in there, if he could get to a car, he could still make it out of this mess in one piece.

What the hell is going on? the accusing voice in Kobin's head screamed at him. *How did you screw this up, Andriy? It was going so well!*

It was obvious in hindsight. He'd made a grave miscalculation about the potency of Nabil's paranoia, and now this whole scheme was falling to pieces. Not only had the gang-lord come here tonight with murder in mind, but it looked like Delim shared the same impulse. These madmen were only interested in tearing each other to bits, in hopes that one of them would be the last asshole standing.

Both sides thought that Kobin had betrayed them to the other. As of now, he had a target on his back for every punk with a shiv from here to the Sahara.

"Never liked this country anyhow," he grumbled, fiddling with the door handle. "Too damn hot. Too much sand. I'm leaving!"

Fortunately, Kobin learned from experience. He had prepared for an occurrence like this. The door thudded open, and he scrambled down the shallow steps into the brightly lit space of the garage.

To his surprise, one of his men was down there, gripping a SPAS-12 combat shotgun, eyeing the entrances. "Boss?" he said.

"Cover the doors!" Kobin yelled. "We're getting out of here!"

Kobin dashed past the line of parked vehicles to the sleek

Jaguar E-Type in the far corner. He popped the sports car's hood and reached into the engine compartment. The Jag was actually a reproduction, and rather than use it to drive, Kobin kept it around for another reason. He'd stashed a go-bag out of sight inside, containing everything he needed in the event of an emergency – fake passports and identity papers, bundles of US dollars and gold coins, everything he needed to get across the border.

But he had to get out of the villa first. Kobin scanned the other parked cars, the Porsche, the Benz, and the Beemer, all shiny and gorgeous. His heart sank. He could only take one; the others would have to be sacrificed to the fates.

He grabbed the keys for the off-road Porsche 911, looking back toward the guard at the doorway. "Emil! Come on!"

"My name is not Emil," said the guard.

"I don't give a shit, come on!"

"But I–" Not-Emil did not have the chance to finish his thought. The door behind him burst apart as gunfire punched through it, catching him across his torso. He fell without firing a shot, the heavy SPAS-12 clattering across the floor.

Kobin wavered, one impulse pushing him to grab the shotgun, another crying out to get in the car and go. He gave in to the latter, and pulled the Porsche's driver-side door open, but the hesitation cost him.

Bleeding but held up by raw fury, Nabil stormed into the garage with a handful of his surviving men. He turned the PKM on the Porsche and blew apart the windshield and the hood. Kobin threw himself to the ground as the machine gun riddled the car with bullet holes.

"The dog… tries to run," said Nabil, panting hard as he took his finger off the trigger, a pennant of smoke rising from the gun's muzzle. He advanced on Kobin, using both hands to point the PKM in his direction. "No way out, animal. Not for you."

His body shaking, Kobin pulled himself to a kneeling position. "Nabil... don't kill me. I didn't betray you! I wanted to make peace!"

"So do I." Nabil coughed out a glob of bloody spittle. "Starting with Delim and his nobodies feeding the maggots. I take over... No more war on the streets. I win. And that means you lose." He took a deep breath, and in the pause Kobin heard the sporadic snarl of gunfire outside. Nabil's men were finishing off their enemies.

"I can help you!" Kobin brought his hands together in a pleading gesture. "You need me! I get you whatever you want, right?" His heart hammered in his ears, his last seconds of life ticking away. This was not how he wanted to go out.

"You have been useful," admitted Nabil.

"I have!" Kobin nodded rapidly.

"But I cannot stand the sight of you," said the gang-lord, with a deep sigh. "You're a parasite, Andriy. Our business is concluded."

Fisher dropped from the top of the villa down to the lower level of the garage's roof, and he risked a look through another narrow skylight set in the concrete ceiling.

He saw a semi-circle of parked cars and his quarry on his knees, surrounded by a bunch of gun-thugs blocking any escape route. Kobin's desperate bid for freedom was at an end, and his death would make this entire mission worthless.

The odds were poor, but Fisher had faced worse. Securing a nylon rope around a free-standing ventilation pipe with one hand, he tapped his mike pad. "Panther, Lynx. Kill the genny."

"Lynx copies," said Sarah. *"Lights out."*

The ripple-fire of multiple grenade detonations sounded from the far side of the villa, and a brief plume of black smoke and orange flames rose up and fell back. Inside the building, every room was immediately plunged into darkness, including the brightly lit garage below Fisher's feet, and it caught Kobin's gang-banger friends off guard.

Clipping on to the other end of the black rope, Fisher flicked down his tri-focal goggles and activated the sonar pulse function, sending an invisible wave of energy down through the walls. The garage interior was immediately revealed to him in a wash of gray, the gun-thugs standing out as red outlines against the sleek shapes of the cars.

He moved fast and smooth, jumping off the frame of the skylight, boots-first through the glass. Shielding his face in the crook of his arm from any tumbling shards, he dropped four meters down to the hood of a BMW roadster, landing squarely in the deepest shadows.

He killed two men with as many rounds in the first half-second, going for headshots to make sure his targets went down and stayed there. The shock and surprise of the power cut wore off and the other criminals began fighting back, but they were blind firing, shooting in every direction and at every jumping shadow.

Ignoring the stark flashes of muzzle flares, Fisher ducked low and slipped behind the BMW, taking down three more of the thugs with careful, accurate hits. Sweeping right, he found the tall man cradling the heavy machine gun, the one in charge. His men dead or dying around him, the gang-lord swore in gutter Arabic and sprayed bullets in Fisher's direction.

Fisher dodged and lit off two snapshots in return, his SC-IS semi-automatic planting rounds through the machine-gunner's thigh and belly. The tall man fell screaming bloody murder, pinned to the floor by the weight of his own weapon.

Across the room, Fisher heard the throaty roar of a 300-horsepower engine and the screech of tires as one of the vehicles came to life. A wash of stinging light near-blinded him as the off-roader's headlamps blazed on at full beam. He recoiled, flipping up his goggles.

Before Fisher could stop it, the bullet-riddled Porsche vaulted forward and crashed through the garage doors, out into the darkness.

A wave of elation came over Kobin as he stamped the Porsche's accelerator pedal into the floor and felt the car pick up speed. The steering was mushy and at least one of the safari tires had been holed, but the off-roader was tough, built to the same specs as a Paris-Dakar rally car.

Escape tasted *sweet.* There was something so rare and perfect about being on the edge of dying, only to give fate the middle finger and speed off in a cloud of dust. Kobin had been there more times than he cared to remember, and when the terror faded, the afterglow of cheating death lingered.

He laughed and put the Porsche into a skidding turn, his go-bag bouncing around on the passenger seat next to him. "Time to get gone," he told himself, shooting a glance back at the receding villa. "So long, assholes!"

He did wonder who had kicked in the skylight and come in shooting, though. That didn't seem like Nabil's or Delim's style. *So, who could it have been?*

His good mood soured as an unpleasant possibility occurred to him; but before he could think it through, a muffled bang sounded from the Porsche's right front fender and the car bucked wildly.

Blowout! He'd lost another tire. The vehicle slid across the road, fighting him as he tried to keep it steady. Then a heartbeat later the rear tire on the same side came apart in a second crash of noise and Kobin knew his celebrations had been premature.

The Porsche spun out into the elbow of the turn that led to the main highway, skidding into a ditch. The airbag in the steering column burst open into Kobin's face and he gagged, getting a mouthful of powder.

For long, dizzying moments, Kobin fought to hold on to consciousness, before finally dragging himself and his go-bag out of the vehicle, to collapse on the dirt track. He rolled over, coming to rest against the ruined car, the hot metal of its frame clicking as it cooled.

He waited for the shot that would end him. There had to be a sniper out there, there could be no other explanation for the two blowouts in quick succession. Aside from the Porsche, he had no cover. If he got to his feet and ran – as if he had the energy to do that – they'd gun him down.

Kobin fumbled at the go-bag's zipper. He'd packed a revolver in there, and a phone. There might still be a chance he could call for help.

Out in the darkness, a shadow moved, growing more

defined as it came closer. Kobin made out the shape of a man with a gun, and he froze.

It wasn't the threat of a weapon that filled him with fear. It was the three eyes staring back at him, glowing green like those of some monster out of the fables his old *babulya* had told him as a child.

He knew that mask, and he knew who would be wearing it.

"Oh, no." Kobin tensed, afraid he might lose control of his bladder. "Oh, fuck no! Not him!" He scrambled back to his feet, the threat of the sniper forgotten. Unseen killers and furious gang-lords, neither of them frightened Kobin as much as this specter did.

"Hello, Andriy." Sam Fisher stepped into full view, reaching up to deactivate the unblinking tri-goggles. "Long time no see." Then he cocked his head, speaking into a hidden mike as he holstered his gun. "Panther, all call-signs. I have Target Jackal."

"Ah, shit." Kobin let the go-bag drop, then made a desperate change of tack and forced a shaky smile. "Sam! My friend! Glad you could drop by!" As he spoke, something back in the villa exploded, and he let out an involuntary groan.

"No need to thank me," Fisher told him, coming up to kick the bag out of reach. "We need to talk."

Kobin spread his hands, trying to maintain some composure. "As much as I would love to catch up, this is a really bad time."

Fisher nodded. "No doubt. You've pissed off some nasty people."

"What can I say, it's a gift." Kobin gave a weak laugh and shuffled in the direction of the highway, trying to put as much distance between them as possible.

"This won't take long," Fisher insisted. "Tell me what you know about Dima Aslanov."

"Who?" Kobin lied automatically, but he couldn't stop the flush of color to his face that betrayed the truth. There were only a few men who terrified him as much as Fisher did, and Aslanov was one of them. "Never heard of the guy." He started walking away. "Look, this has been fun, but I gotta jet…"

Kobin heard a sound like the drone of a hornet, and a patch of ground in front of him burst into a fountain of dust as a bullet struck it. He wheeled around.

Fisher's pistol was back in its holster. Kobin peered into the dark and swallowed hard.

"Like I said," Fisher went on. "Dima Aslanov. Tell me what you know."

"Uh…" Kobin weighed his options, and every one of them was shitty. He could see vehicle headlights on the highway now, more cars coming up from Rabat toward the villa. He couldn't tell from this distance who they belonged to – reinforcements from Delim's gang or Nabil's – but whoever they were, they would not look kindly on him.

"Copy that," said Fisher, responding to a voice that only he could hear. He glanced at Kobin, then in the direction of the approaching vehicles. "You know what? Forget it. If you don't know anything, I don't need you."

He started to move off, and Kobin saw a black 4x4 jeep come rolling in from the opposite direction, out of the darkness beyond the burning villa. Fisher signaled to the driver, and the jeep lumbered toward him.

"You're gonna leave me?" Kobin grabbed his go-bag and held it tightly. "They find me out here, they'll cut me to pieces!"

"Likely," agreed Fisher, as the jeep halted.

"OK, fine!" Kobin came running after him. "Aslanov, yeah. I know him. I wish I didn't."

"Know where he is?"

"I might." Kobin tried to maintain his composure. He only had one card to play here, and he couldn't afford to waste it.

Fisher let the moment hang for far longer than Kobin was comfortable with, and over the hum of the jeep's idling engine, the wind carried the angry shouts of the men back in the villa grounds, and the occasional gunshot.

Fisher relented and gestured at the back of the vehicle. "Get in."

Kobin ran to the jeep as fast as he could and clambered inside, trying not to think if he had just picked the worst of his choices. He dropped into the vehicle's flatbed and looked up.

The driver turned to stare back at him, a woman with dark hair, hard eyes, and an unforgiving set to her features – and for the second time that night, Kobin saw a face he had never wanted to see again as long as he lived. "*Sarah?* Oh shit, is that you?"

"Hello, Kobin," she said coldly. "Haven't seen you since you faked my death."

"You, uh, you look well," he said lamely, as the woman stepped on the gas and the jeep shot away into the night.

ELEVEN

National Route 1 – Skhirat – Morocco

The Toyota 4x4 sped through the night, weaving in and out of the slipstream of dusty cargo trucks as it headed back toward the Paladin's staging point, a few hours south of Kobin's villa.

They had got away clean. None of the vehicles belonging to the gangs pursued them, and they had attracted no attention from the local police. Still, Fisher didn't want to push their luck, and he told Sarah to keep up the pace. Fortunately, Moroccan drivers seemed to treat the speed limit as more of a challenge than a rule, so no one looked twice at the black jeep racing along the highway.

Fisher secured his gear and slipped back from the front passenger seat and into the rear cargo bed. Kobin sat on the floor, his head propped up on one hand, a dejected cast to his expression.

Fisher almost felt sorry for him, but not quite. Andriy Kobin was no angel, and some might have said that he deserved to be left behind and picked apart by vicious gang-bangers. But he had his uses, and that kept him alive.

Fisher tapped his mike. "Paladin Actual, Panther. You read me?"

Lea Kade's voice sounded in his ear. "*Go ahead, Panther.*"

He briefly wondered why Kade had taken over running comms from Grim, but let it pass. "I'm debriefing the asset. Keep the channel open, speak up if you have any specifics. I'm not waiting to get back to the bird."

"*Understood,*" said Kade.

Fisher sat down on the metal bench over the rear wheel and gave Kobin a level look. "Cheer up. You're still breathing."

"Yeah." Kobin drew out the word. "Lucky me." He straightened. "OK. First thing I want is a shower and some coffee. Then we can talk about what kind of deal you have for me–"

"Whoa there." Fisher held up a hand. "Are you under the mistaken impression that you get to set the terms?"

"Not how it works," added Sarah, from the driver's seat.

"Quid pro quo," Kobin countered, making a to-and-fro gesture. "I have information you need, I ask for some reasonable compensation."

"Compensation." Fisher echoed the word. "Like I said, you're still breathing. Consider that your fee." He leaned in, his manner hardening, and nodded toward the road flashing by out the back of the jeep. "You talk or you walk."

Kobin blinked, taking that in. On other occasions, Fisher knew he'd been willing to beat answers out of Kobin, so by those standards he was practically being reasonable. "OK," Kobin said.

Fisher wasted no time getting to the point. "Dima Aslanov. Considering everyone in the intelligence community thinks he's dead and buried, you didn't seem surprised to hear he's still alive. Why is that?"

"I... I've known about Aslanov's whole Lazarus act for around three years." Kobin looked away, staring at the floor.

"You kept that quiet," Fisher said, holding back his irritation.

"Of course I did, I'm not fucking stupid," Kobin retorted. "I know his reputation! I know his history with the CIA and with you... He's a damned horror story! So when he came to me–"

"*He* came to someone like *you*?" Fisher frowned at the thought.

"Don't say it like that! Makes me sound like I'm small-time..." Kobin scowled. "He wanted to stay off the grid, right? Low-key. He needed weapons, hardware, he paid me in cash... I was shit-scared of him, so I did the deal."

"If you knew Dima Aslanov had resurfaced, why didn't you say anything?" Sarah threw in the question, pitching her voice up to be heard over the sound of the engine. "You have to know he's on the kill lists of a dozen different agencies!"

"Eyes on the road," Fisher admonished his daughter, then turned back to Kobin. "Answer her."

"I didn't want any of the heat on him aimed at me! What do you think would happen if word got out that one of the KGB's boogiemen was back from the dead, and in *my* shop? Anyone who wanted his head would go through me to get to him! I figured I'd say nothing and let the big kids work it out. He'd slip up sooner or later, and they'd call you in to deal with him."

"More like you hoped we might take each other out," said Fisher.

"Who can tell?" Kobin gave an insincere smile that made Fisher want to smack it right off his face.

Kade spoke up. "*We need intel on Aslanov's current whereabouts.*"

Fisher nodded to himself. "Where is he now?"

"No idea," Kobin replied. "It's been over a year since we last spoke, and I'm happier for it!"

"*That tracks with the CIA's intel on the killings,*" said Kade. "*They started around ten months ago. Enough time for Aslanov to set up and start hunting.*"

"He tell you why he needed the hardware?" Fisher held Kobin's gaze.

"I didn't ask."

"Make an educated guess."

"Everything he bought from me was top-end kit. You do the math." Kobin blinked, and Fisher recognized the tell.

"What are you hiding from me?" Fisher shifted position and put one hand on Kobin's forearm. "I don't have time to drag it out of you. Talk."

"I am talking!" Kobin insisted.

"Sure. You're just not telling me anything," said Fisher. He gave Kobin's arm a savage twist and his captive cried out, falling sideways.

Fisher kicked open the jeep's tailgate, grabbed a fistful of Kobin's shirt, and shoved him out of the back of the vehicle. Kobin screamed as he dropped face-first toward the blacktop speeding past, his fall halting centimeters from the highway.

The only thing stopping him from becoming roadkill was the material of his sweaty, blood-soaked silk shirt in Fisher's vise-like grip. It began to tear.

"Stop stop stop!" Kobin yelled at the top of his lungs. "OK! I'll tell you everything!"

"Better," said Fisher, and hauled him back into the jeep.

Shuddering with adrenaline, Kobin sat heavily on the deck and started talking, barely pausing for breath. "Aslanov was on empty," he said, the words spilling out of him. "He'd been in the gray too long. Spent everything he put away in his dark money bank accounts before he decided to play dead after Kuwait. Like, dollars don't go as far as they did in the Nineties, right? So, I figured out he found himself a new gig, nothing tied to any nation or government. Aslanov has gone full-on private sector. He's freelancing for a Fortune 500 company, if you can believe it…"

"I need a name," Fisher insisted.

"The Teague Technology Group," Kobin added, with a nod of the head.

Fisher had heard of the corporation in passing, mostly from news items about their continual clashes with the government over monopoly issues.

"T-Tec! They have more money than half the countries in the G7," continued Kobin. "I read about it in *Wired*! And with that kind of cash around, there's always questionable shit that needs to get done, right? You don't get rich without getting dirty. So Aslanov's working for them now."

"*That puts a different light on it,*" said Kade. "*Keep him talking, Panther, I need to push this new information up the chain…*"

Kobin kept talking, unaware of the voice in Fisher's ear. "I tried to get in on that action myself, you know? I mean, I saw an opportunity! But I got greedy-stupid, and Aslanov… That asshole ripped me off!"

"My heart bleeds," muttered Sarah.

"He took my contacts, man," Kobin grated, shaking his head. "My little black book. All the names and numbers I've worked for years to put together, he stole them. Left me with next to nothing, which explains my present circumstances..."

Fisher eyed him. "Why?"

"Why did a ruthless killer working for an amoral corporation steal my list of terrorists and assorted shady motherfuckers?" Kobin blew out an exasperated breath. "Not for anything good, obviously. I thought about trying to get the book back, but it was too late. I wasn't dumb enough to go chasing after Aslanov. I had to let it go."

"Smart call," said Fisher. "He'd eat you alive."

"Yeah," Kobin said dejectedly. "So, that really *is* all I know." He met Fisher's gaze again. "You gonna toss me out now?"

Fisher gave a shrug and turned to Sarah. "What do you think?"

"Don't ask her!" Kobin yelled. "She hates me more than you do!"

"True," said Sarah. "But let's keep him around. I like making him sweat."

Kobin seemed to shrink as the reality of the situation settled in on him. "Every time..." he said quietly. "Every time you people turn up in my life, it all goes to hell..."

Málaga–Costa del Sol Airport – Málaga – Spain

To the casual observer, Anna Grímsdóttir would have seemed like any other person waiting in the airport's arrivals lounge, flicking idly down the screen of her smartphone. She still wore the same jacket she had in Berlin, and despite the lateness of the hour, the clammy air inside the terminal made her uncomfortable. Hot climates weren't exactly her thing – a legacy of her Icelandic roots, perhaps – but there hadn't been time to change into something better suited for the sultry Spanish night.

An observer would have thought something was off about her if they were close enough to see that the smartphone she held was actually a military-grade OPSAT device, connected to a discreet radio earpiece. The digital pages she scrolled through on its screen were not some vapid social media feed, but the uplink of speech-to-text files from Sam Fisher's impromptu interrogation of Andriy Kobin.

It took a lot to make Grim cut and run, especially in the closing phase of an active operation like the Morocco recovery, and hopping a fast flight to Málaga was motivated in many ways by Grim's desire to balance a debt. To be brutally honest with herself, it was to assuage her own guilt.

But that wasn't the only reason. As with everything in the shadow world where Grim existed, there was a larger agenda at work.

A voice over the airport's public address system had announced the arrival of the last flight from London, and now the first few disembarked passengers were making their way through. Maintaining her disinterested manner, Grim scanned the faces of eager British holidaymakers pushing luggage carts piled high with suitcases.

Her target immediately stood out among them. Dressed in a dark hoodie pulled up over his head, he carried a satchel over a shoulder but no other items of baggage. He kept glancing behind him, as if he was afraid someone would drag him back into the customs hall for a strip-search and body-cavity probing.

Grim stared fixedly in his direction, waiting until his searching, nervous gaze turned her way. Their eyes met and she gave a slight nod, which he returned.

He made a vague attempt at tradecraft by coming around to the lounge on a roundabout path, by which time Grim had already purchased two take-out coffees from a nearby vendor and returned to her seat.

"Charlie," she said, by way of greeting, pushing one of the cups toward him as he sat down opposite her.

"Anna." He dropped heavily into the chair. "Are we, uh, *secure* here?"

Grim placed her OPSAT on the table and activated a localized frequency jammer built into the device. The range was limited but enough to encompass their corner of the near-empty lounge. "Secure enough," she told him.

"Thanks for coming." Charlie Cole bent forward, elbows on his knees, cradling the coffee cup. "I wasn't sure you would."

"You asked for my help," she replied.

"Yeah, but you don't have to give it," he said. "I mean, I don't work for 4E anymore."

"We take care of our own," said Grim.

But that wasn't always true, and they both knew it.

In fact, it had been the reason why Cole had quit the NSA and Fourth Echelon a few short years ago. An operation in Tehran, where Charlie had been deployed in the area of activity as field support for Isaac Briggs, had self-destructed when a local contact doublecrossed them. Grabbed by enemy agents and held hostage for days, his captors kept the hacker awake and beat him half to death while they tried to figure out the Splinter Cell's plans in the Islamic Republic.

In the end, Grim, Briggs, and the rest of the team found the location where Charlie was being held, but the experience was profoundly traumatic for the young man. Plagued by nightmares of his ordeal, he resigned soon after his rescue, too fearful to go back to active duty and risk the same thing happening again.

What made it personal for Grim was the responsibility. She had sent Charlie into the field, into a threat environment he wasn't ready for. He had been taken on her watch, and she carried the blame.

But being the woman she was – cool, stoic, calculating – Grim let none of that show. Inwardly, she wondered if she was getting soft, the same thing she had accused Sam Fisher of back in Berlin.

"I listened to your message," she said. "If I can help, I will. But you need to be completely open with me, Charlie. Don't hold anything back."

He nodded woodenly. "My friend is dead and the guy who murdered her almost killed me. I'm not about to play games, Grim." He took a wary sip of the coffee.

"I want everything Jan Freling gave you," she told him. Grim had gone through Charlie's message a dozen times since departing Morocco, her lips thinning into a hard line as she saw the clear lines of connection between what had happened in London and the confession that spilled out of Kobin.

Charlie's eyes narrowed as he caught on to her tone. "I reached out to you because I need protection. You told me to get the first flight out of England, so I did." He lost momentum. "I thought…"

You thought I'd help you because I'm guilty about what

happened in Tehran. Grim held in the words, saying nothing. *And I am. But the mission is always the first priority.*

In the face of her silence, Charlie gave a weary nod. "OK. Where do you want me to start?"

Ben Slimane Airport – Casablanca-Settat – Morocco

"Huh, this thing is still flying…" Kobin offered up the comment as Fisher marched him aboard the Paladin, craning his neck to look around at the jet's interior. "You made some improvements."

"Keep walking," Fisher told him.

"Sure, sure…" Despite what happened on the highway, Kobin had recovered some of his former swagger. "Listen," he said, with a sniff. "You need me to pilot this thing again for you, I could do it. Just like old times, right?"

Ahead of them, Sarah halted on the cargo ramp and looked back at her father. "You let *him* fly the Paladin?"

"It was an extreme situation," Fisher noted, recalling the moment. Hacked by the terrorist group known as the Engineers, the jet had been stuck in a terminal dive toward the ocean, and he had to reluctantly admit that Kobin had made good on getting the Paladin back on a stable heading. But it was important to remember that the criminal had been saving his own life along with everyone else's.

"I get one of those little crew cabins this time, right?" Kobin looked up at Fisher as he guided him through the cargo bay. "Right?" he repeated.

"Not so much." Fisher halted by the Paladin's holding cell and opened the hatch. Kobin started to complain, but before he could get anything out he had already been shoved inside. "Just like old times," said Fisher, slamming the hatch shut and keying the magnetic locks.

He walked past Sarah, who stood back, arms folded. "When I look at Kobin, I think about what I lost because of him," she said quietly. "Two years of my life living under an assumed name, with some anonymous corpse that he provided lying in my grave."

Fisher understood her sentiments, but they didn't change anything. "This is the job," he told her. "Sometimes wolves need to run with dogs."

"You mean a jackal," she corrected, and moved off. "I'm gonna take a shower, I need to wash off the smell."

Fisher carried on to command-and-control, where he found Lea Kade manning the strategic mission interface.

"Kade."

"Sir." She nodded a greeting.

"Where's Grim? She went off-comms after Kobin's exfiltration."

The ex-Marine gestured at one of the secondary screens. "Something came up. She's taking care of it personally."

"That right?" Fisher walked to the monitor, looking over the shoulder of Drew as he worked the keyboard in front of it. Ignoring the operator's reaction, he leaned in and studied the screen. He saw the interior of an airport terminal, via a feed co-opted from a security camera.

A familiar figure sat in the middle of the image. Grim was in a conversation with a man in a hoodie. As he watched, the man reached up and rolled back the hood.

"Cole…" Fisher shot Kade a hard look. "That's Charlie Cole

she's talking to. Someone want to explain this to me?" Then he frowned and poked Drew in the shoulder. "I want to hear what they're saying."

Drew gave Kade a questioning look, and she returned a nod. With the flick of a switch, a scratchy capture of Charlie's voice issued from a speaker.

"*Brody Teague and T-Tec are into something serious,*" he was saying, "*and they're killing people in order to cover it up.*"

Málaga-Costa del Sol Airport – Málaga – Spain

Grim listened carefully as Charlie relayed the discoveries made on the GreenSea and T-Tec corporate computer servers, everything from the shifting assets and dark money to the apparent murders of the freelance consultants and other employees involved in project Gordian Sword.

Everything he told her lined up alongside the information that Andriy Kobin had given up regarding the assassin Dima Aslanov, each piece slotting into place. It was the break that could put them ahead of the game, if they used the data carefully. All too often, the gathering of actionable intelligence came down to moments of confluence like this, of coincidences spotted and acted upon. The key was setting the right conditions and acting decisively when the time came.

Grim tapped out a command on her OPSAT, bringing up an image from one of the partly redacted files supplied by the CIA. She turned the device so Charlie could see the screen, a copy of a KGB identity document from the early 1980s. "This is an old picture," she began, "but the man in the photo..."

She trailed off as she noticed the color drain from Charlie's face. "That's the guy who came after me," he said. "He works for Brody Teague. His name is Stone."

"His name is Dima Aslanov," she corrected. "He's an assassin."

Charlie gave a slow nod. "That makes sense. I couldn't shake the feeling that I knew him from somewhere. I must have run across his picture while I was with the NSA."

"*This is a new wrinkle.*" Sam Fisher's low growl sounded in Grim's ear. "*When were you going to tell me Cole was involved?*"

"The situation is fluid," said Grim, her voice picked up by the OPSAT. "We have an audience," she explained to Charlie. "Say hello. Sam's listening in."

"Sam?" Charlie's eyes widened. "Whoa. Is he here?"

"*You need to get him someplace safe,*" Fisher insisted. He, like Grim, knew the full story of what happened in Tehran. "*He's a civilian now. He's not up for this.*"

"Duly noted," Grim said firmly, dismissing the suggestion for the moment. "All right, let's lay out the facts." She thought aloud, as much for Charlie's benefit as for everyone monitoring back on the Paladin. "T-Tec have been using GreenSea as a covert blind to move money and assets. Aslanov's killing anyone who finds out about that, along with several technical experts who have previously consulted for Teague's company on some secret project."

"He's clearing up the loose ends around this Gordian Sword thing," said Charlie.

Grim nodded, turning the words over in her thoughts. "What does that codename suggest?"

"*Alexander the Great and the Gordian Knot,*" said Sam. Off her silence, he continued. "*Don't act surprised. I read a lot in my downtime.*"

Grim was familiar with the ancient legend. The tale went that there was a knot so complex, the oracles said anyone clever enough to untangle it would rule the continent of Asia. When confronted by this impossible test, the famous Macedonian warrior-king Alexander simply cut the knot in half with his sword, solving the problem with a single stroke.

"Brody Teague's not exactly the subtle type," noted Charlie. "A Gordian sword would be one that cuts through any knot, any barrier. In the context of a digital technology corporation, that suggests a lot of worrying possibilities."

"We need hard facts, not assumptions and word games." Grim studied Charlie, gauging how far she could push him. "Your friend found those files on ghost servers in the dark net. Where would Teague keep his most sensitive data?"

"T-Tec's main server is in Portugal, at the European head office in Lisbon," he noted. "It's fully secured, air-gapped, the works." Charlie hesitated, suddenly catching up to Grim's train of thought. "Wait, no. You can't be thinking about penetrating that building?" He shook his head. "It can't be hacked remotely! It would have to be on site, a physical incursion, in person!"

"You could figure out a way inside," she said, making it a statement, not a question. "You know how to access the servers directly."

"*Grim. Don't.*" Fisher's voice sounded once again. "*We'll find another way.*"

Her face showed a flicker of irritation, and Grim reached up and pulled out her wireless earpiece. She turned the full force of her icy gaze on the hacker. "I know it's a lot to ask. But we're ten steps behind here, and we need to know what we're up against. If what you're telling me is right, Teague's plans are already in motion. We can't wait for him to make the next move."

"I can't go back in the field," Charlie said firmly. His eyes lost focus, and she knew he was recalling the terrible hours of his abduction.

But Grim stamped down on any sympathy she had for him. *The mission is always the first priority.* And right now, Charlie Cole was her best shot at getting to the heart of this.

"Look at me," she demanded, and he did. "You're the only one who can do this. If you're with us, we can keep you safe."

There was an unspoken warning in those words that Charlie didn't miss. Finally, he gave a wary nod. "All right. I guess I don't have any choice."

"You don't," she told him, picking up the earpiece and replacing it.

"*That was cold, Grim,*" said Fisher. "*Even for you.*"

"Get the Paladin in the air," she replied. "We'll rendezvous in Lisbon in ten hours."

TWELVE

T-Tec European Head Office – Lisbon – Portugal

Charlie's hand shot out as they crossed the street and closed in on their target. "Stop. We have to abort!" He grabbed Sarah by the wrist, squeezing it uncomfortably hard.

She unpeeled his fingers and shot him a hard look. "Keep it together."

"Lynx, Paladin Actual. Is there a problem?" Grim's voice droned in Sarah's skull, and she winced.

Rather than the usual earpieces typically employed by Fourth Echelon agents, Sarah and Charlie were using mastoid conduction devices, so radio signals were beamed directly into their ears by tiny vibrations through their bones. Hidden behind their earlobes, it made the communicators almost impossible to detect by anything other than a close-up, finger-tip examination, but the downside was it felt like having a constant, low-level toothache.

"No problem." Sarah subvocalized the reply, glaring at Charlie. "Right?"

"You see that?" Charlie halted on the street corner, inclining his head toward a line of parked vehicles a few hundred meters away.

She looked without making it obvious. Standing out from the rest of the evening's traffic was a line of three identical Bentley Bentayga sport utility vehicles in shiny blood-crimson. Each one had tinted windows and sat low on their shocks, a telltale indicator that the SUVs had heavier-than-standard engines and armor plating. Two men in dark windbreakers stood nearby, scanning the street in both directions. Sarah imagined that if she walked closer, she would see the bulge of firearms under their jackets.

"That's Brody Teague's private motorcade!" Charlie's voice rose an octave. "Which means he's in there right now!" He jabbed a finger in the direction of the building in front of them. "I can't do this…"

"*All call-signs, Paladin Actual.*" Grim's words buzzed around them. "*We knew this was a possibility…*"

"Did we?" snapped Charlie. "I don't remember it coming up during the pre-brief!"

Grim ignored him. "*This changes nothing. We're on the clock and we have to act now. Proceed as planned.*"

"No…" Charlie shook his head and started to turn away.

Sarah reached out and drew him close. To anyone passing, they would have looked like a young couple sharing an intimate moment. She leaned in and spoke into his ear. "You're worried about Aslanov."

"Yeah, no shit." He stiffened. "I get recognized, we're both done."

"That's why I'm here," Sarah said firmly. "To keep you safe.

Come on, Charlie, this is your operation. *You* designed it."
She'd been impressed by the hacker's work in developing
the mission profile for this intrusion, but without him it
would fall apart. Sarah reminded him of that fact, and of
one other hard truth. "Your friend Jan is dead because of
these people, and she's not the only one. We can't let that go
unpunished."

He eyed her. "You're using emotional blackmail."

"Is it working?"

"Yeah," he said, making a face. "You're not fazed by any of
this, are you? You know, when I saw you back there on the
Paladin after Grim brought me in, I couldn't believe it. *Sarah
Fisher*. The girl who used to be an art history student, now a
dark-ops badass-in-waiting. I think I missed a memo or two."

"It feels right to me, Charlie," she told him. "We all change."

"Not always for the better." He scowled. "You know, if your
dad needed me to do something I didn't want to, he'd just
intimidate me. But somehow your way is worse." He took a
deep breath, steeling himself. "OK. For Jan's sake. Let's do this
before I have a panic attack."

The two of them carried on, with Sarah leading the way
toward the office building. The ten-story tower rising up
from the Avenue Pacifico had a smooth, rounded shape that
reminded her of coral or carved bone. A strikingly modern
creation in a city better known for the bright colors and
tiled forms of boxy Pombaline architecture, the European
headquarters of the Teague Technology Group blended in
with the other constructions along the edge of the Tagus
Bay that bisected Lisbon. Centered in the Parque das Nações
district – what the locals called the Expo – and close to

the Vasco da Gama Bridge, it was one of several futuristic buildings meant to signify Lisbon's march toward progress.

Brody Teague had purchased the tower in its entirety from the city, for an undisclosed fee that allegedly included certain "permissions costs", such as allowing T-Tec to have their own private security force on call, and overlooking certain other legal requirements.

Sarah looked up along the tower's curved flanks, noting that each floor was illuminated, despite the lateness of the evening. According to the breathless publicity text on the company website, the staff in the Lisbon building's vertical campus operated on a 24/7 program, constantly in synch with T-Tec's other offices around the globe. At the top, where the curves formed into a shape like a frozen wave, she saw anti-collision lights blinking on a large satellite antenna.

"Here we go," she said, as they entered the cavernous glass lobby and headed to a security console.

Beneath their feet, transparent tubes revealed fast-flowing streams of seawater going out to the bay from the hydroelectric power plant in the basement. On its way in, the flow of cold water powered underground turbines, and pumped around the floors to keep the building cool in the subtropical Portuguese heat. According to Charlie, it also chilled down the tower's constantly running computer servers.

"Moment of truth," muttered the hacker, as he used a near-field transmitter in his phone to spoof an ID scanner. Instead of logging in Charlie Cole's biometrics, his face and his gait, the scanner registered him as someone else.

"Who's Gary Borden?" Sarah studied the device's screen, reading off the false identity.

"He's a knobhead," Charlie replied, duplicating the same hack for her. "Who I'm now impersonating, okey dokey?" He made a very poor attempt at a British accent, and Sarah shook her head.

"Don't do that again."

"Fair enough." He finished his work, and they moved away. "You're logged in as Gary's plus one. That should be enough to get us up to the security floor."

"Paladin Actual, Lynx." Sarah subvocalized again. "Passing Waypoint Alpha."

"*Copy*," said Grim. "*What's the duration on that fake ID?*"

"A good lie has maybe thirty minutes in it," said Charlie, "so we've gotta motor."

"Proceeding to Waypoint Bravo, going silent," said Sarah, tapping the tiny patch behind her ear to render it temporarily inert, and Charlie did the same.

Before the elevator bank that would take them to the upper levels, they passed through the arch of a T-wave security scanner and turned over all personal items to another unsmiling guard for temporary safekeeping. Teague was so paranoid about industrial espionage that no devices of any kind, or anything that might contain even the smallest data chip, were allowed in from the outside.

All of which meant that Sarah and Charlie had been forced to leave every item of Fourth Echelon hardware back on the Paladin. Their intrusion would run on intelligence and cunning.

There were no buttons inside the elevator to indicate what floor the passenger wanted; the car would take you only to destinations preprogrammed and permitted based on security clearance. Sarah felt the floor tremble and they began to ascend.

"You know, I can only get us to the right level," Charlie said quietly. "Getting into the security area is a different matter."

"I'll handle it," she told him.

Fisher swam close to the bottom of the bay, kicking gently with his flippers to propel himself through the water, being careful not to stir up the silt.

He moved away from the glowing underwater structure of the Oceanário de Lisboa, giving the aquarium's lights a wide berth, using it as a marker to navigate toward the nearby quay. He checked the air meter display on the waterproof OPSAT clipped to his wrist. The small tank on his back was down to its last quarter.

He'd swum the entire way across the bay from Montijo Air Base, where the Paladin was parked in a hangar belonging to the Força Aérea Portuguesa. They had used the same cover story as in Morocco, mimicking a USAF transport flight making an unscheduled stop caused by engine trouble.

The effort of the swim had been greater than he expected, and Fisher knew he was running slightly behind schedule. By now, Sarah and Charlie would be inside the office tower and moving to their primary objective. That meant he had to be in place when the word came down to begin phase two of the intrusion.

Viewing the world through tri-goggles clipped to a specially modified scuba mask, Fisher quickly located the heavy safety grille across the inlet vents leading into the T-Tec building. Floating close by, he felt the pull of the pumps inside dragging down the water.

He pulled an item from a sealed pouch in his tactical suit,

resembling two syringes side-by-side with a shared nozzle. Each cylinder contained an inert chemical component, which, when mixed together, became a sticky gel that reacted on contact with metals. The exothermal compound burned even underwater or in a vacuum, reacting violently enough to chew through steel in seconds. Fisher applied a fat blob of the combined goop to the industrial-grade lock holding the grille shut, and watched it fizz and crumble.

Within a few moments, the lock fragmented, and he levered open the grille to slip inside, detaching his flippers as he went. Fisher's slim, athletic build filled the pipe beyond, and he worked his way down it with his hands and feet.

The inexorable pull of the water pump increased. Ahead of him, visible as a flashing disc through the tri-goggles, a bladed intake fan in the duct spun too fast to see, sucking seawater into the building's power plant. The fan operated on a pre-set sequence, spinning up to full speed for sixty seconds and then down to idle for fifteen.

Fisher waited for the down-cycle, flicking his air tank off its back mount as he watched the glowing clock on his OPSAT. When the moment came, he kicked off hard and squeezed through the gap, mentally counting down the time as he made himself as narrow as he could. His feet cleared the narrow gap as the fan started to move again, and the blades caught the air pipe from the tank floating behind him. Fisher yanked it hard to pull the tank free before it could become entangled, pulling it along with him. The drag of the intake pump grew in force, pushing him back toward the next set of filter grilles and the narrowing throat of the pipes.

Pulling out the tank had turned him around. Fisher rolled

over and planted his hands on the inside of the curved inlet channel, scanning the dark, turbulent water for the shape of a maintenance hatch along the top of the pipeway.

He found it by feel, gloved fingers tracing the edges until he came to the hinges. The next step was difficult to accomplish while underwater, in the dark, and being buffeted by a fast-moving current.

Flipping up his tri-goggles, Fisher pulled a black-clad flexible cable from another pouch. The cable ended in a tiny micro-camera, small enough to fit through a keyhole gap in the hatch. Connecting the other end to his OPSAT, he fed the snake-camera rig through until it relayed a grainy image of the mechanical room above the pipes. Wedging himself in place, Fisher panned the optic cable around, and didn't proceed until he was sure the room was empty.

Reeling the cable back in, he used the chemical gel again, burning out the hinges on the hatch. Fisher slowly lifted it free and pulled himself out of the pipe.

Panting, he secured the hatch as best he could and then stood silently, letting the water from the bay run off the tactical suit's fluid-resistant outer layer. He put his mask and air tank in a dry-bag and reactivated his goggles. The machine room appeared before him as a gray maze of rectangular shapes and twisting tubes.

Fisher tapped the mike pickup at his throat. "All call-signs, this is Panther. Passing Waypoint Zulu."

"*Copy,*" said Grim. "*What's your situation?*" That was her way of saying *you're late, so pick up the pace.*

"No opposition so far. Proceeding," he replied, moving toward a service walkway. He was still sore about the conversation they'd had on the Paladin, after Charlie had explained the nature of their objective. "Status check on Lynx and Merlin?" The hacker had grinned like an idiot when that random call-sign was selected for him, cracking a joke about *Dungeons & Dragons* that had gone right over Fisher's head.

"*In motion,*" noted Grim. "*Time to target, ten mikes.*"

"Right." Fisher chewed on a reply, then let it fade. He was too much of a good soldier to let his reservations show once the starting gun had been fired, but he wasn't afraid to make his concerns known at the planning stage of a mission – and he'd done exactly that on board the Paladin, even to the point of drawing Grim aside to question the way things were going to play out.

The hard reality of it was clear. Charlie Cole was the best shot to get Fourth Echelon the access they needed from Teague's servers, but to do that required him to be inside the threat zone and *that* meant someone had to cover him. Years ago, Charlie had been trained up to minimum field rating as an NSA technical officer, but he had never been *operational*, not in the true sense of the word. Then the incident in Tehran had come along and smacked any confidence out of him.

Fisher had seen the same thing happen to accomplished soldiers. They would have their first encounter with death at close hand, and something in them broke. They saw how close they came to dying and could not recover from the revelation. Some people could look into that abyss and stare it down. Others never got over the shock.

Charlie had been to that same brink and recoiled from it. Not his fault, Fisher thought. He wasn't trained for that. He was in over his head.

But for this mission to work, Cole had to be in the field, and Fisher had to be elsewhere. Which mean Sam's daughter drew the chaperone duty.

The strength of Fisher's initial reaction to that had surprised even him. He was vehemently opposed to the idea and made no bones about demanding Grim find another solution.

But there isn't one, she told him, *and you know it.*

The situation rang with echoes of that horrible moment back on the embassy terrace in Tbilisi, when Aslanov had coldly threatened the life of Sam's future wife. If he closed his eyes, he would be back in that memory, powerless and furious, but this time it was Sarah in the firing line.

Ever pragmatic, Grim summed it up with clinical precision. Sarah might not have been technically mission-cleared as a Splinter Cell operative, but the risk to her was worth it to gain direct access to Brody Teague's plans. Whatever influence Sam Fisher had at the upper levels of Fourth Echelon, Grim had more, and she overruled his misgivings.

There was one more factor to all this that Fisher had almost lost sight of, in his focus on the safety of his only child, and now he considered it as he stalked along the walkways above the water pumps.

Grim isn't telling me everything about this op, he thought. *The speed she's pushing this, the shortcuts she's taking... There's more going on here than I know.*

Voices from below wafted up toward him, snapping him out of his musings, and Fisher reacted by reaching up to smother a lightbulb casting illumination across his path. He froze, listening to a pair of guards chatting in rapid-fire Portuguese. His Spanish was good enough to follow most of the conversation in the sister language, picking out the salient points from context and guessing the rest.

They were sharing complaints about the boss being in town unexpectedly, and how that had messed up their plans for a lazy shift. Everyone was expected to work twice as hard, and both men resented it. Fisher stayed out of sight until they passed into the next area, then set off again as quickly as he could along the walkway toward the main stack for the cooling pipes.

He tapped his mike again. "Paladin Actual, Panther. Overheard chatter here that we have Target Blue on site. Repeat, Target Blue is in area of operations."

"*Actual is aware, Panther.*" Target Blue was Brody Teague's operational designation, with his second-in-command, Samir Patel, color-coded as Target White, and Target Red reserved for the elusive ex-KGB agent, Dima Aslanov. "*Confidence is high,*" added Grim, confirming that the team back on the jet were certain Teague was in the building.

"That's a damned complication," he said, with chilly understatement, irked that Grim hadn't told him first. "Target Red status?" Where Teague went, the Russian couldn't be that far behind. "Confirm or deny?"

"*No new intel at this time, Panther. Proceed as planned.*"

It was exactly the answer he expected to get, and exactly the job he had been trained to do.

Splinter Cells were expert in handling deployments where actionable intelligence was thin on the ground, where changing circumstances in the AO meant that they had to adapt on the fly to new threats, as and when they emerged. Splinter Cell operatives had the autonomy to make tactical choices in the moment that would keep the United States safe, even if those choices were extreme ones, even if they broke laws in order to defend them.

In training, Fisher's instructors had referred to that deadly liberty as the Fifth Freedom. The term spun out of a speech given in 1941 by the then-president of the USA, Franklin Delano Roosevelt. He spoke of the four fundamental freedoms that humans "everywhere in the world" should possess – to be free in speech, and in religion, to be free from want, and free from fear.

The Fifth Freedom allowed any actions to be taken, any lines to be crossed, any means to be employed in order to preserve the other four and protect the Free World.

There were days when Sam Fisher questioned what all of that meant, and his place in it. But for now, he would become what he needed to be, and what his government and his commanders required of him.

He moved on in silence, letting the shadows swallow him.

THIRTEEN

T-Tec European Head Office – Lisbon – Portugal

Brody Teague walked into the center of the open space and spread his arms wide. He turned in place, letting the mapping sensors hidden in the curved walls read his body shape and limb position. Fans of laser light washed over him, and he tipped back his head, as if he were accepting some kind of electronic benediction.

The walls showed a test pattern, becoming one seamless video screen, and presently a digital avatar of Teague formed before him. It moved when he moved, gestured when he gestured.

"Just two more minutes, Brody," said Eighteen, looking down at her tablet computer, anticipating his question before he asked it. "We're on schedule for the link-up." Teague's assistant stood outside the spherical chamber at the heart of the room, watching him through the open side. She knew well enough not to step inside the space; this was his realm, and it belonged only to him.

And besides, another person inside the perimeter would confuse the scanners. They were still working on the ability to map multiple users in real time, something that Teague was pissed off about on a daily basis. He poured millions of dollars into this virtual/actual environment simulator, and as much as he loved the idea of the thing, it had yet to be anything more than a clever toy.

Rich people always had their pet projects. Diana messed around with her socially conscious coffee plantations, Natalya overcompensated with her private army, and Jace had his creepy drones. But Brody's simulator actually *meant* something. When they got it right, it would change lives forever – a full and free recreation of anything and everything was the goal. The freedom to explore in a world without borders and arbitrary limits.

But there were a lot of petty little complications to be dealt with first, and not just with the technology. People are the problem, Brody told himself. They need a shock to the system to kick them out of their idiotic complacency.

He shot Eighteen a look, like it was her fault. It irritated him that he couldn't remember her name, because he wanted to yell it at her. "Go get me my chai latte," he barked, making do with the demand. "Right now!"

"Sure thing, Brody." She nodded, showed that brittle smile of hers, and backed away.

On the way out, she passed Samir Patel walking in, followed by the Russian. Teague gave them a dismissive grunt and went back to letting the V/AE's scanners do their work.

"The last of the participation fee deposits have been made," said Patel. "Just thought you'd like to know."

"Whatever." Teague shrugged. "Give the money to charity. Sick kids in Africa, or something, I don't care. It's not like I need it." Patel made a disappointed face, and he mimicked it, mocking him. "I told you before, Samir, this is bigger than dollars in the bank. Shit, you know what? I would have given out the invites for free if I thought anyone would have taken them up. But no, it turns out paranoid people don't trust it when you offer them something for nothing!" He looked in the Russian's direction. "You know all about that, Mister KGB?"

Aslanov mirrored Teague's dismissive shrug. "Sometimes it is easier to make the mark pay for their own funeral."

Teague gave the Russian a second look, as if he had just realized who he was. "What are you even doing here, anyway? Where's that nerd, what's his name? Cole?" He made a throat cutting gesture, and his virtual avatar copied the movement. "Aren't you supposed to bring me his head?" Aslanov gave Patel a glance, and that annoyed Teague even more. "Don't look at Samir! I write your checks, not him!"

"Indeed," said the assassin, folding his arms behind his back. "Cole dropped out of sight in London. The Freling woman warned him before I eliminated her. I believe he escaped into Europe... We are searching."

That did not satisfy Teague. "How the hell did he get away from you?"

"Well, Cole worked for the NSA before GreenSea hired him," Patel noted.

"As an analyst!" Teague snapped back. "For crying out loud, he's some beta geek, not Jason Bourne!"

"Exactly," said Aslanov. "He may have gone to one of his

former contacts for help. Depending on what he knows about the Gordian Sword asset, that could present a problem."

"No Such Agency?" Teague spat the words across the room. "More like *Such Bullshit!*" He paced in circles, talking up his defiance. "I'm not worried about some government attack dogs and their script kiddies. They're old news. Nation-states are dinosaurs, too slow for the modern age…"

"They'd be the perfect target for a demonstration of the asset's capabilities." Patel offered the suggestion so guilelessly, it couldn't have been anything but deliberate. The sneer fell off Teague's face; Patel had long ago learned how to call him out without making it obvious.

"We're not doing that," Teague replied, changing tack. "They want a sneak preview, they should have paid for a ticket like everyone else."

The redheaded assistant returned, offering up a steaming cup to her employer. He took it without comment, and she glanced at her tablet computer once again. "Almost ready," she said, with a practiced smile.

Teague straightened his shirt, and his mercurial mood shifted again, this time toward smug confidence. "OK. *Showtime.* Let's change the world."

"Tell me you have a way to get us in there," muttered Charlie, keeping his voice low and his eyes down as the elevator ascended to the security floor.

"A nice smile and a sunny attitude work wonders," said Sarah, as the lift halted with a melodic ping and the doors opened. She started laughing loudly as they walked out into the upper level lobby, as if in response to a joke that Charlie had told. "Oh my god, stop!" Sarah giggled. "That's hilarious! I can't believe she said that!"

Charlie gave a sheepish grin and tried to play along. "Yeah, huh. Crazy, right?"

"Crazy!" Sarah deliberately walked without looking where she was headed, bumping straight into another woman in the middle of a group coming the other way. She made a performance out of stumbling over her feet and grabbed the woman for support. "Oh no!"

"*O que você está fazendo*?" The woman reacted with surprise.

Sarah's cheeks reddened convincingly, and she appeared confused. "I'm, like, so sorry! I don't speak Portuguese!"

With a frown, the woman switched to English. "Are you all right?"

"Yes!" Sarah brought up her hands in front of her face, as if mortified. "I'm, like, such a Klutzy Kathy!" She dialed up her accent, adding a little upward intonation at the end of the sentence to play into the role of a clueless American.

The woman stepped back and gave the two of them a severe look. "You need to watch where you are going."

"Sure, sure." Sarah did her best to sound contrite and stepped aside to let the other people pass. "Sorry!" She drew out the last word, watching as the group boarded the elevator they had vacated.

"*Turista estúpido*," said the woman, drawing a snigger from her colleagues as the lift doors closed.

"Not sorry." Sarah dropped the act and strode over to the mag-locked security vestibule leading to the rest of the working floor. Charlie trailed after her, his fingers tapping nervously on his thighs.

"So, what now?" He cast around, becoming more agitated by the second.

"Now we walk right in." Sarah revealed the plastic bracelet she had surreptitiously removed from the woman's wrist. The thin strip contained a radio frequency ID chip that responded to a lock pad by the door, and with a cursory swipe, the vestibule opened. "Quickly, before someone else comes." She pulled Charlie through the door after her.

A corridor extended away from them, branching off into alcoves that led to individual workstations. Numerical codes on plaques designated the functions of each area, but to Sarah they were incomprehensible.

"Which way?"

Charlie gave a start at the question and blinked at her. "What?"

"Where do we go?" she asked. "Focus! I need you on your game for this."

"I…" He shook his head. "I don't think I can do this. I thought I could, but I was wrong. Let's go, before we get caught…" Charlie turned back to the security door, but Sarah caught him before he could take another step.

"Charlie, look at me." She met his gaze, sensing the deep fear rising in him. Grim had given her the high points of what Cole had suffered during his abduction and she knew he had to be on the verge of panic, terrified that it would happen again if they were caught. "I'll keep you safe. I promise you. But you've got to meet me halfway."

"Halfway. Halfway." He repeated the words, nodding to himself, staring into the middle distance. "OK. Sure. I can do that."

"Where do we go?" she asked again.

Charlie took a deep breath and pointed. "This way."

Sarah trailed after him into one of the dimly lit rooms and reactivated her mastoid communicator with a tap of the flesh-colored pad behind her earlobe. "All call-signs, this is Lynx. Passing Waypoint Charlie."

"*Paladin Actual copies.*" Grim's voice buzzed in her ear. "*Any problems?*"

She glanced at the hacker, as he dropped into a chair in front of a rack of computers, the blinking LED lights on the panels reflecting off his face. "Negative."

"*ETA on Merlin's first objective?*" Sarah's father joined the conversation, his voice barely louder than a whisper.

"Stand by, Panther." She leaned in over Charlie's shoulder. He was already cracking his way through layers of the smart building's internal security network, pulling up page after page of digital controls. Whatever hesitation the hacker had shown before, it melted away once he was back in his own element.

"I'm in," Charlie told her. "Isolating the cooling systems command array... Here we go." On the screen in front of him, a series of code strings scrolled up, and he went to work editing their functions. "Done."

"Passing Waypoint Delta," said Sarah. "Panther, you're good to go."

"Copy that."

As Fisher said the words, the maintenance gantry in front of him clicked and retracted back into the wall, revealing a dark void amid the tight snarl of water pipes. He dropped into the gap, using the gantry frame to re-orient himself.

Shifting from horizontal movement along the tops of the crawlways, the next leg of Fisher's infiltration required him to ascend a narrow concrete shaft that ran the full height of the office tower. Lined with bunches of pipes carrying water coolant to every floor, he had precious few hand-holds other than the odd support beam or protruding bolt.

He called on his core strength to make the climb, using the tri-goggles in low-light mode to find purchase in the dimness. His muscles pulled tight as he rose, and the shifts became more difficult, forcing him to jump over wide gaps. If he fell, he would be dashed against the concrete floor at the bottom of the shaft.

Fisher concentrated on what was directly in front of him, the next step, and the next, and the next. He didn't permit himself to dwell on what would happen if he missed a ledge.

Finally, a glow-in-the-dark number painted on the shaft wall told him he was in the right place. Moving from a vertical position to a horizontal one, Fisher made his way along the lines of the chill-to-the-touch pipes, to a narrow air vent overlooking a room filled with computer servers. He used the snake-camera once again to make sure it was unoccupied, then dropped in through the vent into a silent cat-fall.

Finding his way to the main server control unit, he crouched low and tapped his microphone. "All call-signs, Panther. Standing by at Waypoint Yankee."

Charlie took his hands off the keyboard and rubbed them together, before reaching up to press the radio pad behind his ear.

"OK, everyone. Uh, I mean, all call-signs?" He frowned.

Radio protocol wasn't his strong suit. "Merlin here. We have a complication. This system has been updated, the software isn't the version I was expecting… Things are going to be trickier than we thought."

"Define *trickier*," said Sarah, standing at his shoulder.

"It's not all bad news! I can still use this terminal to access the main server core where, uh, Panther is. Then we siphon off any data we want into his OPSAT's memory, as planned." His throat felt dry, and he swallowed hard. "But for that, I need root access, and with these updates in place I can only get it through a security protocol reset."

"So do that," Sarah told him.

"*He can,*" said Grim. "*But a reset only happens after the intruder alarm goes off.*"

"*Say again, Merlin,*" said Fisher, and Charlie could hear the scowl in his voice. "*You want me to deliberately trip an alert?*"

"That is affirmative," he nodded, despite the fact that Fisher couldn't see him. "And obviously, do not get caught. It needs to look like a system error."

"*Understood,*" said Fisher. "*Wait one.*"

Sarah leaned closer. "You sure about this?"

"No," he said truthfully. "To be honest, I'm kinda winging it."

Adapt and improvise.

Fisher frowned as he felt around the edges of the computer server. A panel covered the access port where he needed to plug in his OPSAT for the download, with a visible warning sensor that would log if it opened without authorization.

"Good enough," he said aloud, and flicked the panel down.

Immediately, an indicator on the server's screen began blinking red.

"*That's done it,*" said Charlie. "*Security alert has been tripped in the server core. Guards are on their way to your position, Panther.*"

"Understood."

"*Just don't punch anyone,*" offered Sarah. "*This has to stay quiet.*"

"Not my first rodeo, Lynx." Fisher looked around, judging the position and depth of the shadows in the room. He spotted a gloomy corner from where he would have a good view of the whole space and folded himself into it.

As he pressed his back to the wall, the door on the far side of the room slid open and two men entered. Both had stun batons held close in and at the ready, and they moved around with care, covering one another as they went. Fisher recognized the patterns; these men were using Vympel tactics, procedures created for the FSB's special operations unit. *Had Aslanov trained them?*

He filed that information away for later consideration and held his silence.

The guards found the problem in short order, and one of them growled into a hand-held radio as his colleague deactivated the alert.

"Nothing in here," said the taller of the two, as he holstered his baton. He spoke Muscovite Russian with a gruff accent. "False alarm. Go ahead and reset."

"They have us jumping at shadows," said the other man, with a shake of his head. "You know why?"

"Because the American is here," retorted the tall guard, putting away his radio. "He sees enemies everywhere."

The other guard shrugged, stepping back from the server stack. "Rich men are always looking for robbers. My mother used to say that."

"That's because there are more men who want to be rich than men that are." The tall guard glanced around the room, his gaze passing right over the deep shadows where Fisher silently waited. "Let's go."

He held his breath until he was alone again, then released a long, slow exhale. Your turn now, Charlie, he thought. Don't screw it up.

"Did it work?" Sarah watched the endless waterfall of data streaming down the screen in front of Charlie, but she couldn't make any sense of it.

"Perfectly." For his part, the hacker seemed to be operating on a different plane. His tone of voice had lowered, his body language relaxed. It was as if Charlie Cole had briefly forgotten that they were deep inside a threat zone, losing himself in the screen-glow of cyberspace. "Reset is cycling… Here it comes."

A panel popped up on the screen showing the words REINICIALIZAÇÃO EM ANDAMENTO and a fast-filling progress bar. Charlie's fingers clattered across the keyboard as he input new commands.

"Sixty seconds and we're golden," he said, out of the side of his mouth.

But the next voice belonged to a stranger. "Who are you two?"

Sarah turned to find a younger man standing at the alcove entrance, tanned and thin, with dark curly hair and a serious expression. He didn't have the thuggish quality she would have expected from a security guard, but his gaze was intense, and he didn't seem like the type to be easily distracted. *A technician,* she guessed, *a sharp one.*

"Hi." She flashed him a smile. "We're with Mr Teague's entourage. I'm Linda and this is Bob."

"Lynx, Merlin, do you have a problem?" Grim immediately picked up on the situation.

"We're fine," Sarah went on.

"No," said the man, assuming the reply was meant for him. "I don't know you, and this floor is off-limits to unauthorized people." He jabbed a finger at Charlie. "Tell him to stop what he is doing and show me some ID."

"It's all good," Sarah continued, taking a step closer. "Like I said, we're with Mr Teague. We're here to check on security while he's in the building."

"Brody," insisted the man, eyeing her suspiciously. "His name is Brody! He never lets anyone call him *Mr Teague.* He says titles foster outdated notions of hierarchy that get in the way of the true creative process. Haven't you even read his autobiography?"

"Waiting for the movie version," she offered.

"You don't work for T-Tec." The technician shook his head firmly. "I'm calling security!"

"Can't let you do that." Sarah spoke over him and swept forward before the man could react. She hooked his leg with her foot and knocked him off balance.

The technician stumbled and tried to throw a wild left hook at her, but she pivoted out of the way, and he hit nothing but air. Sarah fired a shotgun punch into the man's solar plexus and winded him, blasting the breath out of his lungs with a wheezing gasp.

Grabbing a fistful of his shirt, Sarah dragged the man into the workstation alcove, keeping him unsteady. "Stop it!" he cried out, belatedly realizing how much he had misread the situation. "Let go of me!"

"No." She slammed his face into the wall, leaving a smear of blood as his nose cracked wetly under the impact. As he recoiled, Sarah got her arm up around his throat and pulled him into a sleeper hold. Within seconds, the man went limp. Panting with exertion, she let him drop to the ground.

Charlie's eyes went wide. "I thought you said we weren't punching people."

"Shut up and do your thing," she retorted.

"Lynx, Paladin Actual. Advise status."

Sarah sighed. "I had to neutralize a civilian. I don't know how long we'll have until he's missed."

"Work fast," said Grim.

FOURTEEN

Montijo Air Force Base – Lisbon – Portugal

Grim glanced at the mission clock in the corner of the Paladin's SMI screen and chewed her lip. With every step of the operation, they were bleeding time, and it set her teeth on edge. She had each phase of the T-Tec intrusion planned out down the last detail, or so she thought. But like the old military adage said, *battle plans never survive first contact with the enemy.*

Bad enough that one or more of their high value targets were on site, at the same time she had two elements infiltrating an office building in the middle of a heavily populated city, but now they were rewriting the operational plan on the fly. With each unexpected change, the mission's chances of failure grew.

But we can't abort, she told herself. *Too many eyes on this. Too much at stake.*

People way above her were watching this operation, and any blunders would get their immediate attention, perhaps even threaten the future of Fourth Echelon. For now, she kept that fact to herself.

Grim had learned to accept her lot in life a long time ago. It was a core part of the job to keep secrets, not just from outsiders but from members of her own unit. She did it because that was what it took to make this organization work, but that didn't mean she liked it.

Lea Kade walked back into the command-and-control center, taking her station at one of the consoles. Grim gave her a questioning look, nodding in the direction of the holding cells at the back of the aircraft. "Did he give you any static?"

Kade shrugged. "Nothing I couldn't handle, ma'am. Kept telling me he was part of the team, and that I should let him out so he can help us."

"That's not happening any time soon," Grim replied. "I won't deny Kobin has his uses, but he's not to be trusted."

"Oh, I got that loud and clear," Kade noted. "I read his file. He changed his tune pretty quick when I told him that."

"Good. But don't underestimate him. He's smarter than he looks."

Kade nodded. "I'll keep that in mind."

"*Paladin Actual, this is Panther.*" Sam Fisher's curt whisper issued out of a hidden speaker. "*Green light at my end. Ready to connect OPSAT.*"

"Proceed, Panther." Grim gestured to Kade and Drew. The two mission technicians would be able to remotely monitor the progress of the data uptake to Fisher's OPSAT device, but the lack of bandwidth between the jet and the agent in the field meant that the data itself would have to be carried out of the T-Tec building by hand.

It frustrated her, but the sheer volume of information to be sifted through would have overloaded their covert network, and broadcasting encrypted communications using a more powerful signal would risk detection.

Like draining a lake through a straw, thought Grim. *We can only take a little at a time.*

"Good telemetry from Panther," reported Drew. "Data sweep is off and running, search parameters include Gordian Sword and other relevant keywords."

Grim nodded and went to the SMI table, pulling a digital panel to her across the haptic surface. The page showed a blur of filenames whipping past, as the OPSAT's seeker software raced through the contents of the T-Tec databank, trawling for the intelligence they needed.

"So… can we get out of here now?" Once more, Charlie Cole's radio protocol was non-existent, carrying on as if this were a casual phone conversation.

"Negative, Merlin," she reminded him. "We need you and Lynx to remain in place until search and recovery is complete, in case there are any complications."

"We have it covered," said Sarah.

"Uh, ma'am?" Kade raised a hand to attract Grim's attention. "I don't want to disagree, but…" She looked to Drew, and the other tech nodded his agreement. "We have an issue."

"Explain." Grim marched over to Kade's station, frowning at her screen.

"See here?" Kade indicated rising-falling waveform on the display, resembling a line of saw teeth or a range of narrow mountains. "That's the movement of communications traffic leaving the T-Tec building. Based on what we know, it should be around this level…" She indicated a midpoint. "But there's something else running in the background."

Grim saw what she was getting at. "This?" She pointed at a tall, narrow spike that towered above the other, much smaller peaks.

"They're running a very heavy transfer through there right now," Kade went on. "We're talking terabytes of uncompressed streaming video and audio."

"Now we know why Teague's here," noted Drew. The other tech was a former DoD intelligence analyst, and he didn't talk much, but Grim had learned to pay attention when he did. "The Lisbon office is the only T-Tec building in Europe with the right gear to communicate with their company micro-satellites in low orbit."

Grim turned that new conclusion over in her thoughts. A few months ago, Brody Teague's corporation had launched a series of communications satellites, known as a cluster, as part of a bid to gain a foothold in the telecom market. The possibility that those orbiting devices might have another, more clandestine function sent a chill up her spine.

She glanced at Kade. "Can we link into that traffic? Can we see what Teague is sending?"

"Possibly." Kade tapped her headset, looping her into the comms net. "Paladin Two, Merlin. Are you seeing this high-range data spike?"

"*Uh, yeah.*" Charlie replied. "*Looks like someone's binge-watching their favorite show in 4K hi-def,*" he went on, with a weak chuckle.

Grim ignored his attempt at levity and concentrated on the important question. "Merlin, can we intercept?"

Charlie snorted. "*With our current bandwidth? No way in hell. But I might be able to separate out a portion, maybe tap the audio element.*"

"Do it." Grim told him.

"*I'll need, uh, Panther to input some commands at the server. He can add some new temp protocols, split the feed… *"

"Panther, do you copy?"

"*I'm listening,*" said Fisher. "*Most of what you're talking about is outside my skillset.*"

"*Not a problem,*" said Charlie, his confidence rising a little. "*I'll walk you through it.*"

Grim folded her arms across her chest and fell silent as Charlie began to lead Fisher by the hand through the improvised hack. *More mission creep,* she thought, *another step past our operational parameters.*

If, as she suspected, this intrusion *was* being shadowed by the higher-ups at the NSA, how far would they let her go before they pulled her back? Unconsciously, her hand went to her throat.

Just how long a leash are we on?

T-Tec European Head Office – Lisbon – Portugal

"So, what's the count?" Teague stepped back into the middle of the spherical chamber and shook out his arms, watching his virtual avatar on the curved walls mirror the motion. "I want you to wow me."

Outside the perimeter of the chamber, Samir and the redhead assistant exchanged looks, while the Russian silently looked on. "The final uptake for the conference is eleven participants.

All entrance fee NFTs have been successfully transferred via blockchain to our TecCoin hubs." As Patel spoke, the curved, semi-continuous screen surrounding Teague sectioned itself into equal elements, each one displaying a test card pattern with the words PLEASE STAND BY rendered in multiple languages.

"Buy the ticket, take the ride," said Teague, bouncing on the balls of his feet. His buoyant mood rose with anticipation of what would come next. "We're gonna blow their minds!" He snapped his fingers. "Names, names, I want names."

The woman consulted her digital tablet. "Invites were accepted by WatchGate, and by representatives of the Phoenix Group and the Continuity JBA. From the Russian Federated States, we also have associate interests from Voron and the Raven's Rock organization. In addition, the October Resistance, Red Sun Brigade, White Masks, Kawakiri, and Islamic Vanguard have provided envoys."

Teague clapped his hands together and grinned. He couldn't have hoped for anything better. The list was a rogue's gallery of terrorists, criminals, and mercenaries from across the globe. It was a witch's brew of hate, avarice, and extremism that represented some of the worst impulses in society.

It was *exactly* what he wanted. A pack of hungry wolves, howling for the bloody meat he had to feed them.

"Wait, that's ten. You said *eleven* participants." Teague shot Patel a look.

"The last applicant paid an additional non-disclosure charge to mask their involvement from all other parties," said the other man.

"Huh." Teague knew what that meant. Only one group were that paranoid about their activities. "Megiddo want everyone to believe they're gone? Fair enough, we'll play along." Years earlier, the conspiratorial cadre of old money power-brokers had tried to strong-arm Teague into joining them, but he had refused. It amused him that the pack of aging, hidebound fools had to come to him in some desperate attempt to remain relevant. He went on. "What about those cartel guys from Bolivia? I liked their ink." Teague gestured at his face.

"I'm sorry, Brody," said the woman. "They declined to pay the application fee."

"Oh, well," he snapped, with a dismissive flick of the hand. "It's their loss." Teague adjusted his shirt and took a deep breath. "OK. Spin up the satellite link and count me down from ten to go live. I want no mistakes, people, you get me?" He glanced back at Patel. "No more alarms! You fixed that shit, right?"

"Of course, Brody," said the other man, his head bobbing in agreement. "A minor glitch."

Patel's understatement annoyed Teague. The earlier security alert from the server core had threatened to jeopardize everything, and now he made it sound trivial, as if someone had tripped over a wire.

"Nothing is minor!" Teague ground out the words. "Not tonight! I've put too much time and money and effort into this for some *glitch* to cause trouble."

"It was a false–" Teague's assistant started to speak, but he silenced her with a look.

"Send someone down there to check," he demanded.

"I already did," said Patel, with a sigh. "A couple of Stone's men." He nodded toward the Russian.

"So, make them double-check!" *Can't these idiots understand how important this is?* Teague scowled. It had been a source of constant frustration throughout his life to be surrounded by slow thinkers, but that was the burden of always being the smartest person in the room.

"I will handle it." The Russian walked away. "It is better I am not present for your demonstration," he added. "I have an unpleasant history with some of those you have invited."

"Whatever," said Teague to his back as he left. "Just be sure!"

The woman's tablet computer pinged, interrupting his rant before it could build a head of steam. "All participants are logged in," she reported, and gestured at the curved screens. "At your discretion, Brody."

He schooled his expression, shuttering away his annoyance and replacing it with the bright, eager smirk that was his trademark. Teague was about to address a group of hardened killers, fanatics, and mass murderers, but he did not fear any of them. When they saw what he had, they would beg him for his indulgence.

The curved screens lit up, each one filling with the form of a new avatar figure. The participants were seeing the same thing Teague did, but for each of them it was relayed through a set of virtual reality glasses. No matter where they were in the real world, the system brought them together in this shared, augmented reality space where they could converse in real time.

There was no way that any of these guarded, ruthless men and women would have agreed to meet Teague in the flesh, and even less of a chance of them coming together at once. *There would have been blood*, he reflected. Some of the invited groups were rivals, but part of the contract for the meeting had been a stipulation that all parties declare a truce for the duration.

"It's a good day for all of us," began Teague, smiling his winning smile. "Thank you for being here! Today's auction is a one-time opportunity for you, a select gathering of individuals representing groups operating outside the restrictions of certain legal frameworks. You're here because you know who I am and what I can do." He let that sink in. "Right now, you're connected to this virtual conference space by an untraceable signal, transmitted from a proprietary encrypted sat-comm rig built to T-Tec's exacting standards. Consider it my gift to you!" He chuckled. "Now, I know this is unusual, but I promise, it will be worth it. And to prove I'm serious, at the end of this conversation, I am going to return the fee you paid to enter this very exclusive club!"

Teague heard Patel give a sharp intake of breath; he had neglected to inform the other man of that detail.

"All I ask is a little of your time, and a willingness to listen. Because let me tell you, what I have to offer is access to a weapon of mass destruction, with a potential unlike any other."

Montijo Air Force Base – Lisbon – Portugal

"Did he say what I think he did?" Kade looked back at Grim, pressing fingers to her headset. "This Silicon Valley jerk is auctioning off a WMD?"

Grim disregarded the question. "Merlin, who is he talking to?"

"*Hard to get a read without more data,*" said Charlie, after a moment. "*But there are incoming signals buried in the feed. I can only get approximate locations… Russia, the Middle East, Europe, North America, South East Asia…*"

She thought about what Teague had said at the start. "Groups operating outside legal frameworks. Another way of saying criminals and terrorists."

"*He's hosting a video chat with the world's worst,*" offered Sarah.

Grim turned to Drew, covering her mike so her next words would not be transmitted to the agents in the field. "I need the Black Box on a direct line," she said, referring to the NSA headquarters in Maryland. "Then get the pilot to prep for emergency take-off, we may need to get out of here in a hurry."

"*Paladin Actual, Panther.*" Fisher's voice sounded in her ear, his tone terse and unforgiving. "*What have we walked into? Were you aware of this?*"

"All call-signs are to hold position and stay off comms," Grim replied, ignoring the obvious challenge in his manner. "Teague likes the sound of his own voice, so we are going to let him talk."

T-Tec European Head Office – Lisbon – Portugal

"I gotta admit, I had a whole video presentation made up for you folks."

Teague smiled around the words, turning in place to study the avatars circled around him. "Cool CGI and a narration by a movie-trailer guy with a deep, gravelly voice. The works. But then I thought, *what's the point?* You're not here for a dog and pony show, you don't want me giving you the slick performance shit. That's for my shareholders and the other low-IQs, am I right?"

He studied the digital avatars looking back at him, almost

but not quite anonymous, crafted to suggest certain faces without being accurate renditions of them.

It was a deliberate choice. The avatars could see each other in the virtual space, and he wanted the men and women behind them to know, or at least *suspect*, the identities of their fellow bidders. These people knew one another by their deeds and their bloody reputations, and that helped underline the seriousness of this little performance.

"I like ancient history," he told them. "I particularly like the story of Alexander the Great. He disrupted the old order, like me, like all of you. He did what he wanted, and along the way he made the world come to heel. I've been doing the same thing in the tech community for years now, but I have my sights set on bigger things." Teague made eye-contact with his audience. "And for that I need money and I need power."

The first part of that sentence was an outright lie. T-Tec's corporate holdings were massive and Brody himself was one of the richest men in the world. He needed more money like the Atlantic needed more water. But people like these didn't understand the abstracts that Teague was really attracted to. He had to put it in terms they would be comfortable with, and that was where the second part of the statement, the truthful part, came in.

Brody Teague wanted to reshape the world, and he needed *power* for that. But it was a rare bloom, one that only really flourished in conflict. So, if conflict equaled opportunity, and opportunity equaled power, the smart thing to do was to stimulate *chaos*.

He couldn't do it directly, of course. As the Russian had said, he had to keep his hands clean. Like most rich people with a dirty job in front of them, he planned to get someone else to do the messy work for him.

"Alexander and the Gordian Knot," he went on. "You know the tale? Who cares? The high points are what matter. The Gordians told Alexander no man on earth could untie their knot, so what did he do? He cut that shit *in half*. You gotta love the directness, right?" Teague gestured at the air. "We live in a world full of knots now. Access to everything is tied up with encryption that can't be broken by conventional means. Firewalls are dirt cheap and impossible to bypass! You need the best hackers in the world to bust into anywhere, and I hate to tell you, those top kick nerds have already sold out to the nation-state players."

He let them chew on that, then started in on the wind-up to his pitch. "But what if you didn't need them? Automated solutions are the future, my friends. We use drones and smart-bombs and self-driving vehicles. Why not a machine to hack other machines? A computer that cuts through any encryption like a blade through a knot! A Gordian Sword, if you will."

"*A clever name.*" Flattened by digital transmission, a voice with a hissing inflection broke the silence. "*But we've seen the promise of digital weapons before. A computer virus? That does not impress us.*"

Teague glanced in the direction of the avatar that spoke. It was the Red Sun Brigade envoy, the representative of the radical pro-communist, anti-establishment faction from Japan. "I get your caution. We've heard of Stuxnet, right? The malware program that screwed Iran's nuclear ambitions by messing with its enrichment laboratories. Then there's the Masse Kernels used in the thwarted cyberattacks on America and East Asia. Or my personal favorite, Petya, which pretty much forced Ukraine back into the Stone Age by killing their power stations, communications, and infrastructure. Imagine being able to do that at the push of a button. Not with a virus, not with malware that has to wait for some idiot to plug in a USB drive."

He grinned again, his eyes alight with the idea of it. "I'm talking about a lock-breaker that can eat through any firewall in existence, anywhere in the world, accessed by microwave transmission direct from low orbit. Something that can beat *any* encryption known to man. Imagine that! No digital system would be safe! You want to crash a stock exchange, wipe trillions off a currency value? *Done.*" Teague snapped his fingers. "You want to break into secret government files, erase every record they have on you? *Done.* Pull the plug on the power for a whole country? *Done.* It can be as small-scale as hacking a local ride-share app to track an assassination target, all the way up to causing a nuclear meltdown. The possibilities are as far-reaching and as fucked-up as your nasty imaginations want them to be!"

He took a breath. "*That* is what I'm offering. Think of it as your all-aspect, on-demand attack vector. Pick your target package, pay the fee, and watch it fall." Teague let his grin widen. "Oh, and in case you worry that someone else might have this? Don't. Aside from a few personnel vital to the running of the hardware, everyone involved in the creation of it has been eliminated. What I have is unique."

"*You promise much,*" said another voice, this time from the faceless avatar of the White Masks terror group. "*But how exactly does it work?*"

"So glad you asked," Teague replied, with a flourish. "Gordian Sword isn't just software. It's not just hardware. It's beyond both. I'm talking bleeding-edge tech that is two decades past any conventional systems currently in operation. It's called a *quantum computer*. You might have heard that name thrown around, right? The Chinese government and a certain internet tech giant claim they're a couple of years from a working prototype... but those guys are the Model T Fords in this game. *I've built a motherfucking dragster.*"

It was all he could do not to laugh out loud.

"Gordian Sword can out-think any software lock and penetrate any firewall in existence. You want cold, hard numbers? It's capable of processing over a hundred *trillion* times faster than a regular supercomputer. You do the math."

Sarah shook her head and glanced in Charlie's direction. "Tell me that's bullshit."

The hacker looked back at her, his face pale in the glow of the screen. "Not so much. Quantum computing is exactly what Teague says, a massive leap forward in processing power. Like, a password that would take a normal computer a thousand years to go through every possible combination could be cracked by a quantum machine in hours." He paused, and in the brief silence the only sound came from the humming machines in the other alcoves. "Quantum is the holy grail of next-gen tech. Everyone is trying to build it, but so far nobody has been successful. It's too delicate, too sensitive for prime time."

"So, Teague is lying about Gordian Sword?"

"I never said that." Charlie shook his head. "Don't get me wrong, the guy is a massive tool, but he's also a next-level genius. If he says he cracked it, I believe him." Charlie blinked as another thought occurred. "Those dark money transfers we stumbled over at GreenSea… That has to be where the funding came from."

"Then there's the killings," added Sarah. "The murdered computer experts the CIA were tracking. I guess now we know the reason for their deaths. They built this thing for Teague, and he's protecting his investment."

As if mentioning his name summoned him, Teague's voice returned over the audio ripped from the communication stream. "*I don't want to bore you with a lot of jargon,*" he said. Sarah could hear the shit-eating grin in the man's voice, and it made her fists tighten. "*But here's the science bit: quantum computers use the exploitation of the collective properties of quantum states, like super-positioning and entanglement, to perform calculations. Seriously, that's pretty much what it says on Wikipedia, look it up.*" She heard him blow out a breath. "*No one here gives a damn about that lab coat crap, am I right? No, you people are results oriented. So, I'm going to give you a live demonstration.*"

"Oh, man," said Charlie. "I do not like the sound of that."

FIFTEEN

T-Tec European Head Office – Lisbon – Portugal

Fisher leaned forward over the server console, his expression stony. Most of what was being talked about over the comm channel went over his head, but he knew enough to understand the reality of the danger.

A technology that could break through any digital firewall in existence was just as lethal in the wrong hands as a rogue biological weapon or a nuclear device – and worse, if Teague's promises were true, it could be deployed from anywhere in the world with the click of a mouse. It wasn't the first time Fisher had faced a threat like this – *a ghost in the net* – and he knew full well what chaos could come in its wake.

For a moment, Fisher put aside his own feelings and tried to place himself in Brody Teague's expensive, handmade shoes. He'd overheard what Charlie told Sarah about the quantum computer tech being fragile, so that meant it wasn't something that could be deployed out of a backpack or carted around on a truck. It probably wouldn't be mobile. It would have to be kept in a protected location, hidden from the world at large.

Is it here? He looked at the building around him, then shook his head, dismissing the idea. *Teague's not stupid. He's too paranoid to hide his prized technology in plain sight.*

Fisher had always thought that most billionaires were one volcano lair away from being a Bond movie villain, and he suspected that the founder of T-Tec was a lot further down that path than most people realized. With this quantum computer in his hands, Teague would have the monopoly on cyber-threats.

"*Panther, confirm OPSAT scan status.*" Grim's voice sought his attention.

"Sixty percent complete," he reported, glancing at the device's screen. "There's a lot of ground to cover."

"*We need data on probable locations for Gordian Sword,*" she said. Grim was clearly following the same train of thought as Fisher.

He nodded. That was the smart play, find the thing and then call in an airstrike. Problem solved. That would leave Teague at the mercy of those terrorists whose time he had wasted, and they weren't the forgiving types. But experience told Fisher this wasn't going be that clear-cut.

"*Heads up,*" said Charlie, his anxious voice rising. "*Something's happening.*"

Without warning, every indicator on the server stacks in the room went bright green, and suddenly Fisher was surrounded by hundreds of flashing firefly lights, blinking wildly.

•••

Teague knew he had them.

He had stood in front of enough crowds and dragged money out of enough marks to recognize the point of tip-over. His audience might have been made up of killers, but they were still human, and still susceptible to a little razzle-dazzle, a little theater.

For the demonstration, he selected two of the participants, the representatives of the Islamic Vanguard and the Kawakiri groups. "I'd like you both to look up the passenger planes currently in transit through Portuguese airspace. Then pick one."

"*Why?*" said the Kawakiri envoy.

"Because a terrorist attack has to be *terrible.*" Teague eyed the envoy's avatar image. "And that's what I'm going to give you. I mean, one jet lost at sea, most people will skate past that on the news. But two? At the same time? That'll get the world's attention." He shrugged. "Oh, and feel free to claim responsibility after the fact."

The Vanguard's representative showed no such hesitation, and she offered up an aircraft identifier. "*Atlantic International, flight zero-zero-five-seven to Los Angeles.*"

There was a nod from the Kawakiri envoy. "*We designate Yamato Airlines eight-eight to Hong Kong.*"

Satisfied, Teague turned away, toward his assistant. "Time to code in," he told her, and held out his hand.

The redheaded woman hesitated, holding her tablet computer firmly, her knuckles whitening around it. Teague scowled when she didn't immediately obey him. She lacked spine when it came to making hard choices, he had noted.

"I've got it." Patel stepped forward and wrenched the device out of the woman's grip, before handing it to Teague. "Here you go, Brody."

"Thanks, pal." Teague activated the palm-print scanner built into the digital pad and placed his hand on it. "Bio-lock," he said to the representative's avatars, by way of explanation. "Gordian Sword's key operations are linked to my biometrics, in case any of you were toying with the idea of murdering me and taking it." He smiled as he tapped in the relevant data with his index finger. "Here we go."

Patel consulted another monitor screen, and gave a nod. "Confirming, target infiltration packages are outbound."

"Get lost," Teague told his assistant without a glance, in a brisk, spiteful voice. "I'm sick of looking at you."

The woman kept her composure, but she almost fled to the door to leave. He watched her go, then shot Patel a look. "We got a clock on this?"

"Gordian Sword has the target data. Intrusion vectors are being calculated." Patel nodded to himself. "We'll have full autopilot override on both aircraft in less than five minutes."

"Or your money back," said Teague, with a snort of amusement. "Let's start the bidding, shall we?"

Montijo Air Force Base – Lisbon – Portugal

"Can he actually do that?" Drew stared at his operations screen, his face turning pale as the reality of the situation began to sink in.

On the main display of the strategic mission interface, a portion of the panel had become a map of the area over the Bay of Biscay, crisscrossed with the flightpaths of dozens of civilian airliners. Highlighted in brilliant crimson, the lines for the Atlantic International and Yamato Airlines flights were clearly visible. The Japanese Airbus was flying south, while the American Boeing 777 was on a westerly course, heading toward open sea.

Kade looked at Drew, whose expression was rigid with shock. "I think we're about to find out," said the other technician.

"Yes sir. That's correct, sir." Close by, Grim talked into an encrypted handset, speaking directly to the director of National Security Agency operations. "We're monitoring the situation as we speak. Yes sir, I do believe the threat is credible."

Kade caught her eye, but the other woman looked away. She turned back to the SMI display and the technician's skin prickled with a sudden chill. The two red trails indicating the airliners showed sharp turns taking them off their assigned paths. The American flight descended quickly, dropping out of its transatlantic flight corridor, while the jet bound for Hong Kong entered a steep climb.

Grim held the handset away from her face. "Give me a projection based on those paths," she demanded.

Drew had already anticipated her requirement, and with a few keystrokes from his panel, a bright yellow line sketched itself in over the display. Kade watched the new line connect the two flightpaths and terminate in a jagged marker some eighteen thousand feet over the ocean.

"How long until the merge?" said Grim. She couldn't bring herself to use the word "*collision*". If the two jets met in midair, hundreds of people would be killed instantly.

The question jolted Kade into action and she checked

her screen. "If both aircraft maintain their current speeds… approximately twelve minutes and thirty-one seconds." She blinked. "How do we stop it?"

Grim held up a hand as she resumed her conversation with the Black Box. Kade knew that the higher-ups back in Maryland were seeing the same data they were. She felt sick inside. *We can't stand by and do nothing!*

"I concur," Grim told the voice on the other end of the line. "We have assets in play. I'm confident we can intervene with a high order of success. Do I have your permission to proceed, sir?" Off the reply to that question, the other woman nodded and folded the sat-phone closed.

"Orders?" said Drew.

Grim didn't answer him. Instead, she picked up her headset from where it lay on the SMI and looped back into the active comms net. "All call-signs, Paladin Actual. As of now, your previous mission directives are scrubbed. Utilize all means at your disposal to interdict and shut down the remote operation of Gordian Sword from that building."

Sam Fisher's reply was immediate. "*Give me a target.*"

Kade looked up. "Can we get to Teague?"

"He'll be heavily protected," said Grim. "It's a bad option."

"*The roof!*" Charlie cried out. "*The satellite antenna up there! It's gotta be how Teague's directing the hack. Wherever Gordian Sword is, he's controlling it in real time through T-Tec's micro-satellite cluster, using them to beam the intrusion signal down to the planes! It's the only thing that makes sense!*"

Grim's eyes narrowed. "Merlin, if you're mistaken, we won't have time to deploy another alternative. Are you certain?"

"*No.*" Kade heard the doubt in Charlie's voice. "*I mean…*

even if we cut the signal, there's no guarantee that the hack will be cut off too. If it's self-executing…"

Sarah spoke up. *"Brody Teague strikes me as the type who likes the power of life and death in his hands. He's not gonna delegate that to some button-pusher… No offense."*

"Hey, none taken," muttered Charlie.

"There's another thing to consider," said Kade. "Panther's OPSAT. He leaves, he'll have to disengage it from the servers. The sweep won't be complete. We won't get the data."

"Then we'll have to work with what we have." Grim nodded to herself, and continued, "Panther, Paladin Actual. Abandon your current objective, find that antenna and destroy it." She paused, waiting for Fisher to respond. "Panther, Paladin Actual, do you copy?"

"Panther, please respond!" Sarah called out to her father.

Something crackled over the communications net, and then Kade heard a grunt of pain and the crash of shattering plastic.

T-Tec European Head Office – Lisbon – Portugal

The server room door opened as Grim gave Fisher's call-sign, and then the rest of what she said was lost to him as the two guards rushed in.

It was the same pair from earlier, the Russians with the Vympel training and the Moscow accents; one tall with a flat-top haircut, the other broad-shouldered and rat-faced. They pulled their stun batons as they came at Fisher, each half-meter rod ending in a pair of metal tines that sparked with electricity.

If he'd had the benefit of a little more thinking time,

Fisher would have drawn his pistol and put them down with snapshots, but he reacted with fluid motion instead, jerking back from the active server console, increasing the distance.

As he pulled away from the computer, the data cable connecting his wrist-mounted OPSAT to the machine disconnected and automatically reeled itself back with a buzzing click. He didn't pause to see how far along the scan had progressed. It wouldn't matter, if the two Vympel goons beat the hell out of him.

The guy with the broad profile had been first through the door and he closed the distance, swinging his baton down and to the right. Fisher took advantage of the sloppy, reactive opening, rushing into the attack. With one open palm, he deflected the weapon away, and with the other hand he struck at the man's neck with a fang choke, grinding his thumb into the soft tissues of the guard's throat and applying crippling compression to his collarbone.

The guard grunted in pain and tried to jab him with the flailing baton, but missed, instead stabbing it through the protective panel over another of the servers. Increasing the pressure, Fisher felt bone break in his iron grip, and he hooked the broad-shouldered man's ankle, pulling a foot out from under him. The guard crashed backwards, stumbling over an office chair on castors, and went down.

His taller comrade danced back out of Fisher's range and reached up to tap the radio mike clipped to his jacket, intent on calling in a warning. Fisher reacted, kicking another chair, sending it spinning across the room and into the other man.

Knocked off-kilter, the guard let go of the radio to steady himself, and in those split seconds, Fisher crossed the distance between them and executed a flawless Krav Maga hook punch. The blow landed, but the guard chewed down the pain and stood his ground. The glowing tines of the stun baton came up at Fisher's chest in a stabbing motion.

He blocked with his forearm and felt a tingle as the aura of the electric charge raced over his tactical suit's protective outer sheath. The baton strike failed to connect, the sharp tines skidding off his arm. Fisher reversed the move, grabbing his opponent's wrist and breaking it. The taller guard howled and lost his grip on the prod, the weapon falling to dangle from its lanyard.

Fisher used an elbow strike to knock the man into a server stack, and he kept up the momentum, hitting him again and again until the guard's eyes rolled back, and he slumped forward.

Movement flickered at the corner of Fisher's vision, and he grabbed his semi-conscious opponent, swinging him into the path of whatever was coming. The other guard, one arm hanging limply where his right collarbone had been broken, reacted too slowly to stop himself from jabbing his baton into his comrade's belly. Blue sparks crackled and Fisher smelled burnt cotton as he slammed the second guard into the first.

"*Bastard.*" The guard with the cracked bone spat the epithet in gutter Russian, and he went at Fisher again, using the baton like a short sword.

Fisher let the man come in close. Ducking a wild swing, he planted a hard blow from his palm heel right into the broken collarbone.

This time the guard screamed as the jagged edges of the split bone ground against one another, but not for long. Fisher sent another hit into the man's throat and this time he went down and did not rise again.

Fisher knelt next to the unconscious guard and pulled the radio loop from his ear, holding it up to listen.

"*Team Two, this is One, do you read?*" The voice speaking Russian over the open channel seemed familiar, and it triggered a sense-memory. For a moment Fisher was in another time and place, decades ago, on a terrace on a rainy night in Tbilisi. "*Two, answer me.*"

Fisher grabbed the mike clipped to the guard's collar and muffled his reply with his hand. "We are down," he replied, hoping his accent would be convincing. He faked a strangled cough to cover himself. "Intruder... heading to ground level ..."

If he was lucky, it might be enough misdirection to gain him an advantage, but there was no guarantee. And if that voice on the other end of the radio was who Fisher thought it was, the odds of getting out of this alive were narrowing. He tossed the radio aside and rose.

Fisher scrambled back up into the maintenance shaft he had used to enter the server room. He started to climb, as fast as he could.

Teague held the tablet computer out in front of him and used his index finger to manipulate the directions and headings of the two airliners. Their controls were reduced to a simple D-pad layout like something from a video game, and he grinned as he pushed the jets through steep turns well outside their normal operating range.

He wondered what was going on in the passenger cabins at that moment. He pictured panicking tourists strapped into their seats, screaming and wailing; terrified flight attendants desperately trying to hold back the tide of fear; and the crews on the flight deck, ashen-faced as they realized they no longer had any influence over their aircraft.

A scrolling text bar flashed up new updates, showing him each attempt the pilots made to reset their auto-flight systems, and the immediate counter generated by the Gordian Sword mainframe. Every life up there was his to control, and Teague liked how that felt. He watched the distance between the jets shrink. Both crews would have seen the other plane on their radar by now, and they would have some inkling of what was coming.

He looked up, catching sight of the screen where the bids were displayed. The number rose steadily as the men and women behind the virtual avatars put their money on the line, angling to be the first to take advantage of his technology. Even the ones who had voiced their doubts were opening their wallets.

"Bidding closes at the point of impact," he said, smiling around the words like a salesman on an infomercial. "Don't wait too long to put in your offer!"

Behind him, outside the projection sphere, Patel cleared his throat, loudly and deliberately.

Teague looked his way, his smile dropping. "What?"

"Radio traffic from both aircraft is increasing," said the other man, glancing at his own screen. "Should we take their communications offline?"

"No," snorted Teague, irritated at the question. "We *want* people to be calling for help! There's no point doing this if nobody knows about it."

Patel didn't respond, his attention drawn by the buzz of a cellphone in his jacket. He cupped the handset to his ear, and his face fell as whatever he heard registered with him.

Teague's annoyance grew as the other man urgently offered up the phone for him to take. "I'm right in the middle of something, Samir." He gestured at his audience.

"You need to hear this," insisted Patel.

"Fine." He turned his smile back on and bowed slightly to the line of bidders. "My apologies, ladies and gentlemen, this'll just take a second." Teague muted the audio pickup inside the virtual space and then snatched the phone from Patel's hand. "You're making me look unprofessional in front of these people," he snarled, his back to the VR camera. Teague raised the phone and spoke into it. "This better be important."

"*It is.*" Aslanov's reply was ice-cold, enough to draw the ire out of Teague in one go. "*We have a penetration. My men reported an intruder inside the building, and one of your technicians appears to be missing.*"

Teague's mind raced. "That alarm before…"

"*Your instincts were correct. It was not false. There is more. I discovered an anomaly in the entry logs. Two passes dated less than half an hour ago, neither of which match. Look at the footage I have sent you.*"

"Damn it!" Teague stabbed angrily at his tablet screen, flicking away from the hacked flight controls to another panel that brought up a video playback. His eyes narrowed as he watched the feed from a security camera in the lobby, tracking a man and a woman as they entered the building. The woman was a stranger, but he knew the slight, curly-haired man. He'd ordered his assassination that night in London.

"What the fuck is Cole doing here?" Teague spat out the question, his color rising, but before Aslanov could answer, he carried on. "No. Not important. He can tell me himself! Do your job! Lock down the tower, find that little shit and his girlfriend, bring them to me alive!"

Without waiting to hear the Russian's reply, Teague angrily threw Patel's phone back at him, and then resumed his role as salesman, unmuting the virtual scanner.

"Sorry, sorry," he said, smirking as he glanced at the rising bids. "We're dealing with some staffing issues."

SIXTEEN

T-Tec European Head Office – Lisbon – Portugal

Emerging in the tower's elevator core, Fisher found himself on a ledge jutting out above a dark, yawning abyss that went all the way down to the building's sub-levels. He flicked his tri-goggles down over his eyes and switched them to low-light mode, revealing the flat, featureless concrete walls and the complex cable mechanisms controlling the lift cars.

There was a safety ladder bolted into an alcove on the near side of the open shaft, but it would be a long, slow climb to the roof level and the satellite antenna, and he had no time to waste. With each passing second, the two hijacked jet aircraft under Teague's control were moving closer to a fatal collision.

Ignoring the terminal fall in front of him, Fisher edged along the narrow sill, squeezing through a gap between two service gantries to reach the opposite end of the shaft, where the express elevators raced up and down.

A rush of stale, grease-scented air pressed down on him, and he ducked back as one of the high-speed lift cars dropped out of the gloom, speeding toward the ground floor level. As it fell, a second express elevator rose quickly on the next gantry over; Fisher saw it coming, a flash of motion blurring as it approached.

The tri-goggles made it hard to gauge distance, so he flipped them up and went on instinct. Another wave of warm air buffeted him, and he rocked on the balls of his feet. Mistiming the leap would send him bouncing off the side of the elevator and tumbling to his death.

Fisher counted down and jumped, arms wide, hands out. His gloves slapped the rising elevator and he hung on, landing with his face pressed to a vent in the top of the car. Luck was on his side – the elevator was empty – and he scrambled up to crouch by the whirring cable rig.

Re-activating the tri-goggles, he watched the top of the shaft come racing down at him. For a moment, Fisher feared the elevator would crush him into the blank concrete panel, but at the last second the empty car slowed to a smooth halt. Through the vent, he saw a couple of technicians step aboard, talking in rapid-fire Portuguese.

But before he could listen in on their conversation, an alarm echoed through the building and a synthetic voice issued out of the elevator's public address system.

"Alerta de segurança. Todos os funcionários, por favor, relatam aos seus supervisores de departamento imediatamente."

Something about a security alert, he translated mentally, *all staff need to report in.* That could only mean that a lockdown had begun.

The elevator jolted, and with a lurching motion it began its descent to the lower floors. Fisher grabbed at a service catwalk as the elevator dropped, and then used the momentum to swing himself up and to safety. Moving on his belly in the crawlspace, he worked his way to a maintenance hatch and gave it an experimental push.

Locked. And with the last of his acidic binary compound used up, Fisher's options were limited. He peeked through the gap between the hatch and its frame, looking out on to the building's roof. The tower's topmost level gently sloped away into the wave-like structure of its design, and he caught sight of the red anti-collision lights blinking around the antenna.

The crimson glow illuminated figures in black jackets, each clutching the compact, angular shape of a silenced Heckler & Koch MP7 sub-machine gun.

Fisher drew his own weapon, changing position to point the SC-IS pistol's muzzle at the lock. He no longer had the luxury of a stealthy approach.

The shot cracked the mechanism, and Fisher shouldered the hatch open, coming out of nowhere to pivot toward the closest of the gunmen. The guard saw the movement and was bringing up his MP7 when Fisher's next two squeezes of the trigger put 5.7mm rounds through his throat.

The guard's hand twitched as he perished, and a burst of fire chattered from his weapon as he crumpled to the roof, the shots sparking harmlessly off a line of ventilation ducts.

As Fisher rolled from the hatch and out of sight, he heard two voices shouting. *Three of them up here, then*. He mentally recalculated his tactics as the remaining guards snapped on the tactical lights beneath the muzzles of their SMGs, sweeping the beams back and forth.

He weighed the SC-IS in his hand. The magazine was still three-quarters full, which gave him some options, and the gun's integral sound/flash suppressor would hide his firing position.

Fisher moved right and popped up over a waist-high air-processor unit, firing a shot into a metal panel near to the spindly gantry of the antenna. The bullet ricocheted off with a flash of sparks, drawing the attention of the closest guard. Fisher saw the tactical-light beam veer away, and as soon as it was pointing in the wrong direction, he sent three more bullets into the spot where the guard was standing. He heard a pain-filled cry and the second man fell.

The last guard fired a burst in Fisher's direction, meant to drive him out of cover. He scrambled around the edge of the air-processor and sprinted toward the antenna. There was no time to engage in an extended gunfight up here. He had to finish this quickly.

Fisher threw himself over a duct and landed hard, scant meters away from the third gunman. Both men squeezed their triggers simultaneously, but Fisher let himself drop out of the line of fire, as a spurt of cordite flame licked the air.

He hit his mark in the belly, and the guard toppled like a felled tree, disappearing out of sight.

"All call-signs, Panther," he said, panting hard. "At the target. How long do I have?"

"*Less than four minutes,*" said Grim. "*Hurry it up.*"

"Copy." Fisher unzipped a pouch on his rig and removed two breaching charges, compact tubes containing C-4 plastic explosive and a wireless detonator. Gearing up back on the Paladin, Fisher had considered leaving the charges behind on this operation. Now he was thankful that he had brought a little extra overkill.

Acting quickly, he surveyed the antenna and picked out the weak points on the supports, where the charges would do the most damage.

"Stand by," he said, "and get ready to go loud."

Aslanov booted open the security alcove's door and saw a man sprawled on the floor, with the dark-haired woman from the security video standing over him. Cole, the elusive hacker from London, sat at a workstation, his eyes wide with fright.

The woman reacted, looking back at Aslanov and his men with a guileless expression. "Thank god you're here, this guy collapsed–"

He didn't allow her to finish. Her tone and her manner didn't match with the way she moved toward him, stepping close, her hands coming up, telegraphing that she was going to try to disarm him.

Aslanov hit her across the cheek with the butt of his pistol, hard enough to send her reeling into the wall.

"Oh, shit!" The hacker jumped out of his seat, shocked into motion by the savage attack. With nowhere to go, he fell back against the far wall of the cramped workspace.

"Mr Cole," Aslanov said coolly. "Hello again. What possessed you to come here tonight? You have made a catastrophic mistake."

"Y-yeah," stuttered the younger man. "Been suh-saying that all along…" He crouched and helped the woman to her feet. "There was no need for you to do that," he added, showing a spark of defiance.

The dark-haired woman had a hand pressed to the new cut on her face, fingers reddening with oozing blood. Her eyes were full of fury.

"Who is this?" Aslanov cocked his head. Something about her seemed faintly familiar, but he couldn't place it. "NSA? CIA? What has this man told you?"

"Who am I?" The woman's lip curled, and too late Aslanov realized her next words were not meant for him. "I'm the one who brought the thunder."

"Panther, do it now!"

Fisher heard Grim's call and double-tapped the trigger pad on his OPSAT. "Fire in the hole!"

The breaching charges detonated together in a quick ripple of noise, and the supporting spars holding up the antenna came apart in twists of broken metal. The spindly mast lurched under its own weight, then teetered backwards across the office tower's canted roof.

Fisher dropped behind a machine unit as the thing came down and broke apart, the anti-collision lights along its length going dark. Thick cables tore free from their mountings and whip-cracked through the air, arcing over his head. The antenna broke its back across the roof, shredded wiring spitting blue sparks, pieces of it tumbling over the edge and down to the street below.

He could hear fire alarms sounding as he rose to his feet. "Paladin, how copy?" Fisher pressed the mike tab at his throat. "Antenna's down. Did we make it?"

"Stand by, Panther," said Grim. *"We'll know in a few seconds."*

Merge Point – Bay of Biscay – Altitude 18,000 Feet

The flight crews aboard Atlantic International zero-zero-five-seven and Yamato Airlines eight-eight were all experienced aviators, each of their senior pilots having dealt with in-flight emergencies during their careers.

But nothing had prepared them for the danger they faced tonight. Desperation gripped both crews as they realized their aircraft were under outside control. Any attempt to deactivate the autopilots aboard the Airbus and the Boeing Triple-Seven failed. Each time the system was disengaged, it retook control a second later, forcing them back into the terminal path leading both aircraft toward a fatal impact.

Aboard the American airliner, a frantic attempt was under way to physically disconnect the entire autopilot module by removing the unit from the console before it was too late – but as the seconds ticked away, the mess of complex wiring made the attempt impossible. Aboard the Japanese aircraft, the crew saw the crimson fuselage of the other jet as it dove toward them, their Airbus rising inexorably into a collision.

Then, without warning, as quickly as it had begun, the malignant override was severed, and the flight crews regained control.

Acting on instinct, the Yamato pilot slammed the Airbus's side-stick controls full forward, and the jet's nose dipped sharply. In the cockpit of the Atlantic International aircraft, the pilot acted a heartbeat slower, putting his weight into wrenching the flight yoke into a hard turn.

The Airbus crossed beneath the Triple-Seven, the tip of its tail fin making contact with the underside of the other jet. Metal shredded and the top quarter of the Yamato airliner's tail tore away; the damage was serious, but flight eight-eight was still airworthy. Trailing debris and shuddering though a turbulent descent, it would still be able to make an emergency landing.

The Atlantic International jet was not so fortunate. Like a knife slicing through the belly of a fish, the Airbus's tail tore open a wound across the centerline of the Boeing, severing hydraulic cables and feed lines. In less than a second, volatile jet fuel combusted, wrapping the fuselage in a halo of fire.

Tumbling out of control, flight zero-zero-five-seven plummeted toward the ocean, coming apart as it fell. Those among the passengers and crew who did not immediately perish were conscious of their fates until the jet finally struck the waves.

T-Tec European Head Office – Lisbon – Portugal

"Paladin, respond." The delay was only moments, but it felt like an eternity.

Grim spoke again, her tone bled of all emotion. "*Tracking one target aircraft now, veering off. The other... we lost the other one.*"

"Damn it!" Fisher snarled out the words. A white-hot surge of anger welled up in him, but he held it in, keeping it back to direct toward his enemies. He sucked in a breath and forced himself to concentrate on the mission. "Status on Lynx and Merlin?" He'd been too busy staying alive to follow all that was going on over the comms net, but now he had the sense that something was wrong.

"*Lynx, Merlin, do you copy?*" Grim's voice became urgent.

When nothing came back but dead air, Fisher's misgivings were confirmed. He strode to the edge of the roof. "What's their location?"

"*Six levels down from your current position,*" said Grim. "*Security floor. Panther, they may have been compromised.*"

Fisher shut away his doubts, overriding the dread that rose

when he thought of his daughter's life in danger. He pulled a bunched rappelling line from a pack on his belt and secured one end around the antenna's broken base. Clipping on his descender, Fisher jumped up to the roof's raised edge and looked down. He had a hundred meters of line, and it might not have been enough to reach ground level, but that wasn't his immediate priority.

Sarah is, he told himself, stepping out into the open air.

The long echo of the explosion resonated down through the frame of the office block, causing the lights to flicker and the floor beneath Aslanov's feet to tremble.

"Where did that come from?" He demanded an answer, but no one had one. One of his men marched Cole and the American woman out into the corridor, while another remained in the alcove, attempting to revive the unconscious security technician. His new prisoners remained silent.

He stalked toward the woman, turning his pistol in his hand, making it clear he intended to strike her again with it. "How many more of you are there?"

"Dozens," she said thickly, around her swollen cheek. "We brought a marching band." There was a defiance in her eyes that warned of steel beneath, and Aslanov decided to keep the gun on her, just in case.

"Sir!" One of the guards pointed toward the far end of the corridor, which ended in a floor-to-ceiling window. Pieces of metal and cable tumbled past on their way down to the ground. "Something on the roof?"

Even as the Russian assimilated that new detail, his radio earpiece buzzed annoyingly. Grimacing, he reached up to activate it, knowing exactly what voice he was going to hear. "Speak," he said.

"*What the fuck is happening to my building?*" Teague shouted the question, then charged on without waiting for a response. "*We've just lost communications with the satellite cluster, do you know what that means? No Gordian Sword, no VR link, no tele-conference! Who did this to me?*"

"I have Cole and the woman in custody," he explained.

Teague didn't hear him. "*Do you realize how this makes me look? Those terrorist assholes are laughing at me right now!*"

Aslanov said nothing, letting him rant. But this was the reaction he would have expected from the petulant billionaire. Teague's first and only metric was the same for everything in his life. *Does this inconvenience or benefit me?* The arrogant genius had no interest in anything else.

"*I have to find a way to unfuck this situation and save some face,*" he went on. "*You make sure those two go nowhere!*" Teague disconnected.

"Sir…" The guard grabbed Aslanov's shoulder, and he reacted irritably, shaking off the hand.

He turned to see the other man pointing back at the window. A shadow hung out there, framed by the lights of Lisbon's skyline. Black-clad, with a face of three alien eyes that glowed emerald.

"Get down!" Aslanov shouted the order, but the words were lost in the crash of shattering glass.

Fisher kicked away, and at the farthest point of his swing on the line, he unloaded three shots into the window, turning it into a fractured spider-web.

He curled into a ball as he punched through the glass, slapping at the quick-release on his descender to disconnect him. In a torrent of fragments, Fisher hit the carpeted floor shoulder first and rolled into cover behind a desk. Without pause, he grabbed two grenades from a loop on his tactical suit and tossed them underarm, pulling the pins as he went. The first was an SC-82 flashbang, the second a smoke canister, and they bounced out into the middle of the corridor, going off with a resounding report and a blinding burst of light.

Fisher was closer than he would have liked to the detonation, and the flashbang's discharge made his ears ring. Executing a tactical reload on the go, he vaulted out of cover and moved up, keeping his pistol close in as he pushed into the thickening cloud of gray haze.

"Lynx! Merlin!" he shouted, sweeping the corridor for any sign of Sarah or Charlie.

A figure stumbled awkwardly out of the smoke, and Fisher saw the pistol in their hand. The guard tried to shake off the effect of the flashbang, his eyes blurry and trickles of blood oozing out from his burst eardrums – but he saw Fisher, saw the threat he represented.

Fisher reacted first, firing twice, hitting center mass at close range, and the guard fell on to him. He staggered back as a second figure appeared in the wake of the first, this one carrying the same H&K MP7 the men on the roof had used. Using the wounded guard as a shield, Fisher pivoted and fired downward, planting shots in the second gunman's legs. He screamed and toppled before he could get off a shot.

"Dad!" In the heat of the moment, protocol was forgotten as Sarah came rushing toward him, pushing Charlie ahead of her.

"Get out of here," he snapped, shoving the hacker in the direction of the shattered window. "Go, go!"

A jagged burst of fire flared in the midst of the haze and Fisher flattened himself against a wall as pistol shots droned past him. He had the impression of a man, a shape of shadows and fluid motion, as a third shooter ducked into one of the workstation alcoves. He returned fire, keenly aware that his moment of shock and awe was fading by the second. Fisher backed up the way he had come, his pistol at the ready, waiting for a target.

As he reached the window, Sarah was already tying on to the rope still dangling outside. He saw the ashen, worried look on Charlie's face and slapped him on the shoulder before advancing back into the fray. "Good to see you," he told him. "Just do what Sarah says, you'll be OK."

With a hiss, the security floor's sprinkler system belatedly surged into action, dousing the corridor in a sudden deluge and damping down the smoke. The man in cover used the distraction to bolt out and into view, firing as he went. Fisher dodged away. He caught a glimpse of a wolfish face lined by hard-won experience, and a gaze that had no pity in it.

Aslanov.

It could not have been anyone else. The man Fisher had thought buried under tons of rubble, the first enemy who had reached into his life and put a blade to the throat of someone he loved.

There was a part of Sam Fisher that hadn't really believed Dima Aslanov was still alive. A part of him that wanted it to be a mistake, a falsehood, some imposter mimicking the Russian assassin's reputation for their own gain. That hope crumbled as he met the other man's gaze, and recognition flashed between them.

Then Aslanov did something unexpected. He *smiled*, as if he had just seen an old friend for the first time in years.

"Panther, we gotta go!" Holding Charlie close to her, Sarah kicked out and dropped through the shattered window, the nylon rope fizzing as she rappelled downward toward safety.

Her father didn't hear her. Time had frozen for him, he and Aslanov aiming at each other through the downpour. The Russian's smile faded, and he pulled the trigger.

Fisher did the same, pacing shots across the corridor as he moved back toward the window. He had no cover, and nowhere to go but out. Twisting into open air, he leapt the narrow gap between the ledge and the shifting rope, snatching it with his off-hand.

Gravity took hold of Fisher and he dropped, friction burning hot through his gloves as the rope shrieked through his grip.

SEVENTEEN
Corinthia Hotel – Lisbon – Portugal

Samir Patel walked swiftly down the corridor leading to the presidential suite, weaving between the guards posted at the entrance. He was sweating, his thoughts churning in expectation of how things were going to go.

His employer did not deal well with failure. That was as true now as it had been when they first collaborated on the digital infrastructure start-up that had grown into the Teague Technology Group.

Back then, the company had a different name and Patel had been an eager partner along with Brody, Josh, and Sung. Four MIT graduates with bright ideas and sharp minds, they dreamed of being the force that would reshape Silicon Valley and the tech industry for the twenty-first century.

But reality – or rather, Brody Teague's idea of what reality should be – got in the way of that. He was always the smartest of them, and the most ruthless. In hindsight, the way it would play out was obvious from the start.

First Josh was ousted, then Sung soon after, both of them bought out and ejected under circumstances that would not be spoken of in public, under penalty of injurious legal action. Only Patel stayed, too meek to object, afraid for his own future. On paper, he was still a co-founder, but he was as much a servant as Brody's endless numbers of assistants. Little by little, he had gone from partner to vassal, in too deep to get out.

He steeled himself as he reached the suite, hesitating before knocking. He could hear Brody's voice coming from inside, an indistinct yell and then the crash of something breaking.

Sighing, he tapped lightly on the door. The redhead, the one Brody dismissively called Number Eighteen, opened it and for a split second she showed him a glimpse of fear. Like Patel, she knew that she was one bad moment away from being tossed out with nothing. The woman had already earned Teague's displeasure once tonight.

Patel tried to summon some sympathy and came up empty. People like her came and went, and he had learned not to invest too much in their fates. He had to concentrate on keeping his own position secure, even if that meant directing Brody's bad moods at others.

Entering, Patel made his way into the opulent suite's day room. Teague's money had bought out not only the presidential suite of the most exclusive hotel in the city, but the entire floor surrounding it. He leaned heavily on his relationship with certain local politicians, making sure that the incident at the T-Tec office was spun by the media into something that benefitted him.

A large television on one wall showed a Portuguese news channel, with shaky footage of wreckage crashing to the street at the foot of the T-Tec office building. It cut to a live feed of ambulances and fire engines crowded around the entrance, and police officers sealing off the reception. The reporters covering the story had been told that the collapse of the antenna was the result of a terrorist attack.

The lie dovetailed with other reports coming in, one on the airliner that had been diverted to the air force base up the coast at Monte Real after an unspecified emergency, and the other about an American jet that had dropped off radar. All the unanswered questions and supposition clouded the truth and cast T-Tec as the victim.

Brody would get what he wanted soon enough. By dawn, the news would be full of shots of weeping families in arrival lounges waiting for a plane that would not land, and rescue ships and helicopters circling bits of broken fuselage floating in the Bay of Biscay. But he wasn't satisfied. He rarely was.

Patel walked past Aslanov on the way to the suite's study, where Brody was in the middle of an angry telephone call. The assassin wore his usual unruffled expression. He sipped from a glass of expensive vodka and raised an eyebrow.

"The child is throwing his toys out of the crib," said the Russian. "You will have to pick them up."

A flash of anger cut across Patel's face. "This is your fault," he hissed. "If you could just do your bloody job and deal with the problems Brody told you to!" He glanced around, making sure that the assistant was out of earshot. "You let yourself get identified in Canada, you lost Cole in London, and tonight you fail to catch these intruders?" His hands tightened into fists. "What good are you?"

Aslanov gave him a slight shake of the head. "Careful. You do not want to say anything to me that you may later regret. You cannot judge a game you do not know how to play." He sighed. "I admit, the appearance of Cole's allies was an unpleasant turn of events, but every problem has the seed of opportunity within it."

"What's that, some sort of Soviet proverb?" Patel wrung his hands and jerked his head toward the office. "He wants results, not excuses!"

"Calm yourself." Aslanov drained the rest of the contents of his glass. "This will work in our favor. You shall see."

"See what?" Teague fairly spat the words at them as he strode out of the study. "Another fuck-up?" His expression was thunderous. "Do you know what I've just had to do? I've been on the line with a half-dozen self-important pricks listening to their agenda-this, jihad-that bullshit!"

"You spoke to the, uh, attendees, then?" Patel backed off a step, showing passivity in his attempt to appease the other man. "That's good, Brody."

"That's good, yeah, that's good," echoed Teague, his tone mocking the other man. "WatchGate and Megiddo dropped out, but to hell with them." He snorted. "Do you know what they said to me? *We prefer to deal with professionals.* The sheer audacity!"

Patel said nothing. Teague's inability to see the similarity between his own monumental arrogance and that of others remained undimmed, despite the night's setback.

He turned on Aslanov. "And as for you! Are you, like, working for the enemy or something? Because I can't think of another reason why you are so shitty at the job I pay you to do!" He advanced on the Russian, until he was inches away from his face, his voice rising into a shout. "Are you actually trying to sabotage me?"

"Sit down." Aslanov's patience faded, and he did something with his hand, striking Teague in the neck with two outstretched fingers, so fast that Patel barely saw the movement.

Teague gasped, clutching at his throat, and dropped on to a sofa. His face reddened, and for a moment he strained at his breath, unable to speak.

"You are a dilettante," Aslanov told him, ice forming on the words. "Your wealth and your status has insulated you from the harsh realities of the world. But you have entered an arena where that does not matter as much as you believe it does. This is not a game, Mr Teague. For those men you spoke with, it is *war*, and in war there are losses. You get bloody." He shot a look in Patel's direction, then back again. "Do you understand?"

Still unable to make a sound, Teague managed a wooden nod.

"You hired me to work for you because I know this world. I understand it." Aslanov went to the wet bar and poured himself another drink. "It was only a matter of time before your activities attracted unwanted attention. Cole's escape merely accelerated that eventuality." He paused, framing his next words. "Based on what I have learned from tonight's events, it is clear that the American National Security Agency has deployed operatives from their Fourth Echelon division to investigate Gordian Sword. They call them Splinter Cells, and I must be clear, they are a threat you are quite unprepared to deal with."

"H-how…? How'd you kn-now all this stuff?" Teague struggled to form the question.

"You pay me to know these things," Aslanov told him. "And I will deal with them. But you need to stay out of my way and let me work." He leaned in. "And do not question me again."

Teague fell silent for a long moment, before he nodded again, showing a rare flash of deference to the Russian. "All right. Fine." He took a deep breath and regained his composure. "This whole performance with the demonstration was a pain in the ass, anyway." He got to his feet and straightened his jacket. "You know what? If the NSA are sniffing around, I say we cut to the chase. No more sideshows, we go straight to the main event." He threw Patel a sideways glance. "You have the details of the bids?"

Patel nodded, summoning the assistant. She handed him her tablet computer, and he input his passcodes, bringing up the relevant data. "So, it appears that Voron and the White Masks group offered the largest fees before the signal was disrupted, each at a figure of twenty million US dollars, and–"

"Don't care." Teague cut him off with a flick of his hand. "It doesn't matter who put up the most cash. What matters is who put in bids."

Patel frowned. He didn't know where this conversation was going. "Well… Brody, aside from the ones who dropped out, they *all* put in a bid."

"And they're all going to win," Teague replied, a grin splitting his features. "I'm not going to sell Gordian Sword to the highest bidders. I'll be honest, I never intended for it to be exclusive! I'm going to let everyone have it, every last one of those fanatic assholes. We're talking *open-source* terrorism." He paced back and forth, his words gaining momentum. "Don't you get it? This is not about money! That's just numbers, that's how we keep score! This is about *the reset*, Samir. This is how we are going to reboot the world."

"Are you mad?" Shock widened Patel's eyes, and for an instant, he forgot who he spoke to. "One or two clients, we can control that, but granting access to all of them, it would be like… like giving every street thug their own battle tank!"

Teague cocked his head, showing surprise at Patel's outburst. Then he chuckled. "Samir… there's a good brain on you, but, man, sometimes I forget how limited you can be."

"If this technology can do what you say," said Aslanov, "would it not be better to restrict access to it? Profit from how it is used?"

Teague pointed at the Russian. "See, that kind of thinking? I expect it from him. Dinosaur behavior! He's set in his ways, with that Cold War, maintain-the-status-quo mindset. But where has that got us, really? Nowhere. Society plays the same notes over and over, we've been doing it since before I was born! The performers change but the music stays the same. We need a fresh start."

When Teague stood up and straightened his jacket, Patel recognized the gesture; Brody was going to lecture them. He said nothing, having sat through such diatribes on many occasions.

Teague turned his attention on Aslanov. "Did I ever tell you, that when we were first starting out, I offered my skills to the United States government? I told them what the Teague Technology Group could do for them. I told them about my plans to develop quantum computing systems… Do you know what happened?"

Patel had heard this story a hundred times, but he sat quietly, letting it spool out.

"They laughed me out of the room." Old resentment came back to the surface, and a nerve jumped in Teague's jaw as he relived the moment. "They told me it was impossible. Treated me like a child, for crying out loud." Brody neglected to mention that he had barely entered his twenties when that meeting occurred. He took a breath, pushing away the memory. "They're going to be sorry they did that."

Aslanov raised a questioning eyebrow. "Does that mean you are doing this out of petty revenge?"

Teague snorted with derision. "Nothing I do is *petty*."

Wisely, the Russian didn't challenge that. He shrugged. "Explain it, then. I am the Cold War animal, like you say, and I do not see what you see. Enlighten me."

It was exactly the impetus Teague needed. If there was anything that Brody loved more than being right, Samir reflected, it was the sound of his own voice.

"Gordian Sword goes active at full operational capacity," began Teague. "What will come next? People are going to freak out! Markets will crash, governments will collapse. *It'll be global chaos.*" He couldn't hold back the wild grin that spread across his face. "I mean, let's face it, this shit has been happening in slow motion for the past forty years… I'm not starting it, I'm just pressing on the fast-forward button." He made a shoving motion. "I'm giving history a little push."

Patel watched the Russian give a slow, studious nod. "And what happens then?"

"What?" Teague answered distractedly, fishing a bottle of mineral water out of an ice bucket on the table in front of them.

"What happens after you have created the anarchy you desire?" Aslanov's tone hardened. "Have you considered that?"

"Oh wow, no." Teague took a drink, then made a mock-worried face. "In all the time I've been planning this, I never did once think about the consequences." Sarcasm dripped from every word he said. "Don't talk to me like I'm a moron! *Of course* I considered it. That's the best part." His grin returned. "I get to save the world."

"How?" Patel let the question drop. Teague had never gone this deep into his plans before, and now Aslanov had goaded him into revealing his endgame, Patel was desperate to learn more.

The other man jerked his thumb in the direction of the study, where his encrypted smartphone lay abandoned on the desk. "Every one of these creeps we're dealing with, pushing their personal little wars and using Gordian Sword to do whatever nasty shit they have planned ... I get their number." He chuckled again. "Not that they'll ever know it until it's too late." Teague made a vague gesture with his hands. "Client users can only access the Gordian Sword system through a proprietary tech interface, the satellite comms units I provided. But they map and record everything going on around them. Every second they're using the com units, I'm tracking *them*."

Aslanov stiffened. "If any of those groups suspect you are surveilling them, they will kill us."

"If any of them had above-genius IQs, I might be worried," Teague shot back. Then he leaned in, returning to his theme. "See, when the day comes the world is on fire and people need someone to save them, that's when I will step into the light..." He spread his hands. "The hero of the day, the man with all the data needed to go after these assholes exactly where they live and put them in the ground. A few airstrikes later and I'm getting a goddamned medal. Believe me, give it a few months of daily cyberattacks and Washington, Beijing, Moscow, whoever, they'll be *begging* for someone to give them a quick and easy solution."

"Suppose it does work." Aslanov looked away, out of the suite's window and into the night. "What of the CIA, the NSA? They will not simply forget the part you played in bringing about this anarchy."

Teague clapped his hands together, as he always did when he had a *"gotcha"* reply prepared for those who dared to question him. "See, in programming, we'd say that's a feature, not a bug. I'm sure your countrymen in Voron, or the White Masks would love the chance to strike at the heart of the US intelligence community, right? We'll make sure they remove anyone ill-disposed toward T-Tec. Burn down this Fourth Echelon thing you're so worried about. And if there are any lingering doubts after the fact, well… We'll hang the blame on the North Koreans."

"They'll deny it," said Patel.

"Sure they will! And that'll only make them look guiltier."

"You have thought of everything," said the Russian.

"Yeah." Teague gave a self-satisfied nod. "I've been planning this for a long time. And when it's over, when I'm in a position of true power, that's when the real work starts. *Technology unchained.*" Patel saw a fire kindle in his eyes. "We'll build a better world from the ruins of this one. We get all the obstacles out of the way and we fix… *everything.*"

Obstacles meant *anyone who didn't see things Brody's way.* Patel said nothing. He had always suspected Brody Teague of having a messiah complex, but not on this scale. Brody looked Patel's way, interpreting his silence as assent.

"This isn't about money, Samir," he went on. "That's old world thinking. It's *limited*. Stick with me, and we'll go down in history."

"I don't know if I want that." Patel found his voice again, but his denials sounded weak. "I don't want people to know my name… I just want to be *rich*."

Teague snorted and shook his head, as if the idea was foolish. "Small picture, Samir. Small picture in a big picture world. Besides, with your T-Tec stock options you already *are* rich. How much more money do you really need?"

Patel said nothing and looked at the carpet, but deep down inside him a dark ember of seething bitterness burned brightly. Brody's right, he thought, I don't just want money… I want his money.

For a brief moment, he hung on to a fantasy of Brody Teague ruined and penniless, a broken man sitting in the ashes of his failures. Then Patel blinked and dismissed the thought, surprised by the vehemence of his own reaction, and fearful that Teague might somehow sense what he was thinking. He covered the moment with a nervous laugh. "You always think big, don't you?"

Teague took that as a compliment. His mood had shifted around the compass to the opposite of where it had been when he entered the room. Anger and bitterness were replaced by confidence and superiority. The man's total belief in his own rightness was something to behold.

"I need you to go out to Site Five." Teague turned his attention back to Aslanov. "Pushing up the timetable means locking that place down *tight*." He made a fist. "Once we start this baby up, we can't take our foot off the gas. I want to be sure that Gordian Sword is one hundred percent secure."

The Russian nodded. "I will make arrangements."

"This is your last chance to impress me," Teague continued. "No more mistakes."

The specific needs of the Gordian Sword quantum computer and its associated hardware meant that the machine's hidden location had a number of very specific requirements. Site Five had been chosen precisely because it ticked those boxes; indeed, the whole reason for the targeting and hostile takeover of the GreenSea Corporation had been to make sure no one but T-Tec could access it.

"Should I, uh, go out there with him?" Patel blinked. Now the moment was upon them, he felt uncertainty crowding in.

"No," sneered Teague, as if the word rhymed with *idiot*. "We have enough techs to run the operations. I don't want you getting in the way."

"Then … what am I supposed to do?"

"Honestly? I don't care." Teague shrugged and walked away. "By tomorrow night, I'll be at my alpine place sipping cognac and waiting for the fireworks."

What Brody euphemistically called the "*alpine place*" was actually a fortified estate in the Swiss Alps, a half-bunker, half-mansion built into a mountain that could serve double duty not only as a vacation home, but as a hardened retreat in the event of a major disaster. The beachside house Patel owned in Malibu looked like a shoebox in comparison.

The other man halted by the door, throwing out one final comment before he left the room. "Piece of advice?" said Teague. "If I were you, I wouldn't go anywhere near any major cities in the next few days. Once we unleash Gordian Sword, it'll be open season out there."

Patel's throat went dry as he considered that grim possibility, and Aslanov walked away, gathering up his jacket as he went. Patel reached out to him, but the Russian shook him off.

"This is it," he managed. "I'm not ready!"

"Hold your nerve." Aslanov gave him a hard look. "This changes nothing. I will contact you when it is done."

"Yes." Patel's gaze dropped to the floor once again, and when he was alone in the room, he closed his eyes and searched for that ember of old, rancorous hate.

EIGHTEEN

Montijo Air Force Base – Lisbon – Portugal

The rumble and hum of idling jet engines stirred Fisher from a dreamless sleep, and he opened his eyes in the dimness. Carefully, he dropped out of the hammock strung across the Paladin's cargo bay and rolled his shoulders, working out the stiffness. Force of habit made him run through a self-check in the same way he might have looked over a weapon that he'd disassembled for cleaning. He tested his muscles and joints with a few stretches, frowning at the places where they felt tight, where they ached.

His body was a good machine, well maintained and trim for a man of his age. There were men twenty years younger than him who weren't as fit as the ex-SEAL, but Fisher wasn't about to delude himself into thinking that age did not affect him. He felt the ghost of arthritis in his bones, the minute delay in reactions that used to be instant. He didn't like it.

Fisher went to one of the oval windows in the jet's hull and looked out. It was early morning, and the Paladin remained in the same spot it had occupied through the night, on the far edge of the Portuguese air force base, across the bay from the city. He could see a couple of the aircraft's crew conducting a walk-around, making their final checks before the bird got airborne.

Boots clanked on the deck plates behind him, but he didn't turn. He knew the pattern of the tread.

"Sleep well?" said Sarah.

"Dark and silent," he told her.

"We'll be wheels-up in twenty," added his daughter. "Grim says the locals are asking too many questions, especially after what happened last night."

Fisher turned toward her, greeting Sarah with a nod. "Guess we don't want to outstay our welcome."

Two major terrorist incidents taking place virtually at the same moment would be enough to raise the alert level of any nation well past the red line. And while it was true the collapse of the T-Tec office's antenna in downtown Lisbon and the long-range hijacking of a pair of passenger jets *had* been connected, the matter of *how* was still unclear to the local authorities.

Officers of Portugal's intelligence agency, the Security Information Service, would already be deploying in crisis mode to get to the bottom of those events, and it wouldn't be long before they examined the Paladin's presence a little more closely than Fourth Echelon would prefer. The jet's cover as a USAF transport plane making an unscheduled technical stop at an allied airbase would not hold up to close scrutiny.

Without being aware of it, Sarah said what was on her father's mind. "We should be able to tell these people what happened in their backyard. It's not right to keep them in the dark. The families of the passengers who were on that plane deserve answers."

"True," he agreed, "but if we open that can of worms right now the Portuguese will lock us down here, and rightly so. By the time we get it straight..." Fisher let the unfinished thought hang and beckoned her to follow him. They made their way forward, heading toward the command-and-control section.

She cleared her throat. "Listen, Dad... After the exfil, I didn't get the chance to thank you. Charlie and me, we were jammed up back there. We wouldn't have made it out without you."

"The team always comes home," he told her. Fisher wanted his words to sound firm, but it was hard to keep a thread of emotion out of them, especially where his only child was concerned. He pushed on, changing the subject. "What about the intel I downloaded to my OPSAT? Anything we can use in there?"

Sarah ducked as she stepped through an open hatch and into the next section of the Paladin's interior. "I talked to Lea. She said the take is badly fragmented because we had to cut the download short. She and Charlie have been up all night trying to make sense of what you got. Neither of them slept a wink."

"I know the feeling," said a wry voice, as they passed by the Paladin's holding cells. Inside, Kobin climbed up off his narrow bunk and put his arms through the bars of the door keeping him penned. "How much longer do I have to stay here, Fisher? Seriously, I'm starting to think you have something against me."

Sarah turned on her heel and glared at him. "Funny. Keep it

up. See how well sarcasm does for you. Maybe I'll ask the pilot to drop you off at Guantanamo as we pass. Without a chute."

Kobin turned to her father. "Well, she certainly has the Fisher charm, that's for sure. Lucky for her, she didn't inherit your looks."

Fisher approached him, sizing up the criminal. "Is this your idea of talking your way out of there?"

"Is it working?" Kobin's expression shifted, hinting at desperation.

"Not really."

The other man cursed under his breath, then changed tack. "Look, Fisher, I know something's up. I have resources, none of which I can use from in here." He banged his hand on the bars. "Give me a little liberty, I'll tell you everything I know about Dima Aslanov and his playmates."

"You give me an honest answer to something, I might be inclined." Fisher took a step closer, and Kobin backed away, despite the presence of the cell door between them. "Tell me this, Andriy. After we pulled your sorry ass out of Morocco, how long was it before you considered selling us out to Teague?"

"Not that long," Kobin admitted, then gave a reluctant nod. "Sure, I thought about it. But then I decided otherwise. Because I have a target on my back and you people are my best shot at being alive this time tomorrow."

"That actually sounded believable," offered Sarah.

"Fear does that," said Fisher. He went to the keypad controlling the cell's locks and input a code. "All right, come with us. You make yourself useful, you stay out of the doghouse. But you test me—"

"Yeah, I get the picture." The door retracted, and Kobin

gingerly stepped out. "You won't regret this," he managed, with a weak smile.

"That," said Sarah, "remains to be seen."

Inside the confines of the Paladin's C&C, the air was tinny with the odors of sweat, stale coffee and ozone from the overworked computers.

Fisher found Grim at her usual spot, poring over a web of interlinked images on the strategic mission interface. In the frosty light cast by the digital table's screen, she looked every inch the warrior queen from the myths of her Icelandic heritage.

She was giving orders without looking up. "Kade, go through the mode four sectors of the take again. If you can't clean up the noise in there, we may have to bypass it entirely."

"I can try a reflection sorting algorithm," said the technician, stifling a yawn.

"Do that." Grim glanced in another direction, to where Charlie hunched over a panel of his own. "Cole, dump whatever you have that's coherent to the SMI, I want to see it myself."

"Copy that." Charlie's hands blurred over his keyboard, and a new torrent of digital panels unfolded in front of her.

Kobin made a face as he entered with Fisher and Sarah. "Ugh. Smells like nerds in here."

Grim's head snapped up, like a missile launcher locking on to a target. "What is he doing out of his cage?"

"I'm taking him for a walk," said Fisher. "I figure we should use every asset we have on hand, right?"

"I suppose so." Grim eyed the criminal gravely, then looked away as a tone sounded on her panel. "Go ahead." She tapped the comm-net earpiece she wore, then nodded at a voice only she could hear. "That was Drew," she explained. "He says Montijo tower are still withholding departure clearance. We may have to risk an unauthorized take-off."

"And go where?" Sarah offered the question. "Do we actually have a target location?"

"Not exactly," said Charlie, popping a caffeine tablet into his mouth. He spoke around it as he crunched down. "We have a whole lot of possible vectors, but it's like trying to nail smoke to a wall."

Fisher took that in with a nod. He didn't remark on the fact that Charlie seemed to have slipped seamlessly back into his old role on board the Paladin. He was even sitting in the same chair.

Old habits die hard, I guess, he told himself, *and hackers love a challenge.* Right now, they needed Cole's skills more than ever.

Fisher stepped up to the SMI "pool table", across from Grim. "OK, then. Here's how we're gonna do this. We go around the room, we show our cards, and we make our best guess as to the location of Gordian Sword… and go from there."

"Clever name," said Kobin, in a way that made it clear he thought the exact opposite. "Why does everyone with a classical education need to flaunt it?"

"Yeah, let's start with Brody Teague," said Sarah. "Where's he at right now?"

Kade brought up a series of images on her screen. "He got out of the T-Tec building before the Lisbon police sealed it. Despite a promise from his lawyers that he would make himself available for interview, he left the city soon after." She flicked across to a video window, showing the interior of a railway station terminal. "The CIA field office in Madrid determined that Target Blue and Target White both boarded a private train a few hours ago, heading north toward the Spanish-French border."

Fisher saw grainy footage of Teague and his long-suffering colleague Patel climbing into the carriage of a sleek, high-speed train. Teague looked as cocky as ever, but Patel's body language was all nerves. He also noted that there was no sign of Aslanov in any of the pictures. "Where's Target Red?"

"Unknown," said Kade. "We lost track of him at Teague's hotel in Lisbon."

"Aslanov's a ghost," said Charlie. "He knows we're looking for him." He paused. "More than that, he knows *Sam* is looking for him."

"Teague is riding the rails." Grim considered that. "He hates to fly, that's a known variable. What's the train's route beyond Spain?"

Kade brought up a map of Europe, and a crimson line drew a shaky path over it. "If they follow the agreed-upon transit, the train will cross Southern France and then enter Switzerland. The final destination is logged as Bern, but there's nothing to stop them diverting to a secondary route before they reach there."

"He's not going to Bern." Charlie gave a curt shake of the head. "Teague has a lot of pull with the Swiss government, enough that he can go wherever he wants inside their borders."

Fisher prompted him. "And that would be?"

"He has an estate in the Alps, one of those stealth mansions beloved of the paranoid rich," said the hacker. "You know the kinda thing, off-limits to everyone, built for a disaster prepper with an unlimited budget and a private army of goons. A place where you could ride out the end of the world in a heated swimming pool with a piña colada. He gets up there, nothing short of a nuke strike will dislodge him."

"Is that where he's hiding this Gordian thing?" Kobin stepped closer to the SMI, peering at the map. "In his basement?"

"Possible," admitted Grim.

Kobin shrugged. "Well, you guess wrong and you're screwed, yeah? You're on a tight clock, so if that turns out to be a dry hole…"

"Thanks for stating the obvious," said Sarah.

Fisher nodded at the screen. "What else have we got?"

Grim cast away the digital pages on the SMI with a sweep of her hand and brought up an assortment of new images, some of them partially corrupted, each one a complex construction diagram for a highly detailed device Fisher didn't recognize. "This is from the data recovered via Panther's OPSAT," she told them. "Blueprints for the Gordian Sword quantum computing array and its associated support systems. Could be some detail in here we're missing."

"Way out of my league," said Kobin, scanning the plans.

Fisher picked out a central mechanism around which everything else was built, a spherical pod in a shock-resistant frame, pierced by dozens of thin tubes. In the abstract, it resembled something grown rather than manufactured, like a giant seed sprouting metallic roots. He saw a thick jacket surrounding the quantum computer, and recognized one familiar set of components.

"That." He pointed at the screen. "Those baffles. I've seen something like it before, on nuclear reactors."

Kobin gave him a sideways look. "How do *you* know what the inside of a nuclear reactor looks like?"

"I get around," Fisher noted.

"Sam's not wrong," said Charlie. "Those are fast-fluid coolant modules."

"These quantum computers, they run hot?" Sarah asked. "Could we track it that way?"

"Actually, no to both questions." Charlie shook his head. "It's more that QC systems are hyper-sensitive to any variations in operating temperature, we're talking like millikelvins here."

"And fragile, too," added Kade. "That's why we know it has to be in a static location. A mobile set-up would have too much vibrational interference."

Sarah folded her arms across her chest. "So, if you need a lot of water to keep this thing cold, has Teague got that up in his giant alpine chalet?"

"Unlikely," said Grim. "Unless he owns an underground lake we don't know about."

"OK …" Sarah cocked her head, a gesture Fisher recognized from her childhood, as she chewed on a thorny problem. "Can we put a map up showing T-Tec's holdings? Look for any sites with power spikes, water supplies nearby, construction traffic …"

Grim exchanged a look with Kade and Cole. "We've been down this road already." She signaled to Charlie, who sent a world map to the SMI. Dozens of bright markers popped into existence on the screen, each accompanied by a text flag identifying it. "That was our first thought too. But T-Tec doesn't have anything that fits the profile."

"Teague's corporation is all about distributed, low-mass,

low-impact infrastructure," added Kade. "Aside from the Palo Alto campus and the tower in Lisbon, it's all small constructions."

"He'd never put that thing in a city," said Kobin. "Too many eyes on it."

Fisher scowled. He could sense an insight lurking at the horizon of his thoughts, but he couldn't grasp it. After a long moment, he looked in Charlie's direction. "We're seeing this the wrong way." He circled the SMI table, pacing out his thoughts. "How did we make these connections to begin with?"

"Charlie reached out to me," said Grim. "I saw links with what CIA were tracking."

"Charlie sent up a flare because of what happened at GreenSea," said Sarah, "which Brody Teague now owns."

"Technically, he's owned it for the better part of a year," said Charlie. "In secret."

"In secret," Fisher repeated, "for months. More than enough to time to use it as a front."

Grim snapped her fingers at Kade as she caught on. "Show us GreenSea's eco-reclamation sites."

"Wait one…" Kade busied herself at her panel, and in a few moments the map indicators were replaced by a handful of new tags. "Here we go."

Fisher immediately saw potential hiding places for Gordian Sword – a mothballed power station on the Japanese coast, a failed wind farm in the Cascade Range – but one in particular stuck out to him. "*There.* Oil rig in the North Sea. That's our best candidate."

Grim threw Fisher a questioning look. "Why that one?"

"It fits the bill. All the seawater you need. No eyes on it.

And it's isolated and alone out there," said Fisher. "If this was my gig, it's the location *I* would choose."

Grim remained unconvinced. "With all due respect, Sam, we can't go on a hunch."

As she spoke, Kade pulled the details of the rig on to the SMI screen. "The decommissioned Nyx Oil Platform stands in deep waters east of the Shetland Islands, beyond the northern coast of Scotland. Formerly owned by McFarlane Energy, shut down and abandoned in place five years ago when the well ran dry. Bought by GreenSea Incorporated, for conversion into a test-bed for wind, solar, and wave power solutions."

"I remember that one," said Charlie, with a sudden burst of energy. "Morant called it S-5... *Site Five*. It was gonna be a showpiece for the company, but they were bogged down with delays and technical issues."

"Ah, *shit*." Kobin's muttered curse escaped all but Fisher's attention, and he turned to fix the criminal with a hard, pitiless stare. "What?" Kobin added, making a poor job of acting the innocent. "I didn't say anything."

"You know something." Fisher crossed the cabin in three quick steps, backing the other man into a corner. "Spill it," he growled.

"It's probably a coincidence," said Kobin, as beads of sweat appeared on his brow.

"In our line of work, there's no such thing," said Grim.

Kobin sagged and stared at the deck. When he started speaking, his words came machine-gun fast. "One of the last jobs I did for Dima Aslanov was to get him a consignment of *Okean Kobras*. Russian anti-submarine munitions, Soviet-made copies of the US Navy Mark Sixty Captor."

"What's a Captor?" said Charlie. "By the look on Sam's face, I'm guessing it's not pleasant."

"It's any submariner's worst nightmare," said Fisher, recalling threat briefings on the weapon from his days as a SEAL. "Hunter-killer torpedo in a can with a bunch of sensor gear. Deploy them on the seabed and they sit there, silent and inert, waiting. When a sub comes into range, the torpedo activates and locks on. And the mark never sees it coming."

"Whoa." Charlie blinked as he took that in. "Like a sniper. By the time you hear the shot, you're already dead."

Fisher didn't take his eyes off Kobin. "And you made bank putting them out in the wild, huh?"

"Aslanov didn't give me much choice, Fisher!" Kobin retorted hotly. "It was that or get my throat slit! Look, I tried to keep a handle on where the Kobras went, but he was too smart for that! All I knew was that the final destination for them was someplace codenamed S-5."

"If that's true, the Nyx rig just went to the top of our list," said Sarah. "Firepower like that would only be used to protect something valuable."

"It also means we can't call the Navy and ask them to blow it up," added Kade.

Grim shook her head. "That was never an option."

Fisher wondered what she meant, but he didn't call her on it. "How quickly can we spin up an infiltration package for S-5? I can board the rig, find Gordian Sword, and destroy it."

Kade let out a weary breath. "Getting access to the quantum computer is going to take more than kicking in some doors, sir," she told him. "Fourth Echelon hacker-ops will only be able to provide minimal assistance to Splinter Cell assets on site.

The core control is linked to a standalone security system we can't break into."

Charlie raised a tentative hand. "Well, that's not strictly true…"

Fisher turned toward him. "What do you have?"

"There *is* another access path," continued Charlie, "but it presents its own set of issues, which is why I hesitate to mention it…" He swallowed another caffeine tablet. "OK. According to the files we accessed in Lisbon, Brody Teague has a hardened digital tablet computer with a personal override that can unlock the core commands. It's the same device he used to mess with those airliners last night."

"Yeah, maybe he'll hand that over if you ask politely," said Kobin.

"We won't *ask*," Sarah said firmly.

"It's biometrically locked," Charlie insisted. "Teague has to be alive and breathing for it to work."

"And Teague is on a train speeding through Europe, hundreds of kilometers away from the rig," added Kade. "Panther's skills are good, but even he can't be in two places at once."

"He doesn't need to be," said Grim, glancing at Sarah.

"No." Fisher stepped between his daughter and Grim. He knew what was coming, and he didn't like it.

"Two operations," continued Grim, "simultaneous deployments. Panther drops on Site Five to deal with Gordian Sword. Lynx boards the train to interdict Target Blue and secure the asset."

"No," repeated Fisher, grinding out the word like sparks from flint. "Find another way."

"Did you mistake this for a democracy?" Grim met his gaze,

measure for measure. "The NSA and the President granted me operational authority over every aspect of this mission, and I'm exercising it. You don't get a vote. You get to do your job or hang up your goggles. Those are the choices."

"She's not ready." But even as Fisher said the words, he knew that was a lie. Sarah *was* ready, she *was* capable. But that didn't stop him fearing for his daughter's life. If anyone on board the Paladin truly knew how deadly and unpredictable the work of a Splinter Cell could be, it was him. He knew *exactly* how much danger she would face.

"Dad, I can do this," Sarah spoke quietly. "I will do it."

Finally, he broke away from Grim's rigid stare and went back to the mission interface. In that moment, more than anything in the world, he wanted to close the book on this and walk away, take his daughter with him, and let the chips fall.

But I can't, he told himself, *and she can't. Because there's too much at stake, too many other lives at risk… and Sarah's more like me than I want to admit.*

Fisher spoke again. "Lynx gets the close support from the Paladin. We don't know what to expect on board Teague's train, she'll need the cover. I'll get another aircraft to fly me out to the rig, something fast and untraceable. And I'll need a pilot." His eyes fell on Kobin. "Time to earn your keep, Andriy."

NINETEEN

Montijo Air Force Base – Lisbon – Portugal

Sarah pulled herself into the black tactical suit and zipped it up. Form-fitting and lightweight, it hugged the curves of her body, the dense material providing protection without restricting her movement. She went through a series of stretches, then moved to the equipment station where her mission gear was waiting. Weighing each item of hi-tech kit in her hand, she considered each piece carefully, thinking through the pros and cons.

Once Sarah committed to the operation, she would be stuck with whatever choices she had made for her loadout, and the wrong pick could mean the difference between life and death. One more concussion grenade clipped to her rig meant one fewer pistol magazine in her pouch, and in a pinch those bullets might keep her alive. She rolled a cylindrical chaff discharger in her gloved hand, studying it carefully.

"Want some advice?" said a voice.

Sarah's father had entered the armory space without a sound, and despite herself, his approach drew a brief smile.

He'd done the same thing for as long as she could remember, even back when she was a little girl. *Daddy has cat feet*, she'd once told him. "Sure," she replied.

"Leave the chaff," he told her. "Dispersal is unpredictable. If in doubt, carry more ammo."

He moved to stand beside her, becoming the instructor once more as he surveyed her loadout with an approving nod. Sarah noted that her father was also in his tactical outfit, but hidden beneath a long gray overcoat. He had a gear bag hanging off one shoulder.

"You're good to go?" she ventured.

He nodded. "Kobin worked his magic and sourced a Gulfstream to get us to Site Five."

"Huh. That was fast."

"I made sure he was well motivated." He picked up the stun gun she had selected, frowning at it.

"Something tells me I don't want to look too hard at how that gunrunner managed to find you a private jet on such short notice."

"Good instinct," said her father. He picked up on the change in her tone and shot her a look, the invitation to add to her thought implicit in his eyes.

"I trained at the Farm to be considered for the Splinter Cell program," she told him. "But I've learned more about what Fourth Echelon really is in the last few days than any training could teach me."

"And you don't like what you see." It was a statement, not a question. Fisher knew his daughter too well not to be direct with her. She appreciated it.

"I'm not sure. I mean, Splinter Cells are supposed to be

virtually autonomous, right? That whole thing about exercising 'the Fifth Freedom'... But that's not really true, is it? I feel like someone's pulling our strings here, that there's more going on than we know. This whole thing with Teague and his key-breaker? I can't believe he's kept it a secret from the world all this time. Someone had to know."

"This is the gray, kid," said Fisher, without humor. "It just gets deeper from here."

"I remember Uncle Vic always said, *operate in honor and morality without compromise.* Do you think that's possible, or was he being naïve?"

Her father's lip curled in a half-smile. "Victor Coste is a lot of things, but naïve isn't one of them." He sighed. "You know where the line is, Sarah. Your mom and I, we taught you that. If the moment comes you have to decide if you're going to step over it, or step away... I know you'll make the right choice." He let his words lay for a moment, then gestured with her stun gun. "This thing, though, is the wrong one."

Fisher replaced it with a pistol case, flipping it open to show her the weapon inside. Slender, with custom grips, holo-sight, a long barrel, and integrated silencer. She picked it up; it felt comfortable in her hand.

"Volquartsen Scorpion," he went on. "Lightweight, chambered in .22 long rifle, accurate and stealthy. Figured it would fit you good."

She gave him a wry look. "You know, when other dads give their girls a gift, it's usually, like, flowers."

"I prefer something that'll keep you safe." He turned serious again. "If you're going out there, I want you equipped to come back alive."

"Aww," said Kobin, as he stepped past the open hatch on his way through the compartment. He wore a khaki green flight suit and a self-amused expression. "That's sweet, in a dysfunctional kinda way."

"If you want to stay *any* kind of functional, keep walking," said Fisher.

"Whatever." Kobin made his way toward the aft of the Paladin, throwing another comment over his shoulder. "Just hurry it up, the Ice Queen is five steps behind me."

"The Ice Queen is right here," corrected Grim, entering the armory.

"Gotta go!" said Kobin, quickening his pace through the next hatch and out of sight.

"Sam," said Grim. "A word before you deploy?" The way she posed the question made it clear that it wasn't actually a question at all. The other woman looked pointedly in Sarah's direction, dismissing her with a glance.

Sarah met her father's gaze, and she could tell he was searching for the right thing to say to her, something that would make them feel better. But both of them were too pragmatic for any platitude to do anything other than ring hollow.

He put a hand on her shoulder. "I'll see you soon."

She returned the gesture and stepped away, cramming her fears into a box and closing the lid tight.

When they were alone, Fisher sat back against the equipment bench and eyed Grim with a scowl. "Any time you talk to me one on one, it doesn't bode well."

"Comes with the job," she told him. "I learned that from Lambert."

Invoking the name of Irving Lambert brought serious baggage with it for both of them. The man had been the operations coordinator and de facto mission commander for Third Echelon, the previous incarnation of the current team, and Grim and Fisher had greatly respected him. His steady, thoughtful presence was sorely missed, and Fisher couldn't help thinking things might be going differently right now if Lambert was still around.

"So talk," said Fisher.

"I'm reading you in on a detail that does not go beyond us," Grim told him, her voice dropping. "A directive has come on stream from NSA Tailored Access Operations." The division she referred to was the National Security Agency's unit of hackers, the virtual world's equivalent of a covert strike force, established to monitor, infiltrate and interdict the computer networks of America's enemies. "The hijackings and the crash in the Atlantic have made it clear that Gordian Sword is a viable and ongoing threat to US interests. We can't have a tool that powerful in the hands of rogue states and hostile actors."

"No argument here." Fisher noted that she called Teague's machine a *tool*, not a *weapon*, and he couldn't help thinking he was hearing the echo of someone else's words from Grim's mouth.

"Once you board Site Five, your primary objective is to ensure Gordian Sword remains intact and secure it for extraction."

"That thing is the digital equivalent of napalm," said Fisher. "It burns everything it touches. But you want me to leave it up and running?"

"That's affirmative. NSA are preparing a team to deploy to the rig once you've locked it down. They'll disconnect and relocate Gordian Sword if they can, or if not, fortify it in place under US control."

"It should be destroyed," he insisted.

"That decision will be made above your pay grade," Grim told him, "and mine."

Fisher shook his head. "We have a chance to deal with it before anyone else is killed."

"You have your orders," she replied. "Your priority is to preserve the quantum computer technology. All other considerations are secondary."

He eyed her coldly. "How long have you known they wanted it taken intact? From the start? Or did they wait to see if it actually *worked* before they decided?"

Grim looked away. "The airliner that went down… That proved it can operate as a targeted system. The order was given then."

"You've known more about this than you've been saying, all along." Fisher cut straight to the heart of it. "Putting us in jeopardy, hiding another agenda, involving my daughter. You know, ever since Charlie explained how that thing works, I've been asking myself why Brody Teague didn't sell it to the government." He nodded at the thought. "I think he tried. But they didn't believe it was real."

"We know better now," said Grim. She took a breath and drew herself up. "Just get it done."

Site Five – Nyx Oil Platform – North Sea

The rotor blades of the big Sikorsky S-92 chopped at the wet, cold air as they raced back up to speed, buffeting Aslanov with a wintry downwash of rain as he marched across the rig's landing pad.

He bent forward against the rush of wind as the helicopter lifted off and pivoted away, turning in the direction of its home base in Aberdeen. The Sikorsky's crew had been quite eager to make the return trip across the gray expanse of the North Sea as soon as possible, troubled by the threatening approach of a heavy storm cell moving in from the Norwegian coast.

Aslanov looked eastward, staring the oncoming tempest in the eye. The wall of menacing cloud had already swallowed the horizon and it would soon be upon the oil rig.

He felt a buzz of vibration in his pocket and recovered his cellphone. Despite insistence from Patel that he should carry an executive-level T-Tec branded TecPhone, the Russian stuck with a characterless, stripped-down device of deliberately uncertain origin. It consisted of little more circuitry than it took to send and received heavily encrypted voice calls and text messages, which was all Aslanov ever needed.

He scanned a line of writing in Cyrillic on the phone's tiny screen and frowned. The message came from an old comrade in the FSB, who currently worked for the Kremlin's information security division. In return for a fee paid monthly into an untraceable Swiss bank account, that comrade kept a weather eye on digital intelligence reports pinging back and forth around the globe. If anyone out on the net showed too much interest in one Dima Aslanov, an alert tripped and the Russian was informed.

Someone was looking into him, and the search parameters used revealed a likely source of the intelligence.

Andriy Kobin. He was the only one who knew about certain

deals and particular locations cropping up in the search parameters. It had to be the oily little gunrunner, most likely spilling his guts to the Americans.

Suddenly, the incident back in Lisbon took on new meaning. Aslanov had gone over the moment a hundred times, and with each consideration, he became more certain that his instinct was correct. It had been Samuel Fisher there, in the corridor. After all this time, his old adversary had returned.

The circularity of the other man's appearance at this precise moment amused the Russian. He enjoyed the idea of fate intervening and offering him the chance to correct a previous mistake.

I should have killed them when I had the opportunity, Fisher and Kobin alike. He smiled thinly and put away the phone. *An oversight I will deal with when tonight's work is complete.*

Gusts of wind pushing ahead of the storm cell rattled through the obsolete wellhead tower dominating the platform, pulling at the black, fin-like solar panels that had been retrofitted along its height. Clustered around the flanks of the derrick were spindly vertical windmills, thin ribbons of curved metal that blurred as they spun rapidly about their axes. As the droning of the departing helicopter faded, a low, eerie humming made itself apparent over the crash of waves.

"Resonant oscillation," said a man with a nasal voice, gesturing at the air. He walked quickly over the landing pad toward Aslanov, clearly unhappy with the harsh weather. His name was Bray, one of the senior technicians on the Gordian Sword project, a figure swamped by a heavy-weather parka three sizes too big for him, the fur-lined hood flapping around his neck. "From the panels. When the wind speed is high enough, the rig, ah, *sings*." He nodded to himself, trying to conceal his nervousness. "Mr Stone, while the team appreciate you coming out here, I must say that I'm not sure the trip was worthwhile. Couldn't this have been discussed over a video-link?"

"No, Mr Bray." Aslanov returned the nod, ignoring the rain sluicing off his jacket. "Your concerns are very important to the company. I was sent here to address them in person."

"Well. Oh." Bray rocked on his feet, then made a *follow-me* gesture. "We appreciate the effort."

We. Aslanov logged that mention for further consideration, and turned away, making no effort to head down the walkway and out of the rain. "You have some issues regarding the operation that took place last night."

"The operation …" Bray echoed, blinking at the thought. "That's right. I mean, ah, we were told that the array would be operating through a test phase. A virtual environment, simulating a threat scenario. A demonstration for a buyer. Two airborne early warning aircraft, to be neutralized using Gordian Sword in direct-attack mode."

"That is what you were told." Bray and his team were typical of the scientists Aslanov had met in his career. Intelligent, to be sure, but myopic with it. Rarely looking up from their work to understand where it collided with the real world – and so, easy for someone with the charisma of Brody Teague to manipulate. He had told them that Gordian Sword was still a proof-of-concept, not a functioning weapon. But that lie could only go so far, and the edges of it were fraying.

"Certainly, a different situation from the network intrusions we've done over the past few months," added Bray. "But the details of it are very troubling."

His doubt was clear in his voice. Those other intrusion simulations were nothing of the sort, of course. Every one of them had been a live exploit – killing the power to a particular house in Berkley, the reprogramming of traffic signals on a highway in Quebec, co-opting the controls for a ride-sharing app in London, and more – all to aid Aslanov in murdering members of the team who had devised Gordian Sword in the first place.

But with most of the location and identifying data scrubbed, there should have been no way for the technicians to know what they were attacking.

"Go on," prompted Aslanov, reaching into his jacket pocket.

"Well, ah, putting aside the matter of the outage that halted the last test prematurely, there's the question of…" Bray's voice dropped to a hushed whisper. "You must have seen the news? There was an *actual* plane crash that night! And when we checked the details, the circumstances were so close as to almost be identical!" He gulped in a breath of wet air. "It *was* just a simulation, wasn't it? I dread to think that we might be responsible for something like that!"

"Of course." Aslanov found what he was looking for and palmed the object. "Those events are a tragic coincidence." He gave Bray a questioning look. "Do you think otherwise?" He allowed uncertainty to enter his tone, encouraging the other man to bring him into his confidence.

"Some of us have suspicions," said Bray, coming closer. "We can't be sure that the earlier tests were actually conducted offline. I know, it makes me sound paranoid! But they may have actually been *live!*"

The Russian feigned shock. "Who else knows about this?"

Bray indicated himself. "Myself, Diaz, and LeBeau." He gave

a weak smile. "You've no idea how good it is to have someone take this seriously."

Aslanov knew the names of the other programmers. Like Bray, they were useful but replaceable. He glanced around, making sure there was no one else in sight, then pointed at the derrick and the storm beyond it. "Do you see that?"

When Bray turned to look in the direction that he had indicated, Aslanov let the *karatel* knife concealed in his hand drop into position. In a quick double-strike, each hit a violent jab-twist motion, he stabbed Bray through the fur hood and into his throat.

Bright crimson gushed, soaking the heavy coat's collar, and Bray fell to his knees. He managed a look at his killer before he fell back on to the landing pad. Bray choked and grasped feebly at a walkie-talkie clipped to his chest, but his movements slowed.

Aslanov delicately removed the radio and examined it, as Bray gurgled out his final, blood-drowned breaths. When he was dead, the Russian rolled Bray to the edge of the hexagonal helipad and then over it.

The programmer's body clanked off a support beam and disappeared into the gray waters far below. The puddle of red he left behind was already being washed away by the rain.

"Hello?" Aslanov spoke into the radio as he set off toward the walkway that led into the rig's core complex. "This is Mr Stone." A voice in the operations center acknowledged him and he went on. "Please contact technicians Diaz and LeBeau. I would like to speak to them immediately."

He cleaned off the *karatel* with a handkerchief, then slipped it beneath the cuff of his shirt to await its next use.

•••

Gulfstream G350 – Atlantic Ocean – Altitude 15,000 Feet

"This is your captain speaking. Welcome aboard Kobin Air Flight *who-the-hell-cares*, from Lisbon to the middle of nowhere. We'll be cruising at an altitude of *way-too-high* before doing some frankly idiotic maneuvers and hoping we don't wind up dead, so please keep your seatbelts on and your tray tables *yadda-yadda-yadda*. We know you have a choice for your clandestine aviation needs, and we thank you for choosing us today."

Fisher rolled his eyes and glared forward, down the Gulfstream's passenger cabin toward the cockpit, where Andriy Kobin sat in the pilot's seat with the door wide open.

"No movie?" he asked.

Kobin shrugged. "Nope. But help yourself to the minibar." He held up a tiny vodka bottle, wiggling it in his hand. "I did."

Fisher scowled. "That's the last of those you're gonna have."

"You think I'd actually do this sober?" Kobin shook his head.

He grunted and looked away. Fisher had half-expected Kobin's travel option to be some fifty year-old rattle trap better suited to a museum than powered flight, but the criminal had surprised him by using his illegal contacts to supply a modern private jet, fully fueled and ready to roll.

The Gulfstream's interior had been decked out expensively, the passenger cabin complete with deep chairs patterned in rich leather, and wood paneling inlaid with what had to be real gold. When Fisher investigated a little more, he found signs that made him picture some trust fund kid's airborne party cut short; there were half-full bottles of flat champagne in a bucket of melted ice water, a mirror with streaks of what could only be cocaine residue on it, and the top half of a discarded bikini.

"Where did you get this bird?"

Kobin chuckled and tossed back a final gulp of vodka. "You don't want to know."

Leaving his gear bag belted in to one of the seats, Fisher walked forward to stand in the cockpit vestibule, looking across the glow of the control panel and out of the canopy. Dark clouds filled the sky before them.

Kobin's self-amusement waned, and he gave Fisher a sideways glance. "OK, I know what you're gonna say…" He paused, then did his best impersonation of Fisher's gravelly tones. "*If you doublecross me, you'll regret it.*"

"You're thinking about it," Fisher noted.

"No!" Kobin's retort was heated. "And let me tell you why that is, as out of character as it may seem." He sighed. "Aslanov terrifies me, man. I mean, you? You're pretty scary, but you got a code. You have principles."

"Stop it, I'm getting misty."

"I mean it! Aslanov is the coldest son-of-a-bitch I have ever had the misfortune to meet, and you know the kind of people I hang out with. So that's a high fuckin' bar." The other man took a breath. "I figure you're the only one who might be able to stop him in his tracks."

Fisher cocked his head. "Might?"

Kobin shifted in his seat. "Well… I know you two have history."

"I don't make it personal," said Fisher, but even he heard the lie in his own words.

"That's bullshit," Kobin retorted flatly.

He's right, said a voice in Fisher's head, one that sounded just like his late wife Regan. *If you let that get in the way of this mission, you've already failed.*

"I guess we'll find out soon enough." Fisher checked his watch, then turned back to the cabin. "Wake me when we get there."

TWENTY

Domazan – Canton of Redessan – France

The railway station on the outskirts of the town was a blink-and-you-miss it place, little more than a couple of concrete platforms around some sidings, and a building housing a ticket office that rarely opened. Almost all the trains passing through didn't bother to slow down, much less stop, instead carrying on along the line of the river Rhône toward Avignon.

But a peculiarity of the French rail network meant that a high-speed TGV service powering north toward Paris had right of way. That meant the private train on this line was forced to dwell a while, short of the junction a few miles north where the TGV would soon pass.

Brody Teague's train rolled to a halt at the empty station right on time, a testament to the precision of the computer-controlled navigation system that guided the driver.

Sarah Fisher watched it from the shadows of a thick stand of trees several meters away, her black-clad form hidden from sight. A cloudy evening sky over the South of France meant no moonlight, reducing visibility, but that suited her fine.

"Lynx has eyes on the prize," she said, subvocalizing the words into the audio pickup adhered to her throat.

"*Merlin copies.*" Charlie Cole's voice sounded in her ear, as close as if he were crouching next to her in the damp grass.

He had reluctantly agreed to a temporary return to his old role with Fourth Echelon until the Gordian Sword situation was resolved, but Sarah sensed that he was more comfortable in the operations center than he wanted to admit. She knew about the blown operation in Tehran that had driven him away in the first place, and found herself wondering: if this job gets its hooks in you, can you ever walk away?

Her father had tried, she reflected, but in the end he came back. After metaphorically walking a few miles in Sam Fisher's boots, his daughter was starting to understand why.

"*OK, there's literally one CCTV camera for miles around,*" continued Charlie. "*Looking over the crossing. But other than that, I have no visual.*"

Sarah found the camera in question, a dusty white box marked with bird shit mounted atop a pole. It pointed toward the strip of road that passed over the railway and the automatic barriers on either side of it – likely linked to some distant operator who only checked once in a blue moon, to make sure none of the tractors from the local farms were stuck on the line.

She saw men in black jackets climbing off the train, taking up positions where they could see one another and scan the area for any threats. The men made no effort to hide the Beretta semi-automatics they carried. They were on alert, ready to shoot first and not bother with questions.

"Wait one," said Sarah, reaching back to a pouch on her

rig. She removed a couple of metal spheres, each the size of a baseball, and rolled them in her hand. The units had tiny whip antennae and a small lens that stared back like the glassy eyes of a doll. Powerful adhesive pads on the outer skin of the devices allowed them to stick to virtually anything, allowing the camera inside to be deployed anywhere a Splinter Cell operative needed a different angle on a situation.

She slipped out of the shadows, closing on the station. When Sarah had the position she needed, she tossed one sticky camera up high, landing it on the eaves of the ticket office roof. The second she lobbed up into the frame of a signal box.

"*Eyes on,*" Charlie reported. "*Whoa, I have multiple hostiles! Watch your step, Lynx.*"

Sarah shrank into the gloom behind an overgrown planter as one of the armed guards walked by her. To her dismay, he wore an image intensifier rig that would turn the dark evening daylight-bright. The shadows were no longer her armor.

She held her breath and waited for the man to pass. He was close enough that Sarah could easily have put a round from her Scorpion pistol right through his heart, but this had to be a zero-footprint approach. No alarms raised, no traces left behind. If Brody Teague got wind that Fourth Echelon were coming for him, there was no way to know how he would react.

"*OK, you're clear,*" said Charlie, watching the feed from the sticky-cams. "*Go to the platform edge directly in front of you, drop down.*"

"Moving." Sarah slipped out of cover in a quick, loping run that took her down to the rail bed. Teague's train stood on the next track over, amber light spilling from its windows. She hugged the rails, risking a glance up. She could make out shapes moving around behind the tinted windows, but nothing definite.

"*Ah, shit.*"

That was exactly not what she wanted to hear from her handler. "Merlin?"

"*We have another guy coming around the back of the train, he's ten seconds away from making the turn. He'll see you for sure.*"

Sarah drew the Scorpion and held it close to her chest. If she was spotted, the mission would be blown.

"*Five seconds, still coming.*"

"*Lynx, get out of there!*" Grim came on the line, snapping out the order.

But Sarah could see what Grim could not, a third guard looking right at the spot where she would emerge if she moved. There was literally nowhere she could go.

Sarah exhaled half a breath, and then braced the pistol with her other hand. She aimed down the length of the train, not toward the spot where the roving guard would appear, but at the bulb of a flickering sodium lamp illuminating one of the station's signs.

As the guard came into view, she squeezed the trigger. The sound of its discharge smothered by the Scorpion's integral silencer, the pistol shot shattered the bulb with a tinkling of broken glass.

The two guards reacted, both pivoting toward the sound and away from Sarah. She burst into motion, dashing across the median strip between the rail tracks, and in the fractions of a second before the guards dismissed the noise, she slid down and into the darkness beneath the train, secreting herself between the axles.

"*Close one,*" said Charlie, releasing the breath he'd been holding in a plosive exhale.

"Easy," she whispered. "Lynx is in position." Sarah found footholds among the machinery on the underside of the carriage and maneuvered herself into place. She peered at her OPSAT, bringing up a diagram of the train cars. There was a hatch in the floor a few meters away. "Good to go."

"*Lynx, Paladin Actual,*" said Grim. "*Hold position and stand by.*"

Sarah nodded an affirmation, even though Grim would not have been able to see her. She could hear faint sounds coming from the train above her; raised voices arguing, indistinct in their anger.

"Damn it, I wish I had something less tasteful to throw at your sorry ass!" Teague glared across the cabin at Patel, scanning the well-appointed lounge car for an object he could use as a makeshift missile.

He snatched up a heavy paperweight and menaced the other man with it. "You are a drag, Samir. A slow-walking, time-wasting, pointless drag of a human being! You weigh me down like an anchor! Why are you even here if you don't anything?" Teague changed his mind about the paperweight and slammed it down on a desk to underline his point. "*Yes* just isn't in your dictionary, is it?"

Patel said nothing, letting Brody blow out his annoyance. He'd been in this exact same conversation more times than he could remember, acting like the other man's verbal punching bag while the mercurial genius let rip and blamed him for everything wrong in his life.

Nearby, Teague's redheaded assistant clasped his secure digital tablet, eyes downcast, afraid to draw her employer's attention lest she become dragged into the argument. Right now, the source of Teague's anger was the fact that the train's wireless communications and data was running slow, and somehow that was Samir Patel's fault. More of the satellite cluster that carried the signal would be overhead in a few minutes, but that wasn't good enough for Brody. He wanted it *now*, like the petulant man-child he was.

The words almost slipped out into the air before Patel caught himself. He tensed, realizing how close he had come to actually voicing the treacherous thought. That wasn't like him. Usually, he could bury his contempt for Teague down deep, but today that didn't work. It bubbled up to the surface.

And not before time, Patel told himself. *That arrogant, spiteful prick deserves everything he's going to get.*

"Are you listening to me?" Teague demanded. "Shit, I'm talking to myself here." He stalked across to the bar, pushing his assistant out of the way, and found a bottle of mineral water.

"I'm... I'm sorry, Brody, I'm just distracted."

"By what?" Teague twisted off the top of the bottle and gulped down the water.

"Everything!" Patel threw up his hands, his exasperation finally poking through. "I thought we had a plan for Gordian Sword, Brody! A program to monetize that technology for years to come! I mean, no one else is even close to where we are with quantum computing, we're decades ahead of our closest rivals!"

He didn't need to add that they had cemented that lead by assassinating the lead researchers in the team who had developed Gordian Sword, so that no rivals could duplicate the technology or find a way to neutralize it. Patel thought of that as akin to the commands of ancient pharaohs, who killed the architects of their treasure-laden sepulchers so that no grave robbers would know how to breach the tombs.

Teague made a *talky-talky* motion with his fingers. "Listen to you go on. You just proved my point." He shook his head, as if he were disappointed in the other man. "You're so basic, buddy. Money doesn't matter. Never did, never will."

Patel's jaw hardened at the monumental conceit in the other man's declaration. Only someone like Brody Teague, who had grown up wanting for nothing on the teat of his family's inherited wealth, could possibly believe that was true.

He carried on, spouting inane catchphrases about his plan for a *worldwide reset*, for his ideal of *technology unchained*, but Patel didn't register the words.

Teague had never been hungry a day in his life, never wanted for something he couldn't get. Not like Samir Patel, the son of poor immigrants who had suffered and gone without so their brightest son could study at MIT. Teague had the luxury of his idiotic pipedream, because even if it failed, he would still be cocooned in his privilege and his parents' riches. He was happy to take the money-printing machine that was Gordian Sword and sacrifice it to a whim, without considering for one second those who would be left with nothing.

He will not understand, thought Patel. *He's incapable of it.*

A soft chime sounded from his smartwatch, and Patel scrutinized the device. The message displayed was from one of the Russian's men, curt and to the point.

Ready for pick-up.

"What now?" demanded Teague. "Are we moving? Why the hell did we even stop in the middle of this crappy country, anyhow?"

"We'll be on our way again in a few moments," Patel told him, soothing his irritation. "I'll, uh, check with the train crew."

"Do that," said Teague, moving to snatch the tablet computer from his assistant. "Oh, finally, we have some bars. Great!" He was already forgetting about the conversation, losing himself in the screen.

Teague didn't even notice when Patel left, walking away into the empty dining car. Unseen by anyone, Patel went back to his smartwatch and tapped out a quick text message.

Tell Stone to go to phase two.

With a satisfied nod, Patel paused to grab the bag he had left by the door and went into the vestibule. But instead of moving down to the next carriage, he turned right and stepped off the train, on to the deserted platform.

Nîmes Garons Airport – Canton of Saint-Gilles – France

"Ah, crap." Charlie's curse echoed around the inside of the Paladin's C&C deck, drawing a hard look from Grim over at the SMI display.

He heard the same scowl in Sarah's response over the comm-net. "*Merlin, you gotta learn some radio protocol.*"

"Sorry," he replied. "It's just, we may have an issue here." He leaned forward, staring into the black-and-white video streams coming from the sticky cameras she had deployed. A recognizable figure in a business suit made his way along the station platform, as if he were some commuter returning home after a long day at work. Except this station was in the middle of nowhere, and the closest town was hardly the kind of place where a man like Samir Patel would find himself.

Grim immediately cycled into the conversation, appearing at Charlie's side. "Explain."

"I have positive ID on Target White," he continued, pointing at his screen. "He just got off the train. He's heading toward the road crossing… Is that expected?" He looked up at Grim's rigid, fixed expression. "Did we expect that?"

"*No,*" said Sarah. "*Checking OPSAT feed… OK, I see him. Where does he think he's going?*"

"Vehicle, there." Grim indicated a dark shape in the far corner of the other sticky cam screen, and as she spoke, headlights winked on. Charlie guessed it was a 4x4 or something similar, but he couldn't be certain.

On another screen, a gust of diesel smoke puffed from an exhaust grille on the flank of the locomotive at the head of the train, and the guards standing around quickly scrambled back aboard. Up ahead, signal lights changed color, indicating that the TGV had passed by and the route ahead was now clear. But Patel kept walking, making no attempt to return as the train started to roll.

"*Merlin, Lynx,*" said Sarah. "*We're on the move. What's the call here, stay or go?*"

"Target Red is the priority," Grim said firmly. "We can let Interpol gather up Mr Patel when the job is done."

"*Lynx copies.*"

Charlie muted his mike so Sarah wouldn't hear his next words. "I don't like this, Grim. Patel never leaves Teague's side,

I mean, like, *ever*. He follows the guy around like a whipped dog. It's out of character."

Grim nodded. "I don't disagree. And if we had the time and the manpower, I'd have an agent drag Patel in for some enhanced interrogation. But we don't, so he gets to walk." She hesitated, watching the screen. "For now."

On the monitor, the train picked up speed and sped away into the evening, while the tiny figure of Samir Patel approached the waiting car and climbed in. They watched the vehicle reverse off and disappear into the gloom.

"Track him," Grim ordered.

"Already working on it," said Charlie, as his hands flew across the keyboard in front of him. "But unless he takes a main highway, odds are thin we'll keep eyes on him."

"Do what you can," she said, and unmuted her mike. "Lynx, Paladin Actual. Nothing changes. Secure Target Red and the asset. Without it, Panther has nowhere to go. Understood?"

"*Roger that*," said Sarah.

Gulfstream G350 – North Sea – Altitude 8,000 Feet and Descending

Fisher's OPSAT buzzed against his wrist as the pre-programmed alarm stirred him from his sleep. He hunched forward in the overly comfortable seat and rolled the kinks out of his shoulders, casting a wary glance out of the cabin's portholes.

Silver streaks of rain lined the oval windows, dragged by the rush of wind over the fuselage. The Gulfstream vibrated from nose to tail as it turned through a pocket of turbulence, and from the cockpit, Fisher heard Kobin spit out something guttural in Ukrainian, cursing the foul weather.

As if sensing his attention, Kobin risked a glance over his shoulder. "You awake back there, Fisher? Had enough shut-eye?"

"What's our location?" He moved forward until he could see the jet's control panel.

"Time to target, two minutes and change." Kobin blew out a breath. "Y'know, I'm having second thoughts about this. I mean, there's a storm right under us. If this goes wrong..."

"Make sure it doesn't," Fisher told him. He clapped Kobin on the shoulder. "You're a good pilot, Andriy. I believe in you." His tone was flat and matter of fact.

"That's the worst encouragement I've ever had," Kobin retorted. "I mean, seriously, you're not even *trying* to sell it."

Fisher gave a shrug and went back to his stowed gear, pulling on a pack over his back. "Well, whatever happens, I'll be OK." He slapped the pack and arranged it so the strap with a black anodized D-ring was within easy reach. "I'm the one wearing a parachute."

"We could turn this bird around and fly to Norway! I know a great akvavit bar in Bergen."

"Tempting," Fisher offered, "but no." He double-checked the rest of his kit, making sure everything was cinched in tight and squared away. He couldn't afford to lose anything on the way down. "You strapped in? Masked up? 'Cause this is happening."

Kobin grimaced. "If I die, I swear I'll haunt you forever."

Fisher tapped his radio earpiece. "This is Panther. Comm check, over."

Lea Kade's voice responded a moment later. "*Solid copy, Panther. We read you, five by five.*"

Grim spoke up, giving the go-no-go confirmation. "*Panther, you are clear to commit.*"

"Panther concurs." Fisher started back down the length of the Gulfstream's narrow cabin. "I'm on my way."

Behind him, Kobin cursed again under his breath, agitatedly locking in the two point harness that secured him to the pilot's seat. He scrambled to pull down a breather mask over his face, adjusting the pipe to an oxygen cylinder at his side. "You really want to do it like this?"

"It's gotta look like an accident," called Fisher, as he moved to the emergency exit hatch over the Gulfstream's wing. "Aslanov's not stupid, he'll be monitoring local air traffic. You need to sell the lie."

"Believe me, that won't be hard." Kobin steeled himself. "OK, go for it. Good luck, you madman!"

Bracing himself against one of the seats, Fisher grasped the emergency release handle and pulled the bright red toggle. The window hatch vibrated, and he slammed his hand into the frame to dislodge it.

Then everything happened at once; the hatch disappeared into the night as the jet went into catastrophic decompression, and a howling tornado came in through the black square in the side of the cabin.

Anything not tied down was caught in the shock. Discarded magazines, glasses and other bits of debris blew out past Fisher's face as the interior of the cabin tried to equalize itself with the air pressure outside.

He could hear Kobin yelling indistinctly – the gunrunner

was either crying out in terror or laughing like a lunatic, it was hard to tell. The jet began a steep turn which became a half-roll, putting the Gulfstream into a knife-flight attitude with the wings pointing straight up and down.

Fisher let gravity push him into the wall of the cabin as it became the floor. Now the open hatch was beneath him, a dark abyss barely large enough to fit through. He waited until the last possible moment before dropping out and into the blackness.

There was the fleeting impression of a winged shape above him vanishing into the thick cloud, and then Fisher fell through layers of freezing air, rain lashing against him as he plummeted toward the turbulent waves of the North Sea.

Turning his body, Fisher pivoted until he could see the screen of his OPSAT. The device showed his descent path, and it ticked away the altitude as he fell. He was off course by a few degrees, and Fisher pitched over in the right direction.

Without warning, the clouds momentarily parted and he glimpsed a shimmering field of black far below, the surface of the sea like a mottled expanse of volcanic glass.

Somewhere down there was his target, thirty thousand tons of steel jutting out of some of the roughest water on the planet. If he missed it, the waves would take him and leave no trace.

TWENTY-ONE

Private Train – En Route – France

Studying the diagrams of the train cars on the flight through French airspace, Sarah had committed to memory the path she would take up along the underside of the carriages. But there was a world of difference between examining a virtual model on the strategic mission interface and doing it for real.

Hanging from the bottom of the trailing car, she tried not to think about the rail bed speeding past a few centimeters from her head. If she lost her grip, if she put a single foot wrong, that would be *game over*. There would not even be time for her to scream, before her body went under the spinning bogies and the life was crushed out of her.

So, no pressure. Her internal voice sounded a lot like her father's, and she frowned. Sarah remembered what he had taught her, to narrow down each challenge she faced into its smallest component parts and overcome them, piece by piece.

That became one step, then another, then another. Move after move, placing each handhold or foothold with care, testing it, then advancing. Like free-climbing, she thought, upside down, in the dark, at a hundred kilometers per hour.

Sarah sensed they were picking up speed, but she pushed that out of her mind. She was close now, right beneath her objective.

Looking up and to the right, she picked out the edges of the service hatch in the floor of the cargo wagon, and ran her fingers around it until she found the release mechanism. On a three count, she jerked the handle and felt the hatch slide back. Dim light fell through the open space, illuminating the sleepers blurring by beneath her.

"Now or never," she said aloud, and shifted her weight. The split second between releasing her grip and grabbing the lip of the hatch seemed like forever, but then she had it, and Sarah strained to pull herself up and into the wagon.

The tip of her right boot clipped the rail bed as she moved, causing a shock that ran up through her leg as if she'd touched a live cable. Sarah grunted and hauled her legs up, all the way inside. The jolt of pain was like an echo along a steel rod, and she gritted her teeth, waiting for it to subside. The hatch slid back into place, and Sarah took a deep breath, surveying her position.

The narrow cargo wagon was largely turned over to Brody Teague's mercurial needs, with a couple of large refrigerators for food and drink, and racks holding bottles or crates of ingredients for whatever rich scumbags liked for dinner. The weak glow from glass-fronted fridges lit the space, and beyond that were luggage racks and the far end of the train. But what Sarah was after lay in the other direction, toward the locomotive.

She tapped her mike pick-up. "Merlin, Lynx. Successful ingress. Proceeding to—"

The words were barely out of her mouth when the sliding door at the other end of the carriage clattered open, and a heavily-built man in a chef's tunic entered. He flicked on the lights, drenching the interior of the wagon in a harsh fluorescent glow. All shadows suddenly dispelled, Sarah was revealed in plain sight, a lithe figure in matte black crouching on the deck.

"*Merde!*" The cook gave a start as he spotted her, his eyes widening. A big guy, bald and clean-shaven, he had thick, dark eyebrows that gave him a cartoonish expression.

"*Excusez-moi,*" she offered, with a sheepish smile. Sarah was competent in a half-dozen languages, but her French was limited to little more than a handful of tourist phrases. She said the first thing that came into her mind. "*Où sont les toilettes?*"

"*Qu'est-ce que?*" The man's moment of confusion was the only advantage she had, and while his brain caught up with what he saw, Sarah launched herself off the deck and flew at him, leading with a punch that gained hard momentum.

The cook took the blow square in the jaw and his head rocked back, bouncing off the metal wall. It was enough to shock him out of his surprise and he snarled angrily, grabbing wildly, trying to pull Sarah into a bear-hug.

She danced back, avoiding the grab, but not quickly enough to get away clean. The cook snagged her wrist and yanked on it, stopping her from gaining any distance.

Should have brought that stun gun after all. Sarah had to deal with this guy quickly, before he could raise the alarm. She went for the closest thing to a weapon she could see, snatching up a champagne bottle by the neck.

As the red-faced cook pulled her closer, Sarah pivoted and struck him with the heavy bottle, once on the swing out, and again on the backstroke. The glass didn't break, and the big guy took the hits, releasing his grip and spitting epithets back at her.

Shaking it off, he grabbed at a tray of vegetables on one of the racks, pitching it at Sarah, sending the contents everywhere. She cast up her hands instinctively to deflect the throw as the cook rushed her. Before she could dodge him, the big man shoulder-charged Sarah, dragging her off her feet and shoving her into the loading door in the side of the wagon.

Blinking furiously through his pain, the cook pinned her to the panel. She still had the champagne bottle in one hand, but the angle was all wrong to hit him again.

Fighting for breath, Sarah turned the bottle in her hand and flicked off the wire cap with her thumb, then aimed it at the cook's face and applied pressure to the cork. The champagne popped, firing the dense stopper point blank into the man's eye, spattering them both with a gush of foamy liquid.

He howled, both hands clutching at his face, momentarily blinded by Sarah's makeshift weapon. She dropped out of his way and let him stumble into the loading door.

He collided heavily, jarring loose the handle that secured it in place. The door rattled open and the night flashing past outside sounded into the wagon. The cook flailed wildly, clawing at Sarah. She dropped, striking out with a scissor kick that knocked the man's right leg out from under him. He fell back, arms windmilling, and skidded through the open door. With a startled cry, he tumbled away into the dark.

Panting with effort, Sarah pulled the hatch closed, hoping for his sake that the big man would land on something soft.

She became aware of Charlie's agitated voice in her ear. *"Lynx! Respond! Are you all right?"*

"Fine," she told him, gathering herself, wiping her gloved hands on a discarded kitchen cloth. "Just a little sticky."

Site Five – Nyx Oil Platform – North Sea

Fisher had waited until the absolute last second before deploying the chute, stretching the moment out before giving the D-ring a hard pull. It was a calculated risk, committing to the low opening, and even as the black canopy unfurled above him, he knew he was coming down too fast.

The rig rose up, a collection of metal shapes on three thick pillars that vanished into the churning sea, lit by floodlights blurred by the downpour. The towering central derrick, festooned with solar panels and surrounded by an orchard of skinny windmills, glowed in the red haze from its marker lights.

Fisher worked the chute's lines, bringing himself in to a curving turn over the rig's empty helipad and the roof of the habitat block. Both were too brightly lit for his liking, without a patch of shadows to aim for. Aware of the height he was losing with each passing second, he went around the top of the derrick and scanned for somewhere to put down. He counted on the foul weather to be keeping the crew inside, but that didn't mean he could loiter too long. Every second in the air risked detection.

Out of nowhere, a blast of wind filled the chute and shoved Fisher off his line, jerking him in the direction of the wellhead. The metal gantry filled his vision, and he twisted his body, dragging hard on the lines to pitch the chute away before the gust slammed him into the tower.

The move avoided the collision, but lift bled out of the canopy and Fisher dropped quickly. He aimed as best he could at the nearest landing spot – the rain-slick surface atop a cube of cargo containers – and descended.

He skidded as he touched down and fell forward into a roll. Lines and chute gathered around him, threatening to wrap Fisher in a deadly embrace, but he managed to arrest his momentum before it carried him over the edge and down to the steel deck.

Flicking out the karambit blade sheathed at his wrist, Fisher cut himself free of the black canopy and gathered up the material before the wind could fill it again. He tied the mass into a bulky bundle, and after climbing down to the deck, he stowed it out of sight.

Taking a moment to survey the platform, he held his breath and listened for sounds of approaching boots; but aside from the steady hiss of the falling rain and a rumble of thunder, there was nothing. He was down and safe, unseen and unheard.

Fisher tapped his throat mike. "Paladin, Panther. On site, no contact."

"*Paladin Actual confirms,*" said Grim, her voice a cool whisper. "*Clear to proceed.*"

He nodded at that, putting away the knife, exchanging it for his SC-IS pistol, checking over the gun. "Status check on Lynx." *How is Sarah?*

"*Lynx is optimal, Panther.*" The unspoken part of Grim's reply was clear. *Stay in your lane and concentrate on your own mission.*

"What about Jackal?" Fisher glanced up at the low, heavy clouds. The call-sign had been Sarah's idea, and although

Kobin hadn't liked it at first, the name had grown on him. "Did he make it?"

"*We lost radar contact with Jackal's aircraft shortly after your egress.*" Drew briefly cycled into the conversation to relay the relevant information. "*Last known position had it heading east toward the Scandinavian coastline.*"

"He'll make it," said Fisher, half to himself. "He's too damn irritating to die."

Putting aside all thought of Kobin's fate, he held his pistol close, raising it to eye level. Two pinpoint shots doused a pair of caged lights casting a pool of illumination ahead of him, giving Fisher a corridor of darkness to follow.

As he moved through the lashing rain, he heard the creak and bang of a metal hatch opening and closing on the level below. Fisher froze, looking down through the open lattice of the deck's gridwork, and found the source of the sound.

A muscular man in a rain slicker bearing the GreenSea logo walked out into the driving rain, with another person in a white lab coat draped over his shoulder. Fisher saw immediately that the figure in the white coat was very definitely dead, their eyes open and staring at nothing.

A technician, he guessed. *Did they piss off the wrong person?*

The man in the slicker came to a guard rail, beyond which there was only the long drop to the sea below, and he let the body fall to the deck, pausing to adjust the hood keeping the rain off his face. Fisher noted two more details; slicker-guy had a PP-19 Vityaz sub-machine gun on a rig across his chest, and the dead man's manner of dispatch had been the slitting of his throat, the mess of gore from the wound across his neck soaked across into the front of his lab coat.

Throat cut, mused Fisher. *Aslanov's style.*

He'd known from the get-go that there was a good chance the assassin might be on site at the rig, but seeing the aftermath of the man's handiwork confirmed it.

A new tension settled into his bones. How many times had he been this close to Aslanov before, only for his enemy to slip through his grasp?

Not tonight, he vowed. *Tonight, I finish what I left undone in Georgia.*

Waiting for the optimal moment, Fisher stayed in the shadows until the man in the slicker bent down to the luckless technician's corpse. He had to use both hands to gather up the body, and once he did, Fisher slipped off the upper level and dropped unseen to the deck behind him.

In two quick steps, he was at the man's back, the blocky muzzle of the SC-IS jammed into his throat.

"*Chyort!*" Cursing in his native language, the man stiffened in shock and let go of the body, letting it tumble away into the darkness.

Switching to Russian, Fisher snaked his free hand around the man's waist and pulled the PP-19 off its sling. "Try anything stupid and I'll open your skull."

The man in the slicker gave a jerky nod.

"Who was he?"

"Uh… LeBeau," came the wary reply. "One of the geeks from the tech core."

"Why did Aslanov kill him?" Fisher threw out the name to confirm his theory, and the reply did exactly that.

"Said he is… dealing with troublemakers."

Fisher filed that bit of information away. "Where is he now?"

"The core." The man tried to move his arm, to point toward where the rig's lower decks met sea level, but Fisher pushed the pistol deeper into the flesh of his neck and he halted. "Down below. See?"

From this vantage point, on one of the higher tiers of the platform, Fisher could pick out the enclosed access shaft several decks below that led to Site Five's deepest levels. But to reach it would take him across a wide open stretch of floodlit surface, an arena-like space surrounded on all sides by high walls. A perfect kill box.

As if intuiting his thoughts, the man in the slicker sneered. "You won't get anywhere near him. He'll cut you too!"

The bigger man made his move, the inevitable flex that Fisher knew would come. He tried to drive his elbow into his assailant's gut, but he lost his breath when the Splinter Cell agent put the pistol frame across his throat and choked the air from him.

A bullet would have been quicker to do the work, but this way was quieter, and with a wet crackle of breaking cartilage, Fisher snapped his neck.

Pausing only to send the dead man and his gun into the sea after the luckless LeBeau, Fisher set about continuing his descent.

Private Train – En Route – France

The vestibule that connected the cargo wagon and the kitchen carriage was a narrow, flexible tunnel of rubber and plastic, constantly in motion as the train clattered along the rails. Sarah could have continued to move through it, forward in the direction of the locomotive, but she knew that with each step closer to Teague, the greater her chances became of running into a serious problem.

Fighting off the angry cook had been an unexpected complication she didn't want to repeat, and it was likely that anyone else she encountered on the private train would be armed.

She pulled her knife from its sheath – a custom Splinter Cell-issue Protector with a serrated spine and a fractal edge – and set to work. The blade went cleanly into the material of the vestibule, allowing her to make a cut in it large enough to fit through. Widening the hole, Sarah climbed up and wriggled back out into the open air, this time sliding on to the top of the train.

She flicked her tri-goggles down, switching to low-light mode, grateful to have the biting, cold wind deflected away from her eyes. Then, ducking low to avoid the overhead electrical wires, Sarah crouch-walked up the roof of the carriage, with the same sure-footed advance she had used when dangling beneath it. A blur of countryside rolled past either side of her, dark trees, fields, and the distant lights of towns lost in motion and speed.

She sensed the movement of the train up through her limbs and went with the rocking motion, advancing in a zigzag rather than straight up the middle. Skirting a skylight in the roof of the kitchen car, she quickly made her way to the next vestibule. According to the diagrams, the connecting carriage was the lounge car, and the most likely place she would find Brody Teague.

Sarah radioed in her position, but didn't wait for Charlie to confirm it, and after a three-count, she stepped lightly over the gap and kept moving.

Like the kitchen car, this carriage had skylights, but rather than avoid them, Sarah pressed herself flat on the roof and crawled to the closest one. Activating her OPSAT in surveillance mode, she attached one end of a flexible snake camera to a port on the device, then fed the tiny sensor cable through a gap in the skylight's frame.

The video feed from the camera appeared on the OPSAT screen, while the audio component went directly to Sarah's earpiece. She heard footsteps and saw Teague's assistant walk into frame. The redheaded woman's body language was closed off and fearful.

"Merlin has sound and picture," reported Charlie. *"Can you pan it around?"*

Sarah adjusted her position, staying as low as she could against the buffeting winds, and manipulated the snake-cable. The image moved to find Teague himself, reclining in a wide chair with a tablet computer in his hands. Behind him, near the far doorway, she saw a granite-faced bodyguard.

"Lynx has visual confirmation on Target Blue," she whispered. "He's right below me."

She watched him flick across the tablet's screen with his index finger, occasionally sneering at whatever he was looking at.

"Can you believe this crap?" Teague asked the question aloud, but not in a way that invited an answer. "I'm giving these idiots the opportunity to hit any target in the world, and what do they pick? Gridlock in Times Square. Shutting down hospitals in Germany." He sighed. "This is dull. They could be launching ICBMs and starting meltdowns!"

"Perhaps… they are starting small," ventured the assistant.

Teague didn't bother to look up at her. "Did I ask for your input?"

"*He's reviewing a target list,*" said Charlie. "*Oh man, this is moving faster than we thought.*"

Sarah found herself wondering how far this could go. No one in Fourth Echelon doubted that Gordian Sword worked – they had seen it in real time, and, like the rest of the world, witnessed the harrowing footage of debris from the Atlantic International flight being pulled out of the ocean.

But how much mayhem could the machine unleash at full operating capacity? If Teague's creation was capable of initiating multiple attacks at once, the world would never know a moment of peace.

It was a horror of the modern society that too many major cities around the globe lived with daily terrorist attacks. Teague's machine had the power to extend that tragic reality to all of them.

Sarah felt for the Scorpion pistol in its holster on her thigh. If taking the man's life right this second would stop the threat, she would have done so.

"You know what?" Teague was talking again, as if performing for his own sake. "Maybe I'll add some spice myself. Burn down the Pentagon. Nuke the Kremlin." He chuckled and shook his head. "I mean, I can't build a road to the future without chopping down the dead wood."

Sarah watched as Teague looked up from the tablet, glancing around the room as if searching for something. Sensing a need, his assistant stepped closer, and the billionaire thrust the computer into her hands.

"Can I get you something, Brody?"

"Where the fuck is Samir?" His expression shifted, becoming annoyed. "Did I say he could go back to his cabin and jerk off, no I did not!" Teague's voice rose as he realized his long-suffering friend was not within earshot. "Find him!"

The assistant held the tablet to her, protectively. "Well, it's just that–"

"*Did I ask for your input?*" he barked. "This is not a conversation, this is me telling you what to do!"

The assistant shook her head. "I'm afraid that's not possible, Brody." And then, for the first time, Sarah saw the ghost of a smile on the other woman's lips.

TWENTY-TWO

Site Five – Nyx Oil Platform – North Sea

Aslanov let Diaz walk ahead of him into the dimly lit operations room, but the technician kept looking back over his shoulder every few steps, unwilling to take his eyes off him for even a minute. Diaz was terrified of him, and with good reason.

The assassin had made the technician stand by and watch as he murdered LeBeau, forcing him to witness the other man take his last breath. As object lessons went, there were few better ways to instill obedience. With Bray and LeBeau both feeding the crabs, there would be no further outbreaks of conscience among Gordian Sword's programmers.

"This is the trench." Diaz was sweating, despite the temperature-controlled environment, as he took in the control center with a sweep of his hand. "From here we can monitor the unit's functions in real time."

Aslanov gave a nod, taking it in. Stepped like the tiers of a theater, the room was divided into three levels, two of computer consoles, and the lowest opening on to a set of heavy, see-through pressure doors. The console levels were tended to by a handful of other techs in lab coats, who barely looked up from their work as he passed. Their screens showed complex waterfalls of digital code that meant nothing to the Russian. He looked away and focused on the cylinder of brushed steel and frosted glass on the far side of the double doors. Surrounded by a thick coolant sheath, it was fed by pipes that disappeared into the decking.

The weapon itself; the Gordian Sword in all its subdued glory.

Stepping past Diaz and the other techs, Aslanov went right up to the glass barrier so he could look down into the bowels of the rig. Beneath the steel cylinder, through gridded deck plates, huge tanks full of brackish liquid rippled in the reflected light. Pumps worked ceaselessly, dragging the cold water of the North Sea in from outside, filtering it through the tanks and into the cooling system. Aslanov could hear the low rumble of the waves against the outer walls of the operations room; they were below sea level here, inside a giant metal module suspended beneath the rig's main superstructure on huge vibration dampeners.

"It's secure," insisted Diaz, his voice going up an octave. Ever since Aslanov deigned to let him live, the man had been falling over himself to assure the Russian that Site Five was totally protected from any outside influence. "We're following Brody's protocols to the letter."

"Good," allowed Aslanov. That would make it easier to assume control when the moment came. He checked the battered Pobeda watch on his wrist, noting the time. *Not long now.*

Diaz hovered nearby, clearing his throat to draw the Russian's attention. "I want you to know, I didn't want any part of Bray's complaints." The words fell out of him in a rush. "I mean, there were some anomalies in the taskings, but I was quite happy to follow orders."

The man was frantically back-tracking, desperate to make sure he didn't share the fates of Bray and LeBeau. Aslanov didn't care. Anyone vocal enough to question what Gordian Sword had done was now dead. Only the timid worker ants remained, and those he could easily deal with.

He glanced at Diaz. "You knew Drake and Virtanen, yes? And the others on the project development team?" Aslanov had been close enough to them to hear their last breaths, each one put down on Brody Teague's orders.

Diaz nodded, and he grew pale. "Yes."

"Do you know what happened to them?"

Diaz couldn't bring himself to answer, but that was more than enough to show that *he did*. He licked his lips and when he spoke again, it was the plea that Aslanov had expected. "Please, sir, I… I have a wife and a family."

Aslanov nodded. "If you want to see them again, return to your duties."

The other man nodded again and slunk away, relieved to be dismissed at last. The Russian felt a vibration in his jacket pocket and retrieved the old flip-phone, snapping it open.

"Mr Patel." He pressed the handset to his ear, catching background noise in the moment before the other man spoke. Aslanov heard the hum of a car engine. Teague's long-suffering business partner was on the road somewhere.

"*Mr Stone,*" came the reply, the alias barely registering with him. "*Are we ready to proceed?*" He could hear the hesitation in the other man's words.

"Are *you*?"

Aslanov turned back to study the steel cylinder inside the core chamber. Within that casing, the Gordian Sword quantum computer ran its trillion-fold calculations in the blink of an eye, effortlessly outpacing every other digital device on the worldwide web. For such a prosaic-looking piece of machinery, it was incredible to consider the huge destructive potential it contained.

He wondered if this must have been what it was like for the men of Russia's *First Lightning* program, the Soviet equivalent of America's Manhattan Project, when they stood in the presence of the original atomic bombs. He was looking at a weapon that would change the face of the world forever.

"This technology is too valuable to be left in the hands of that arrogant child Teague," continued Aslanov. "He will squander its potential, and for what? Some foolish dream of remaking society in his image."

The Russian was, as his people often were, a pragmatist. Teague's fantasy of technology unchained was unrealistic and doomed to failure, tethered to a fool whose monumental ego would drag it down. But a more cunning man – one, perhaps, who had spent his life navigating the darkest, most dangerous shadows – could use what Teague had created to become rich beyond his wildest dreams.

"*He won't listen to me,*" said Patel. "*He never did.*" His dejection was pathetic.

Patel had spent years of his life hanging on to Brody Teague's coattails, only now aware of all that he had wasted. Predictably, that sadness swiftly changed into anger.

"*To hell with him! Let's finish this.*"

"That is the spirit." Aslanov had more to say, but an alert flashed on one of the technician's panels and he saw Diaz dash across the room to take a look. "Go to the safe house, as we planned," he added. "I will contact you when it is done."

Patel started to reply, but the Russian had already snapped the flip-phone shut. He advanced on Diaz, seeing the trepidation in the other man's expression.

"One of the guards missed his check-in," said the technician.

"Raise the security level to yellow." Aslanov's eyes narrowed, his hand instinctively reaching for the *karatel* blade sheathed under his cuff.

Taking the stairwell down risked being spotted on any one of a dozen security cameras, so Fisher weighed the risks and took a more direct route to the rig's main deck. Descending hand over hand, he worked his way down the patchwork of welded metal sheets cladding the outside of the platform, his fingers finding handholds around the edges of the ice-cold steel panels.

The rain bombarded him from above, accompanied by booms of thunder, each one closer than the last. The salt spray from the sea lashed at him from below, becoming fiercer the lower he went.

Meter by tortuous meter, he made his way down until his boots thudded on to the deck. Shaking off a shiver, Fisher found a shadowed corner to gather himself and briefly rest the aching muscles in his arms.

Out of nowhere, an alarm high on one wall let out a single, strangled whoop of noise, echoing across the open expanse of the rig. Fisher tensed, waiting for the sound to continue, but it didn't.

So, not a full-on alert, he guessed, but a warning. He scowled at the thought. A higher level of vigilance made his job that much harder. *Better move now, while I still have some advantage.*

Flexing his hands, Fisher shifted position, scanning the area ahead of him. From above, the arena-like space between him and the core access had looked risky, but now he was right on top of it, the reality was even worse. Cover was minimal and barely a square meter wasn't drenched by the amber glow of the floodlights overhead. The ally of a Splinter Cell was the darkness, and he lacked it here. Shooting out each individual light up above would take too long and give away his position, but the notion was sound. If there were no shadows, Fisher would have to create them.

He flicked his tri-goggles down over his face and cycled through the vision modes. Low-light was a blurry, useless mess, and thermal, with its blooms of red-orange against cold blue-black surfaces, was little better. The third mode turned Fisher's world into a shimmering, ghostly framework of edges and lines, showing the invisible fields of electromagnetic energy all around him.

Peering up with the EMF mode engaged, Fisher tracked the paths of seething white that were the power cables leading to the floods. They congregated in a glowing rectangle twenty meters away across the deck, a regulator unit that fed power from the main generators to the hissing lamp heads above.

Flicking up the goggles again, Fisher drew his pistol and aimed at his target, bracing the gun over the crook of his other arm. He fired three rounds to make certain, but the sudden gout of brilliant blue sparks from the regulator told him he was right on the money. The lights around the deck faded out, turning the lower level of the platform into a maze of hulking black shapes and depthless gloom.

Pulling the dark to him like armor, Fisher broke from his cover, executing a tactical reload on the go. The gantry that would take him the rest of the way down to Site Five's core levels was a quick sprint away, and he ducked under a support girder as he moved, picking his way through the blackness.

He was halfway there when a flare of interior light spilled out across the deck, announced by a hatch banging open. Fisher ducked back behind a heap of crates and waited for the hatch to close again, not willing to risk his night-adapted eyes against the brightness.

Rusted hinges squealing, the hatch slammed shut, and Fisher heard the clank of the dog levers being pulled to seal it. Whoever had come out looking for him was smart enough to block the way behind them. That suggested a level of forethought that gave the Splinter Cell operative pause.

Dropping low, Fisher chanced peering around the edge of the crates in a brief flicker of distant lightning.

Framed by the lashing rain, two muscular figures in helmets and combat gear surveyed the deck, looking for any sign of intruders. Their outfits had the same matte black sheen as Fisher's tactical suit, but they had the extra weight of an assault pack and a light plate carrier vest. Each one gripped a sound-suppressed SR-2 Veresk at the ready, the long snouts of the Russian-made sub-machine guns panning left and right.

Fisher calculated his angles, figuring out the lethal math that would allow him to take these men out of commission as swiftly as possible. Just that quick glance told him that these were not common rent-a-merc types. Like knew like; they carried themselves with the self-assurance of professional tier-one operators.

Then the odds shifted again as a familiar, distinctive sound reached Fisher's ears, a sharp metallic click followed by the high-pitched whine of electronics powering up. The gunmen pulled down vision rigs, bulbous crimson-eyed sensors that covered one side of their face – Voron-issue goggles, as capable as Fisher's own triad optics.

He threw a glance in the direction of the gantry. *They'll nail me for sure if I make a run for it.* Fisher took a silent breath and steeled himself. *So, we do this the hard way.*

For a brief moment, the lights in the operations room flickered, and a warning flashed red on a screen in Aslanov's sightline.

"What is going on?" he demanded.

Diaz rushed to check, and with a nervous frown, he looked back at the Russian. "A power surge from the main generator," he explained. "One of the regulator units went offline unexpectedly. It won't affect Gordian Sword!" Diaz waved in the direction of the core module. "Everything down here operates off its own separate electricity supply."

"Show me." Aslanov marched over to the technician's side to look at the screen. A wireframe graphic of the Site Five rig showed a blinking tag over the location of the errant regulator. Instinctively, Aslanov looked up. It was located a few decks above them, close to the support gantry.

"It happens sometimes," said Diaz. "The bad weather out here can play havoc with–"

"It is not the storm." Aslanov cut him off, a chilly certainty settling in his mind. "We have a trespasser." He activated the radio handset he had taken from Bray's corpse and switched to speaking in Russian. "Go to alert level red, weapons clear. All stations report in immediately. Any unverified presences are to be considered hostile, repeat *hostile*. Shoot on sight."

He listened to the guard posts sounding off one by one as he marched across the room, pushing Diaz aside. Aslanov found the control console he was looking for, manned by another of Teague's worker drones, a middle-aged woman with auburn hair pinned up in a severe, unflattering style.

"The current target packages," he told her. "I want to see them."

Reluctantly, the technician gave a nod and brought up the two attack programs that were currently cycling through Gordian Sword's matrix prior to activation.

The first upload was the objective selected by the anti-globalist terror group called the White Masks, who had paid to target the electrical grid in the heart of New York City. Once engaged, Gordian Sword would slice through the firewalls surrounding NYC's vital power lines, plunging businesses and homes into darkness, trapping countless people in traffic jams, stalled elevators, and subway trains.

The second upload had been chartered by the Phoenix Group, a cadre of ruthless anarchists based in Europe. Their attack was a massive denial-of-service strike against the German national health network, programmed to crash every computer in every hospital and clinic from Hamburg to Munich.

"Delete both of them," ordered Aslanov, producing a memory stick from an inner pocket of his jacket.

"Sir?" The woman blinked in confusion. "I don't understand.

Brody gave us these directives himself." She indicated her screen. "We're less than five minutes from trigger point."

"Circumstances have changed." He offered her the memory stick. "You are to upload the replacement target package on this." The new data on the stick had come directly from Samir Patel, diligently programmed by the man after Aslanov had carefully maneuvered him into thinking it was his idea. It had been a simple enough task for someone with Aslanov's skills to use Patel's petty jealousy to manipulate him.

The technician looked in Diaz's direction for confirmation and got an agitated nod in return. "Do what he says!"

"Very well," she sniffed, plucking the stick from the Russian's fingers. With a few quick keystrokes, the woman shut down the active programs running through the quantum computer and brought the machine back to standby mode.

Lines of data vanished, eating themselves as the Phoenix and White Mask attacks were stalled before they could begin. Aslanov wondered what the men who had paid their blood money would make of that.

They will believe Teague has cheated them, he imagined. *A lie that may have use to me, if he somehow survives the next few hours.*

The new attack package loaded in swiftly, filling the screen with new variables, target data, and hacking vectors. The Russian glimpsed pieces that he recognized – a rail network map of Southern France, a series of wireless communications protocols, the control panel functions for a high-speed locomotive. A faint smile played on his lips.

"Package is viable," said the technician.

"Activate it," he ordered.

"Understood." The woman highlighted a digital tab showing

the word COMMIT and with a single click of her mouse, Gordian Sword went to work.

Aslanov couldn't stop himself from looking up at the steel cylinder beyond the pressure doors, as if expecting to see some showy flash of light, some visual cue that the quantum computer was fully engaged. But there was only the same train of green indicator lights blinking steadily up and down its flanks.

He smiled in cold self-amusement. To an old soldier like him, weapons of war were meant to instill shock and awe, to radiate lethality like the heat of an inferno. But this quiet, humming machine had fired a shot in a very different kind of conflict, one operating in the ghost world that underpinned his reality, deep in the dark web battleground of ones and zeroes.

"System compromise successful," said the technician, reading the result off her screen. "We have full control of the target."

"First blood," said Aslanov, to himself. "Now, shall we twist the knife?"

Vitali advanced across the rig's deck, his heavy combat boots thudding against the platform as he stared through the driving rain. Thunder boomed high above, and the downpour drummed loudly on his helmet, sluicing off it and down his plate carrier.

He tuned out the noise. Through his right eye he saw a red-lit version of the world, the sensors in the Voron optics rendering the area around him in shades of blood.

A few meters away, Georgy signaled him silently, making the signs for *spread out* and *search* with his fingers. Vitali nodded his assent, and the two men split up to cover the rain-swept deck.

He adjusted the optics, scanning shadowed corners for any signs of movement. At least three people had failed to report in at the latest headcount, and while it was possible that the storm might take the unwary, the odds on so many suffering that fate at once were slim.

Vitali hoped for action. On Aslanov's orders, he and Georgy had been stuck on this rusting steel island for the past month, with no one but these computer geeks for company, and his patience was diminishing. He wanted to be at the sharp end, in the fight, like the good old days.

Adjusting his grip around the butt of his SMG, Vitali turned his head, and a sudden shock jolted through him.

There! From the corner of his eye, the gunman saw part of the crimson shadows break off and drift away. He turned sharply on his heel, bringing in the SR-2 high and tight to aim the weapon's barrel in the direction of the ghostly shape.

A man in black, a face hidden behind glowing optics; that was all Vitali had time to register before the angular shape in the intruder's hand released a brief jag of muzzle flare.

He tried to veer away, but the mass of his gear slowed his reactions. Two bullets smacked into Vitali's body armor above his left breast, and distantly he knew that the rounds would have hit his throat and face had he moved a heartbeat slower.

Reflexively, Vitali jerked the trigger of his weapon, spraying a burst of fire in his attacker's direction. The rushing hiss of the rain swallowed the sound of the muffled discharge, the bullets sparking off the metal walls.

Heat and pain bloomed across Vitali's chest where he took

the hits, but the rounds had not penetrated. The rain sizzled as it spattered against the damaged armor, and he recovered with a shaky, agonized breath. Through the optic, he saw nothing. The intruder had vanished.

"*Report!*" Georgy called out from the far end of the open deck, his voice coming over Vitali's headset.

"Single target with sidearm," he replied. "Come to me, we'll trap him between us."

"*Moving!*" He spotted a shape in the middle distance and saw the red glow of the Voron goggles as Georgy jogged back toward him.

Vitali went low, as another shot came out of the darkness, ringing harmlessly off a steel support post near his head. Once more, he fired two bursts in the rough direction of his attacker, but it was like trying to snatch clouds out of the sky.

In the wet and the dark, cradled by the roaring storm, every gunshot was smothered, every footstep lost. Vitali's senses prickled. He was breathing hard, laboring with the pain spreading down his chest. Finding cover, he dropped and probed his torso beneath the distorted armor plate, finding several cracked ribs.

"*Where did he go?*" Georgy whispered in his ear. "*I have no target.*"

"He's a man, not a ghost," Vitali said firmly, chewing on his pain. Checking the remaining ammunition in the SR-2's magazine, he drew a deep breath of rust and razors, and ventured out of his concealment.

The storm cell was on top of the rig now. The lightning flashed, the answering rumble of thunder barely a half-second behind it. In that brief moment of sharp-edged illumination,

Vitali looked through his naked eye and saw the figure in black atop a low mound of crates, training a pistol in his direction.

This time he wasn't quick enough to save himself from the shots that took him down. The first round hit him in the head, the shot shattering his cheekbone and ripping open the side of his face. The second round went through Vitali's neck and sent out a spray of arterial blood.

The waterlogged deck came up to meet him and Vitali felt numbness gathering at the ends of his limbs. Burning with agony, he tried vainly to press his hand to the ragged wound in his throat, but hot fluid flowed through his fingers, filling his nostrils with a coppery reek. He was bleeding out, fated to a protracted, excruciating end.

Vitali's attacker came into view at the edge of his fogged sight, and the only clear detail visible to him was three, unblinking green eyes. The intruder's gun came up again, and the next shot was a mercy.

TWENTY-THREE

Private Train – En Route – Approaching
French/Swiss Border

"*No*" was not a word that Brody Teague heard often. In fact, he had built a life for himself that revolved around never having to be told that he could not have what he wanted, whenever he wanted it. That was the thing about being born into money, living with it each day of your life, breathing it in like the air around you.

You grew to expect the world to work for you. And when it didn't, when you were actually *refused* something... That wasn't supposed to happen.

Teague rose to his feet, glaring across the lounge car at his assistant, his irritation growing by the second as she maintained a vapid, porcelain-doll expression. "What's your name?"

"I've worked for you for the last six months," she said, her eyes widening. "I've been around you fifteen hours a day, every day. You don't remember it?"

"Of course not," he said dismissively. "I don't pay attention to details that don't matter. But I want to know it now. I want to know who is wasting my time!"

"Katya," she said, looking away. "My name is Katya."

Teague clapped his hands together. "Well, honey, if you don't find me Samir Patel in the next five minutes, your name will be *fired*."

"I am not aware of his exact location," she told him. An electronic chime sounded, and the woman glanced at her smartwatch. The faint, infuriating smile on her face returned. "You have an incoming video call."

"Is that him?" Teague turned to the far wall as a panel slid back to reveal a widescreen monitor concealed behind it. A test pattern flicked on, and he recognized the familiar start-up routine of a T-Tec encrypted satellite link. "Did he get off the train? That little shit!"

But the face that appeared on the monitor did not belong to Samir Patel. *"Good evening, Mr Teague."* The craggy face of the old Russian agent filled the screen, and in the background, the consoles of the Site Five operations room were clearly visible. *"I am sorry to tell you that there has been a change of plans."*

"What are you talking about? I make the plans!"

"Not presently. Gordian Sword is no longer under your control. The choices you have made with it are… self-interested. You have been removed from the decision loop."

A contemptuous snort escaped him. *"You're* trying to push *me* out? You goddamned fossil! Old farts like you can't work a TV remote without having a stroke, what the hell are you going to do with a quantum computer?"

"I admit, I lack the required knowledge in some areas. Mr

Patel is handling the technical details," Aslanov explained, and Teague's hands balled into fists. *"While I have been promoted to a management position,"* continued the Russian.

Teague swore violently and kicked over a coffee table, scattering debris across the carpeted flooring. "Samir betrayed me!" He shot an acidic glare at his assistant. "You knew about this?"

"Mr Patel asked me to relay a message," said Aslanov. *"His exact words were:* You had this coming, asshole. *Succinct and to the point, I feel."*

"Whatever he's paying you, wring his neck and I'll double it." Teague said the words without thinking, but Aslanov grunted with amusement.

"I do not want your money, Mr Teague. I have what I want." He gestured at the steel cylinder visible behind him inside the core chamber, then shook his head sadly. *"I warned you in London, but you did not listen. Your scheme is a fantasy. You think you can set a fire across the world and then be the hero for putting out the flames. It is a child's plan."*

Teague spat back his reply. "Don't patronize me! Please don't tell me you're doing this *for the Motherland* or some basic shit like that! Nation-states are obsolete!"

"Men like you... Always so clever, but so short-sighted. You cannot see past the magnificence of your creations. And now I take it from you."

"No," Teague shouted. "Without my biometrics, Gordian Sword is a fucking paperweight!" He gestured sharply at his assistant, pointing to where his tablet computer lay on a nearby desk. "Bring me that! I'll lock him out, and that ungrateful prick too!" But Katya made no move to obey.

Aslanov looked down from the screen, shaking his head like a disappointed parent with an idiot child. *"Arrogance is blindness, Mr Teague. Yours blinded you to the fact that the man you have been denigrating for the past decade bears a grudge. Enough that he colluded with me to bring you down. Enough that he programmed a backdoor into Gordian Sword's codebase that not even you were aware of."*

"That... little... *bastard*!" Teague spat out the words; then in a sudden flurry of movement, he dashed to the intercom on the wall of the lounge and jabbed the talk button that would connect him to the driver's compartment. "I want this thing stopped right now, do you hear me? Get me a helicopter, I'll go out there myself..."

"The intercom is offline, Brody," Katya said calmly, and in response Teague took out his anger on the panel, smashing it in with his fist.

"Your machine is an impressive tool," the Russian was saying, *"the quickness with which it was able to co-opt the control systems of your train is quite remarkable."*

"What?" The color drained from Teague's face in a rush. Then he shook his head. "No, you can't do that. You're bluffing."

"Am I?" Aslanov signaled to someone offscreen, and a moment later Teague was almost thrown off his feet by a sudden jolt of acceleration. Outside, the dark mass of the countryside passing by became a blur as the train gathered speed.

Teague grabbed at the wall for support as a sickening, creeping fear rolled over him. He had planned for something like this, making sure that Gordian Sword's attack programs could not be turned against him, could not access the control permissions for his homes, his cars, his plane, his yacht, and his private train.

But he'd been too busy to handle the task himself. With growing apprehension, he remembered that he had delegated the job to Samir Patel.

That only left him with one other option. It was the most extreme of his choices, but there was no other path open to him. It would be complicated, but with the right series of commands, Teague could remotely connect to Gordian Sword's core modules, perhaps even brute-force a shutdown of the entire mainframe.

But first he would need to access it. He burst into motion, dashing toward the desk on the other side of the swaying carriage, where his encrypted tablet computer lay out of reach.

The woman – Eighteen, Katya, whoever she was – stepped in front of Teague and blocked him.

"Oh, *no*." She shook her head, and like a mask falling away, her insipid mien became something stony and unforgiving.

Teague instinctively recoiled. He'd seen the same pitiless, predatory expression on Aslanov's face.

The man on the screen looked right at the redhead and said something in Russian that Teague didn't understand, but the bleak finality of his tone made the meaning clear as the screen went dark.

"*You* work for *me!*" Teague bellowed the words, at a loss for anything else to say.

Katya shook her head. With a deft flick of her wrist, she produced a double-edged *karatel* blade. "I really don't," she told him.

"What just happened?"

Sarah heard Charlie's voice rise in alarm, but she had no

time to respond. The train's unexpected burst of speed sent a tremor along the roof of the lounge car, and she lost her grip on the frame of the skylight. She felt her boots scrape metal as the rush of cold night air grew from a hard gust to near-gale force.

Her stomach knotted and she felt herself sliding backward, toward oblivion, to be cast off the fast-moving train and into the darkness. But at the last moment, a shock of pain went through her arm, over-reaching it to full extension as her fall was arrested.

Pulled taut, the cable connecting the snake-camera head in the skylight's frame to the OPSAT on her wrist was the only thing keeping her from tumbling to her certain end.

Sarah felt it start to give. The cable wasn't designed to bear the weight of a person being dragged back by gravity and a force-ten windstorm. She scrambled forward, grasping for a handhold, and her fingers finally found purchase. Relief flooding through her, Sarah let the twisted cable disconnect and grabbed on to the skylight for dear life.

"*If I'm reading this right, someone has accessed the train's auto-drive controls,*" said Charlie, his words coming a mile-a-minute. "*The locomotive was just cut off from the rail network. It's not supposed to be going that fast, the line isn't rated for that speed!*"

Underlining the point, Sarah felt the carriage tremble as they thundered over a set of switches, the steel wheels throwing out sparks as they scraped the rails.

"*All call-signs, be advised, Teague's train has been hacked.*" Grim broke into the radio conversation, relaying the sober reality of the situation. "*Gordian Sword is no longer under Target Blue's control, but that changes nothing. Panther, Lynx, your mission objectives remain the same.*"

"Easy for you to say," Sarah muttered, dragging herself up to the corner of the skylight. Looking down into the carriage, she saw the man himself gesturing wildly at the assistant she had seen in surveillance footage of the billionaire.

And then Sarah noticed the sliver blade glinting in the woman's hand, saw her advancing on him with murderous intent, and the whole situation spun through a one-eighty.

Her mind immediately parsed the situation. *If Teague is dead, the tablet's biometric lock is useless; if the lock is useless, Dad won't be able to access the Site Five core; and everything we've done will count for nothing.*

"*Lynx, do you read? Acknowledge.*" Grim's voice called for her response, but Sarah ignored it, yanking a breaching charge from a pack on her belt.

She slapped the explosive against the skylight and pulled the arming tab, turning her face away into the ice-cold metal of the carriage roof. The charge was configured to take out heavy-duty locks or cut through door hinges, but against the polymer glass of the skylight it was a hammer-blow.

The roar of concussion tore the skylight apart and Sarah grimaced through the ringing in her ears as debris blew past her. Rolling over the edge of the broken frame, dropping straight through into the carriage's smoke-wreathed interior, she landed off balance, crunching on a mess of broken plastic and damaged furniture.

Knocked down by the discharge, Brody Teague lay sprawled over a long leather sofa, floundering as he tried to pull himself back up. The woman who wanted to kill him was still on her feet, shaking off her daze from the confined blast.

"Who the fuck are you?" Eyes wide with shock, Teague yelled the question at the new arrival.

"I'm the one who has to keep you breathing, dumbass," Sarah told him, but his slack, uncomprehending expression told her he had been half-deafened by the noise of her violent entrance.

The redheaded woman didn't need to ask the question; the intruder was in her way, and that made Sarah her enemy. Flicking her blade up and around, she lashed out with a horizontal slash that hummed through the air, and Sarah barely flinched back in time to avoid a deep cut across her bicep.

The other woman gave Sarah no time to react and came running at her.

Site Five – Nyx Oil Platform – North Sea

Georgy heard his comrade Vitali's last gasp of breath over the radio channel, and his jaw set. He knew the sound of death when he heard it.

The intruder stalking the decks of the rig moved in the middle distance, a ghost in black. Georgy swore under his breath and switched his SR-2 to single-shot mode, snapping off a couple of rounds in the enemy's direction. He saw his target go down into a slide, skidding out of the line of fire.

He stormed across the deck, through the lashing torrent of icy rain, the steel-walled arena briefly illuminated by another flash of lightning. He fired again into the following bellow of thunder, trying to keep the intruder off balance.

On the deck, Vitali's body lay in an expanding puddle of pinkish water, the dead man staring up sightlessly into the stormy sky. Georgy barely spared him a look, intent on avenging his comrade's brutal end.

The intruder had nowhere to go, forced back behind a pile of crates by Georgy's shots, into a blind corner of the deck with no exits. The gunman came around fast and ready, aiming with his SMG – and found his prey nowhere to be seen.

Impossible. He swept left and right, before catching the sound of a low whistle over the rush of the rain. Georgy raised his head and the barrel of his gun.

The man in black was astride two tiny footholds up on the wall, balancing like a gymnast on the bars. He dropped, leading with a balled fist, striking a stunning knockback blow that smashed the delicate electronics of Georgy's Voron optic into his face.

Howling in agony, he fired again and heard the intruder grunt with the impact of a bullet at point-blank range.

Georgy staggered back, his face wet with blood, and reached up to tear away the smashed vision-rig. New flares of pain shocked through his skull, and by touch alone he flicked the SR-2 over to its fully automatic setting. Squeezing the trigger, he unloaded the rest of the SMG's magazine in a braying flare of fire, carving a line of lead in his attacker's direction.

He couldn't see the man in black drop to the deck, one hand clutching at the wound in his side, the other gripping a pistol. The gun chugged twice, and sent rounds through Georgy's shin and ankle.

His scream became a drawn-out moan, and he collapsed as his legs gave out under him. Georgy heard the SR-2's breech lock open over the spent magazine, and he fought against a wave of agony, fumbling to reload the weapon.

He heard heavy steps splashing toward him, but with his eyes gummed with fresh blood, he couldn't see the man in black.

"*Prashai*," said a flint-hard voice from close at hand.

Fisher executed the second merc with a final round through the forehead, and then exhaled hard, releasing the pained breath he had been holding in.

He dropped into a crouch by the dead man and gingerly probed the hit on the side of his torso, hissing as his fingers found the open wound. A centimeter to the right and the bullet would have torn through his kidney, tearing an ugly exit on the way out of his back. The round had creased him, expending its kinetic force cutting through the ballistic material of his tactical suit and gouging a bloody furrow across his belly.

Crouching forward, Fisher pulled a self-adhering dressing from a gear pouch on his webbing and folded it into place over the injury. The matte-colored bandage was more like duct tape, but it would keep him together. He chewed on the burn of the pain, taking a shaky breath, as a new sound reached him.

It took him a second to realize he was hearing a muffled, tinny voice speaking over the dead man's radio earpiece. He heard a single word, being repeated over and over.

"*Fisher.*"

Warily, he pulled out the earpiece and held it up, uncertain if his mind was playing tricks on him. Then the voice spoke again, and he recognized the steely, metered quality of it.

"*I know you are out there, Fisher. I know you are still alive.*"

"Aslanov." There was no-one else it could be. He looked up, scanning the walls around him.

"*I sent my two best men after you,*" the Russian went on. "*Their silence answers my next question. Clearly, you have lost none of your skills.*"

He wanted to bite out a snarling retort, but Fisher reined in the impulse. Aslanov was trying to goad him, to manipulate him here as he had all those years ago in Tbilisi.

"*Do you hear me, Samuel? It must enrage you to know I have been alive and well all this time. The man who outplayed you. The target you could never hit.*" He paused, and when he spoke again, there was a note of false sorrow. "*I was so sorry to learn of Regan's passing. Yes, if you are wondering, the KGB kept a weather eye on you and Ms Burns after the Belov sanction... Terrible business, cancer. You could protect her from a poisoned blade but not from that, eh?*"

Fisher stiffened, his aspect turning cold. His wife's face rose and fell briefly in his thoughts. He remembered the smell of the rain in her hair, then shook off the memory before it could fully form, before it could distract him.

"*Come below,*" said Aslanov. "*We can raise a glass to her and talk of old times.*" Fisher heard the smile in his voice. "*I will be waiting.*"

He tossed away the earpiece and rose to his feet. Fisher reloaded his weapon, double-checked the field dressing, and then advanced toward the gantry that would take him down to the half-submerged module suspended beneath the rig.

"Paladin Actual, Panther." Fisher spoke into his throat mike. "Target Red knows I'm here. He'll be digging in."

"*Understood,*" said Grim. "*Be advised, confidence is high that Target Red is now in direct control of Gordian Sword.*" She paused, framing her next words carefully, doubtless aware that Charlie, Lea, and everyone else in the Paladin's C&C could hear what she was saying. "*We'll lose comms once you enter the core. You know your mission, Panther. Execute and secure.*"

"I know my mission," he echoed, weighing the last conversation he had shared with Grímsdóttir. "I know what has to be done."

Private Train – En Route – Approaching
  French/Swiss Border

The wicked little blade in the redhead's hand cut swift, curving paths through the air in front of Sarah, forcing her on to the defensive. The rocking motion of the train made it hard to stay on an even footing, and each time the lounge car rattled over a set of points, the floor shook.

She dodged to one side, barely avoiding a jabbing attack, only to realize too late that it was a clever feint. Her opponent brought up her other hand, but it was no longer empty. The redhaired woman had conjured a second *karatel* knife, seemingly out of nowhere, intent on planting it in Sarah's neck.

Sarah threw up her forearms to block the incoming strikes, instinctively defending her upper body, and one of the daggers struck her, slashing across the side of her wrist and scraping over the screen of her OPSAT.

She snarled in pain and tried to open the distance between her and the other woman, but to her dismay, the redhead reeled back of her own accord, bringing up her arm to throw the other blade.

Sarah twisted out of the way – but the thrown knife had not been meant for her. The *karatel* whistled past her head and buried itself in Brody Teague's chest with a meaty thud.

Wheezing in shock, Teague fell back into the leather sofa and sat there, twitching and gasping. His face turned milk-pale, and he tried to reach for the handle of the knife. A great crimson bloom grew across the designer T-shirt and jacket he wore, glistening in the half-light.

Sarah's opponent gave her no time to dwell on Teague's circumstances, grabbing a handful of her raven hair and yanking it savagely. She twisted around, fighting to keep her balance, one hand snatching at the butt of the Scorpion pistol in her hip holster.

The gun cleared leather and swung up in a tight arc, but the other woman saw it coming and struck with a vicious downward slash over the back of Sarah's hand. The razor-sharp tip of the *karatel* sliced through the material of her glove and cut across her knuckles. The pain shocked through Sarah's fingers, and she lost her grip on the gun, hearing it bounce away over the carpet.

The redhead did not let up, maintaining her momentum with a wild flurry of fast, slashing advances that threatened to slice Sarah open if they made contact. Blood oozing through the tear in her glove, she made a split-second calculation.

There was no room to keep avoiding the other woman's attacks. She had to take control of the fight for herself.

Sarah left a deliberate opening for the knife, and it came in toward her neck in a fast, stabbing pass. She pivoted, hands coming up to trap the other woman's arm before she could press the blade home.

The redhead put her weight into it, trying to twist free, but she and Sarah were equally matched. Their arms locked and it became a stalemate, strength against strength as each fought to overcome the other, their faces a few centimeters apart.

Sarah looked into the other woman's eyes and saw nothing.

Then, the icy smile she had witnessed before etched itself over the redhead's face.

Her opponent opened her fingers and let the *karatel* drop, down into her other hand, free to cut and slash and tear.

The knife rose again in a back-handed grip, a rising curve of shiny steel that would have cut Sarah from belly to throat had it made full contact. Still, the arrowhead tip came close enough to slice through the dense ballistic nylon of her webbing vest and into the black material beneath, leaving a line of fire across her sternum.

Sarah turned the bolt of pain into energy and fired off a reflexive upward kick, hitting her mark, but the move robbed her of her balance, and she fell back, crashing through the remnants of a broken coffee table.

Among the wreckage, she saw a familiar, long-barreled shape – the Scorpion pistol. Sarah reacted without thinking, rolling toward the fallen gun, snatching it up.

She turned the weapon on the other woman, and the moment froze. Sarah's blood glistened on the edge of the knife in her opponent's fist. The woman's blank, doll-like eyes stared back at her.

Sarah took a breath and felt the cold of a crisp November day in the Colorado wilds prickling her skin. The memory of that hunt with her father came back to her as if it were happening right that second.

The deer in the sights of her rifle. The decision to pull the trigger or release it.

To willingly take a life, or not.

Then the redheaded woman's smile grew large, and her arm came back to throw the *karatel* at Sarah's throat.

She was dead before she could hurl the blade. Sarah shot her twice through the chest, the impact of the rounds kicking the woman back and away across the shuddering floor of the train carriage.

"You... got her." Teague coughed wetly, bringing up dark blood. "She. She's fuh-fired." He gave a tortured rasp and looked down at the fluids soaking his shirt. "This is... isn't right." He managed a shake of the head. "Brody Teague doesn't... Brody doesn't *die*."

Sarah rolled to her feet and snatched up the encrypted tablet computer. Picking her way through the debris, she dropped into a crouch by the blood-smeared sofa.

She had seen men die before, and the pallor of Teague's face told her he was too far gone to be saved. His murderous assistant's aim had been true, her blade piercing his heart.

"Give me your hand," she told him.

"Whuh-why?"

Sarah grabbed his wrist and twisted it, forcing Teague's thumb against the tablet's biometric reader. The device bleated, showing a panel that read ACCESS DENIED. She swore to herself, then looked him in his eyes. "Brody. Listen to me. You're going to lose, do you understand that? Aslanov and Patel, they're going to win. Is that how you want to go out?"

"No." He choked out the word, grabbing hold of the tablet with every last bit of strength he could muster. Sarah saw it in his eyes; in that moment, all he cared about was destroying everything he could not have.

"I don't... *lose*." He mashed his thumb on the reader and the device chimed.

ACCESS GRANTED.

ACTIVATE GORDIAN SWORD CORE MODULE EGRESS Y/N?

"Paladin Actual, Lynx." Sarah panted as she spoke into her throat mike. "Objective secured. Panther can proceed."

"*Copy that,*" said Charlie. "*What about, uh, Target Blue?*"

She looked back at Teague, now silent and unmoving. "Brody's logged out," she replied.

TWENTY-FOUR

Site Five – Nyx Oil Platform – North Sea

"The lift," said Gera, pointing upwards. "It's coming."

The cage-like elevator platform slowly descended the shaft leading from the rig's main deck, dropping down into the sublevels.

Aslanov studied it as it drew closer. "That is bait," he said.

Along with his comrades Vova and Alik, the mercenary Gera was armed and armored, ready for violence at a moment's notice. But they had no idea what they were about to face.

"Fisher is on his way," continued Aslanov. "Do not underestimate this man."

He directed them to take up firing positions around the reception area outside the operations room, quickly throwing a glance back to where Diaz and the other technicians were still at work.

It was imperative that the American not be allowed to interfere with the takeover of Gordian Sword, but at the same time, Aslanov found himself eager for the confrontation. He rarely allowed himself an indulgence, and this piece of unfinished business was such a moment.

In the beginning, he had given little thought to Samuel Fisher after the assassination in Georgia. For the younger American, that night had been a defining moment in his life, but for Dima Aslanov, it was just another mission. The elimination of Maxim Belov sent the message his KGB masters desired, and he moved on to his next kill.

But over the years, Fisher had continued to dog him, with a tenacity that Aslanov almost admired. Again and again, their paths had crossed, but each time the assassin had slipped through the other man's grasp. It was a game of sorts, in a life where there were few pleasures to be had.

Events had overtaken him, in the end. One too many breaches of protocol, one too many incidents of disobedience, and Aslanov had earned the displeasure of the Politburo. He took the only way out he could, letting the world believe he had been buried in the chaos of a NATO bombing raid. The perfect finishing touch was making Fisher a witness to it. After all, if the man who had hunted him for so long believed Dima Aslanov had perished, so would everyone else.

But even the best-laid plans could go awry. Aslanov's enforced retirement grew stale, his secret coffers of money slowly emptied, and so he took the opportunity to re-invent himself for the new age of cyber-warfare and digital espionage.

The sins of the past, though, he thought, as the elevator drew level and slowed to a halt. *They will always catch up with you.*

The doors across the gantry drew back, revealing the interior of the wide metal platform inside the lift shaft. A figure in black combat gear lay slumped and unmoving in the far corner, their face turned away.

The mercenaries exchanged suspicious glances, but none of them moved. Aslanov made a *tsk* sound and gave Alik a shove in the back. "You. Take a look. And be careful."

"Sir." The mercenary steeled himself, then stepped gingerly into the elevator, panning around with the muzzle of his SMG, aiming up in case an assailant hung from the roof. "Empty," he added.

Alik approached the body on the floor and prodded it with the tip of his boot, before dropping into a crouch. Shouldering his weapon, he checked over the corpse.

"No booby-traps," he confirmed, then turned the dead man's head so they could see his ruined face. "It is Georgy. His equipment has been stripped."

"What is the point of this?" said Vova. "Is Fisher trying to intimidate us?"

A melodic electronic chirp sounded inside the elevator, and Alik stiffened, turning toward the source of the noise. "Something up there, in the corner. Stuck to the frame." He pointed with his gun. "Like a ball. Is it a camera … ?"

"Get out!" Aslanov shouted the command a half-second too late, his words smothered by the metallic crash of a detonation emanating from the top of the elevator.

A shaped charge severed the support cables, and suddenly there was nothing to hold the elevator in place. With the dead man and the mercenary still inside, the steel cage plunged the last ten meters down into the service area below, striking with such impact that the elevator was crushed under its own weight.

On the level above them, perched on the far side of the open shaft with a gun at the ready in his hand, Fisher tossed away a spent radio detonator and started shooting.

Vova recoiled in shock, and his sluggish reaction cost him. Fisher knocked him down with hits to his thigh and the armor plate carrier over his torso.

Aslanov's own gun barked, the blunt-nosed Grach semiautomatic spitting fire at the intruder, but he had no desire to engage the American on his terms. "Fall back," he ordered, retreating beyond Fisher's angle of attack. Gera sprinted across the floor and grabbed the loop on the back of his comrade's body armor, dragging Vova out of the firing line.

Fisher's persistence in pursuing his old enemy remained undimmed, however. The American holstered his pistol and in a flash of black, he threw himself bodily across the width of the shaft.

A harsh, derisive laugh burst from Aslanov's lips as he watched the other man grab for the lip of the open hatch and *miss* it.

Fisher misjudged the distance and landed badly, hands grabbing at the ledge to stop himself falling into the mess of wreckage at the bottom of the elevator shaft.

Taking his time, Aslanov pushed past his men and walked back to the edge, his grin widening. "That is the problem with aging, Samuel," he said, switching to English from Russian. "Inside, we think we are still the same men we were in our thirties! But the body betrays you! No matter how hard we work, we can never be what we once were." Aslanov shook his head, his grin hardening into a pitiless glare as he watched Fisher struggle to hold on. "When you were young you might have made it. But you are no threat now. You never really were."

He raised the Grach to deliver a killing shot, but before he could draw a bead, Fisher did the last thing Aslanov expected of him: *he let go.*

The American fell, vanishing over the edge.

The Russian wasn't a fool.

He didn't take the risk and peer down the lift shaft himself, he sent a man to do it for him. The taller of Aslanov's mercs – the one with the buzz-cut – craned his neck out to take a look, expecting to see the Splinter Cell agent's broken body lying amid the wreckage of the broken elevator car.

What he found was Fisher half-hidden in the shadows below him, balancing on a tiny ledge, one hand gripping the edge of a bent panel and the other holding the wicked curve of a "Panther Claw" karambit knife.

His muscles burning, his jaw locked hard, Fisher dug deep for his resolve, channeling a decades-old enmity for the man he had never been able to kill into his will to survive.

With quick slicing motions, Fisher slashed deep into the calf muscles and sinews of the man standing over him, then hooked the blade in and pulled hard. The mercenary screamed as he toppled forward, tumbling over Fisher's head and down to the bottom of the metal shaft.

Exchanging his knife for his gun, Fisher threw himself up and over the edge of the deck, rolling level with Aslanov and the merc he had tagged moments earlier. The SC-IS pistol bucked in his hand as he fired on the move, shooting more for effect than for the hope of a solid hit.

The unexpected assault forced Aslanov and his wounded comrade to retreat back into the operations room. Fisher heard cries of alarm from the civilian technicians inside and saw them diving for cover behind their consoles.

From his webbing, he pulled one of the smoke grenades he had taken from the corpse in the elevator, ripping off the ring and tossing it into the control room. As the white haze filled the enclosed space, Fisher caught sight of his objective for the first time. The steel cylinder housing the quantum computer system stood on the far side of the operations room, beyond a set of transparent pressure doors.

Fisher's thoughts briefly strayed back to his daughter, bringing a scowl to his face. He had never wanted her to be a part of this life, but now he relied on Sarah not just to *endure* it but *succeed*. Unless she completed her part of the operation on Brody Teague's train, those doors would not open, and Fisher's mission would be stonewalled.

Going low, Fisher reloaded his pistol and slipped into the smoke-choked room, activating his tri-goggles in thermographic mode. Everything changed into a heat-vision landscape of blocky shapes rendered in light blue or sea green – the consoles and computer panels arranged in tiers leading down to the pressure doors. Human figures made of hotter colors – oranges, yellows and reds –appeared in his line of sight, and he tracked them with the muzzle of the SC-IS. He saw only the panicked technicians, and no sign of Aslanov and the injured mercenary.

"You should not have come, Fisher." The Russian's harsh tones echoed around the chamber. "This will only end one way. The same way it always has when you have faced me."

"I'm not the one who had to run and hide." The words slipped out of Fisher's mouth before he could stop himself, and he frowned in irritation. He was letting Aslanov bait him.

Two can play at that game.

Fisher shoved one of the civvie techs out of his way and found the wall, pressing his back to it so his enemy could not blindside him. He took a breath and called out.

"You got sloppy, Dima," he snapped. "All that time out of the life? You've lost your edge. We tracked you down *easy*."

"Is that so?" Aslanov sounded close, but Fisher hesitated, refusing to be drawn out.

The room's odd acoustics and the steady rumble of the sea out beyond the walls of the chamber made it hard to pinpoint his exact location. If Fisher revealed himself too soon, he would be dead before he knew it.

"Forgive me, but perhaps you forget that you are alone here. Reinforcements are on the way. You are outnumbered and outgunned." Aslanov chuckled, and Fisher cocked his head, listening hard, trying to narrow down the Russian's location amid the haze. "Anyone else would have sent an army to take this place," continued Aslanov, "but not Fourth Echelon. That perfect American arrogance at play, so convinced that one man... the *right* man... cannot be stopped."

The technicians were using the lull in the shooting to flee the room, but among their movements, Fisher glimpsed a figure holding a blocky, dark-shaded object.

The merc, he guessed, *trying to flank me while Aslanov keeps me distracted.*

The white smoke began to settle. If a counterattack was coming, it would happen in the next few seconds.

"You have a killer rep, I'll give you that," Fisher said loudly, readying his weapon. "At least, you did. This thing of Teague's, it's your shot at getting back your crown, right? You want people to fear you again." He shook his head. "Not gonna happen. You've been living on borrowed time, Dima. Now the clock's run out."

"I beg to differ," sneered the Russian.

As if his retort was the signal, the mercenary approaching from Fisher's right veered out of cover and opened fire. The muzzle flare from his SMG cut a brilliant white swathe across Fisher's vision as he ducked and rolled.

Fisher responded with his pistol, the bright flickers of ejected bullet cases arcing away. Already injured from their first engagement, the merc was slow on his feet, hoping to put down his target with firepower and the element of surprise. But Fisher had seen him coming, and he knew there was only one approach the gunman could take.

Deactivating his tri-goggles, Fisher dropped prone as the merc executed a badly timed pop-up attack, coming over a computer console with his SR-2 sub-machine gun canted at an angle. The other man fired, but his shots landed where the merc predicted Fisher *would* be, not where he *was*.

Aiming upward, Fisher did not hesitate, placing two 5.7mm rounds up through the bottom of the mercenary's head. The dead man crumbled forward and collapsed across the console, his SMG clattering to the floor.

From nowhere, an alarm tone began to sound, and yellow warning lights strobed around the edge of the pressure doors. Fisher jerked up at the noise, knowing it could only mean one thing.

Sarah did it.

With a hiss of air, the heavy transparent doors parted, opening up access directly to Gordian Sword's core.

Fisher exploded into motion, bolting into the open and down the tier toward the entrance. The moment he showed himself, Aslanov's Grach pistol thundered, ricochets keening off the consoles and the floor beneath his feet as the Russian tried to bring him down.

A round struck Fisher in the shoulder, and he staggered, but he swallowed the shock of pain, pushing through it, dropping into a slide that took him low and through the pressure door vestibule. From behind, he heard Aslanov spit a curse and the metallic clack of a weapon being reloaded.

Inside the computer core, the air temperature was noticeably colder, and Fisher's breath revealed itself in puffs of white vapor. Ignoring the throbbing pulse of agony from his shoulder, he moved deeper into the chamber, advancing over a gridded deck that allowed him to see down into the tanks immediately below. Maintenance crawlways extended away toward heavy duty valves and pump mechanisms that brought in the cold waters of the North Sea and forced them through the computer's coolant system.

He glimpsed movement on the other side of the bulletproof glass walling off the control room from the core. Aslanov picked his way down toward him, pausing to gather up some additional firepower, taking the SR-2 from the mercenary Fisher had dispatched.

"Do you even know what that is, Fisher?" the Russian called out after him. "Do you understand what potential it represents?"

Fisher ignored him, scanning the room, finding a hatch set into the deck. He wrenched it open and dropped down to the level below, where the coolant pipes rumbled in their mountings. Breaking line of sight with Aslanov, he moved into the orchard of pipework and machinery, checking his SC-IS pistol as he went. He took the moment of calm to dress his new wound. It was a messy through-and-through, but survivable.

The steel casing of the computer core rose up in front of him, and he rapped on the thick cylinder with a gloved hand. Nothing short of a demolition charge would be able to crack it, and he would run out of bullets before he even managed to dent the thing.

Grim's orders rang in Fisher's mind. *Secure the objective.* He was here to capture Gordian Sword for the United States of America, to make sure this lethal machine would never be used against that nation.

But Fourth Echelon's directives were not just defensive measures. The device was a weapon – *Brody Teague had put it right there in the name!* – and if even half of what Charlie Cole had said was true, it could radically alter the balance of global power. Gordian Sword could not be allowed to threaten America – but what about the rest of the world?

Fisher thought of the wreckage of the Atlantic International flight floating on the sea, and of everyone this system had been used against. How many more lives would it destroy?

Taken to its deadly conclusion, a nation with Gordian Sword's technology at its disposal would be a superpower in the digital age. America would be able to detonate the nuclear missiles of hostile forces while they were still in their silos; it would be able to cripple vital infrastructure and plunge whole countries into the dark ages without ever firing a shot, transgressing borders, ignoring rules of engagement; and it would become the most hated, most feared nation on Earth, waging a war that would never end.

A shadow war, he thought. *The kind fought by politicians safe in their beds, by men and women who've never known the bloody truth of it.*

Fisher knew in his bones that it wasn't right for one nation, *for anyone,* to wield that kind of power.

From above him, Aslanov's boots rang on the deck. "Consider what choice you wish to make, Samuel." The Russian stalked him across the chamber, and belatedly Fisher realized that the man had followed his blood trail. "If you try to destroy the device, you will fail. Be a realist!" He chuckled. "Shall I guess at what your masters told you? They want it for themselves, yes?"

Fisher moved slowly, bringing up his pistol to aim in the direction of Aslanov's voice. He couldn't see him yet, but the man was close. He had to wait for the right moment to fire; the Russian would not give him a second opportunity.

"You are wounded, bleeding badly. And there is an easier way for this to end. Let us talk like two professionals, and perhaps we can both walk away," said the other man, almost conversationally. "Samir Patel is spiteful, but he is as greedy as he is spineless. If your government paid him well enough, he would make a deal with them and I, of course, would be handsomely compensated. An exclusive contract for the use of Gordian Sword? I imagine the Pentagon would agree to terms, especially now they have seen it in action. And I can assure you, that fool Teague will no longer be a problem."

Fisher seized on the last few words. "What about Teague?"

Aslanov paused on the deck above, weighing his options.

"His usefulness has come to an end. And there is something poetic about using his prized creation to kill him. Mr Teague and his train will be at the bottom of an alpine valley very soon, if he is not already dead."

There was an edge of icy amusement in Aslanov's words, and Fisher knew at once that the Russian would not keep to any deal, no matter how much money was at stake. He liked the power that Gordian Sword offered, and that didn't have a dollar value.

But what chilled Fisher more than anything was the mention of the train. He saw the bleak truth unfolding before him. "You used the machine to hack Teague's train. You're going to crash it."

"You should thank me. I do the world a service by eliminating him." Aslanov was very close now, directly above Fisher's position, but he still hadn't spotted him.

"My *daughter* is on that train!" Fisher bit out the words.

"Ah." Aslanov considered that. "The girl you assisted at the tower, of course." He sighed. "A pity. I am afraid the attack program is fully committed, and anyone who might have been able to halt it, such as Patel, has fled. That does change things, does it not?"

The Russian knew that Fisher's revelation meant the time for talking was over. He opened fire with the SR-2, spraying bullets through the open-weave grid of the decking, bracketing the Splinter Cell agent's position with a withering salvo.

Fisher retaliated with paced shots that sparked off the metal flooring and drove Aslanov back against the wall.

Unknowingly, the assassin had made up Fisher's mind for him. Now the Gordian Sword device wasn't some grand, existential threat to the fate of the world or the balance of global power. The scope of the danger it represented had been reduced to something small, personal, *human* – and no father worthy of the name would be willing to sacrifice his only child to preserve it.

Leaping off the catwalk, Fisher dropped to the next gantry down, running over the tops of churning tanks filled with seawater. Positioned at the far end of the narrow metal walkway was a lever valve control painted in black-and-yellow warning colors.

A sign above the valve read DANGER! EMERGENCY SEA VENT, and beneath it in smaller text DO NOT ENGAGE DURING GALE FORCE CONDITIONS.

As more bullets tore down from the deck above, chipping at the walkway around him, Fisher snatched at the metal lever and slammed it down into the active position.

Alarms sounded and the heavy vents cranked open, overwhelmed by the force of the ocean outside. With a sound like a caged thunderstorm, the black and freezing waters of the North Sea burst from the confines of the tanks and rose to smother him.

TWENTY-FIVE

Private Train – Canton of Valais – Switzerland

Sarah sat in a leather armchair amid the wreckage of the room, her tactical suit drawn down and her gloves off, doggedly working strips of adhesive bandage around the deep cuts across her hand and chest.

Across from her, Brody Teague's corpse sat staring blankly into nothing, still clutching the computer tablet that had been of such critical importance only minutes before. Teague's traitorous assistant lay in a heap on the floor, long red hair pooling around her pale face.

Sarah avoided looking in that direction. She had the Scorpion pistol resting beside her, reloaded and ready in case any hostiles had come back down the train to check on Brody Teague's wellbeing. But no one had, and it was starting to concern her.

"Merlin, Lynx." She tapped her radio earpiece. "You copy?"

Static choked the reply, but she picked out Charlie Cole's voice amid the hissing interference. "*Comms are intermittent,*

Lynx. Long story short, I had to co-opt a drone from the Swiss Air Force as a relay so we could keep eyes on you..." Sarah heard him gulp down a breath before he went on. "*Real talk here, you need to get off that train as quickly as possible, I'm not kidding!*"

She nodded, as a heavy rumble echoed up through the floor of the lounge carriage. Out of the picture window in the side of the train car, all Sarah could see of the countryside flashing by was a featureless blur of black and gray. "We're still picking up speed..."

"*Exactly!*" snapped Charlie. "*You've gotta go, now! Get to the rear car as fast as you can!*"

She couldn't miss the rising panic in his tone. "Merlin, what aren't you telling me?" Sarah went to the window and pressed her face to it, trying to see up ahead along the line of the rails, but there was only the mass of a snow-covered forest and white mountains rising beyond them.

"*There's a curve in the line, about three klicks from your current position.*" Charlie forced himself to meter his words. "*Whoever's messing with the locomotive's controls has deactivated the speed governor subroutines. You're going too fast to make the turn!*"

"It's going to derail..." The realization sent an electric charge through her, and from beneath her feet Sarah heard metal on metal as the carriage's steel wheels scraped against the rails. "Lynx is on the move!"

Pausing to holster her pistol and secure Teague's tablet under her tac webbing, Sarah broke into a run, but the chaotic rocking motion of the train made it hard to keep up her momentum. She skidded into walls and off the adjoining vestibule leading to the next carriage.

Shouldering open the doors, she raced through a dining car

and into the disorder of the private train's kitchen. Cupboards hung open, their contents spilled across the deck, and a pot had been left to boil over on a hotplate, all of it forgotten in the haste to escape the runaway.

A frigid wind whipped around the interior of the carriage, rushing in through an open doorway toward the rear. Sarah realized why no one had come looking after the melee in the lounge. The service crew had already taken their chances and thrown themselves from the fast-moving train.

Charlie's voice crackled in her ear, lost in the howl and hiss of static, but Sarah heard one thing clearly.

"*Two minutes,*" he warned. "*Don't stop for anything!*"

Site Five – Nyx Oil Platform – North Sea

The cold came at Fisher in hard waves, rising every few seconds as each new sea surge forced more water in through the vents. He stumbled over the gantry, the level already at his chest, and then another wave blasted across the chamber, tearing through the safety baffles as if they were made of paper.

The vents were only meant to be opened under controlled circumstances and calm sea conditions, so releasing them in the middle of a violent storm like the one currently lashing the rig stressed the entire structure well beyond its limits. All around, metal moaned like a wounded animal as pressure built in the wrong places.

The next wave gathered Fisher up and hauled him off his feet. He became a piece of flotsam, turned and propelled by the crushing force of the seawater, rising to slam against the underside of the deck above. He sucked in a breath as the vicious undertow ripped him away. Fisher collided with the ladder leading to the open hatch in the floor of the next tier, the impact sending a shock of agony through his injuries.

Grabbing on with both hands, he waited for the wave to ebb, knowing he would only have seconds before the following crest flooded into the chamber. When the moment came, Fisher pulled himself up the rungs and rolled onto the wet deck.

"*Mudak!*" He heard the angry shout and twisted into the blow that came from behind him.

A savage kick caught Fisher in the head and sent him sprawling. Fireworks burst behind his eyes as he struck the deck and rolled away.

Aslanov came stalking toward him. "You have ruined it! Years of work, *for nothing!*"

The Russian fired his pistol at Fisher as the next wave burst through, and this time the surge blew up through the gaps in the deck's metal gridwork, briefly swamping them both as the water level continued to rise. Aslanov lost his balance and slammed into a support pillar, the Grach's shots going wide.

Fisher was ready for it this time, the flooding seawater breaking over him, swatting both men like the hand of a giant.

Unbidden, an old memory flashed through Fisher's mind as the freezing, salt-harsh wave seared his exposed skin. For an instant he was a young man again, fighting his way through the hell week of BUD/S training to make the grade for SEAL selection.

The snarled words of an instructor echoed through the thunder of the sea. *Never fight the water, son. You'll always lose. Let it take you. Become part of it.*

Fisher rolled into the undercurrent and followed that hard-earned advice. Holding his breath, he braced himself against the gantry, while Aslanov flailed and choked on a lungful of seawater. When the surge dropped back, Fisher rose out of the flood with his gun drawn and aimed.

Two shots, center-mass. The SC-IS barked twice, and the Russian reeled back as if he had been kicked by a mule. Aslanov crashed into the rising waters, coughing and groaning.

More than anything, Fisher wanted to finish the man off, to be certain it was done, but the sea had other plans. The succeeding wave came and the flooding continued to fill the decks, rising inexorably. Across the chamber, salt water slopped over the upper edge of Gordian Sword's cylindrical casing and gushed inside, drowning the delicate electronics of the quantum computer. Sharp, braying cracks sounded from inside the machine as wild short-circuits ran through its innards, and the acrid, burnt-hair stink of scorched plastic reached him.

Fisher pulled himself up the next ladder to the control-room level as the wave came again, beating the wounded Russian against the side of the cylinder below. Aslanov clawed at the gantry, hands slipping from the rungs, and then went under again. Fisher didn't see him rise.

Leaving the Russian to drown wasn't the ending Fisher's old foe deserved, but to stay a moment longer risked suffering the same fate as the assassin. Power failed in the overhead lights, panels dropped from the ceiling trailing severed wires and ducting, and the floor of the core chamber canted at an angle, the oil rig's damaged superstructure taking on the weight of tons of displaced water.

Fisher waded away through the flooding, cold-hot agony searing the wounds in his shoulder and his torso. Yellow warning strobes around the pressure doors flickered madly, but the hatchway's hydraulics juddered in place, jammed open by some malfunction of the system.

The water lapped at his knees and kept rising. He estimated that it would quickly engulf the operations room beyond and destroy everything in it. Fisher hesitated at the doors, looking back at the blackened, fizzing wreckage of Gordian Sword.

Well done, Sam, said a voice in his head, a voice that sounded just like Regan. *You've disobeyed a direct order from the President of the United States.*

"Not the first time," he said aloud. Brody Teague's creation was no more, and the insidious threat it had presented was gone – at least for the moment.

Fisher pressed on, fighting through the fallen debris to the elevator shaft that would take him up and out. There was no way to know if destroying the computer would save his daughter's life, if killing Gordian Sword would halt the attack program it had set in motion. He could only hope that she would survive.

You know she can, said Regan's voice. *You know she will.*

Private Train – Canton of Valais – Switzerland

The last carriage sat beyond the cargo wagon where Sarah had first boarded the train, the interior a mess of fallen crates that made progress difficult. Struggling over them, she dragged herself to the door at the far end of the car and peered through the window set into it. Light cast from the speeding train gave the snow an eerie glow, and the black lines of the rails receded away from her into the hazy distance.

"Can't leave that way," she said aloud. At the rate the train was moving, if Sarah struck the rails or the concrete sleepers between them, she would shatter every bone in her body.

She went to the window in the side of the car and looked out, feeling the carriage shifting beneath her as she moved. The floor tilted alarmingly; the train had entered the turn.

Outside she saw only fields of white, the line of trees falling away. A plan formed in her thoughts.

Sarah aimed the Scorpion up at the skylight in the carriage's roof and emptied the pistol into the panel, blasting out the glass, letting a hurricane come rushing in through the hole.

She mounted a heap of fallen containers and bridged the last half-meter to the ceiling with a jump. Her gloves slapped on the edge of the skylight's ruined frame, and with a cry of effort, she hauled herself up and onto the top of the train car. She shook with adrenaline and her breath came in ragged gasps, every fiber in her body screaming for this ordeal to end.

The biting wind dragged on her body, pushing Sarah toward the back of the carriage and the fall that would most certainly kill her. Over the howling gale, she heard the drawn-out screech of the wheels against the track as the train's automatic braking system locked up. Showers of orange sparks jetted from beneath the axles, but nothing could stop what was coming. The metal roof beneath her tilted further as the carriages took the turn too steeply.

Something sped past overhead, moving low and fast. Sarah had the impression of long and narrow wings, and a skinny fuselage bearing the insignia of a white cross against a red disc.

The drone! Charlie Cole's eye in the sky was a Hermes 900 UAV temporarily "borrowed" from the Swiss Air Force, and as she watched, it turned into a circling pattern overhead. Sarah felt the mad impulse to throw the thing a salute, and a wild laugh escaped her.

"Lynx! I see you, go now! Go now!" Charlie's voice made it through the static, shocking Sarah out of her moment of hesitation.

"Easy for you to say," she retorted, the wind tearing the words from her mouth.

Sarah turned to face at a right-angle to the direction of the train, bracing her feet against the broken skylight like a sprinter on the starting blocks. Then with all the strength she could summon, she leapt into the air.

For one dizzying moment, she was suspended in the night as the world turned around her; then a wall of endless, freezing white rushed up to meet her.

Sarah drew in her arms and legs, striking the surface of the deep-packed drift with a punishing impact that threw up a torrent of powder and sent her tumbling end over end. She felt her shoulder dislocate in a red blast of pain, but there was nothing she could do to arrest her forward motion. Sarah skidded and rolled across the snowfield, burning off the velocity of her fall in one agonizing bounce after another, until finally, *mercifully*, she came to rest on her back.

It took a monumental effort for Sarah to sit up, and as she did, a sound like the end of the world boomed back up the valley to reach her.

Thunder, ice, and steel collided as Brody Teague's private train lost its battle with gravity and momentum. In slow motion, she saw it roll off the railway tracks at the apex of the turn, first the bullet-nosed locomotive, and then, in a chain of screaming metal, each of the carriages following on behind it.

There was no explosive detonation, no infernal burst of flame that lit up the night, only a long and drawn out death-screech of grinding steel violently crushed against itself. The wreckage of the train slipped down the steep incline on the far side of the track, gouging black divots out of the snow and earth beneath, before it crumpled against the edge of the forest, uprooting trees with a final crash of noise.

Panting hard, Sarah placed the heel of her good hand against the popped shoulder and rammed it back into place with a jerking motion. The scream that escaped her echoed away into the night. She collapsed back into the snow.

Staring up into the low clouds, Sarah saw the hijacked drone rocket past, dipping its wings so its sensor head could find her against the frozen landscape. It circled back, and this time she managed a weak wave.

"Some guardian angel, huh?" Sarah's words came in puff of vapor. She realized she couldn't hear Charlie's voice anymore, and gingerly she touched her ear. Her fingers came away with blood on them and her earpiece was gone, knocked out of her in the fall.

Sarah pulled herself out of the pit she had made in the snow and began a slow, steady march back toward the tracks. She remembered the train passing close to some alpine hamlet just before she had confronted Teague, and pointed herself back along the rails, doggedly putting one foot in front of the other. A town meant heat and shelter, maybe hot food and a phone.

As she walked, she looked down at the damaged, flickering

screen of the OPSAT on her wrist. It was barely readable, but still active, and without radio it was the only link she still had with the team on the Paladin.

Her hands shook with the cold, but after a couple of attempts, Sarah managed to tap out a message on the OPSAT's touchscreen.

target blue down
lynx injured but mobile
seeking shelter

She paused, sucking in another icy breath before she added the one thing she wanted to know, more than anything else.

how is my dad?

Site Five – Nyx Oil Platform – North Sea

Fisher emerged on the rig's main deck as the frame of the platform began to distort, warping like a piece of rain-bloated wood.

Propped up on three thick legs vanishing into the water, Site Five's main superstructure was essentially a gigantic triangle built out of steel, with a pillar at each point. The southernmost leg twisted and crumpled as the mass of the rig shifted beyond its tolerances. The whole thing listed, with the new weight of seawater flooding the retrofitted chambers below the waves.

A cargo container the size of a school bus strained against the chains holding it in place, and suddenly burst free as the metal links gave way, splinters ricocheting off the walls. Fisher dove across the canted deck to avoid the heavy container as it slid past him, across the open area where he had fought Aslanov's gunmen earlier that night. It slammed into the far bulkhead, the impact crushing the sheet metal panels, and something behind the wall spat out a belch of flames.

Fisher caught a sharp, acrid reek in the damp air. The container had cracked a gas line inside one of the habitation units, sparking a fire already spreading up to the levels above, despite the constant downpour.

With the safety chains gone, other containers lined up along the deck began to shift, gravity giving them the impetus to move.

"Paladin Actual, Panther." Biting out the words, Fisher tapped his throat mike as he limped across the deck. "How copy?" A nasty buzz in his ear told him that he still had radio comms, but the pick-up was poor. "Say again?"

"–*Panther, over–*" Grim's voice faded in and out. "*Visuals from bird are unclear–*"

"Yeah, I bet." Grunting in pain, Fisher grabbed the rungs of an emergency ladder and pulled himself up it.

He knew that far overhead, Fourth Echelon were watching events unfold in the North Sea through the eyes of an NSA spy satellite, using its synthetic aperture radar imaging to peer through the thick cloud cover. They would be able to see the Site Five platform in real time, the rig's desperate and luckless crew cast into the waves, the plumes of outgassing heat as it went into its death throes.

It was hard going hauling himself to the deck above with one arm barely working, but he made it, emerging on to a mid-tier where strobing red lights marked the launch racks for Site Five's emergency lifeboats. Bulky capsules made of bright international orange fiberglass, the lifeboats were mounted on sloping rails that would send them out and over the side of the rig in the event of an order to abandon the platform. Once in the water, they could sail away in any weather and wait for recovery.

The pods were gone, each launch rack yawning empty. Grimacing at his ill fortune, Fisher hobbled to the edge of the gantry and looked down over the long drop to the sea. Amid patches of lost containers and burning debris he could make out a cluster of brilliant white stars on the water, the rescue strobes on the lifeboats, tossed about in the ten-meter swell of the dark waves.

There were other lifeboat stations in other sectors of the rig, but it would be a tough march to reach them, and Fisher had no guarantee that the others hadn't also been taken by the technicians who fled the operations center.

"–*Panther, over?*" Grim's clipped tones sounded once again, slicing through the static. "*We're getting conflicting ISR data. Can you confirm mission status?*"

"Target Red has been neutralized," he replied, drawing back from the edge.

"*Panther, advise condition of Gordian Sword.*"

Wrecked. Fisher almost said the word aloud, but before he could frame a better reply, the rig's superstructure shuddered and dropped a half-meter to the starboard as the south support leg buckled. The rig's central derrick rising up over Fisher's head bent out of shape, shedding retrofitted solar panels and knocking down a clump of fast-spinning windmills beneath it. Metal and plastic cascaded down around him, steel rods spearing through the deck.

A cold claw of fear tightened around his heart. "Time to go," he told himself.

"Panther, please repeat last."

"Panther is on the move!" He shouted back the reply and started running. Lines of fire raced along Fisher's nerves from the site of his injuries, but he ate the pain and turned it into fuel.

As he reached the edge of the gantry, he bounded up and used the safety rail as his jump point. Boots slapping against the wet steel, Fisher pushed off and away from the rig in a powerful leap.

He resisted the momentum pulling him into a head-over-heels tumble, and controlled his fall with the skill of an Olympic high-board diver. Fisher turned his body into a dagger – legs straight and feet pointed, head up and back. The drop seemed to go on forever, the wind screaming in his ears, the black of the night swallowing him whole.

Then he hit the freezing waves and the breathtaking impact hammered up through his bones and joints as he went under. Fisher spread his arms and legs to slow his descent and looked up. He could see the lights of the rig and the fires above him on the roiling surface, twinkling and distant.

He had nothing in his lungs. His chest burned. His muscles felt leaden, the stunning cold leeching the energy from them.

Never fight the water. The voice in his head admonished him, pushing out of the past and into the moment. *Become part of it.*

Fisher reached up with his good arm and carved his way through the sea, rising up and up, kicking against the undertow. The half-collapsed rig caused riptides and unpredictable currents that threatened to pull him back, but he defied them, struggling on.

Then he burst into the air and sucked down a wheezing gasp. The waves slapped him violently, and he fought to keep steady.

I need to get out of the drink. Fisher cast around, finding no sign of the lifeboats but more than enough pieces of floating wreckage that would do the job. He swam toward a curved section of broken roof, reaching for it. If he stayed in the icy water too long, he was doomed to hypothermia and a slow death.

Fisher grabbed the edge of the debris and felt metal and insulating foam beneath his gloved fingers. *Not a Zodiac, but it'll do,* he told himself.

But as he started to haul himself on to the makeshift raft, Fisher's leg was jerked back by a powerful grip around his ankle. The wreckage drifted out of his grasp, and he slipped back into the sea, falling into the trough between the steepening waves.

A figure in a waterlogged coat, with a face masked in streaks of blood loomed over him out of the water. A claw-like hand dragged Fisher down into the cold murk.

Aslanov. For an instant, shock locked Fisher's mind into a denial of what he was seeing. *Not possible!* He had left the Russian to drown, trapped inside the flooded operations center. *How could he be here?*

Fisher wondered if the pain and the fatigue were making him hallucinate; but then Aslanov's other arm came up with a glistening silver blade in his fist, stabbing the *karatel* at Fisher's chest. Somehow, against the odds, his nemesis had made it out.

He blocked the attack, but with only limited success. The knife cut into the ballistic nylon webbing over Fisher's torso and a length of it entered his flesh, lodging there, caught on the dense material of his tactical suit.

The Russian shouted a curse at him as a wave gathered them both up and engulfed them. Heedless of the danger, Aslanov wrestled with Fisher and clawed at his face.

They sank, twisting around one another in a murderous embrace, vital breath leaving them in froths of air as they traded blows. Aslanov had the strength of a madman, his face close to Fisher's through the gloom as he screamed into the sea.

What does it take to end him? Fisher had lived with that question for years when he had hunted the Russian, and even after he had believed the man was buried in that Coalition air raid, a part of the American had never truly accepted Aslanov's death.

Time after time, shot after shot, Fisher had tried to avenge himself on this man. Not only to seek justice for the murder of Maxim Belov and his family, but to prove that the unkillable man *could* be killed.

Now the ocean would be the grave for them both. Two war-dogs, trained by their nations to be lethal weapons, two cold warriors long past any expectation of survival. By any sane measure, Sam Fisher and Dima Aslanov should have been dead a hundred times over. Perhaps it was fitting that the clock would run out with them at each other's throats.

Fisher would be willing to accept that. He would be willing to give his life to make sure this ice-hearted sociopath was crossed off for good, *for certain this time.* The world would be a safer place without a man like Dima Aslanov in it.

"You will die!" The Russian spent the last breath in his lungs shouting out the drowned words in a gush of bubbles, and he grabbed at Fisher's throat, fingers like iron rods tightening around his neck, squeezing.

A depthless black void shrouded them as they continued to sink. Fisher's world became pain and shadows, and he knew that Aslanov's furious eyes would be the last thing he saw.

No.

The denial lit a fire inside him. Fisher reached for his final reserves of strength, and grabbed blindly at the trapped knife. He ripped it free with a jolt and grabbed the back of Aslanov's head before the Russian could stop him.

Fisher rammed the *karatel* through Aslanov's skull with a crunch of shattered bone, forcing it deeper with the heel of his hand, pressing the Russian's head into the weapon so he could not escape the killing strike.

Aslanov's talon-like fingers released their grip on Fisher's throat and the other man twisted away, his body shaking as death finally took him.

Fisher's last glimpse of the man was the black mass of his coat swirling around his body, before he vanished into the deep.

There was nothing left in Fisher's lungs but acidic vacuum. His chest ached as if bands of steel were contracting around him, the pressure of the water squeezing out his last seconds of life. His mind fogged, his vision narrowing to a dark tunnel. He tasted copper in the back of his throat.

In the struggle, Fisher had lost his sense of up and down. Buffeted by the currents, his fate would follow the Russian's if he did not act.

No.

He kicked against the icy waters surrounding him, making one last push in what he hoped was the right direction.

Twinkling lights sparkled in front of him, seemingly

suspended in the water. In their glow he thought he saw Sarah and Regan. Fisher kept pushing, kept fighting, even as his body betrayed him, his energy ebbing.

The sea gathered him up, and its darkness engulfed him.

TWENTY-SIX

RAF Lossiemouth Air Base – Moray – Scotland

A thundering roar dragged him back into the light.

He opened his eyes, and that action alone took an effort that he felt all the way to the ends of his limbs. A small room with pale green walls surrounded the bed he lay on, and watery, cloud-thinned sunlight came in through a window to the right of him. Beyond it, he saw the tops of nondescript buildings and above them, climbing into the sky on lines of jet thrust, the source of the sound – a pair of delta-winged Typhoon interceptors.

Where was he?

Military hospital. The words pushed themselves to the front of his thoughts. He'd been in places like this before, too many times than were good for him. He recognized the texture of the over-starched bedsheets and the faint odor of heavy disinfectant.

He took a slow breath, mapping the injuries to his body. Bandages wound around his chest and his torso, in the places where the mission had cut a little blood out of him. His throat felt desert-dry. He tried to speak, but only a husky croak emerged.

Someone was in the room with him. He turned toward the presence he sensed and focused on a young woman with dark hair and her arm in a sling, dozing in a chair by his side. Her eyes opened, as if she knew he was watching her, and she blinked.

"Dad?" Sarah leaned forward, reaching out to him. He saw her hand wrapped in white gauze, and an old instinct took over.

"You all right?" said Fisher.

A crooked smile broke over her face, and it lit up the room. "Am *I* all right? I'm not the one they fished unconscious from the North Sea."

"How long was I out?"

"This is the fourth day."

"Huh." He struggled to remember what had happened, but there was nothing but the recall of disjointed images and odd sounds. The last thing that was clear to him was Aslanov's rage and the blade. The thought clouded his features.

Sarah gave him something to drink, and despite her protestations, she eventually agreed to help her father climb out of the bed and get dressed. As he did so, Fisher caught a glimpse of himself in a mirror above a washbasin on the far wall. He looked gray but hard, like ancient, weather-beaten granite.

I'll take that, he thought, dwelling on the comparison. Still here. Still alive.

"I'll get the doctor," she began, turning toward the door.

"Not yet." He put a hand on her arm. "Tell me what happened first."

Frowning, Sarah filled him in on the days that had vanished into the haze. Drawn by mayday calls and flares from the lifeboats, a frigate from the British Royal Navy patrolling nearby had arrived at Site Five after the strike mission, and gathered up the survivors in the water, Fisher included. A savvy junior officer had taken one look at his wounds and his gear and isolated the Splinter Cell operative before calling it up the chain of command.

By the time the frigate returned to the Moray Firth and Fisher's unconscious form had been choppered over to the medical center at the local RAF base, the NSA were in the loop with the Brits. Grim had diverted the Paladin to Scotland after recovering Sarah from some Swiss backwater along the way.

She didn't say much about her mission on Brody Teague's train, beyond vague details of the crash that destroyed it and the tech billionaire's bloody end, but the sling, the bandages, and the stiffness in her walk told the rest of the tale.

And there was something else, another tell that Sarah might have kept hidden from someone who didn't know her well. She couldn't conceal it from her father, however, and when he put his hands on her shoulders and searched her eyes, he knew for certain what it was.

She had a new distance in her gaze, a length to her stare that Sam Fisher knew intimately, because he saw it so often in himself.

Somewhere on that mission, his daughter had crossed a line she would not be able to walk back from. She had taken a life.

A surge of irrational anger kindled inside him, a fury at the circumstances that had forced his child to make that choice. He stamped it down, dispelled it, then asked the question that came next.

"You want to talk about it?"

She eyed him and deflected. "No offense, Dad, but we've never really been the sharing types."

"Don't do that," he said, with a shake of the head.

"Don't do what?"

"Don't push away." Fisher remembered countless times when the faces of those he had killed in combat came back to haunt him, and all these years later the first of them still returned now and then, in the dead of night. He carried that burden in silence, and it pained him to see Sarah shouldering it too.

His daughter spoke again. "She didn't give me a choice." Sarah looked down, and he knew she was reliving it. "It was me or her."

There were a million things Fisher wanted to say to his daughter. He wanted to take her away from this, to make his child safe from ever having to make such a decision again.

He said the only thing he could. "You did what you had to. Now leave it behind and push on. Because if you stay in that moment, it'll eat you alive. You understand?"

Slowly, she let out a breath, staring off into the distance. "I always wanted to know what you were feeling, Dad. Now I do."

He drew her into an embrace, and for a while they held it in the quiet, saying nothing, just maintaining the simple act of being present for one another.

There came a knock at the door, and it opened to admit

Charlie Cole and Lea Kade. The two of them looked sheepish, aware that they had interrupted something personal.

Sarah broke away and beckoned them in. "He's awake," she said.

"I see that." Charlie cocked his head, giving Fisher a brisk look up and down. "Geez, Sam. You look like fifty miles of bad road."

He shrugged. "That pretty? Lucky me." Fisher took a few more steps, testing his limbs, feeling for the places where the pain still lurked.

"It's good to have you back in one piece, sir," added Kade. "We thought we might lose you."

"Sam Fisher?" Charlie snorted at the idea, glancing at the other woman. "You're pretty new to 4E, right? So maybe you haven't caught on yet, but Panther here is way too ornery to die. I could tell you stories…"

"Those are classified," Fisher said firmly. "And last time I checked, you were still a civilian, Charlie."

"True," said the hacker. "But my, uh, *consultancy* during this operation kinda puts me back on the team. Maybe I'll stick around for a while. We'll see."

Kade gave him a look. "You're going to give up the lucrative private sector and come back to government work?"

Sarah made a face. "Well, technically Cole doesn't have a job anymore, because the Teague Technology Group no longer exists."

Fisher frowned, feeling like he'd missed a step. "How's that?"

Charlie rubbed his hands together. "While you were sleeping off that dip in the North Sea, T-Tec's share price sank to the bottom. Turns out, an unidentified whistleblower was happy to share records with the media of Brody Teague's dealings with known terrorist groups. The brand turned toxic, the shareholders cashed out in less than forty-eight hours... I hear Jace Skell's company swept in and bought out their assets for chump change."

"That whistleblower wouldn't happen to be a certain disgruntled hacker formerly on the payroll, would it?" said Fisher.

"Let the punishment fit the crime," Charlie intoned, with solemn affirmation. "And it's the least I could do, after what happened to Jan and the others they murdered, right?"

"No argument there," agreed Kade.

Fisher glanced between the two techies. "Charlie. Lea. You did good out there. Couldn't have ended this without you, don't forget that." He looked at Cole. "I know it was tough for you to come back in, after what happened in Tehran." He turned to Kade. "You kept us alive. That pretty much proves you're Fourth Echelon material."

"Yes sir. Thank you, sir." Fisher could tell the ex-Marine was resisting the urge to salute him.

"Nice words," said another voice, clipped and brusque. "Just stop short of the high-fives, if you please." Anna Grímsdóttir stepped into the room and jerked her thumb at the doorway. "All of you. out. Get back to the Paladin, I need to debrief him."

Her tone did not brook any argument, and the others left them to it. Sarah gave her father one last look before she closed the door behind her, a dozen unspoken words in the simple glance.

When they were alone, Fisher went to the window, staring out across the airbase, finding the sea in the near distance. "I have you to thank for that navy frigate?"

He saw Grim's reflection in the window give a shrug. "I asked a colleague at MI6 to make sure a surface ship was in the area. In case it went sideways."

"What happened to Kobin?"

"Andriy?" She shrugged again. "The Norwegian Intelligence Service found the Gulfstream, abandoned at an airfield north of Trondheim. But Kobin's in the wind."

Fisher smiled slightly. "He'll turn up. He's too dumb to stay quiet for long."

Grim folded her arms across her chest, a gesture Fisher was only too familiar with. "So you're aware: Fourth Echelon has used the fallout from the revelations about Brody Teague to build our own narrative as to what happened here. His interaction with the White Masks, the Islamic Vanguard, the Kawakiri and the rest of them, that doomed his corporation from the moment the news dropped. Most of the world believes that one of those groups is responsible for Site Five and the train crash, and we'll let it stay that way. But any information pertaining to the existence of the Gordian Sword quantum computer has been categorized Above Top Secret. As far as anyone knows, it did not exist."

Fisher thought about Teague's hard-done-by colleague. "What about Target White? He got away."

"He didn't," she corrected. "Samir Patel is currently in a French detention center, pending extradition to the United States. They arrested him attempting to board a flight to Qatar."

"And what's his punishment going to be?" There was more venom in the words than Fisher had intended.

"Patel has a genius-level IQ and he's spineless. It won't take him long to figure out that he should play ball with the agency and tell us everything he knows, in exchange for a light sentence." She paused. "Of course, we wouldn't need him if you had followed orders."

Fisher ignored the comment, nursing the annoyance inside him. "So, Gordian Sword gets classified deep black, what about the people whose lives it destroyed? Drake and Virtanen, Charlie's friend, those passengers on the flight that went down? What bullshit are we going to feed their families?"

"You already know the answer," Grim retorted. "Those people will never know the truth, not even the smallest fragment of it. We live in a wired world now, and we can't un-ring that bell. If the existence of something like Teague's computer was made public, there would be mass panic. People need to believe that digital security works. That their secrets and our infrastructure are safe."

"Even if it's an illusion?"

"Everything we do is shadows and lies, Sam."

His lip curled. *She's right about that.* After a moment, he turned away from the window and spoke again. "I need something from you, Grim. A promise."

She raised an eyebrow. "About what?"

"*Sarah.* I want her off field duty. Put her on the Paladin or one of the other operations teams, but not at the sharp end. Not again."

"I can't do that–"

"Yes, you can," he snapped, cutting her off. "You're in charge of field ops, you can do it with the stroke of a pen."

"Sarah volunteered to be part of this." Grim eyed him. "You want me to bench her?"

"What I *want*," he said firmly, "is to make sure she doesn't become like *me*." Fisher remembered that distance in Sarah's eyes once more, and it chilled him. "I can't change what I am, but I'm damn sure not going to let my daughter follow the same path."

"You're the senior agent, you could put in a report and fail her evaluation," Grim shot back, challenging him. "Technically, she's still a probational operative."

"There's enough of a gap between us as it is. I don't need to make it worse."

Grim fell silent, considering the demand. She knew Fisher well enough to have no doubts that he would go over her head if she refused, all the way to the top. After everything he had done for Third and Fourth Echelon, there were a lot of markers he could call in.

She gave a reluctant nod. "All right. I'll make sure she stays off the line. But I warn you, Sam. Sarah is her father's daughter, and sooner or later she's going to figure it out. And when that happens, it won't be an easy conversation for either of you."

"I'll take that risk," he said firmly.

"You're on thin ice as it is," Grim noted. "The director and the rest of the chiefs at the Black Box are not pleased. You were ordered to take Gordian Sword offline, not send it to the bottom of the ocean. Want to explain it to me?"

"The situation at Site Five was fluid," he said. "I had to act in the moment."

"That's all you're going to say?" Irritation flared in her tone. "I have to go back to the higher-ups, to the President, and give them an explanation."

Fisher felt his strength returning, his fatigue fading. "Teague's nasty little toy is best gone. You know it and I know it. A weapon that powerful... something that can cut through any firewall in existence? It's too dangerous, even in the hands of our side."

Grim's manner softened. "Damn it, Sam. I don't disagree. But you can't put the genie back in the bottle. Teague was twenty years ahead of the rest of the world with Gordian Sword, but sooner or later someone is going to catch up and build what he did."

"Maybe so," Fisher allowed. "We'll face that threat when it comes. Lambert told me once, the Splinter Cells were created to take extraordinary threats off the board before they fully manifest. Well, we did that. We did our job. If the suits back at Fort Meade have a problem with it, tell them to read the charter again."

Her frown deepened. "Is that what we do, Sam? *The right thing*?"

"If we don't, Grim... who will?"

Fisher turned back to the window, watching the clouds over the water, looking out at a world that was – at least for now – safer than it had been a week ago.

"The doctor's outside, waiting to check you over," said Grim. "I'll call him in..."

"No need," Fisher told her. "I'm ready to get back to work."

ACKNOWLEDGMENTS

Cards on the table: I've been a reader of Tom Clancy's novels for years, and an avid player of the "Clancyverse" video games for almost as long. With *Splinter Cell*, I was in from the start of the series, drawn by the mix of stealth action gameplay and hi-tech espionage themes. Ever since I first met Sam Fisher, I've wanted to see more of his world, so I dove into the games, I read the tie-in books, and I even got the wristwatch… *Yeah, you could say I'm a fan.*

It's been a while since Sam has had a new adventure of his own. We've had recent missions with him in *Ghost Recon*, *Rainbow Six* and elsewhere, and as I write this, work is proceeding on an animated show for Netflix that will open up a whole new series of *Splinter Cell* stories. I look forward to the day when I can slip into Sam's tri-goggles once again, but for now I'm honored to have been given this opportunity to write a novel about a character that has been a big part of my gamer landscape over the years. I hope you have as much fun reading it as I did writing it.

Of course, like covert agents out in the field, authors never operate without support – be it editorial, inspirational or educational – so in that spirit I'd like to give credit where it is due...

My thanks to Gwendolyn Nix, Marc Gascoigne and the hardworking team at Aconyte Books; to Etienne Bouvier, Lauren Stone, Richard Dansky and everyone at Ubisoft and Red Storm Entertainment; to JT Petty, Clint Hocking, Mike Lee, Matt MacLennan, Raymond Benson, Grant Blackwood, and Peter Telep, in whose footsteps I follow; to Derek Kolstad and the writers on the *Splinter Cell* animated series; to Abandoned Berlin, the DDR Museum and the contributors at the *Splinter Cell, Rainbow Six, Ghost Recon,* and Black Belt Wikis; and finally, with much respect to Michael Ironside for breathing life into such an enduring and iconic character.

ABOUT THE AUTHOR

A *New York Times, Sunday Times* and Amazon #1 bestseller, and a BAFTA nominated scriptwriter, JAMES SWALLOW is the award-winning author of over fifty novels, including the internationally bestselling Marc Dane thrillers *Nomad, Exile, Ghost, Shadow, Rogue* and *Outlaw*, the *Sundowners* steampunk westerns and fiction from the worlds of *24, Star Trek, Watch Dogs Legion, Warhammer 40,000*, and many more.

His other credits include several scripts for videogames, including the Tom Clancy titles *The Division 2* and *Ghost Recon Wildlands*, along with the *Deus Ex* series, *Phantom Covert Ops, Disney Infinity* and *No Man's Sky*.

He lives in London, and is currently working on his next book.

jswallow.com // twitter.com/jmswallow

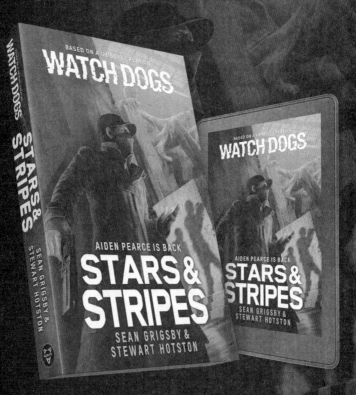

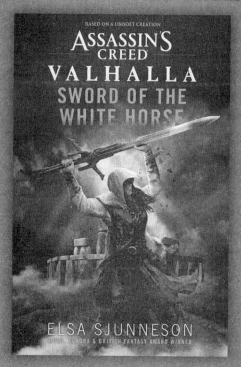

WORLD EXPANDING FICTION
Have you read them all?

ASSASSIN'S CREED®
- ☐ *The Ming Storm* by Leisheng Yan
- ☐ *The Desert Threat* by Leisheng Yan *(coming soon)*
- ☐ *The Magus Conspiracy* by Kate Heartfield *(coming soon)*

ASSASSIN'S CREED® VALHALLA
- ☐ *Geirmund's Saga* by Matthew J Kirby
- ☐ *Sword of the White Horse* by Elsa Sjunneson *(coming soon)*

TOM CLANCY'S THE DIVISION®
- ☐ *Recruited* by Thomas Parrott

TOM CLANCY'S SPLINTER CELL®
- ☑ *Firewall* by James Swallow

WATCH DOGS®
- ☐ *Stars & Stripes* by Sean Grigsby & Stewart Hotston

WATCH DOGS® LEGION
- ☐ *Day Zero* by James Swallow & Josh Reynolds
- ☐ *Daybreak Legacy* by Stewart Hotston *(coming soon)*